Dedication

To my patient husband and my beautiful children
and to God whose promises are new every morning

*For you shall go out with joy, and be led out with peace; the
mountains and the hills shall break forth into singing before
you, and all the trees of the field shall clap their hands.*

Isaiah 55:12

Perched in the rafters of the old stone barn, Avery Kaler swung his legs back and forth, unspoken curses hanging on his chapped lips. Sweat poured from his temples, lingered at the tip of his graying widow's peak, then slid down his forehead. His knees knocked against the mortar-bound beams as he flicked straw into the empty stalls below, aiming for a rusty metal bucket. How dare Frank McMillan take the farm?

The first hint of sunlight poked between cracks in the roof, a cheerful intrusion to his surliness. Time to get the girl to the campground before her strung-out friends started missing her.

As relentless rays crept closer, he caught a solid oak beam, lowered to a stall, and steadied his feet on the half wall so he could drop to the floor. He stomped a square of sunlight, like that might send the sunrise fleeing back into night. Bits of hay fell from his gray trousers and landed on his waterproof boots.

He reached over his badge into his right shirt pocket, drew out a pack of wintergreen gum, and popped a piece into his mouth. Though the minty aroma persisted, for a moment, he could taste a brief hint of the old-school Teaberry gum Frank had given him as a youth. Stifling a scowl, he tossed the wadded wrapper at a spider, sending it skittering up its web. Frank's sudden appearance posed a serious problem. He needed to be eliminated before he spilled too many secrets.

Avery crossed the barn, lifted two floorboards, and unlatched a trapdoor. The musty underground tickled his nose, and an epic sneeze nearly tumbled him down the concrete stairs. Minutes later, he ascended with the unconscious blonde flung over his shoulder like a rag doll. Her thighs poked out from a too-short cocktail dress. A beauty, but no Pandora.

Squinting from the brightness, he slid through the barn door and carried her to his cruiser. He slung her into the backseat, knocking her against the opposite door. She briefly stirred as he brushed a wayward tendril behind her ear. Poor thing. Her head would likely ache tomorrow.

He lifted his key to the ignition and held it mid-air for a moment. With a grimace, he dropped his hand to his lap. How many years had it even been?

Yawning, he removed the wrinkled photo from his pocket and traced the profile of the smiling girl posing in her college softball uniform. A petite brunette who looked nothing like the pudgy girl she'd once been. He'd snag her as she pulled into town. With luck, no one would recognize her, and she'd disappear before anyone knew she'd arrived.

He fingered his Glock and laid it in the seat, suppressing the rage that could consume him. First, he'd capture Pandora. Next, he'd take care of Frank. Then, he'd skip town for good.

His gaze landed on the old stone church nestled across a shallow valley behind a crumbling fence. Vines crept up the side, clinging to windows and twisting around balcony rails. He tightened his grip on the steering wheel as twenty-eight years fell away. The wicker basket, the rumbling thunder, and the wiggling babe screaming while its mother ran in tears... And Frank watched from the bushes. Avery should have killed them all then.

Didn't matter. This time, they'd never stand a chance.

Chapter One

Savannah Barrett pressed her sandaled toes against her apartment door as she edged it open a sliver and balanced her mug against her chest.

"Hello, Pandora."

She spewed cinnamon tea over her crisp, white shirt. Who would show up here on a Thursday morning, calling her that name? After fourteen years.

The tea she'd managed to swallow rolled in her stomach. Clamminess spread over her as she squinted through the peephole at the frail gentleman teetering outside her apartment. Taking several deep breaths, she cracked the door to a whirring noise. "Who are you?" *And how do you know I'm Pandora?*

The gentleman steadied himself with his cane. "Someone who can help you find your roots." His painfully thin body quaking, he turned to the thirtyish blond man in the three-piece suit who stood next to him. "Show her the papers."

"Perhaps you've mistaken the address." She closed the door in his face with her free hand and fastened the chain. A fumble with the deadbolt sloshed more tea on her sleeve. She must have heard him wrong. At least she hoped she had.

Through her peephole, she eyed the plastic tube that climbed the old man's torso and wrapped around his face. It extended from a thick canvas strap secured to a black bag, which explained the whirring. Poor guy. So feeble, standing there with a worn cardboard box. Shame to not at least offer him a seat and explain he'd mistaken her for someone else.

Only he hadn't. Two pink rosebuds poked out from his shirt pocket.

Covering her mouth, she smothered a gasp and pressed her other palm against her chest. Surely not the same roses. Identical to the ones left in her basket at birth? It couldn't be. She slumped against the wall. "I'm not ready for this."

Rapping drowned her whisper. The door shuddered against her spine, and chills coursed to her toes. Who was this man? And why now?

"Ms. Barrett? Pandora?" The deep baritone resonated. The younger man.

She stood and pressed her ear to the wood. What would she miss if she didn't open the door?

"We have information about your biological family. Please, allow us a few minutes."

Relaxing her grip on the mug, she peeped through a crack, letting the chain catch. "My name is Savannah." Her heart throbbed like drumsticks pounded on it, the racing blood roaring in her ears.

"Of course you're Savannah. You're also Pandora." The old man slipped into a coughing fit. The younger one braced him.

"Look, I don't want to be Pandora." He had no right coming here dredging up her wretched past, not when she'd worked so hard to start over and forge a new life. "You should go."

Withered fingers squeezed into the opening as she tried to slam it.

The younger man pushed the door wider. "Please, Ms. Barrett. Listen a few moments, and then decide. Mr. McMillan traveled a long way to see you."

Wheezes overcame the older man. The box slid from his hold.

The younger man caught it and tucked it under his elbow. "As you can see, he's ill. It would be better if he could sit."

Savannah set her mug on a coaster and rocked on the balls of her feet. If this man was a biological relative, he'd have answers to her lifetime's worth of questions. A stack of unpaid bills taunted her from the kitchenette counter. Would he offer an inheritance? Something to compensate for her having such a rotten life?

She met the young man's gaze and undid the chain. "Twenty minutes. Then I have to leave for work."

Mr. McMillan placed a pallid hand on her tanned one. "I hoped…" Another wheeze. "…you'd remember me."

"Well, I don't." A distant memory stirred within her, the man talking with her adopted parents. *Had* she always known him?

He fished for his wallet and dug through folded receipts. Seconds passed, and finally he produced a worn photograph and a piece of Teaberry gum.

She stared at her six-year-old self, a chunky girl standing in a group of girls in the church foyer. A younger version of Mr. McMillan handed her a foil-wrapped candy.

Palms raised and fingers curled, she stumbled backward over the trim separating her dingy carpet from cheap linoleum. The Bubble Gum Man.

His companion stepped forward, forcing her into the living area.

She kicked three pairs of discarded shoes away from her tattered couch. Why couldn't he have come when she'd cleaned the place? Not that she ever did. "Mr. McMillan, is it? Sorry about the mess. I've had a rough week."

Clambering closer, he scooted away a pile of junk mail with his cherry cane. "Please call me Frank."

"Frank." A relative? She turned to the younger man. "And you?"

The man extended a smooth right hand with lanky fingers. His left sported a diamond-studded wedding band. "Mr. Anderson. Mr. McMillan's lawyer."

Frank grinned. "Peter."

Peter wrinkled his nose toward the spotted carpet, soiled from a previous tenant's pet. "We have an offer, one I think you should consider."

Geoff Spencer sat on the porch swing, shucking corn and flicking the husks into the brisk wind. His devoted beagle raced around his muddy farm boots and skidded under his seat, the little guy's exuberance not jaded by the impending storm. Geoff dropped the corn and scratched the beagle behind the ears. "Calm down, Cyrus. Save your energy, and I'll take you for a run when the storm passes."

A rusted pickup meandered toward him, and the veins in his forehead twitched. His body tensed. One, two, three... eight, nine, ten. He imagined his mother chiding him from behind the screen door to not release his rage on the messenger. It wasn't the mailman's fault. If only she were still here. Maybe she'd know what to do.

To the left of the long gravel driveway, fallen leaves danced around the silos and swept across the pumpkin patch. They chased after his farmhands, who'd heeded the forecast and packed up for the day. He'd given a decade to build up this farm to its glory. He couldn't lose it all now.

Robert Arnold eased out of his truck and shuffled toward the front porch. Slow as itch. That's what Nana Jean would have said. That, and bless his heart. So many memories. How could he leave them behind and start fresh somewhere else?

Fidgeting with his mailbag, Robert leaned on a wooden column to the right of the steps. He stared toward the shucked corn.

"Good Thursday morning, Robert." Geoff tried not to chuckle at the pudgy mailman's distraction. "Hand me a bag from the chair over there, and I'll wrap a few ears for you."

Robert wiped sweat from his forehead with a wrinkled handkerchief. "You don't need to go and do all that." He grabbed two bags and dropped them at Geoff's feet.

"My pleasure." Geoff stuffed each bag. "Quit being so nervous and give me the letter."

Robert let out a noise—a cross between a sneeze and a gasp. "Who told you?"

A red Camaro whipped into the driveway, stirring up gravel.

Cyrus tucked his tail and bolted into the doghouse. Robert looked after him, as if he might hide in there, too. "Shoulda known. Crazy aunt of yours." Hands shaking, he fumbled with the mailbag clasp and retrieved a certified envelope.

Pressing his thumb into his chin, Geoff stifled a groan. He'd spent all morning trying to get Mona off the phone. She couldn't stand staying out of his business. "Yeah. Mona's a mess." He reached for the letter.

"Wait. You gotta sign." Robert fished in his bag for a pen and shoved the receipt in Geoff's face. "Be fast. Susan's makin' fried green tomatoes for lunch."

Geoff scrawled his name across the page. "See you later, Robert."

"Billy-Bob! How's the redneck delivery biz?" Mona strolled to the porch, laughing as he scuttled down the steps. "Give my regards to Susan. Tell her I hope she chokes on a tomato."

Robert stumbled to his truck, corn forgotten, envelopes spilling behind him.

"Mona, you're awful." And the bane of his existence. If blood didn't bind them…

Geoff chased after Robert, snatched up the letters, and passed them and the bags of corn through the truck window. He dodged broken tree branches and returned to the porch as Robert sped away.

She snorted, draping an arm over Geoff's shoulders and reaching for the envelope with the other. "Why do they let that hayseed keep delivering mail? Aren't you going to open it?"

Lord, please give me patience. "You can open it, if it's bugging you so much."

She broke the seal and eased the paper from the envelope. "Lighten up, nephew." The paper smelled of a strong ink and appeared to be a form. "This is absurd." She scowled. "Like Mary Lou said, it's a declaration of ownership of your property. They're scheduling a transfer."

Geoff rubbed his temples, his chest tightening. If she hadn't called to warn him first, he wouldn't have believed it. There must be a legitimate reason, or the lawyer would have never agreed to send a letter. He gathered the shucked corn and set it in the house. When he came back out, she'd torn the paper into pieces and dropped them on the mat. "Mona!"

"It's nothing. A bunch of nonsense. Frank McMillan lurked around town for thirty years without saying a word. I bet it's a scam."

Geoff knelt and pocketed the loose pieces of the letter. He'd tape them after she left. "Let me talk to Larry before we go getting too upset. I doubt tearing it to shreds makes it any less legal. What do you know about this guy? Does he still live around here?"

"He's a reclusive photographer, without a lick of common sense. One time he set up a photo booth at the town fair, and they caught him trying to force a kiss on some woman. And then…"

As he suspected, gossip. Letting her words blur, Geoff focused on a centipede crawling between the deck cracks. Herb could be ruthless, even criminal when he wanted. Was it possible he'd stolen the farm from Frank and hidden it all these years? When she finished, he stood. "Why would he think he owns my farm?"

"No one knows. He went to the war and didn't return for a while. Herb moved onto the property after he left, and everybody assumed Frank made a legal transfer."

Okay, more than gossip. Theft was possible, and if Herb kept disorganized records like his dad, it would be hard to determine.

Unless… A shadow crossed Mona's tan-wrinkled face, and she averted her gaze. Had she been involved in the theft? He squinted at her, furrowing his brow. "You knew all this and didn't tell me? For how long? And why come forward now?"

"I didn't see the relevance." She marched down the steps. "What will you do?"

"I'll call Larry and see if he wants to bring Anna Leigh by for supper and talk about it."

"That harebrained fool of a lawyer about sent you to prison when Maria died."

"Not his fault. Most people suspect the husband in a situation like that. We won the case, didn't we? They found me innocent." Geoff flicked his gaze to the rain-swollen clouds. "Larry's a well-respected attorney. He'll fight for me to keep the farm, and we'll win this one, too."

"If you say so…" She sauntered to her car.

"See you at church?"

"You know I don't like that place. Those old women are rude to me."

Thunder clapped. His shoulders drooped. He'd tried. Again.

Cyrus darted out from behind a bush, his teeth bared.

"Come on, buddy, let's get out of this storm." Cyrus at his heels, he moved to the living room, dropped to the couch, and cradled his temples in his hands. A meeting on Thursday? What had the letter said?

After removing the paper from his back pocket, Geoff rearranged the torn pieces and taped them together. Yep, Thursday. To discuss the transfer of his farm. Transfer, not claim. Mona had been telling the truth for once. He'd have to talk to this McMillan man. If the guy owned the property, Geoff could offer compensation.

14

He took out his phone, scrolled through his contact list, and tapped the screen. As he waited for the ring, he paced the room. Floorboards creaked.

"Morgan and Morgan, Attorneys-at-Law. This is Sheila. How may I help you?"

He spun and returned to the couch. "Hello, Sheila. It's Geoff Spencer. Can I speak to Larry?"

"You're lucky, sugar. He's getting ready to head out to court."

Larry whistled into the phone. "I meant to call you."

"*You* already know?" Stupid gossip train. "Athena called yesterday from the bank and said they couldn't find the title. Then Mona called, and a few minutes later I got this letter telling me some McMillan guy owns the farm, and I can't stay without his consent."

"I heard so, too. Mr. McMillan lives in town, not far from church. He's private, though he pops in for the morning services on occasion. The old guy who carries the cherry cane."

"Right. Frank." Geoff scratched his head. "The Bubble Gum Man. Why do you think he's coming forward now?"

"Not sure." Larry cleared his throat. "We'll meet tomorrow and look over the details."

What would the details show? From the sound of it, everyone thought the transfer had already been settled. "I hope so. I don't know what I'll do if he wins. What about my men?"

"Well, you can reason it out with him. He's a decent sort. I can't see a man in his nineties wanting to run the farm. Would he let you rent?"

Geoff kicked the coffee table, knocking over an old picture frame. He held up his palms and counted yet again. Losing his temper wouldn't do anyone any good now. "I'm not going to pay rent to live in my home and run my farm. That's crazy."

"He might rent, but if he's the owner, it's not your farm. There's nothing you can do."

Geoff set the frame back on the table, taking in his mother's warm smile. How he missed her. She'd know what to do. Heart heavy, he returned to the kitchen. "This McMillan guy is Herb's age, right? What if he dies? Does he have anyone who'd stand to inherit?"

"He's got a great-granddaughter, and to beat it all, she didn't even know. He's telling her today. Strange family, this is."

As Larry spoke, Geoff turned the faucet all the way on and plugged the drain. He added a drop of soap. "This great-granddaughter—anyone I know?"

"I told you, it's a funny thing." Larry's hard swallow resonated through the speaker. "Her name is Savannah Barrett. You knew her as Pandora."

Geoff dropped the phone in the sink and scrambled for it. "Panda Barrett."

Anyone but her.

He slammed the phone against the counter, jostling the battery free. Thank goodness no water reached the circuitry. "Guess I'd better get packing."

Chapter Two

Savannah flicked bread crumbs from her skirt and examined Peter's three-piece suit. Like one of those TV lawyers, his polished hair shined and his super-crisp tie appeared plastic. How could she trust him? "Do you have any proof? Like lawyer ID?"

Peter helped Frank to her ratty leather armchair. He retrieved a Kentucky driver's license from his wallet and handed it to her. Cheeky grin, salesman eyes, Ken-doll expression.

"What else have you got?" She crossed her arms. "Anybody can fake a license."

Huffing, he swiped his phone and passed her a website advertising a law firm. Fourth name on the list. She smirked. The low man. "What do you want to talk about, Mr. Anderson?"

"Peter. His name's Peter." Frank wet his lips and reached into his front pocket. "Here." He removed a wad of cash, dropping hundred-dollar bills on the carpet.

Peter picked up the hundreds, folded them, and tucked them back into the pocket. "I said wait. Let me handle this."

She eyed Frank's pocket, then her stack of bills. Enough to pay most of them. She could dump her broken furniture on the sidewalk and drive away with the old man in a Lexus. He'd buy her expensive things. Then she frowned. Her chest filled with stifling air. Why approach her now? "Are Mom and Da—I mean, um… are Phil and Rose okay?"

"Your adoptive parents are fine. This concerns your biological family." Peter palmed the cardboard box and lifted the flaps. Dust and brittle pieces scattered to the floor.

She clutched her collar, her shoulders sagging. "What do you know about my biological family?"

He shoved magazines off the oak coffee table, setting it wobbling. After steadying it, he freed a silver half-heart box from the musty cardboard, and set it before her. "Plenty."

"Wha—?" Heat surged through her. She snatched the heart, sheltering the tarnished patina in her hand. Did they break into her apartment? "How did you get this?"

"Relax, Ms. Barrett." Peter stepped over a brown leather belt. "This is the mate. Remember? You have the right side. This is the left."

"Oh." Air gushed from her lungs. "It is the left. Sorry." She traced the silver edge, following its organic shape to the jagged and broken center. Beside hers, a perfect match.

Frank snorted and sat straight. He removed the wad of money from his pocket and fanned it before her like a deck of cards. "What would you like to know, Pandora?"

"Anything. Everything." Why the money? And what did he want from her in return? She landed on her lumpy couch, a pile of unfolded laundry softening the fall. She dumped the clothes on the floor and scooted against the cushion, grappling for the armrest. "What's the catch?"

Peter glanced at Frank. "Mr. McMillan, tell her your conditions."

Frank adjusted his oxygen and took a deep breath. "All you have to do is move back home and complete a scavenger hunt, and you'll have all the answers you seek."

"A scavenger hunt?" He couldn't be serious. She planted the mug on the table. "You want me to *move* back? Quit my job, leave my apartment, and live in the place with only bad memories? No way." Although… Would the answers be worth the agony of facing Geoff Spencer?

Frank shuffled to the couch and dropped on the cushion next to her. He tucked a withered hand beneath her palm. "Yes."

18

Savannah jerked away. How could she ever agree to go to Dreyfus? Then again, how could she not? She eyed the clamshell antique. What could it hold? Pictures of her real parents? Names? She pressed her heels into the carpet. "If I go back, you'll give me whatever's in the silver box?"

He nodded. "And I'll tell you about your biological family. Everything."

Drumming her fingers on the table, she shifted. She could pop into town for a couple days, just long enough to get answers. "Do I have to commit to living there?"

"Of course not." Frank leaned forward. "I'm hoping you'll want to stay."

No. Not ever. As she rubbed her neck, her veins throbbed. "I remember you. The Bubble Gum Man." She frowned. "I last saw you the night before I left Dreyfus. You came to see Phil and Rose and asked them to make me stay."

He smiled. "Good. You do remember."

She puffed her cheeks, held her breath, and then finally released it. How could she have forgotten him? He'd spoken to her every week at church. "Phil called you a nut."

The twinkle left Frank's eyes. A tear glimmered in its place.

"I'm sorry." Savannah pressed her fingers against her mouth. Breathe. Calm herself. Get it together. "You haven't given me any evidence." Twisting a lock of her hair, she shifted her gaze and squared her shoulders.

Peter passed her a faded document. "Your birth certificate. Mr. McMillan took a picture before your real mother destroyed it. We didn't have time to get a new copy."

Black lines obscured the names. She arched one brow. "Are you serious? I can't read this."

Peter pointed. "You can read your surname."

McMillan, like Frank's.

She pressed a shaky hand to her left temple. Blood rushed to her face with the flood of memories—encouraging hugs when she walked home from school and passed him sitting on the bench by the courthouse. He'd always waited, even in bad weather. She'd been too young to wonder why. Had he done so every day?

He reached again for her hand, this time lacing his fingers with hers as she lowered it to the couch. His voice wavered, and his breathing grew shallower. "I'm your... great-grandfather."

Her breath hitched. Could it be true? Tears brimming, she searched his eyes and scraped her teeth over her lipstick. "Why didn't you tell me years ago?"

"I thought I'd have more time." His bottom lip quivered. "I was ashamed."

Peter flipped through the stack of documents and pulled one to the top. "You'll have answers soon. First, let's look over this paperwork."

She accepted the paper he offered and scanned it, chewing the inside of her cheek. Letters swirled into blurs and the words appeared foreign. Something about taxes and property ownership. "I don't know. I haven't had time to process any of this. Plus, I have to get to work."

Frank's chest heaved, and he straightened. "I understand your skepticism. Please, trust me. This means everything." He squeezed her palm. "Indulge an old man while there's time."

His labored breaths tore at her soul. She'd always struggled with compassion. He clearly needed it. "What's wrong with you?"

Giving her a sad smile, he dabbed his mouth with a handkerchief. "Congenital heart failure, emphysema, rheumatoid arthritis..."

Not much time... She slid free from Frank's grasp, wiggled her toes against her sandal strap, and faced Peter. "You're one-hundred percent sure he's my great-grandfather."

"Yes." Peter dug in the briefcase side pouch and came out with a pen.

She ran a hand through her bangs, flicking them from her eyes. "Who are my parents?"

Frank fell into another coughing fit.

"He's not ready to tell you." Peter unzipped the briefcase and removed a laptop. He rested it on the coffee table. "We'll cover the terms of agreement first, and you can sign. Then we'll talk about what you need to do to get your answers."

"Well, hurry. I don't have all day." She glanced at her watch. "I need to call my boss."

"We've spoken to your boss. We explained it was worth his while to give you a vacation day." Peter shrugged. "Do you have a Wi-Fi password?"

"No, I don't have a pass—you talked to my boss?" A picture stuck out from the side of the briefcase, her with a recent ex-boyfriend. Her heart skipped a beat. "You're a stalker."

"I'm the lawyer." He tucked the picture deeper into the pocket then withdrew a portable printer and digital signature pad from the cardboard box. "Ms. Barrett, before we continue, Mr. McMillan requested you agree to a few conditions." Handing her the silver half-heart, he triggered the latch to let her see the interior. "First, I'll need the mate."

"It's in my closet." She leaned closer. Two keys. A car and a file cabinet? Frank gripped her arm. "Tell me what's in yours."

Savannah rocked back and forth on the couch. "A small piece of paper with a Bible verse: 'Where your treasure is, there will your heart be also.'" She lifted her fisted hands, resting her chin against her interlocked fingers. "And old pictures of trees."

"Right. The map." Frank nodded, knocking his propped cane to the floor.

"Give me a second. I might have to dig to find it." She crossed the room to her tiny closet and sifted through clothes until she struck the corner. Old yearbooks, shoebox of pictures, letters from Rose… "Here it is."

When she handed it to Peter, he pushed the two pieces together, forming a perfect heart. A new latch popped out the front, and she gasped as he triggered it. The lid split into two parts, revealing a hidden compartment.

Frank snorted from the couch, and Peter walked over to him. He nudged his shoulders, and the old man's eyes widened. "Frank, buddy, are you with us? It's time. Thought you might like to do the honors."

As Peter held the heart out to him, Frank retrieved a brittle, yellowed page covered with calligraphy and ink blots from Savannah's half.

Her chest ached. She needed to breathe. "What is that?"

Frank gave her a crooked smile. "It's the original deed to Geoffrey Spencer's farm."

An eerie, evil calm spread over her body. "Let me get this straight. If I return with you, I get to take his farm away from him?" The ultimate revenge.

Tears filled Frank's eyes. "Yes. First, you must travel to several locations and sift through the scavenger clues. You'll need to leave Chicago behind."

Her head pounded like it might explode. "Are you serious? How long will it take? I can't be off work long. Besides, I have no desire to move back to Dreyfus."

Peter placed his hand on Frank's trembling arm. "Let's give her space, and let her consider your offer. She's not ready yet."

Barbecue marinade dripped from the steaks, leaving red blotches on Geoff's deck. Thirty days since Robert had brought the letter, twenty-seven days since they'd postponed the meeting, and he still felt his life was on hold. He scanned the distant clouds. Another storm would arrive by late afternoon. He'd let the rain wash the deck. Not that it mattered. He didn't own it anymore, anyway.

Larry and Anna Leigh Morgan sifted through papers under the patio umbrella.

Geoff glanced over his shoulder at them. "Any luck?"

She shook her head. "I've been over every page. There's not a loophole we can see. Mr. McMillan kept meticulous records, pictures, and documentation, and the bank has no record of a transfer from his ownership to Herb's."

"I'm going to lose the farm. Nothing we can do." Geoff slapped the last steak on the grill and carried the blood-covered plate to the house. He took deep breaths until the veins in his neck quit throbbing. When he rejoined the Morgans, Larry cleared his throat, and Anna Leigh gave him her charity smile. Not what he wanted to see.

"Could the old man sell it to you? Have Dale do an appraisal. Then make him an offer." Larry jotted a note on a legal pad. "It's not like you don't have the funds."

Geoff moved foil vegetable packets to the grill shelf above the steaks. "I do, but it will take away from my community projects." He stirred the chopped mushrooms and onions sautéing on the side burner. "It stinks. We've made so much progress."

"It does stink." Anna Leigh tucked a loose tendril of brown hair underneath her eyeglass arm. "Speaking of community projects, does Georgia need more help with the special needs barbecue? Darla said she'd be willing."

"Sure." He lowered the heat on mushrooms and balanced the lid on the pan, leaving a crack for steam. "Tell her we need someone else to take money at the door."

Anna Leigh grinned. "She wants to work beside *you*."

Larry elbowed her. "Annie, you don't try to set a man up at a time like this."

She made a halo above her head with her pointer fingers and thumbs. "Hey. Darla's a sweet girl. She could be a support to Geoff during all this."

23

Geoff forked a steak, lifting it to check the sear. "Darla is sweet, but Larry's right. I can't even consider dating until we take care of this farm stuff."

She winked. "I had to try."

Larry's cell rang. Averting his gaze, he ducked inside the house. After a few moments, he returned to the patio table and propped his chin.

She grabbed his sleeve. "What's wrong?"

"Frank McMillan died."

Geoff dropped the metal tongs. The sharp edge pierced the deck, inches from his bare toes. "He died?"

Larry nodded. "Which means Panda inherits."

Anna Leigh reached for her husband's legal pad. "Now what?"

Leaning over his notes, he traced a circle around the top half of the page. "We go forward as planned. Make her an offer."

Geoff knelt and picked up the tongs. He wiped them with a wet towel hanging from his waistline, a snarl tempting his face. She'd never accept an offer from him. "Dora Barrett wouldn't sell me water if I lay dying in the desert."

Anna Leigh threw him another sympathy smile. "She might. I doubt she'd want to keep the property. After all, she did move away."

"Thanks to me." He checked the steaks again, this time flipping them. "I doubt she'll be in the mood to cut me any slack."

"You were kids." Anna Leigh tapped her pencil against her wrist. "It's been fourteen years. People change." She smiled. "At least you've changed."

Larry cocked his head and twisted his wedding band. "We'll find out Thursday at our meeting."

Chapter Three

Savannah stepped off the plane, blinking. Her eyes burned from hours of trickling tears. She, who never cried. As she passed through the gate, she stopped and donned her sunglasses, drawing a curious glance from the attendant.

"Are you okay?" Peter rested a hand on her shoulder.

"I'm tired. After the delay, I…" Clutching her carry-on bag, she scanned the room. A digital clock hung on the wall behind the attendant. She lifted her glasses and peered at the screen. Six thirty. Twenty-eight more hours, and this would all be finished. "I waited too long to come home. I should have agreed the day you came to my door."

"It broke his heart." He walked ahead of her. "But Frank understood. You had to be ready."

Sniffling, she patted the clamshell box through her leather bag. Why had she been so stubborn? She knew why. She'd rather face a starving tiger than reconnect with Geoff Spencer. "I'm sorry."

Peter led her down a hall, past long glass windows where a frazzled mother wrangled with three toddlers. Her youngest, a cherub-faced boy with a buzz cut, pressed his lips against the terminal window.

The mother took her little girls' hands and turned them toward the gate. "Look, Kayleigh! Carson! Michael! There's Daddy."

Savannah glanced over her shoulder. The man in camouflage who'd sat a few seats back stretched his arms wide, scooping the three kids into a tight embrace.

Her eyes dampened again. What was wrong with her?

25

A restroom sign offered solace. She nodded to it. "I'm going to freshen up if that's okay. I could go ahead and change."

Peter shifted his briefcase from his left to right hand. "We have time to change later."

"I want to be more comfortable." Leaving him standing by the door, she ducked into a stall and shimmied out of her sweatpants, into the navy pencil skirt and silky white tank from her carry-on bag.

A loose thread dangled from the tank's floral embroidery. She bit the string and let it fall to the floor. After swapping her black runners for red suede pump sandals and slipping into her hunter-green cardigan, she stuffed everything in her carry-on and moved to the sink.

Wrinkling her nose, she eyed her oily brown hair. She fished a sample of dry shampoo from her purse and brushed it from the roots to the ends. A quick layer of concealer and makeup popped her cheekbones and faded the blotchiness around her eyes. Much better.

Flashing her white, toothy smile, she winked at her reflection. Skinny, flawless, perfect. Her smile faded. Not good enough to please Rose. With luck, they wouldn't cross paths before she met with Geoff.

Peter chuckled when she emerged. "More comfortable?"

"Yep." She rocked side to side on the heels of her pumps.

"Then let's pick up our baggage and get on the road."

When they reached his car, a hint of red lined the charcoal clouds. She set her bags by the trunk and waited for him to open it.

"First stop, your parents' house."

She flinched. "I told you we aren't going there. I have no desire to see my mother right now."

"Frank's instructions left no wiggle room. You have to talk to your parents, or you don't get the car." He loaded her bags in the trunk and held the passenger door open. "I can't shuttle you around everywhere. I've got a ten-year-old and a wife waiting at home."

26

"I'm sorry. I didn't mean to imply I expected that. I do appreciate everything you've done. You've gone above and beyond the call of a lawyer." She slid into the bucket seat and crossed one sandaled foot over the other. "Don't worry about me. I'll be in Dreyfus. One-stoplight Dreyfus. I walk more miles every day in Chicago than it would take for multiple trips across town and back. I can manage without a car."

He ducked his head as he climbed into the driver's seat. "First, Dreyfus has grown. There are at least eight"—he waggled his fingers—"stoplights now, several around the college area. Second, you're going to walk out to the country? In those shoes?"

She twitched her nose. "I'll get a cab if I have to venture out far. If I go see Rose, she'll nag me about why I still haven't found a husband. Then she'll make me can tomatoes for six hours straight and tell me all the reasons why I need to get back in church. We'd never make it to the courthouse."

"You do need church." Peter grinned. "Frank said so."

Heat crept across Savannah's face, and she turned to the window. She yawned and tilted her head against the glass. "I'm going to sleep."

"We'll be there in twenty minutes."

She closed her eyes. "Then I'll sleep for twenty minutes."

The hum of the tires morphed into a roar of laughter and chants of students screaming, "Panda! Panda!"

She raised clammy hands. Goose pimples dotted her arms. Forcing her weary eyelids to slivers, she squinted. Dawn had overtaken the car, and bright rays peeked over the clouds. She lifted her elbow, shielding her face. "Wow. We're already on the parkway. You weren't kidding."

"You snored through the entire trip. Trust me. I wouldn't call this soon."

27

Savannah faked a smile, mock-punched his shoulder, and glanced at the dashboard clock. "I do not snore. I didn't even sleep. It's only been ten minutes."

He laughed. "Would you like me to build a case and prove it to you?"

"No, thanks." Rubbing her neck, she twisted toward the trees flashing by the window. A forest now swallowed the fields in front of the park where she'd once played.

He signaled as they came upon a familiar interchange, one she'd taken with Rose and Phil many times—the exit to nowhere. The highway ended, going from a four-lane parkway to a two-way bridge, where the thick-trunked oaks, white pines, and silver maples obscured the roadside.

"So, what have you decided? Car or no car?"

She toyed with the hem of her tank. "Can't we please wait and let me visit my parents tomorrow? I need time. I'm not ready to face her. Not when I've been up all night."

Peter drummed his fingers against the steering wheel. "Hmm. Since Frank isn't here to ask, and he didn't specify when you had to see your parents, I guess we operate under the assumption you can visit anytime. His stipulation is you can't drive the car before you've talked at least an hour with them."

"Another stipulation." She gritted her teeth and rested her chin against her fist. "An hour."

"You did sign, Ms. Barrett." He signaled a left turn, stopping for an old tractor to pass, and faced her.

"Have you ever met Rose? She's…" Savannah folded her hands in her lap. "I need time to prepare. I want to focus on Frank's journals, not deal with her drama. I've been wanting these answers my whole life. I've played out every scenario. Right now, I need to know who I am."

"Okay, then. We'll go after the meeting. Want breakfast?" He pulled into the parking lot of a beat-up restaurant.

28

Her heart caught. Mama's Place. Phil had taken her there often. The pale red shutters still hung crooked, and the drive-thru lane bore the boxy brown shingles they'd installed in the eighties. "Returning to Dreyfus feels like opening a time capsule. Nothing's changed since I left."

"It's grown into a good-sized community. This part is older, yes. You'll be surprised when we get to town." Peter yawned, swinging his car wide into a space. "Let's eat in the lobby. I need to stretch my legs." He stepped out, slammed his door, and started crossing the lot.

Savannah eased her sandals to the ground and planted them.

Cheeks puffed, she smoothed her skirt and straightened the waistline of her tank. Cool morning air offered a chill, so she draped the cardigan over her arm. Reaching into her purse for a tube of lip gloss, she checked her appearance in the side mirror.

Peter peered over his shoulder. "You coming?"

She uncapped the gloss and slid some on her lips. "I haven't eaten anything like this in years. I won't even know what to order."

"Bacon." He winked. "You should order lots of bacon." He turned, crossing into the drive-thru lane.

A horn blared from an extended cab truck.

Peter waved an apology to the driver, who whipped into a space two down from her.

She peered into the passenger window. Her breath stuck in her throat.

Geoff Spencer looked at her then turned away.

Jutting her chin, she smirked and let her hair spill down the center of her back. *He has no idea who I am.*

Geoff leaned against his rusty old Chevy, shoving callused hands into his jeans pockets. He jingled a handful of change, poking his finger through a hole in the lining. A coin slipped out, down his pant leg. He shuffled, letting it slide to the ground. What was a nickel if he stood to lose everything?

The school drop-off crowd had started rolling in, the normal line of fathers and mothers picking up breakfast for half-asleep kids. Cars streamed along the drive-thru lane, the occupants sometimes waving and sometimes casting worried glances. Above the restaurant, rays of sunlight burst through cloudy streaks, the pink hue promising storms.

The man with Ken-doll hair held the glass door for an older couple before nodding for the brunette to pass.

A green sweater draped her forearm. She lingered on the sidewalk, gazing at the skyline. Dark curly locks tumbled to the middle of her back, a perfect complement to her deeply tanned arms. The man paused until she crossed the threshold then walked behind her a few feet. Not a couple. Not that Geoff cared.

He waited outside as she approached the counter. She tossed her hair, revealing a slender neckline and bare shoulders begging for kisses. Kisses? The last thing he needed was a woman distracting him. Turning away, Geoff met the gazes of three elderly ladies from church and inwardly winced.

If they had seen him gawking, he'd never hear the end of it. He checked the time on his cell. Six fifty. Might as well go in and order.

When he reached the counter, the brunette stood in front of him in line, close enough he could smell her soft, floral perfume. She distanced herself from the suited man, who carried a briefcase. A business venture of some sort. Definitely not a couple... but an odd connection.

"I'm telling you, you want bacon." The man eased forward, closing the space between himself and the brunette. "Lots and lots of bacon."

"I'll pass." She glanced over her shoulder, the corners of her lips drawing up in a smile.

Her tinkling laughter filled the lobby and warmed his soul. Geoff averted his gaze to Lily, the cashier.

The brunette faced Lily, too. "I'll have two ham biscuits, minus the biscuits."

Lily gave her a blank look. "You want ham. By itself?"

"Ham, and an unsweetened tea."

Her companion shook his head. "Suit yourself. I'll have a sausage gravy biscuit and two sides of bacon." He chuckled. "I should order three sides."

"Peter…" The brunette folded her arms. "You'd better not."

Geoff eyed the counter. If he inched closer, he could steady himself against it. Her voice had a musical quality, too. Like Maria. He needed to get a grip.

"Geoff! Hey, Geoff! You with us?" Lily grinned at him, and he blinked his way back to reality.

"Sorry, Lily. I didn't sleep much last night."

She leaned over the cash register. "Yeah, the storms kept me up, too. Want the usual?"

He scanned the bustling restaurant, finding half his crew. He ought to update them, though from the way they looked at him, they'd already heard. Couldn't keep anything private around here. "No. I think I'm going to eat in today. You still serve the double egg platter that's not on the menu?"

Lily eyed her manager, who nodded. "Yeah. By the way, Dad said to thank you again for the steaks and vegetables. We've been eating like kings this past week."

He turned up the corners of his lips for a brief moment then let them fall slack. With her mother's cancer progressing, Lily's family would need help for the long haul. Could he sustain it if he lost the farm? "My pleasure. I'll send more if you all need it. Tell your mother I'll be praying."

31

Another worker approached the counter, placed ham and tea on a tray, and looked past him to Peter. "Sir, it's going to be a minute on your bacon and gravy. If you want to have a seat, we'll bring it."

"Sounds good." Peter sorted his change, turning all the bills the same direction.

The brunette picked up her tray and pivoted, smiling when she met Geoff's gaze. She passed the tray to her companion and extended her hand. "Well, well, Mr. Spencer. Fancy meeting you here. It's been a long time."

Familiar brown eyes blazed into him. What? How? He lifted three fingers to his parted lips. *This* vixen held the key to his future? Only two words came to mind. "Hello, Panda."

Chapter Four

"It's Savannah." She arched her brows. "Not Dora, not Panda."

Savannah? She'd changed her name? Her too-thin face shifted, replaced for a moment by the tear-stained gawk Geoff memorized years earlier. Had the chunky, awkward girl from eighth grade grown into this sleek woman? She'd never forgive him. He met her fierce glare. "I… um… I'm so sorry. I didn't mean to—"

"She'll talk to you at the mediation tomorrow." Peter stepped between them.

She placed a hand on Peter's shoulder, her irises darkening to a deep brown. "Yeah."

All the workers stood frozen against a blurred backdrop of stainless steel, their focus intent on him. The customers stared as well. He turned to Lily. "Can you please make mine to go?"

"You don't need to leave." Peter gestured to a corner table. "We'll stay out of your way."

"Lily, if you'll take my order to Zach, I'm sure he'll know what to do with it." Geoff tossed a folded bill across the counter. He closed the space between him and the door in three long strides. Dodging cars, he sped to his truck. Veins in his neck throbbed as he slid behind the wheel.

Now what? His appointment with Dale and Larry didn't start until eight thirty. Larry would be late, no doubt. He backed out and peeled onto the main road, heading to the old tobacco warehouse at the edge of town.

When he arrived, he reached behind the seat for the blueprints and examined the artist's rendering. The facade of his dream restaurant towered above other venues he anticipated occupying the neighboring space. Tracing his finger over the planned teen center, he gritted his teeth. Could he pull it off without the farm as collateral?

Mr. Taulbee, an older gentleman from church, hobbled up to his truck with the aid of an intricate wooden cane.

Geoff climbed out, painted on a smile, and extended his hand for a shake. "Morning, Mr. Taulbee. Out for an early walk?"

"Hello, Geoff." Mr. Taulbee pointed to the sidewalk. "Penny lost her coupon pouch on the way home yesterday. I can't find it."

"Between the pharmacy and your apartment?"

"Yes."

"I'll help." Geoff glanced to the fifth floor of the elderly complex. Penny Taulbee stood at the window. The pharmacy could move into one of the empty spaces, closer to the apartments, and the Taulbees wouldn't have to walk so far. He could build them a drive-thru and tear down the old pharmacy to make more parking for the law offices. It would be perfect. After he finished some of his other projects…

He paced the sidewalk, scanning the ground for the bright floral pouch Mrs. Taulbee carried everywhere. There, lodged into the slats of a wrought-iron bench. "Here you go, Mr. Taulbee."

"Thanks."

"No problem." Geoff sat on the bench, chuckling as Mr. Taulbee poked his way back to the apartment, holding the pouch overhead.

Mrs. Taulbee waved with a wide smile. She'd be sending apple fritters soon.

Licking his lips, Geoff grinned. He could already taste them. Then, he frowned. Where would she send them?

A cool breeze tickled his neckline. He scratched his chin. Stubbly. Great. He'd forgotten to shave. He checked his wristwatch.

Not even seven thirty. Plenty of time to run to the farmhouse and take care of it.

Cyrus waited on the front porch. His tail wagged so hard it tipped him. As Geoff fumbled with the keys, the beagle scuttled around his feet and tugged at his pants with bared teeth.

"Sorry, fella. Guess I forgot about you, too." Cyrus raced across the hardwood, followed him to the kitchen, skidded on the linoleum, and smashed into the dog food cabinet. "Whoa, boy." Geoff nudged him aside and scooped a cup of dry food into a plastic dish.

Moving would be hard on Cyrus. Geoff's chest tightened. And him. How could they leave the only home they'd ever known?

He climbed the stairs to the master bedroom he'd shared with Maria, disturbing the dust for the first time since Christmas. He scanned the closet for the electric razor Mona had given him. It would be faster.

Boxes filled three-quarters of the closet. Maria's clothes. The pink-flowered crib he never assembled. The piles of newborn outfits and diapers. Things he should have given away years ago. He filled his lungs and let out a long exhale. Could losing the farm be God's way of telling him to move on with his life?

He lifted the razor from the high shelf. Four AA batteries. Not included. Forget that. He put the razor back and headed to his bathroom for his trusty Mach 3 Turbo blades.

Ten minutes later, scraps of toilet paper sticking to the nicks on his face, he brewed a fresh pot of coffee and scrambled eggs in an iron skillet. Might as well try to eat.

He sat at the head of the hard rock maple table, facing his parents' portrait in the great room. He tried to channel his father's sternness, though his mother's soft brown eyes drew him. Brown eyes like Dora's.

"Have you been on your knees?"

Had her image spoken it aloud? He had prayed—in fact, he'd been up all night uttering selfish prayers for God to let him keep the

35

farm. He knew nothing truly belonged to him and God's will would be done regardless. He hadn't prayed for that.

He turned his chair sideways and bent over, folding his hands and resting his arms against his legs.

"Father, I come to you today, your sometimes-humble servant, scared, and with a burdened spirit. You've been gracious over the years, far more than I deserve. Please forgive my weakness."

He cleared his throat. "Lord, I thank you for the many blessings from this farm, for the opportunities of service to help me make restitution to those who I mistreated in my youth.

"I know you have an underlying purpose here, something to bring glory to you." Squeezing his fingers, he rubbed his thumbs over each other. "And perhaps I've been too focused on my own glory lately. Help me use this situation as a lesson in humility."

His cell vibrated on the counter. He pressed his arms deeper into his thighs. "Above all, give me strength to be gracious to Dora… um… Savannah and ask her forgiveness. Help us both act as adults and, if it's your will, please, let her accept my offer to purchase the farm."

"Amen." He yawned, rubbing his face. His stomach still felt heavy. Had he lost his ability to tap into God's peace? He eyed the dusty family Bible, opened to the book of Luke, as his mother left it years ago. When was the last time he'd read God's word, other than preparing to teach Bible class? When had he last focused on growing his personal relationship with his Father?

He glanced at the clock. Eight fifteen. Dale and Larry should be pulling up any minute.

Savannah's lips quivered as she took the seat across from Peter. "I can't believe he called me that." She inspected her ham, stuffed a straw into her drink, and peered out the window to the spot where he'd glared before revving his engine and peeling out of the lot. "Stupid jerk."

"He's gone now, so get yourself together. Being upset won't make this easier, you know."

"I know." But it would make her feel better.

"Think you can get yourself from the hotel to the courthouse by eight thirty?"

"I'll be there earlier." She forced down a bite of ham. A group of bulked-up farm boys laughed and punched at each other's shoulders to her right. Geoff's friends. His bully partners. Butterflies fluttered in her stomach. Inheritance or no inheritance, she'd made a mistake in returning.

Peter waved a piece of bacon in her face. "C'mon. One bite won't hurt you. It might improve your mood."

The smoky, savory grease filled her nostrils. She blinked and accepted a bite, letting the crisp crumbs roll over her tongue. Perfect. Looking at her tea, she sighed. "I'm ready for today. What then? I mean, I know I'm going to Birmingham. What will I do when I get there?"

Pushing his plate to the side, he reached into his briefcase and removed a green folder and a brown leather journal. "Frank planned to take this trip with you. He wanted to tell you about all of this in person." He lined up the folder with the table edge and set the journal on top. "Three years ago, he realized that would never happen. After his hospitalization, he wrote you letters, describing everything he wanted you to experience—everything he wanted to share with you. He worked on it for hours every day."

"Why did he wait so long? Why not contact me then?"

"He thought you weren't mature enough to handle the responsibility."

Her veins seemed to bulge against her skin. Not mature enough? She'd more or less raised herself since age fourteen. What did he know about maturity?

Nagging thoughts pushed forward—the fit she'd thrown in her realty office a week ago over a vacation day. The stacks of unpaid bills, the times she'd snuck out of work early... Not very mature or responsible. Maybe he had a point. She clamped her jaw shut and accepted the journal.

Within its pages, garage sale stickers sealed divided sections. He broke the seal on the first page and nudged it across the table. "Stubborn old man, he should have died months ago. He managed to hold on until he finished."

"He's paid you for months? Did he pay you to spy on me?"

Grinning, Peter shook his head. "I'm no James Bond." He adjusted his silk tie and straightened his collar. "I do have a family, remember, so I wasn't able to do Frank's bidding twenty-four seven. I've worked for him for a while. You'd never believe me if I told you how many people he kept on salary until the last week or so." He stood and smoothed his suit coat. "I have no idea where he got all his money, or if there's much left. He's left that for you to discover. All the answers you're seeking, he recorded in sealed notebooks. Open one seal at a time, and it will direct you to the next location."

"Will you go to Birmingham?" She traced the journal cover edges and closed it. "How will you know I'm compliant?"

"Credit card receipts, phone logs—you'll be in the right places in the right time." He fingered one seal. "Frank prefers you don't read ahead. At certain checkpoints, someone will inspect the journals and know if you did." He shrugged. "I'm not planning to micromanage your life, Savannah. Follow his instructions. You'll travel four weeks, and then you can do whatever you want. We'd better go. I need to look over my notes for my afternoon clients."

Chapter Five

Savannah paced the lobby of The Grand Stink, as everyone had called it in middle school, marveling at the renovations. Marble columns replaced once-crumbling plaster ones and the tile floors reflected like mirrors. She clutched her room key and took a deep breath. Cherry potpourri filled her lungs.

She deposited her bags on a red velvet couch and plopped beside them while Peter shuffled in his briefcase. "What now? I can't go in the room until eleven. Do I hang out here all day?"

"You can go see your parents. Get the car."

Her mouth felt suddenly dry. She tugged her collar away from her neck and fanned it. "No way."

"Suit yourself." He handed her a green file folder. "Here's your itinerary for the trip Frank put together for you. You can read over it and prepare yourself. You'll leave for Birmingham tomorrow after the meeting." He yawned, staring toward a painted ceramic urn the corner. It stood about four feet high. "Then, you'll follow his instructions until you come to the last stop. If you decide to stay in Dreyfus—"

"I won't."

He huffed. "Anyway, the medical examiner will keep Frank a few days, and then he will be cremated per his wishes. We'll have a memorial ceremony when you return."

She tapped her sandals on the thick Berber carpet. Why couldn't Frank have lived longer? Why couldn't she have returned when he first asked? "I guess all my answers will be buried with him if I don't meet his conditions."

Peter pointed to the journal, which stuck out of the side pocket of her bag. "You have a lot of answers there, but the complete picture comes from following his instructions."

"Okay." Savannah tucked the journal deeper into the pocket. "Although, I still don't understand why I can't read it all today while I'm waiting."

He shook his head. "Don't do that. Be patient. It will be worth it, I promise. You have to follow the sequence of Frank's instructions. He wants you to see the pictures and description when you reach the locations for the first time." He snatched the journal from her bag and tucked it in his briefcase. "I'm going to keep this for a while so you won't be tempted. I'll give it to you after we've met with Geoff."

She spit air. "I can be patient. Well, mostly. I can't wait to see Geoff's face when I walk in that conference room and he signs over his property."

He unfastened the briefcase snaps and placed his ink pen in a zip pocket. "You might consider that Mr. Spencer is an adult. I'm sure he's changed in the past fourteen years."

She snorted and scooted her carry-on bag closer. "I doubt it. He did call me Panda at the restaurant."

Peter frowned. "Savannah, he's not that kid anymore. You're not a kid, either. Frank clearly stated this is not about revenge. It's about getting the farm back to its rightful owner."

"If you say so." She counted her money. Twenty-six dollars. About another hundred on her debit card after paying all her bills for the month, and three hundred on her credit card. "You said all expenses covered, right? Starting today?"

He pulled a plastic rectangle from his wallet. "Tomorrow, after the meeting, I'll give you this prepaid card with a couple grand on it. More will be added after you complete the task at each location."

She gasped. A couple grand? More? "Are you serious?" She definitely made the right decision.

"Oh." He gestured to her leather bag, where the sharp part of the silver heart jutted against the fabric. "The keys. One is to a lockbox in the Dreyfus bank. The second is to the car. This is why we need to go to your parents' house."

"I'd rather not." She eyed the prepaid card. "I'll rent a car."

"Nope. You can't use the money for just anything. Restrictions apply."

"Well, that stinks."

He grinned. "You could always take a charter bus like Frank did when he was young."

She flicked her gaze to the brass and crystal chandelier, losing her vision within the fluted bulbs. Spots danced in front of her, and she closed her eyes, leaning back against the window. "Ten thousand times better than facing Rose."

"If you say so." He picked up his briefcase. "I'm going to go, then. Traffic is a beast this time of day."

Geoff stood on his back porch, overlooking the farm as his mind swam in a pool of eighth grade regret. Panda Barrett, wailing on the gym floor as everyone walked by and refused to help her. Panda screaming insults at him as the bus drove away, leaving her sitting in a mud puddle. His mother chiding him, demanding he stop bullying. He'd listened, but would Dor—Savannah ever believe it?

In the distance, a line of trucks left a trail of dust as they made their evening trip across his fields. Six o'clock. Quitting time. He ran into the house for his Bible and headed to the truck. If he got to church early, he could hide out in one of the offices until it started.

Long tire marks cut into the winding road in several places. He drove past the access road to the old furnace, glancing at the litter by its entrance. College students must have been partying again.

He gripped the steering wheel tighter. He'd planned to build the restaurant with a badly needed youth and college ministry upstairs. An abandoned furniture store downtown would have been the perfect location, and might have even had room for other businesses. But not if he had to spend all his money transferring the farm back to his name.

The truck rattled as he bounced over a broken piece of asphalt and came to rest at a vandalized Stop sign. Dreyfus needed so much attention. Signaling, he looked both ways and edged over the bump onto a two-lane road.

Rain drummed the roof and splashed across the windshield, glistening in his headlights. He activated the wipers, dislodging the spider who'd called the right one home for days. As its small brown body whisked into the shadows, Geoff heaved his chest. That was exactly how Panda would destroy him. He should've found her and apologized. She wouldn't have listened, but the effort might have mattered.

By the time he reached town, bits of hail peppered the truck. Winter would arrive early, like the almanac said. He had so much to do—too much to worry about moving everything to a new location.

He pulled into the church parking lot, in a space facing the gas station, meeting the headlights of a police car. Avery Kaler leaned against it, staring like he could bore a hole through the place.

Avery lifted a hand and waved, offering something between a smile and a smirk.

Geoff waved back, refusing to meet Kaler's accusing eyes. He'd been proven innocent of Maria's death, and Kaler needed to let that go.

Seconds later, he entered the front doors, into a sea of sympathy, and grimaced. He'd forgotten they'd moved the start time up by a half-hour. Good thing he'd come early. He brushed through the lobby and grabbed a songbook from the front seat before taking the bench behind the pulpit.

Cory Baker approached the mic. "Good evening."

42

A handful of members responded. Most kept their eyes on Geoff.

Cory cleared his throat. "Good evening."

A roar of good evenings reverberated across the room.

Grinning, Cory read from the list. "The teens will be having their annual dinner of appreciation for the Young At Heart group on Saturday, November 7. The theme this year is TV Shows from the 1950s. That's coming up in a few weeks. If you'd like to help with donations, see Logan Hamilton."

The undertone of murmurs and whispers soared through the audience.

"We need someone to do communion for the months of November and December. If you are willing, the sign-up sheet is still on the bulletin board beside the water fountain."

Geoff scanned the audience then took vigil of his feet. The murmurs must have been about him. Let them talk.

"Keep the following people in your prayers: Leila Stuart fell last week at the nursing home. She's okay, but bruised up good. She might appreciate a few visitors." Cory shuffled the paper. "Deana Casey had a bad car accident, as most of you know. Crushed most of the bones in her foot, so she's looking at some extensive surgery, I think." He looked out into the crowd. "Carmen, will you ladies start the food train for her family?"

Geoff stretched his arm behind him, bending it at the elbow and rubbing his neck.

"I think that's everything. Any other prayer requests?" Cory faced Geoff. "Brother?"

Words caught in Geoff's throat. He nodded.

"As most of you have heard, Brother Spencer faces a difficult situation regarding his property. We all know how much good he does for this church and community. Let's keep him in our prayers."

Following the prayer, Geoff stood and rested the songbook on the pulpit. He glanced at the song he'd chosen, sounding the pitch in his head. His chest constricted, and his lungs refused to accept a breath.

Maddie Evans escaped her pew and raced up to the pulpit, her blonde curls bouncing. "Mr. Geoff! I want to sing, too!"

Amidst a room full of laughter, he scooped her in his arms. "Hi, Maddie." Thanks, little girl, for saving me.

He handed her to her red-faced mother and moved back behind the mic. "How about we try a different song? Number six seventy-three. 'Jesus Loves Me'."

Maddie's eyes lit. When he started the song, she belted it with all her heart, lifting the burden weighing on his. God is gracious and good. God will have a plan.

Even as he sang with assurance, doubt slithered into his mind. What if God's plan involved letting Panda Barrett destroy him?

Chapter Six

Avery brushed the dust from his dashboard with a crumpled KFC napkin. He stuffed it in the brown bag and slammed the car door behind him. His entire day off, he'd waited in vain for a call that Pandora had emerged from the hotel. Time to figure out another plan.

He wadded the bag, deposited it into a green plastic receptacle, and headed to the bus depot where a dreadlocked redhead sprawled over a paint-chipped bench. Coughing, he kicked one of the wrought-iron legs. What a lump of nothing.

Darren Shepherd scrambled to sit vertical. "Whoa. Kaler. Dude, you scared me."

"Officer. Not Dude." You're supposed to be watching the hotel for me. Letting me know if the grizzly makes a move."

"Right." Darren jerked his thumb toward the hotel lobby. "Well, I can tell you this. She sat next to that window for about three hours, until around eleven. Then she stood up and grabbed her bags." He grinned. "I ran over and peeked into the lobby and watched her take her stuff into the elevator."

What an idiot. "So, she's been in the hotel all day." Avery frowned, and sifted through his wallet until he found a twenty-dollar bill. "Well, she needs to eat sometime." He handed over the bill and eyed the green-striped awning one block away. "Go on home, Darren, and keep watch from your apartment. Let me know if she leaves. I'll be sitting outside Opal's."

He paused at the modern stop light, its plain black pole a stark contrast to the marble stone steps and Corinthian columns of the

45

courthouse. Pressing the Walk button, he tapped his feet and waited for the display to change.

When he entered the bar and grille, he smiled at the hostess, a short, thin-framed girl like the one he'd "saved" a few weeks ago. "Hi, sugar. I need to pick up a gift certificate."

She led him to the plump, cheeky bartender, who tossed bottles around so fast the whole room seemed to spin. Avery waved two ten-dollar bills at her, and she caught both bottles in a smooth instant.

Five minutes later, certificate in hand, he entered the Grand Dreyfus Tower lobby and approached the clerk, a twenty-something blond with a red-checkered bow tie. "Hello, sir. Hope you're well this fine evening."

"Sure am." The young man adjusted his collar. "How can I help you?"

"I've got a delivery from Opal's for one of your guests." He handed over the certificate envelope. "They were busy, so I offered to bring it."

The young man held the envelope to the light. "Should I leave her a note as to the sender?"

Avery chuckled. "It's from Opal's. Says on the certificate."

"Right." The young man picked up his phone. "I'll take care of it."

"Thanks." Avery caught his reflection in the glass double-doors. His receding hairline faded as the queue to a neighboring dance club came into view. So many college girls… too risky to interact with any of them. He returned to his patrol car and drummed his fingers against the dash.

The line to the club dwindled to a trickle. Traffic slowed to its normal evening crawl. Avery's chest rose and fell heavier with each moment. Where was she?

A half-hour later, Pandora emerged. A red dress barely swished over her thighs, and black sandals wrapped around her lower calves.

He swallowed then left his car again, keeping his distance as she neared the restaurant. Shame he'd have to kill her.

"Dora!" A tall girl with jet-black curls secured in a tight ponytail waved from a bench.

Pandora stopped, the skirt settling above her knees, and he froze.

A grin widened her face. "Megan? Megan Carter?"

The girls embraced, Pandora's sleek night attire not quite blending with Megan's black uniform. He ventured a couple steps closer.

"I can't believe it's you!" Megan reached into her apron and came out with a cigarette. "People said you were in town, and came back all skinny. You look incredible."

Pandora smiled, and Kaler pressed his fists against his thighs. Her wispy hair danced around the freckles peppering her nose. She looked so much like… No. He couldn't consider that now.

She dropped to one of Opal's stone benches, extending her long legs and crossing them at the ankles. "You look good, too, Megan. I don't think you've aged a day since eighth grade."

Megan sat and lit her cigarette, her face blurring behind the cloud of smoke. "So, where've you been? Someone said Chicago."

"Yeah. I've been working in this realtor's office since college." Pandora laughed. "I'm a glorified secretary. Wrap his Christmas presents, pick up his laundry, and make sure his kids get off the bus."

"Still sounds better than this gig." Megan flicked her ash toward the restaurant. "Someone else said you taught Zumba, but then I heard you were a softball player."

"I was both." Pandora flexed her toes. The Dreyfus gossip train still thrived. "I started with aerobics when I moved in with Aunt Nellie. Her daughter was the dance team coach at the high school, and she worked with me until I was good enough to make the team. But softball was my true love. It paid for my college. Although, I haven't played in years."

Megan gripped her arm tight. "You have to enter Georgia's dance-off in a few weeks."

"A dance contest?" A distant grin swept her face. "I'll give it some thought."

Kaler pivoted and trekked along the sidewalk a couple blocks before circling back. The dance-off would be a great opportunity to get closer to her. He stumbled into an overzealous couple leaned against the facade of a party store, and draped himself next to them, clearing his throat.

"Um… um…" The boy moved three steps away from the girl and scuffed the sidewalk with his Nike. "Sorry, officer."

"How about you guys take this indoors?" Avery puffed his chest. "I don't want to see you out here again tonight."

He retraced the blocks through parking lots, stopping behind a small ficus, feet shy of the stone bench.

Pandora fiddled with a sandal strap. "So, are you married or do you have any children? Are there more Megan Carters running around town pulling pranks?"

"Not married, no children." Megan tapped her cigarette against the arm of the bench. "You know me. A free spirit."

"Yes, I do. So, you got any good gossip? It's been a while." Pandora's widened eyes twinkled.

"As a matter of fact, I do." Taking another long draw, Megan leaned closer to her friend. "Some crazy stuff about you."

Avery smirked. He couldn't wait to hear.

Savannah unzipped the side pocket of her purse, found her tube of plum lip gloss, and applied a liberal layer. "What have you heard?"

Megan tightened her ponytail and checked her watch. "It's time to get back to my shift. You want something to eat? You can sit at my table, and I'll tell you all about it."

Savannah dug out the gift certificate. "Yeah. I guess. Opal wanted to pay for my meal. They said she sent it over a couple hours ago."

"Opal?" Megan scoffed. "I can't believe she'd do that. One time, a younger couple came in on a date. The boy was fifteen or so, like their parents dropped them off and he couldn't even drive. Well, he forgot his money, and Opal would not comp them a meal. I ended up paying for it out of my tips because I felt so sorry for the kid." She pointed through the window at a group of guys focused on a big-screen TV above the bar. "Do you have a secret admirer?"

Savannah shrugged. She doubted it. Especially not if everyone in town knew she'd come for the farm. "Maybe my lawyer? He was probably afraid I wouldn't eat, and he wants me ready for tomorrow. So anyway, about the gossip…?"

Megan lit another cigarette and peeked over her shoulder like she expected someone to crawl out of the bushes. "I waited Mona and Geoff Spencer's table a few minutes ago. They came in for dinner. More like she dragged him. No one else would serve them."

Ugh. Geoff. Savannah toyed with a wayward strand of her hair. Thank goodness she'd missed him. "I understand. Geoff's such a jerk."

"Actually, Mona's the jerk. Geoff is fine. You'd never believe it, but he turned out kinda decent."

"I doubt that. Mona's his aunt, right? The one who used to work the front desk at school?"

"Yeah." Balancing the cigarette between her teeth, Megan centered her apron and retied the strings. "Anyway, he's all bummed out about losing his farm." She chuckled. "Your fault, right?"

Savannah's cheeks burned. "He deserved it."

"I told you, Geoff changed. You might want to get to know him again before you make judgment."

Megan, too? Was she out of her mind? Had Geoff brainwashed everyone? "After the way he treated you?"

Megan dragged her scuffed shoes as she started toward the restaurant. "Believe it or not, he's paying for me to take classes at Mahoney Cosmetology School. He's apologized about a hundred times. Okay, back to Mona. She said she was your mother."

"What?" Savannah's purse fell to the sidewalk. The contents spilled at her feet. "That can't be true."

"I know, right? The woman is crazy. Geoff called her a liar." Megan knelt to help collect Savannah's things. Smoke swirled around her chin. A tube of mascara rolled onto the street, and she chased it, brushing past two link-armed college girls. She returned to the bench and presented it with flourish. "Voila."

Savannah tucked it in her side pocket. "She has to be lying. What else did she say?"

"She was. He got her to admit to lying, and then she said she named you Pandora. She said your mother asked her to take care of you, and she decided to leave you at the church because she didn't know what else to do."

"That makes no sense. Why would she try to claim to be my mother?" Savannah tried to conjure an image of Mona. Did they even look alike? Vague memories of the handful of times she'd seen his aunt pick him up from school rendered no similarities. Mona had the same sharp nose and jutting chin as Geoff's dad. Savannah resembled her adoptive parents more. It was a crazy ploy to try to con her out of the farm, and it would not work. "Anything else?"

"No. She saw me standing there and went on a rant about our coffee." Megan stabbed the ashtray with the butt. "That's Mona Spencer for you."

"You know I had my name changed when I moved to Chicago. I go by Savannah now."

Megan stood, shaking the ashes off her apron. "Savannah. I like it. You should have told me." She sighed. "I've got to get in there, or I'll be looking for another job. Go through the front door and tell them you want to sit in my section."

"Okay. See you." Savannah walked toward Opal's entrance. She pulled a mirror from her purse and checked her lipstick, narrowly missing a police officer. She looked up to apologize then shivered when she met his icy green eyes. Avery Kaler. Other than a hint of gray in his close-cropped hair, he looked terrifying as usual. The loser had done nothing but watch while all the middle school boys tormented her.

Chills giving way to fury, she clenched her fists, drew in a deep breath, and sidestepped him. "Excuse me, Officer Kaler."

He grinned. "Pandora. Glad to see you back in town. You look beautiful. Will you be staying?"

"Not planning on it." She strode three paces closer to the restaurant. "Bye, now."

He closed the space between them. "I'm having a late dinner. Are you hungry? It's no fun eating alone."

Tingles spread down her arms then moved over her entire body like tiny bugs. He hadn't lost an ounce of his creepy factor. Didn't he realize she was decades younger than him? She flashed a polite smile. "I'm meeting someone. Thanks for the offer."

His shoulders slumped, and a frown distorted his face like Scar from *The Lion King*.

She snatched the door handle and tugged it open before the hostess had a chance. "After you."

He reached over her head and grabbed the door by the edge. "Ladies first."

"Suit yourself." She smiled at the hostess. "I'd like to sit in Megan Carter's section, please."

The waitress led her through cherry high-tops to a red leather booth in the left rear. As Savannah settled into the seat, another girl led Officer Kaler to a seat a few tables away. She cringed.

Megan stopped next to her, frowning. "What's wrong?"

"The cop who used to work in our school. He asked to eat with me." Savannah gave a nervous laugh. "I told him I'm meeting someone."

"Never fear." Megan winked. "Someone coming right up."

"No, Meg…" Savannah groaned. "Wait."

Megan had already resumed waitressing, approaching a table full of drunken college boys. Savannah slid lower in the booth and covered her forehead with the menu. Megan had always gone for the wild boys back in eighth grade. Who knew what taste she had now? Savannah hid her eyes.

She dared a peek between her fingers. Thank goodness. Megan passed the college boys and entered a partition on the opposite corner of the restaurant. She returned, arm-in-arm with another policeman.

Officer Kaler scowled at the younger cop, who countered with a stone-faced nod.

Megan grinned. "Dora, do you remember Nathan Smith? He graduated with us."

Another of Geoff's favorite victims. "I do. Hi, Nathan."

He sat in the booth opposite her. "Hi, Dora." Splaying his ring-free hands, he reached across the table. "Meg said Avery bothered you."

"Not really bothering. He just asked if I wanted to eat with him and followed me in here."

Nathan shook his head. "He can be intimidating. Don't let him get to you. He's just a bully."

A table full of people watched them through the wall divider separating the right side of the restaurant from the bar area. "Aren't you with that big group?"

"My family's celebrating my brother's birthday, but we've finished. So if you want, I can wait with you and see you home."

"That would be awesome." She faced Megan. "I'll get the blackened chicken salad to go." She refocused on Nathan. "I'm staying at the hotel up the street, so it's not far. I hate to take time away from you and your family."

"Not a problem. Like I said, we had finished." He picked up the saltshaker, inspected it from the base, and then twisted the lid tighter. "So, Dora, can I ask the question on everyone's mind? Will you stay in town? If not, will you sell the farm back to Geoff? All his workers are nervous."

She pressed her spine into the booth cushion and squeezed her wrists between her knees. "To be honest, I'm not sure what I'll do with the property. This has all been kind of a shock to me. I'll have to give it some thought, but I'm not planning to stay in Dreyfus." Tapping her fingers against the table, she stole a glance at Kaler, who still stared. "Selling it back to him would be an option."

Nathan's cell dinged. He inspected the screen. "Mom wants to see you. Is that okay?"

No. It wasn't okay. "Sure, I guess."

Nathan's mom, her seventh grade English teacher. The tall lady with boy-cut hair stirred no memories. Three bulky boys, two women carrying babies, and a grumpy-looking older man followed her.

"Hi, Dora."

Savannah stood, extending her hand, scarcely resisting the urge to shrink back. "Mrs. Smith. Good to see you."

Mrs. Smith's thin arms engulfed Savannah. "I'm so glad you've returned. I've worried so over the years." She grasped Savannah's face with both hands. "Have you talked to your mama?"

Retreating, Savannah studied a small round stain on the carpet. "Not yet. It's on my list."

Ten minutes of small talk blended into mush. Her head throbbed.

When Megan rushed up with a take-out bag, Savannah handed her the gift certificate, with the new balance marked in pen. "You can use the rest of it."

Megan took it to the bar station. The redheaded girl running the register eyed Savannah, the certificate, and then Officer Kaler.

Savannah met his stare. Ugh. Surely, it wasn't from him. She shivered. "I'm ready to go, Nathan."

She left the restaurant and headed toward the hotel, accompanied by Nathan and his entourage. When he escorted her into the lobby, she exhaled a breath she didn't know she'd been holding. "Thanks. He's so weird."

"Don't sweat him. He likes to let people know he's all-powerful around here." Nathan shook his head. "Anyway, have a good night. Hope things go well in the morning. Be easy on Geoff."

She tapped the elevator button. Be easy on Geoff? First Megan, now him. Had these people entered a time warp? Didn't they remember?

The steel doors parted and she headed to the fourth floor. She remembered. Nothing else mattered. No way would she be easy on him.

Chapter Seven

Geoff parked his rusty Ford alongside a Lexus in front of the white brick courthouse. Dora's fancy-schmancy lawyer, no doubt. Savannah's lawyer. He'd never get used to calling her that.

A familiar Camaro pulled in on his other side. Mona stepped out, wearing a bright blue pantsuit and reeking of flowery perfume. Of course, she'd show. A smudge of coal-black dye stained her forehead. "Why drive around in that old thing when you have a brand new truck sitting in your drive?"

"Too muddy." Geoff planted his feet on the asphalt. "What's up with the outfit?"

She patted him on the shoulder and fussed with his plaid flannel collar. "You could have dressed more proper yourself, nephew."

"I'm meeting with a handful of people and a judge. I don't know why you're here. They'll read over everything and decide when I have to leave the farm."

"You need my support." She tugged at his shirttail then reached higher.

Geoff shielded his face with his arm. "Stop it! Mona!"

"You've got this long nose hair. Here, let me get it."

He jolted backward into someone and pivoted. "Sorry, Larry."

Mona scrunched her nose. "I smell stink. Lawyer stink."

Larry scowled. "Why are you here?"

Geoff moved between them, holding them apart. "I appreciate you wanting to offer moral support, but you can't come with us."

"I have to come with you." She grabbed Larry by the shoulder. "I tried to tell Geoff last night. I have information."

"You have gossip or drama." Geoff clenched his jaw. "Or lies."

Larry scratched his neck. "We should hear what she has to say."

"It's simple." Mona hung her head. "I had a child out of wedlock. I'm her mother."

Geoff lunged toward her then stopped himself. "I told you last night I'm not buying your nonsense. You don't look like her."

"Even if you are, I fail to see how that changes things." Larry shrugged and walked toward the courthouse entrance. "Mr. McMillan excluded everyone from his will except her."

Mona followed, Geoff in tow. "I'm the next of kin. Not her. I should inherit." Her lower lip protruding, she picked a long black hair off her pant leg. "I don't know why you won't believe me."

"You'd have to prove it." Larry held out his hand. "Fork over that hair, and I'll have your DNA tested."

She rubbed the hair between her finger and thumb, and let it fall to the floor. "No."

They passed through the double glass doors. Geoff draped himself against the interior brick wall, crossing his ankles. "You want to get the farm in your name so I won't lose it. Ridiculous."

She huffed. "I'm trying to help."

Sliding down the wall to a leather bench, Geoff stared out the atrium window. Traffic crept down Main Street. The bellhop at the Grand Dreyfus Tower helped a feeble white-haired lady into a dark sedan. Geoff loosened the button Mona tightened and spread his collar.

Maria's decorative touches remained in the hotel window—red damask curtains and gold plating around the sill. He lowered his hand, covering his aching heart. It had been the only charity project she'd helped him finish. If she'd lived, could he have changed her?

The revolving door spun, and Geoff's breath caught. Dora—no, *Savannah*—emerged, wearing a high-necked sleeveless dress. A black band cinched her tiny waist, separating a teal and white floral pattern from the solid black skirt. Classy. The last thing he'd expected.

She pushed the pedestrian crossing button and rocked on high-heeled sandals. With her tight-pressed lips and darting gaze, she appeared fragile. Beautiful. Dangerous.

Geoff shook his head. He was an idiot.

Larry whistled. "Hard to believe she's even the same person."

Mona coughed. "Stop gaping, fools."

Savannah held her head high and shoulders square, like she walked a tightrope. She planted one foot on the marble courthouse steps and turned toward the window, her forehead creasing.

Geoff stumbled a few paces. "Let's head to the conference room. We can wait there." He glanced at Mona. "Go home. I'll call you later."

When she rounded the corner, Larry shielded his eyes with his palm. "That woman is all kinds of crazy."

"You don't have to tell me anything about that."

The courthouse, like everything else Savannah had seen of Dreyfus, had changed. Where stark white walls had once given the feel of a sterile hospital, they now held bright children's art in thick, bronze frames. One painting caught her eye, a watercolor dancer with auburn hair. It reminded her of her college dancing days. She traced the frame's edge and eyed Geoff across the lobby. If he could have seen her then, bet he wouldn't have called her Panda.

She grimaced. Why did she care what he thought?

A middle-aged woman with a bad dye job marched to her, fists clenched. Savannah shrunk against the wall.

The woman moved so close the pungent odor of a menthol cigarette overtook her strong floral perfume. "You didn't tell me how ugly she was," she called over her shoulder. "She can lose weight, but she can't lose ugly."

Tears burned the corners of Savannah's eyes. She willed them to stay put.

Geoff crossed the lobby in four strides. "Mona, you aren't helping."

His voice, sharp and stern, set her arm hairs prickling. Or was it his general presence? She spun on her heels and clacked her toes against the shiny tile floor.

Where was Peter? He'd told her to arrive early. She approached a short middle-aged woman sitting behind a long, cherry desk.

"Can I help you, dearie?" Ugh. Aramis for Men. Did everyone in Dreyfus wear too much cologne? No doubt, since Rose likely sold it to them and coached them to model her own overuse. Savannah turned her head to the right, inhaled, and faced the woman again. "Have you seen Peter Anderson? My lawyer? He was supposed to meet me here at eight thirty."

The woman lifted her bifocals and placed them lower on her nose. "No. I saw your mama this morning. She looked like she'd been crying all night."

Savannah lifted her gaze to the ceiling and puffed her cheeks. Air stuck in her lungs. "Rose is here?"

"No. She's taking a scrapbooking class at the library." The woman pointed out the window, where Peter shuffled toward the entrance. "There's Mr. Anderson."

"Oh, good."

She stood and patted Savannah's arm. "Don't you remember me, sugar?"

Savannah licked dry lips. "Sorry. It was so long ago."

"I'm Carolyn Howard. I was in your mama's first sewing group."

"Right." Savannah forced a smile. "I do remember you. You made me a black and white sweatshirt." Which led everyone to call her Panda.

"You need to go see Rose. She's torn all to pieces over this. That McMillan man stormed into her house a few weeks ago and told her who he was. She's tried to call you...."

An adorable girl in a yellow sundress and straw hat smiled from Mrs. Howard's desk calendar. October 8. Three months past Rose's birthday, the last time they'd attempted civility. "I'll go visit her. I promise. This was all a shock to me, too. I'm trying to get my bearings."

Digging through her purse, Mrs. Howard whistled "Amazing Grace." She retrieved a white card from an envelope. "Here. Let me give you a ticket to the charity barbecue. I wanted to go, but my arthritis gets to me."

"Sounds interesting, but I'm not sure I'll be in town."

"Of course you will." Mrs. Howard pushed the ticket across the counter. "It'll be at Georgia's in a few weeks. Benefits special needs children, to get them a new playground built." She winked. "Geoff Spencer's going."

Savannah sighed and accepted the ticket. Of course he was. Geoff, the benevolent town celebrity wouldn't miss a benefit like this. Go figure. "I'll give it some thought."

Mrs. Howard glanced up and down the hallway. "Be kind to Mr. Spencer. I know he hurt you, but you need to know he's changed. He does so much good for our community." She leaned closer. "And he needs a good wife."

Savannah held up the ticket, like she could disappear behind it. The woman was delusional. "I'll try to."

The courtroom doors swung open, and a crowd of older women burst out, rushing like a line of ants toward the bathroom.

59

Mrs. Howard grinned and waved. "Agnes! Donna! It's Rose's girl."

Several women marched closer.

Savannah clasped her hands, tapping her fingertips against her knuckles. She eyed the counter trim. Could she melt and slide under it? Where was Peter?

Whispers enveloped her. Holding perfect posture, she smiled and returned the women's embraces.

"Dora." A wispy gray-haired lady in a tent-style dress slammed her walker into Savannah's foot. "We expected better of you."

Savannah poked a knothole in the wood paneling and held her breath. Geoff was Prince Charming, and she was Maleficent.

A few painful minutes later, the crowd parted, and Savannah followed Mrs. Howard's directions to the conference room.

Geoff sat at a table with a portly sandy-haired man. They both met her gaze, and she lost hold of her purse, the strap catching on her elbow.

Larry Morgan was Geoff's lawyer? No wonder he lost the farm. She swallowed. She needed to attack before he had a chance. "Lar-Lar! Look at you, all grown up and... Am I right? You're *practicing* law?"

Larry blew her a kiss. "Pandora Barrett. Look at you all skinny and fashionable. Not at all like we'd expected."

"If you're implying I don't look like a Panda—" She glared at Geoff.

"Ms. Barrett!" Peter hurried to her side and gave Larry a menacing look. "Sorry I'm late. I had to tie up some loose ends with Frank's hospital bills."

Larry stood and shook Peter's hand. Geoff did too, but kept his focus on her.

She shivered. Why did he have such kissable lips?

60

He extended a hand. Their fingers touched for an instant. Her smooth, silky skin brushed against his callused palms. A jolt surged through her body. She retreated, crossing her arms. "Hello, Geoff."

"Dora."

"Savannah."

His chest puffed and fell.

They all sat around the table, and the judge joined them.

"Ms. Barrett, do you remember me? Craig Rhodes. Used to play golf with Phil every week until he threw out his back. You should give your ol' dad a call."

Of course, he had to bring up Phil. "Yes, sir."

"Morning, Geoff, Larry." He faced Peter. "Mr. Anderson. Are we ready to get started? I understand you have documents relating Mr. McMillan's wishes."

"I do." Peter passed copies of a single sheet around the table. "Mr. McMillan wants to allow Mr. Spencer to remain on the property until the first of January. This will give him time to find a new location and prevent his workers from losing income."

Savannah accepted the page from Peter. Geoff could maintain business as usual until the New Year. Frank would pay the cost to move his possessions up to five-thousand dollars. She forced herself to breathe and sat on her trembling hands.

"Sounds fair." Larry jotted on a legal pad. "And you mentioned compensation at our last meeting. Did Mr. McMillan agree to it?"

"We're squared away for this." Peter handed Larry another page. "Mr. McMillan and I discussed the request at length." He addressed the judge. "If you'll recall, Mr. Spencer asked if Mr. McMillan might be willing to counter his loss of property with assistance to one of his charities, since the purchase of a new farm would hamper his ability to meet the needs of those he serves. This is documentation for 2.5 million to be donated to the adult scholarship fund in exchange for the property."

Savannah covered her gasp with a pitiful excuse for a cough. She stole a glance at Geoff. Did he have tears in his eyes?

"Great. Thanks." Geoff's voice cracked. He relaxed his shoulders. "More than I'd expected. This will help a lot."

"Frank applauded your efforts to increase adult education in the county, and he appreciated the donations you'd made to the library." Peter smiled. "He had a lot of respect for you, Mr. Spencer, and a deep regret over hurting you in this process. Now, in exchange for the scholarship fund, he asks you to take a more active role in the transfer."

Larry's cell buzzed, and he silenced it. "What does that mean exactly? An active role?"

"Since Mr. McMillan died, Ms. Barrett is the sole heir to his estate. This is contingent on her honoring the agreement between Mr. Spencer and Mr. McMillan, and one between Mr. McMillan and herself. If she refuses to abide by either agreement, the University gets the estate. Mr. McMillan requested I not disclose the uses." Peter swallowed. "And as discussed, Mr. Spencer is not eligible to purchase the property. The will states the property not be sold or rented to any member of the Spencer family, in perpetuity."

Savannah stifled a yawn as they passed around paperwork and everyone signed. Peter had instructed her not to speak unless someone asked her something, so she listened and gave the occasional smile and nod. After signing her part, she kicked off her sandals and stretched her toes, bumping Geoff's shoe. Her cheeks warming, she gripped the table edge.

Peter leaned forward, passing another document to everyone. "You asked about the active role. Mr. McMillan stipulated the following in exchange for the scholarship fund. Mr. Spencer is to accompany Ms. Barrett on the scavenger hunt, as it would require intimate knowledge about the farm, and also because she may find herself in need of a bodyguard."

"What?" Savannah flicked her gaze to the ceiling and huffed.

"Are you serious?" Larry stood, shoving the papers to the center of the table.

Geoff's brow raised and his jaw clenched. He remained silent, his gaze focused on hers in an unsettling stare.

The lawyers' words became jumbled noise. Savannah closed her eyes and trembled, assaulted by flashbacks of the entire middle school class laughing as she fell through a wooden stage Geoff had built for her. Their chants—"Panda! Panda! Panda!"—rang loud in her ears.

She couldn't go on this trip with him. No way.

The room felt like an inferno. Sweat trickled down her hairline and disturbed her makeup. Couldn't it be over already?

"Are we finished then?" Judge Rhodes checked his watch.

"Yes." Peter stacked the papers and tucked his pen in his briefcase.

"I'm not going with him." She folded her arms and narrowed her eyes at Peter. "Money or no money, it's not worth it."

"You have to go." Peter slapped the signed agreement on the table. "You scrawled your John Hancock across the dotted line, remember? If you don't go, you relinquish the farm to the state."

Geoff closed his eyes and opened them again. He glanced at the judge, then Larry, Peter, and her.

Judge Rhodes laid a hand on his shoulder. "What do you need, son?"

"Sir, I..." He looked at her and swallowed. "Can I talk to you alone for a few minutes?"

Several nervous glances crossed the room. She brought clasped fingers to her lips. "No."

"Dora. Please. For a few minutes."

Peter nodded toward the door. He and the others left, and Geoff moved to the chair beside her. She clutched her purse.

He turned sideways and twisted her seat to him. His wintergreen breath tickled her neck. "I want to tell you how sorry I am. For calling you Panda yesterday and making fun of you in school. For Herb stealing the farm. I'm sorry for everything."

Savannah kicked over a sandal. If she lifted her gaze a hint, she'd brush his lips. How many times had she dreamed of being this close? No, crazy thinking! Focus. "What do you expect me to say? It's fine?" She bit her lip. It would never be fine.

"I don't expect you to accept my apology. I did want to give one, though."

She pressed her spine against the stiff chair and folded her arms. "Then why did you call me Panda?"

He picked at the hem of his flannel shirt. "I don't know. I—"

"Whatever kind of stunt you're trying to pull, I'm not interested in being humiliated again. I didn't come to relive the past, okay?" She pushed her chair back and stood, the tightness in her lungs diminishing as the space grew between them. "All I want is to find the answers and move on with my life."

"Please, if we have to do this together for scholarship money—"

"I don't care about your scholarship money." She spun on her heels and stalked out the conference room door. A digital clock in the courthouse hall flashed 10:47.

Larry held up an envelope. "Your lawyer asked me to give you this."

A bus ticket. Birmingham. She puffed her cheeks, unfolding the note. *Savannah, even if you don't want to go along with Frank's wishes, you should at least take the trip for yourself. Find your roots.* Fine. She'd take the bus to Birmingham. No further. Not with Geoff. She didn't need a stupid farm anyway.

Larry dragged his left hand through his sweat-mopped hair. "Mr. Anderson said he had to run, but go to the Dreyfus bank, and everything will be ready for you there. Call this number if you change your mind, and I'll let Geoff know to start packing. At least give him time to find a new place."

Chapter Eight

Geoff gripped the rain-dampened rail, dodging Savannah's march down the courthouse steps. When she stalked toward the hotel, he let out the breath he'd been holding, whistling as the air passed his teeth. "Birmingham?"

Larry nodded. "Birmingham, bro. No idea why. Her lawyer said to give her the ticket and suggest you follow her there. What did you say to her?"

Geoff flared his nostrils, expelling another blast of air. "I tried to apologize. She didn't want to hear it."

Larry approached his truck then glanced over his shoulder. "I could have told you that."

Geoff hung back. Across the street, the rusty bus depot sign hung cockeyed. "Why would she take a bus? They barely run through here anymore."

"Who knows? Not your business. Go. Get lunch and pack a bag. Follow her, like her lawyer said. You should be celebrating right now. Mr. McMillan financed those scholarships. He gave more than we could have hoped."

Savannah turned left, passing the hotel.

"I guess so." A bottle cap glinted by his feet, and Geoff picked it up, twisting the Miller crest straighter. "Wonder where she's going now."

The courthouse door creaked behind him.

"Geoff, son. I hoped to catch you."

He pivoted and pasted on a smile. "Judge Henry. How are you?"

"Fine, fine." The sixty-something balding man caught up to Geoff in two paces. "Come, sit with me. I want to talk for a minute."

"See you, Geoff. I'll be praying." Larry climbed into his truck and tossed an abrupt wave before backing.

Geoff followed the judge down the concrete steps and the stone path spanning the courthouse perimeter. He walked past bright fall blooms to a cozy sitting area. He settled on the right stone bench, rested his elbows on his knees, and stared at his muddy work boots.

Judge Henry sat on the opposite bench, his mouth thin-pressed. "I've been worried about you. How did things go today? Did you convince her to sell?"

"No. According to Mr. McMillan's will, I can't buy the property. Ever. Even if I could, I doubt she'd sell. She's convinced I'm going to humiliate her like I did in middle school."

"Talk to her. She'll understand. You're both adults now."

"I tried. She has no plans to forgive me." Geoff kicked at gravel with his steel-enforced toe. "I don't blame her. You remember back in high school how you told me I had to make it up to everyone?"

Judge Henry stroked the tuft of fine hair covering his chin. "Of course I do."

"Well, I've made it up to everyone except her. I don't think she's going to let me."

"Give her time." Judge Henry dabbed sweat from his forehead with a white monogrammed handkerchief. "I miss your mama—such a special lady, and so sick herself. I couldn't believe she still ran the farm even after your daddy died. She'd be turning over in her grave right now." He cleared his throat. "You know, we were high school sweethearts for a while. I always thought the world of her."

"She was special." Geoff flexed his hands. "But you're wrong. She'd have said something crazy like I owe all this to Dora for embarrassing her."

"You're right. God has a plan for you two, a possibility you haven't even considered yet." The old judge winked, crossed the garden, and patted Geoff's shoulder. "You two used to play in the yard in front of my house. Everybody thought you'd be forever pals."

"Me and Dora? At your house? I don't remember."

"You were best buds, for sure. Give her space and then, when the time comes, apologize. You'll be close again one of these days."

"I'll try." Geoff stood. "I'll have to find her first. Thanks for the talk."

"My pleasure."

He strolled to the front of the courthouse, shielding his eyes from the bright sun. The old depot sign teetered in the cool October breeze. Dora seemed way too fancy for the bus. Why would her lawyer buy her a ticket? And why Birmingham, of all places?

The once-crowded Main Street had cleared, although Opal's Bar and Grille had patrons lined around the building. No sign of Dora. Where would she go? Her parents' house? Worth a shot.

Phil and Rose Barrett lived two miles away at the dead end of Hibiscus Avenue, in an old yellow Victorian with bright pink shutters. Geoff parked in the street, forced there by the abundance of cars in front of Phil's garage. Mike Puckett's pickup. Katie Henry's Nissan, wrecked again. A Prius parked under a canopy. Make that a brand new Prius on bricks. No sign of Dora.

Around the back of the house, steel hit rock seven times, each with an accompanying, "Argh!" He followed the gravel path.

Rose sat on her knees, stabbing the ground with a spade.

Phil stood behind her, his arms folded over his chest. "I told you, Rosie, I can borrow an auger from someone. Wait."

"I could send Zach Allen over with an auger tonight." Geoff moved closer, and they both faced him.

"What do you want?" Phil scowled.

"Phil!" Rose tossed the spade toward his feet.

Phil turned up his lips, giving his cheeks a dramatic squeeze. "Excuse me. Mr. Spencer! What brings you to our humble abode? Do you need me to do some work on that truck of yours? I thought you bought a new one." He flashed a triumphant grin at Rose. "Better?"

She huffed.

Geoff stifled a chuckle. "I'm looking for Dora. I thought she'd come here."

Rose pushed her sunglasses up onto her forehead. Curly gray hairs spilled around her face. "Is she in town? Have you seen her?"

"She came home to sign paperwork. Frank McMillan died." He winced and glanced from her to Phil. "You didn't know." In this town full of gossips, no one mentioned anything?

"I can't imagine her coming back to support you." Phil extended his hand to his wife, and she jerked away.

"Mr. Barrett, I'm sorry for hurting your daughter. I want to make things right."

"I guess giving her the farm is supposed to accomplish that?" Phil's face softened. "Frank came to visit about six weeks ago. Told us the whole story. He's Dora's great-grandfather, and she'll inherit his estate. He wanted her to make amends with us. Even bought her a car—hers for the taking if she'd visit us for an hour. As you can see, the thing still sits there waiting for her."

The Prius.

"She'll visit soon." Geoff loosened wet leaves from his boots.

"She hasn't been home in fourteen years." Phil spat into the yard, drawing a sharp look from his wife. "I haven't laid eyes on her, other than a handful of pictures my sister sent."

Rose flashed a wide-toothed smile. "Oh. Would you like to see them? I could make you some tea."

"No, thank you."

"Nonsense." She turned to her husband. "Do you want anything?"

"Nah. I've got to fix Hannah's air conditioner. I told her mother I'd have it done by six."

"Suit yourself. Geoff, come on in the house."

"I should go look for Dora."

"That can wait." She put her hands on her hips. "There's always time for tea."

"Well, okay, Mrs. Barrett. I'll have some tea." He stepped across the threshold onto plush beige carpet and followed her around a tchotchke-covered table, the creepy eyes of statuesque kittens staring back at him. One, a black-and-white stood on its hind legs scratching at a ceramic pedestal. Sleek like Dora, who reminded him nothing of a panda now. More like a lioness. She'd be an awesome kisser. His cheeks warmed. Crazy thoughts.

"Sit here on the couch, and we'll have a look. Here's some of your mother I bet you haven't seen."

His mom's thin face, framed in wavy brown locks, smiled with her familiar benevolence. He flipped through the album, finding her sewing, baking cookies, weaving baskets—always some act of service, despite his father's protests.

He tapped his toes inside his boots while Rose described every event in detail. His jaw ached from polite smiles, and his heart ached from forgotten memories. He stretched out his legs. "Phil said you had pictures of Dora. Could I see them?"

Raising her eyebrows, Rose grinned. "You know, she's single. It's been a long time since you two had your... issues."

First Judge Henry and now her mom. This town drove him crazy sometimes. He stuck his lower lip out and drew it back. "Yes, Mrs. Barrett. I'm sure she still hates me. I tried to apologize, and she wouldn't hear it. I doubt Phil would approve if I asked her out."

"Well, we taught her better." She nudged the album closer. "Don't worry about Phil. He's a lion on the outside and a kitten within that tough exterior."

Yep. Which makes Dora the lioness. Trouble Geoff didn't want.

An old grandfather clock chimed from the hallway, and he shifted, sinking lower in the couch. "I think I'm ready for tea."

"Oh. Sorry. I forgot. Be right back."

He flipped the page to a picture of a group of uniformed girls holding pompoms and lifted the album closer. Dora's vibrant, cheerful face far outshone the other girls.

Her genuine smile captivated him. In photo after photo, she held up trophies, a wide grin exposing her teeth. Looked like she found happiness in Chicago.

Rose returned with two tall glasses of iced tea. "Oh, there's a good one." She reached into the plastic sleeve and removed a wallet-sized copy of an individual pose. Dora rested one hand on her hip, clutching a sparkly pompom. Long, tanned legs stood taut beneath a clingy short uniform. "Here. Take one of these."

"Um...thanks." Geoff downed his glass in quick gulps and tucked the picture in his wallet. "Guess I'm going now. I'll try to find Dora in town."

She engulfed him in a hearty embrace until he freed himself from her grasp and jetted out the front door to his truck. The dash clock flashed noon when he turned the ignition. Lunchtime. Wish he'd thought to ask Larry about the time on the ticket.

Savannah's cell buzzed. Peter. She sashayed past a cluster of businessmen and paused by the steps to an accounting office.

"Hello?"

"Ms. Barrett." She could hear the grin in his voice.

71

"I'm walking toward the bank. Where are you?"

He coughed. "I'm on my way to Lexington."

She fumbled her phone, caught it between her knees, and brought it to her ear. "Why did you leave?"

"I had other clients today. Don't worry. I've checked you out of the hotel, and everything is ready at the bank. Go see the woman in the side office."

"You're not returning?" Savannah scanned the facades and storefronts along the downtown strip. Three streets down, the Dreyfus Bank sign loomed above the roof of the neighboring music shop.

Peter chuckled. "I feared you'd changed your mind. I've also taken the liberty of purchasing you a round-trip ticket to Birmingham. Did Larry Morgan get it to you? Unless, of course, you'd like to visit your parents."

"You can be such a pain sometimes."

"Thanks, Mr. Anderson, for helping settle my great-grandfather's affairs," Peter squeaked in falsetto. "Thanks, Mr. Anderson, for helping with my inheritance and paying your *own* money to buy me a bus ticket."

She huffed. "Fine. I'll go to the bank and take the bus."

"Go see your parents."

"No way."

The call ended in response. Savannah shoved the phone in her bag and headed down Main Street, tendrils of her hair dancing in the intensifying wind. She tucked them behind her ear and inspected herself in the glass doors before grabbing the handle and jerking the right one open.

A neon flyer hung on the interior wall—Dreyfus Dance-Off, Only Four Weeks Away. Help Raise Money For Special Needs. She fingered the ticket in her pocket. If she stayed in town, it would be the perfect opportunity to show everyone how much better she looked. Nothing like a panda.

Her heel caught in a crack as she stepped forward. She teetered, momentum throwing her toward the sidewalk. Shaking her head, she chuckled. She wouldn't impress anyone with moves like that.

She passed through the atrium into the bank lobby and stood in line behind scores of men, all dressed in flannel shirts and muddy jeans. The whole room stunk of earth, and bits of dirt clotted on the marble tile floor. She wrinkled her nose, and the men glared back. Geoff's friends. Partners in bullying. Enemies.

She squared her shoulders and walked past them to the offices lining the left wall.

A woman waved through the glass window, then poked her head out the door. "Ms. Barrett?"

Savannah nodded.

"Welcome. Peter Anderson said you'd come see me."

"Yep. I'm here." Her garment bag and carry-on waited in one of the two chairs behind the mahogany desk. She sat in the other. She glanced at the nameplate. Kathy Sanders. One of Rose's sewing partners. "So, you knew Frank."

"Yes, I did." Kathy smiled. "Quite a character."

"I never got to know him."

"My condolences. I knew his illness had progressed more than he admitted. Poor man, he thought he could run around like a teenager." She pulled out a clipboard and dug through a stack of papers. "Okay, Miss Barrett, here are the instructions he gave me. First, I'm going to activate the prepaid credit card Mr. Anderson left for you. Every business day, I will send a list of your transactions to him, and he will authorize me to add to the balance when you've completed certain tasks. For example, your first stop is a museum in Birmingham. When I see the ticket purchase, I'll let him know you've made it."

"So I still get to use the travel money, even though I'm going without Geoff?"

"Mr. Anderson didn't tell me any different."

"Okay." Savannah accepted the card and tucked it into her purse. "What else?"

"The money is contingent, of course, on you being in the right locations in sequence. If we find evidence you've strayed from Mr. McMillan's instructions—skipping ahead or stalling, etc.—the account will be frozen. There will be a total of eight payments, totaling twenty-thousand dollars." She handed over a paper. "Here's the list of permissible purchases."

Savannah snorted. "Reasonable shoes." She lifted her feet. "Like these?" The leather in her four-inch pumps wrinkled as she wiggled right and left.

"I love your shoes." Kathy sifted through a stack of manila folders and retrieved a paper-clipped document. "He also wanted me to give you this. In here, you'll find some information on taxes and inheritance money. There's a card attached for a man who can help you if you have any questions. But I'll hold on to this until you've finished the quest, since you'll be traveling and all."

"Okay, sounds good."

The phone rang, and Kathy raised a finger, picking up the receiver. "People's Heritage Bank, Kathy speaking. How may I serve you today?"

On the window ledge, a picture of a group of women smiled from behind a plastic table at some church function. Sure enough, Rose glared from the center. A pang stabbed Savannah. She should have run by for a while.

When Kathy replaced the receiver, she followed Savannah's gaze, then gave her a stern look. "Have you been to see your mama?"

"No, ma'am, not yet." Savannah focused on the list. "I'll go soon, though."

Kathy touched Savannah's arm. "I know your mother is a complicated woman. She drives us all crazy at church, too, with her worrying, gossiping, and such. But she loves you, and all she ever talks about is how she wishes you'd come home." Kathy walked around the desk and wrapped her arm around Savannah's shoulders.

"It's been a struggle keeping such a big secret from her for all this time."

"I'm sorry. I'm sure she'll understand." Savannah offered a forced smile. Rose wouldn't understand. Rose never understood.

A man rapped the doorframe, holding out a piece of paper with his free hand. Kathy scrawled her name across the page in one quick, flowing loop and turned back to Savannah. "I forgot. Peter said you had the lockbox key."

"I do." She took the right side of the clamshell box out of her garment bag and popped it open. "Oops, wrong one." She lifted the lid on the other half. "Okay, here's the key."

"Those boxes are beautiful," Kathy said. "Real treasures."

"Yes, they are." Savannah pushed them together until they clicked. She undid the latch and slid them apart, revealing the old deed. "This one I've had since birth, and he gave me the second one right before he died." She eyed her bulging garment bag. "How big is this lockbox? Is there room for these in there, too? I'd hate to lose them on the trip."

"There's no room in Frank's safe deposit, but you can rent another. Seventy-five dollars for a year."

"What about for a month?"

"I'm sorry," Kathy shook her head, "but you'll have to pay an annual fee. We don't rent them on a month-by-month basis at this branch. So, would you like one?"

"I guess so. Can I purchase it with the prepaid account?"

"No." Kathy pulled the list back to her side of the desk and scanned it. "You'll have to pay for it out of your own money."

Savannah passed over her credit card.

"Okay, then. Let's go get this taken care of, so you can be on your way."

"Sounds good."

75

Kathy led her down a teal-carpeted hall to a wall lined with steel boxes. She withdrew a set of keys from her pocket and unlocked a midsized drawer. "Here's your new one."

Savannah removed the tree pictures and Bible verse from the clamshell box and tucked them in her purse. She'd look over them on the bus ride. Surely, they had some significance.

Kathy unlocked Frank's box. The musty smell of worn pages stung Savannah's nose. She eased the book out of the box and knelt, spreading it across her lap.

"This Bible belonged to your mother. She left it in the church, and Frank saved it. He thought you might want to read through it on the trip."

Of course, someone had ripped the name page from the front cover. Why all the mystery?

Kathy checked her watch. "You'd better go if you're going to make the two-thirty bus."

Chapter Nine

Geoff honked at the Massey Ferguson spinning mud in the distance. He pulled to the gate and hopped out, leaving the truck running while he opened it. Then he slid behind the wheel, sloshed across the rain-soaked soil, and stopped to close the gate behind him. One of his Charolaise swiped her tail at him, grunting a sorry moo.

"Right back at ya, Bessie." Poor thing. Dried mud caked her, and her legs sunk two inches into the ground.

He made a bumpy trek across the field, his tires spraying the muck. Stopping a few feet shy of the tractor, he frowned at the driver.

"Zach? What's going on?" He reached through the rear window into the truck bed for a bag of pebbles and spread them over the ground, before stepping out and sprinkling them in front of his tires.

Zach glanced over his shoulder. "You don't want to know."

Two pickups shot over the hill at lightning speed, their headlights obscured by mud splatter.

Geoff palmed his forehead. "Let me guess. Racing."

Zach yanked the bill of his cap over his eyes. "Forgive us?"

"Yeah, sure." Tossing a wave toward the pickups, Geoff grinned. "I might regret asking, but I need a favor."

Lifting the cap, Zach raised his brow. "Want me to run her off?"

"Zach."

"Well, they said she wouldn't sell."

"Couldn't. How do you know already?"

Zach loosened dried dirt from the tractor and stepped gingerly to the soft ground. "Larry met me at Opal's. He wanted me to clear those broken trees out of his backyard."

"I think I'm going out of town for a couple days. In fact..." Geoff tossed the pebble sack in his truck. "I'm not sure how long I'll be gone."

"You wouldn't be going to Birmingham by any chance, would you?" Zach punched Geoff's arm.

"Larry told you everything?" Rubbing the punch site, Geoff clenched his jaw.

"He was worried. Told me to look out for you."

He flicked his gaze to the clouds, then back. "Frank agreed to finance the adult scholarship fund if I go on this trip. Besides, I need to talk to her. I tried to apologize, and she wouldn't listen."

Zach scraped his boots against the tractor tire. "If that's what you think you have to do." He paused, boot braced against the tread. "You realize she's going to think you're a stalker, right? What will you tell her?"

"I don't know. Birmingham is a long drive. I'll figure it out by the time I get there. So, you'll take care of everything on the farm?"

"Will do." Zach tipped his cap and hopped on the tractor. "Have a good time, you crazy fool."

Geoff returned to the farmhouse, leaving a trail of deep grooves. He threw together an overnight bag and set out toward the depot, arriving as Dora climbed on the bus. He parked in the courthouse lot while her bus departed, then followed at a short distance.

When the bus stopped, he stopped, careful to park out of sight. Five hours into the trip, he passed her and drove ahead to the gas station/hot dog joint across from the Birmingham depot. He found an empty table and nursed a soda. The redheaded manager stared at him from behind the counter, picking at the hem of her maternity top.

His stomach rumbled, and he left his vigil to buy a newspaper, a couple packs of peanuts, and another fountain drink.

"There's a steakhouse about a half mile from here." She offered a sympathy smile. "They stay open until one a.m. if you need to drown sorrows."

He wadded his straw paper into a ball and tossed it in a bin by the register. "Thanks. I'm good."

She scratched her pregnant bulge and took a sip from a Styrofoam cup with her other hand. "You're waiting on a woman, right?"

Geoff ripped the peanuts open with his teeth. "I've driven about four hundred miles to reason with her." He dumped half the bag into his mouth.

"I've seen many sad travelers over the past few years, most desperate for love." She sprayed the glass countertop with blue cleaner and wiped it. "I hope your story ends well."

"Me too." Across the street, a bus waited to turn into the depot. Way too early to be hers. "Thanks for the pep talk."

He made his way to the window seat and flipped the newspaper to the forecast. Just his luck. Rain.

Savannah met the twinkling eyes of the gray-haired driver in the rearview mirror. He stopped his whistling and nodded to her.

"Not much longer, right?"

"Twenty minutes. The last round of traffic slowed us down."

"Good." Her bag spilled onto the seat as she shifted. She stuffed the small items back in and picked up the journal.

A shiver coursed over her spine as she broke the first seal. Tracing Frank's flowing script, she could feel the lost connection in the pit of her stomach.

May 15, 2014—my dear Savannah, by the time you embark
on your journey, I may be gone from this world. I hope
you'll reflect on who you are. You've lived your life void of
compassion and served those who do not appreciate you.
You have devoted your body to men who have not cherished
you. Time after time, I have watched you suffer heartache
and succumb to emptiness. I do not believe this is who you're
meant to be. God made you to laugh, live, and love.

Savannah's cheeks warmed as memory after memory of casual encounters flooded her mind. She clenched the journal tighter. What right did Frank have to mention her sex life? How did he even know? And yet… she lived an empty, loveless life. It stunk. Still, none of his business.

Love means giving to others, a contradiction to what
I've asked you thus far. If you've followed my instructions,
you're now in ownership of Geoffrey Spencer's land, and he's
accompanied you to Birmingham.

She smirked. Yes, she owned the farm. But the accompaniment? Not happening.

By my guidance, you've taken what Geoff held, but
belonged to me, and yet it still belongs to him, too. I wish
you to offer him compassion and forgiveness. As you journey
together, seek peace.

"Ha! That'll be the day."

The old bus driver gave her a strange look. "Do you always talk to yourself?" He waved a free hand. "Never mind. After six hours on the road with you, I know you do. You even talk in your sleep."

"Sometimes." She ducked into the seat.

I realize you hold a great deal of resentment toward Geoff
and others from your childhood. Do you remember the verse
you memorized for your second-grade Bible class? I can
picture the horror on Rose's face when you ran to the pulpit

and jumped before the preacher to say it. It said to put away childish things. Well, it is time to release your resentment and hatred. Geoff Spencer deserves your kindness.

Doubtful.

A faded picture peeled loose below the paragraph. Three men stood before a half-painted barn. They held a baby between them. One, she recognized. Geoff's father's snarl put Ebenezer Scrooge to shame.

See the rage on each man's face—the rage they passed on to the baby? Your biological clock is ticking, my dear. In a few years, you will wish you were close to your family. Perhaps you will soon be holding a baby of your own. I pray you will pass on a legacy of compassion and love.

She tossed the journal into her bag. Did she deserve such things? She'd tried to love and failed more times than she could count. If Frank still lived, she'd tell him he'd lost his mind.

"About five minutes." The driver signaled. "It's off this next exit."

"Great." She gathered her bags and moved into the front seat, bracing as the bus lurched to a stop. "Thanks for the company."

He opened the door and grinned. "Friend of yours?"

Savannah peered down the steps. "I don't see anyone."

When she planted a foot on the blacktop, her face tightened into a scowl.

Geoff Spencer held his hand out for her luggage. He'd followed her?

The strap of her bag slid to her elbow as her arms went slack. "What are *you* doing here?"

He smirked. "Hello, Dora. Why are we in Alabama?"

She brushed past him, bumping his chest with her garment bag and dropping her carry-on. "It's Savannah. Will you stop calling me Dora?"

81

"Dora, Dora, Dora." He snatched up the bag. "Dora, Dora, Dora. Go on, get mad. I'm going to keep it up until you agree to listen."

The bus driver stopped at the foot of the steps. "Think you two might let me by, so I can run in for a minute?"

"Sure." Geoff scooped her into his arms. "Excuse us."

He carried her to his truck, garment bag, purse, carry-on, and all.

"Hey!" Savannah wiggled and caught the amused grin of a fifty-something couple strolling by on the sidewalk. Ridiculous and embarrassing. "Put me down right now."

"Only if you'll promise to talk to me. Why are you in Alabama?"

She squirmed from his grip, her ankles twisting as she landed on the blacktop.

His smirk disappeared, changing to concern. "Did I hurt you? I'm sorry."

"No." She closed her eyes and counted to ten. It didn't help. "Why did you follow me?"

"You know why. I've got 2.5 million dollars of scholarship money riding on this trip." He rubbed his temple. "Can't we at least go somewhere and talk?"

She threw her garment bag at his feet, stomped away, and glanced over her shoulder at his fallen face.

He tossed the bags in his truck and locked the door. Closing the distance between them, he fell into step with her.

"This is personal business. Family business. As in not yours."

"Mr. McMillan disagreed." He caught her arm at the light, stopping her from stepping in front of a car. "Have you been to Birmingham? Do you know where you're going?"

She jerked away and scraped her fingers across her scalp, catching tendrils of hair in a loose fist. "Fine. I have no idea where I'm going, and I need to find a hotel. I guess you're planning to be my knight in shining armor?"

"Something like that." He winked. "Come on, Dora. Let's go back to the truck, and I'll take you to get something to eat."

"You will call me by my name. Not Dora, not Panda. Savannah. In fact, if you call me Panda even one more time, I'll break into your house and pull a Delilah on you while you're sleeping." She laughed. "My house. I won't even have to pick the locks."

"I'm not going to call you Panda. I'll try to remember to call you Savannah, but you owe me a real conversation in return."

She planted her balled fists on her hips. "And no humiliation, public or otherwise." A shiver coursed through her. Why didn't she pack more sensible clothes?

He slipped off his flannel shirt and draped it over her shoulders. For real? Did he think he could win her over by being chivalrous? She tossed the shirt at him, trying not to notice how his muscles filled out the black tee underneath it.

"Don't be stubborn. You have the rest of your life to hate me. But I can help you right now." He held out the shirt again. "I made peace with every person I bullied. Except you. I want to make the pain up to you. Please, will you trust me, and at least let me buy you a meal? After I've had my say, I'll leave you alone. I promise. I'll drive you wherever Frank wants you to go and stay out of your way."

His eyes seemed full of sadness. Gingerly, she accepted the shirt. Remembering the picture from Frank's journal, she puffed her cheeks. "Okay. One meal. That's it."

They fell into a slower gait back to the truck. She shivered more as he placed a light hand in the small of her back.

Was she insane to agree to a meal with him? Dare she admit his lopsided grin still made her heart flutter the way it had in the eighth grade? And yet how could she walk away and deny him the scholarship money? Not when he helped people like Megan. She drew in a deep breath. "I guess you could drive me a few places. We can try to do this together. Like Frank wanted."

"Good."

He unlocked the passenger door and held it open for her. She slid across the shiny leather seat and tugged the shirt tighter around her shoulders.

Minutes later, he turned the ignition and adjusted the heater. "You won't regret this. I promise."

"I hope not."

Chapter Ten

Geoff eyed Savannah's compressed frame through the rearview mirror. She looked incredible wrapped in his flannel shirt. "This is my treat."

"No thanks. Not a date." She turned to the window.

Of course, it wasn't a date. It was, however, the first time he'd been anywhere alone with a woman since Maria died. He'd be lying if he denied his nerves. Did she think he wanted to date her? *Did* he?

He circled a couple blocks, spotting the steakhouse the gas station manager mentioned. "This okay?"

Savannah shrugged.

He pulled into a parking space and faced her. "Look, I know being together is awkward. It is for me, too, but we need a civil relationship. Too many people are involved in that farm—men whose families depend on the income. We have to work to make it a smooth transfer."

"I know." She glanced at his hand, inches from her shoulder, and shrunk against the door. "I don't want to cause trouble for anyone."

He withdrew, folding his hands in his lap. "There's a big community garden at the western edge of the property. Volunteers tend it, and the food is for anyone who needs it. Would you consider keeping it?"

"Other people do all the work, right?" She tapped her sandals against the floorboard. "Not that I'm opposed to hard work, but I'm not exactly good at gardening."

"Yes. Volunteers run it. A field of cattle backs up to it. We butcher them and give out meat to struggling families. A man from church feeds them."

She fluffed her hair and shook it over her shoulders. "It sounds neat."

"I'll show you around when we get back home. My farm has a reputation for being one of the coolest, neatest places in the tristate area."

"My farm?"

His grin slacked. "Your farm." He opened the truck door and swung his legs to the side of the seat. "But my animals, my employees, my tree house my grandfather built for me, my name etched into the fencepost in the front yard, my acres of soybeans to plant."

She hopped out the passenger door, grabbed her purse, and headed toward the double wooden doors. "I'm not planting soybeans. I'm not planting anything."

He walked a few paces ahead of her then winked over his shoulder. "It can be a challenge living in an older house and managing so much property. Things break, and fences need mending. You'll need someone to take care of it all. Like a farm manager."

"Like you, I guess." She followed him into the restaurant, keeping several inches between them.

A preppy boy leaned across the hostess stand, propping his chin. Dark hair fell around his collar. "Two?"

"Two, please." Geoff placed a hand on her shoulder then withdrew it as she moved away. Worse than a blind date. Had he moved too fast?

The host led them to a booth near the front, next to a college-aged couple holding hands across the table.

"You're everything to me." The girl batted her lashes.

Savannah snorted.

Geoff shook his head. "How about a different table?"

"Sure." The host whisked them further in the restaurant, across from an older couple. A walker hovered next to the man's chair, and the woman stretched over the table draping his coat on it.

"So, were you serious about managing the farm?" Savannah took the seat facing the woman.

Whew. Progress. Smiling, Geoff sat opposite her. He lined his silverware with the edge of the paper placemat and placed his hands on top of hers. "Good. We're on the same page."

"Sorry." Her gaze darted, and she backed from the table. "I can't do this."

Savannah scowled as she crossed to the ladies' room. She didn't need a farm manager, and she definitely didn't need Geoff Spencer being all touchy-feely.

A foul diaper in the trash marred the lavender-scented bathroom. Savannah wrinkled her nose and stepped over a pile of paper towels spilling from the can against the wall opposite the light green stalls.

She tried the first one, her stomach churning when she saw the toilet. She opened the second, the third. Finally, a clean one.

Minutes later she emerged, washed her hands, and turned on her cell. Eighteen missed calls from Rose and six texts from Adam Capesi. Her heart sank. She'd completely forgotten Adam.

"Family… emergency." She typed it on the screen. "Will return… um..." Her reflection glared at her. Fine. Deleting the text, she emptied her lungs. *Death in the family. I'll call as soon as I get back. Promise.*

She tapped send and met her gaze in the mirror. Would she go back to Chicago? She didn't have any reason. With Frank's money, she could start over anywhere. Why couldn't she let Geoff manage the farm? She didn't plan to live there.

Leaning forward, she tugged at the skin beneath her chin. She tilted her head down, checking for neck fat, and then inspected both arms. Flappy. In the morning, she'd find a mall and buy some running shoes. Why hadn't she thought to pack any? Right. Because she never planned to take this trip in the first place.

Butterflies overwhelmed her stomach. How could she face Geoff now? Would he call her fat again? She gripped the counter and drew in several deep breaths, swarms of dizziness surrounding her.

Then came the chants, "Panda! Panda!" Middle school kids, pointing and laughing. Food dripping from her hair. She snatched a paper towel from the dispenser and covered her mouth. Her head throbbed, and she groped past the first two stalls, barely making it into the third before retching.

Tears engulfed her. She wiped the plastic lid with toilet paper. Then she spread some on the floor and sat, clutching her knees and burying her head between them.

The restroom door creaked. "Hello?"

The voice quiet, timid, and raspy. Beneath the stall, a pair of soft leather shoes surrounded swollen feet.

"Savannah? Are you in here, sweetie? Your fella asked me to check on you."

"Yeah." Her voice came out tiny. She grabbed the handle, pulled herself to a stand, and cracked the stall door an inch. The elderly woman from the table next to them stood on the other side, her arms open, brow furrowed, and lips tight.

Shoulders slumping, Savannah emerged and fell into the woman's embrace. Her sobs shook both of them. "I can't go back out there. I can't talk to him. I'm not ready for this."

"Sure you can." The woman tugged her to the mirror. "Let Lola help you. We'll get you fixed up." She smiled at Savannah's reflection. "Okay?"

Savannah nodded.

Lola folded a paper towel and wet it, squeezing out the excess. "You want to talk about it?"

"No." Savannah accepted the towel, wiped her face, and patted her eyes dry. She dug through her purse and set makeup bottles on the counter. Twisting off the foundation cap, she avoided the woman's gaze.

"How long have you had an eating disorder?"

The makeup slipped from her hand, spilling tan liquid in the sink. She wiped the mouth of the bottle and rinsed the makeup down the drain. "How did you know?"

Lola patted her shoulder. "Been there. Here, let me."

"Okay." Savannah leaned against the counter while Lola dabbed a light coat on her face and added blush and shadow accents. When Lola finished, Savannah blinked. "I haven't purged in years. Until tonight. Being with him again...We have this terrible past. Something happened fourteen years ago, and he wants to talk about it."

"You have all this hurt bottled up inside, sugar. Sometimes getting it out and talking about it is how you help it go away. Have you ever tried?"

"No, I ran away. Left town and moved in with my aunt." She slathered a glob of gloss on her lower lip and rubbed it against the top one. "Then my great-grandfather died, and I had no choice other than to come home. Now, to meet the conditions of his will, we're supposed to go on this trip together. But I just can't."

Lola linked arms with her. "Trust me. Talk to him. Even if it goes badly, it helps to say all the things on your heart. Then you can start working past them." She squeezed Savannah's elbow and drew her closer. "That boy is worried to death about you right now. I think he'd do anything to make you more comfortable. Let him try."

Savannah puffed her cheeks. "Okay." She allowed Lola to lead her out of the bathroom, clinging to her as if she couldn't stand on her own feet. When she rounded the corner, Geoff sat across from

Lola's husband, the two men laughing like they'd always been best friends. She had to smile. The elderly couple had plotted and ambushed them. Thank goodness.

As they reached the table, Geoff stood. Lola nodded toward the seat. "Join us."

Savannah followed Lola's gaze to the chair next to Geoff. She obeyed while Lola settled in the one next to her husband.

"Meet Oliver." Geoff grinned. "He's written twenty-eight books. Romantic suspense."

Oliver winked. "Christian."

"No kidding?" Savannah forced a smile. Even the mention of the word convicted her. "Incredible."

The waitress interrupted to take Savannah's and Geoff's orders. Lola winked as Savannah examined the menu.

She chuckled. This woman refused to back down. "I'll have the grilled chicken, smothered, but no cheese, and with house vegetables."

Geoff ordered a steak. "After good ol' Oliver here told me how scrumptious it tasted, I had to try the rib eye." He closed the menu and handed it to the waitress. "Does anyone mind if we pray first?"

Oliver interlocked his thin fingers with his wife's. "We'd mind more if you didn't."

Following the prayer, Savannah relaxed, engaged in continual laughter from stimulating conversation and humorous banter between Geoff and Oliver. She cleaned her plate under Lola's scrutiny and even looked over the dessert menu when she finished.

The waitress approached, and Lola rushed to her, stopping her a few feet away. She whispered in the girl's ear, handed her a hundred-dollar bill, and returned.

"Dinner is on us." Lola smiled and looked Savannah in the eyes. "And pie."

"You didn't have to do that." Geoff stood and hugged her.

"Our pleasure. Thanks for the company." Lola moved Oliver's walker in front of the chair, and Geoff helped him rise.

Savannah stood, too, and took both of Lola's hands. "Thank you so much."

Lola squeezed Savannah's shoulders, pressing their cheeks together. "Eat the pie," she whispered. "Do it for me."

"I will." Savannah's voice quivered.

As Lola and Oliver walked away, Savannah returned to her seat. Geoff moved his plate across the table and faced her.

"I guess you want the whole story from the beginning." She pushed her dirty plate aside and folded the napkin into a square. "I have an eating disorder. I've struggled with it since leaving Dreyfus, and being with you tonight triggered those feelings."

There. She braced for his laughter.

He reached, and she let him slip his fingers between hers. "I am so sorry. I never thought about how talking things out with you would bring back your pain. Please, please forgive me."

She glanced at his fingers, rough and covered in small cuts. "I need you to stop calling me Dora. Every time you do, I see myself standing in the gym again. I'm not that girl anymore." Her vegetables churned in her stomach.

He cleared his throat. "I've wanted to take that day back ever since it happened. My whole life changed in that moment. Judge Henry made me promise never to bully again, and asked me to make restitution to all my victims. When you left town, I started going to church and learned how to serve others." He squeezed her hands. "I became motivated in school and went to college to learn how to turn the farm into a successful business. The Ag professors helped me with a research project on hybridization, and I spent eight years developing a process. A couple of years ago, I sold the patent. To be honest, I owe my success to you."

91

"Oh." Her fingers tingled beneath his touch, perhaps because her wrists pressed hard against the table edge. She freed them and dabbed her eyes with her napkin.

"I'm glad you're back." He sifted through papers in his wallet and withdrew a single page, yellowed with age. "This is one of many letters I wrote you. I asked Phil and Rose for your address, but they refused."

She accepted the paper and unfolded it, her heart pounding.

Dear Dora, Sorry for embarrassing you and calling you names. You are a good friend, and I've been mean. I hope you will forgive me and we can be friends again. If you want, we can hike Death Valley like we used to and pick some rhododendron leaves. Love Geoff.

"Death Valley." She refolded the letter and held the square in her palm. "I bet the place is so overgrown now."

He laughed. "I could take you there. It's not quite as big as we thought back then."

Savannah swallowed. "I think I'd like that."

The waitress placed a single pie plate between them, with two spoons. Shame on Lola.

Geoff handed Savannah a spoon. "How do you feel about sharing dessert with the enemy? Think we can call a truce?"

"Truce." She scooped a spoonful of whipped cream and let it rest on her tongue, the sweetness filling her body with a strange peace.

Chapter Eleven

The digital bedside clock read 4:01 a.m., 5:01 a.m. Dreyfus time. Geoff stretched and planted his feet on the navy pile carpet. He walked to the window and lifted thick paisley curtains. Neon light streaked the dark parking lot.

A Birmingham taxi approached the hotel, disappearing under the carport. Way too early. Yawning, Geoff drew the curtains, flipped on the TV, and switched to the weather. No rain. He'd take it, even if it still rained in Dreyfus. He muted the sound and hit the shower.

Dry and dressed, he scanned the messages on his cell. Fourteen. Larry: *You okay?* Zach: *The old bull got out again.* Of course it did. Two from Mona, plus a handful of people from church—everyone worried. Was he crazy? He could be, but at least he hadn't crossed any lines. For 2.5 million in scholarship money, they'd do the same.

Chuckling, he pressed the top button, blackening the screen. He should send a group text at four thirty in the morning. That would go over well.

Following Savannah might have been crazy, but at least they'd had a civil conversation. She seemed open to continuing the community garden.

He fished through his duffel bag for the leather Bible his mother gave him the year she died. Unlike the worn one he carried to church, the crisp pages stuck together, and the stiff leather cover wouldn't stay open.

Her scrolling penmanship graced the inside cover. *Nothing is so bad you cannot overcome it. Never forget, Psalms 3:5-7. Trust in the*

Lord with all your heart, and lean not on your own understanding. In all your ways, acknowledge Him, and He will direct your path.

How he missed her. She would have drawn Savannah in with easy conversation and made her forget any discomfort. As she'd said, talking to Savannah—facing his shame—eased the guilt he carried for so many years. Could they both move forward now?

Savannah still hadn't explained why she'd come to Birmingham. He turned the Bible to the book of Zechariah and read the passage he would teach from Sunday morning.

The ruler, Zerubbabel faced the daunting task of rebuilding the temple. Geoff faced the task of rebuilding his barns at another location. Not quite as daunting. Challenging, sure, but with newer, better equipment he'd have more productivity. Yes. This whole situation counted as a blessing.

He bowed his head, his lids narrowing to slivers. Before closing them, he sighted a text notification. Mona again. Three chilling words: *I'll destroy her.*

Talk about someone needing prayer.

One foot after the other, twenty-four-hour Walmart shoes pounding pavement, Savannah ran out her nerves through the soft orange glow of Birmingham streetlights. Soon, the sun brightened, and the morning traffic multiplied.

She stopped for breath at the hotel intersection, clutching her chest and clenching her teeth. Five weeks with no running had caught up to her. Shoulders squared, she rounded the corner, spanned the parking lot in a few long strides, and stopped short next to Geoff's truck.

He waited by the driver's-side door, his lips pressed into a thin frown. Two stuffed grocery bags hung from his wrist.

94

"What's wrong?" She bent her knee, extending her foot behind her, and grabbed the toe of her shoe.

"Family stuff. No biggie." When she stood, he held out one of the bags. "I got apples, peanut butter, and bagels. Oh, and plastic silverware, plus an iced cooler full of water for the trip. You want a bottle?"

"Wow. Thanks." She chuckled and accepted the bag. He'd gushed. "You didn't have to do that. I rode a taxi to Walmart early this morning, but I didn't even consider buying food."

Geoff snickered, reached over the truck bed, and retrieved a water bottle from the cooler. "I wondered who would be crazy enough to set out so early." His face stiffened. "Sorry, I didn't mean to imply I think you're crazy."

She uncapped the bottle and started toward the hotel, the grocery bag swinging from her arm. If she'd known he'd be so penitent, she'd have come home years ago. "It's okay. I'm going to shower, and I'll be ready to get on the road soon. Thanks for the food."

"No problem." He followed her into the lobby. "You still haven't told me why we're here. Can I drive you somewhere today?"

She flashed him a bright smile. "Yes. If you're still up for it, we'll do this together. Like Frank planned. I'll meet you in the lobby in a couple hours with the address."

After a quick shower, she slipped into the long-sleeved George T-shirt and jeans and slathered peanut butter on the bagel and apple slices. She sat on the bed with her feet crossed and stared at the beige concrete wall separating their rooms. Did he sit on the other side with his back to her, doing the same thing? They could have eaten together. She pictured him beside her, his legs draped over the thick white comforter, and his lazy grin splayed over his face. He might reach over and dab peanut butter on her nose, like he'd done as a kid. That would be so Geoff. As she imagined him doing so, the thought turned to a kiss.

Kissing Geoff? In a hotel room? Dizziness washed over her. She scanned the room for a distraction.

The corner of her real mother's Bible poked out of her carry-on pocket. It reminded her of her last trip with Phil. He brought his Bible everywhere they traveled. He'd stay up hours into the night reading it. A sliver of guilt raced through her heart, but she shoved it out of her mind. Now she needed a distraction for that, too. She puffed her cheeks and looked at the ceiling. "I'm feeling smothered." Not that God cared to listen.

She brushed her teeth, gathered her bags, and carried them to the lobby. Geoff sprawled in a chair, using a duffel bag for an ottoman, his head propped against the back of the seat.

She cleared her throat. "You ready?"

He straightened. "Yep. Where we headed?"

Savannah took the green folder from her bag and opened it. "I have to check."

"You don't know where you're going?"

"Frank wrote a scavenger hunt for us to follow. At the end of it, I'm supposed to have all the answers about my biological family. I don't know why he wanted you to come with me. I guess he thought you'd need to help me understand the landmarks since some are on your property." She opened the folder and removed the typewritten page. "Here's the itinerary—a list of locations and an estimation of time to spend there. If we go out of order, we lose everything."

"I wonder why he didn't approach me." Geoff examined the page and handed it back, then opened the truck door for her. "He only gave you the towns? Where do you find the addresses?"

"The journal. I open the next seal and find the next address. If I open too early, people at certain checkpoints report to the lawyer, and again, I lose everything. A lady at the bank checks my receipts. See here?" She showed him the introduction, her cheeks warming as his fingers traced where Frank asked her to be kind to him. "I think he wanted me to approach you, same as he wanted me to visit my parents and get this car he bought for me."

"Yeah." Geoff withdrew his hand and walked to the driver's-side door.

96

"After this letter, the next few pages show him posing with a bunch of cameras." She flipped to several faded pictures. "He could have wanted me to understand how much he loved photography. Like this one..." She turned another page.

"Wow. A Kodak vest-pocket autographic. I bet he used Jessop's 127-roll film for these." Geoff's breath warmed her neck.

Savannah cringed, lifting her palms and leaning toward the passenger door. "How do you know?"

He slid back behind the steering wheel. "There's this barrister bookcase in the old farmhouse in the great room, full of different cameras. Herb always wanted to get rid of them. Nana Jean never let him." A shadow moved over his face. "They fascinated me. I got in so much trouble sneaking into the cabinet."

"Do you think they belonged to Frank?"

Geoff started the engine and tapped his foot against the gas pedal. "I'm not sure. It's possible. The farmhouse walls are covered with professional quality pictures predating Herb." He adjusted the rearview mirror and met her eye in the reflection. "I always wanted to learn photography."

"You should."

He shrugged. "Someday."

As she closed the journal, her finger caught on a photo sticking out from the next page. It dropped to the floor, and she strained to retrieve it. "Interesting."

A black-and-white rendering of two men shaking hands. One—dark-headed, clean cut—wore a suit. The other wore a pair of loose-fitting jeans. A button-down shirt hung open over a baggy white T-shirt. On the back, Frank had scrawled a name. "Have you ever heard of Bibb Graves?"

"Nope." Geoff eased the truck forward to the end of the parking lot. "What's the address?"

"Five-Twenty, Sixteenth Street North." She palmed her forehead. "You know, I passed that street this morning. We can walk there."

He found a space and killed the engine. "Sounds good."

While they paused at the hotel entrance intersection to wait for a walk signal, she opened the Internet browser on her phone. "You know, it's never too late to learn to take pictures. I learned how to roller skate last year."

Geoff laughed. "I remember the time you tried to roller skate in seventh grade."

She stuck out her tongue. "Can't you please forget my awkwardness back then, and pretend I'm a stranger?"

He shook his head. "Nah. When I tease you, you get those cute little wrinkles on your forehead. Besides, I didn't promise to forget anything, only to stop calling you a certain name."

"You're impossible. Okay, here we go." She scrolled down the list of links—over a billion hits. "Wow. Bibb Graves served as governor of Alabama, in 1927. This picture is dated 1919, so I'm not sure what it means."

"Someone not-so-important meeting a big-shot? Happens all the time. Are there other pictures?"

"I don't know. Let me check the journal." She broke the seal, careful to turn only one page. "There are several pictures of this other man, but nothing says who he is." She inspected each of them, tracing the edges. "A family member?"

"Can't you look on the next page?"

Frowning, she closed the book, stuffed it in her bag, and resumed her phone search. "I'm not supposed to look at it until we get there. Frank was adamant. Oh, wait. Here's something. Bibb Graves was in the Ku Klux Klan."

The signal changed, and they traveled a few more blocks, to the intersection of Sixth Avenue and Sixteenth Street. Geoff lingered a couple paces behind her. "Hmm… The governor in the Klan?"

"Yep, or so it says here."

He linked her arm and nodded to twin towers at the front of the brick church. "Look at this place. Wow. Those arches and windows. I bet the inside is neat."

"*I* bet it's got a rich history." She winked, continuing toward a long, brick building. "Oh, wait. Here's a plaque with the address. The Birmingham Civil Rights Institute? I don't understand. What is Frank's message?"

"Let's have a look." He started up the steps. "This is only the first of his clues. You can't expect to understand from the beginning."

"Yeah. You're right." She followed him to the ticket counter then into the gallery, halting in front of a brick wall barrier with two water fountains. Her breath caught in her throat, and she dug the journal out of her purse. "Frank did write this verse under one of the pictures." She held the book closer. "'Because of the devastation of the afflicted, because of the groaning of the needy, now I will arise,' says the Lord; "I will set him in the safety for which he longs.'"

As they moved through the exhibits, Savannah made careful notes on the back side of the itinerary page. They came to a church replica. She paused at the threshold, tiny hairs standing up on her nape as Geoff approached the pulpit.

"Come here. You need to see this." He pointed at a Bible under a glass case. "Says it belonged to a man named Fred Shuttlesworth. He participated in freedom rides, worked with Martin Luther King."

Savannah pursed her lips. "No way. I'm not walking in a church, not even a replica. Lightning would strike me dead as I entered." She gripped her bag tighter. "Although, can you tell me the page? Frank has already used a lot of Scripture, so it could be important."

"Isaiah 55. Listen to this verse. 'For you shall go out with joy, and be led forth with peace: the mountains and the hills shall break forth before you into singing, and all the trees of the field shall clap their hands.'"

"Wow. Beautiful. Poetic." Savannah noted it, and they moved on to a photograph of men looking into a rubble-filled hole before a building sign captioned Liberty Contracting. It looked familiar. She consulted the journal—the same picture pasted midway on a page. Anguish distorted the men's faces. Next to it, four sweet, innocent girls smiled back, dressed in church clothes. "Sixteenth Street Baptist Church Bombing."

"This is awful." Geoff rested a hand on her shoulder.

She read the caption then searched the bombing on her phone. Tears welled in her eyes. "These girls died in the blast. It was dynamite, planted by someone in the Ku Klux Klan. They walked through the church when it exploded. A place that is supposed to be safe." Young lives, lost to a senseless act of terror. "How could anyone be so evil, to think bombing a church is right? Who could celebrate the death of little girls?"

"Or who could justify bullying?"

She jerked away, pivoting to him. "I didn't mean—"

"I know. There's one source of evil, Savannah. You know who that is. He blinds people to truth and fairness, and incites rage and indignation where it doesn't belong."

"It's too hot in here. I need fresh air." She darted past him, through the exhibits, out the door, and down the steps. Stopping at the last one, she dropped to sit.

A few seconds later, he joined her. "I think I understand. Frank's message is simple. He wants you to have compassion and fight the injustice in the world."

Savannah fanned her face with the itinerary. "Possible. I don't know." She slid her finger under the picture, lifting it up and finding words on the back side, penned in heavy ink. "Carl T. McMillan, uncle. Joined the Klan to protest crime in the city."

Meeting the hard eyes of the man in the black-and-white photo, she shivered. "Look at this guy. I come from monsters."

Geoff covered her hand with his. "That makes two of us."

Chapter Twelve

"Hamilton's a couple hours from here. Do you want to go on now, or would you rather drive around Birmingham?" Geoff glanced at Savannah's bobbing head and chuckled as it thumped against the window. Poor girl. He'd never seen anyone drift off so fast. Although, she'd yawned all through lunch. His call. Onward to Hamilton.

He drove in silence for an hour, not wanting to turn on the radio and disturb her. Every so often, he stole a peek. What peaceful sleep. His perfect lioness, out like a lamb. He frowned. Not his. But he couldn't get the thought out of his mind.

He could see himself with her so clearly—walking hand in hand with children in tow. Had Frank wanted this? If they fell in love, they could share the farm. Why else would Frank demand he accompany her?

A box toppled off the pickup in front of him, landing about six feet ahead of his left tire. He swerved to the right, hit the grooves at the edge of the road, and jarred Savannah.

She sat up and grabbed the door handle. "What was that?"

"Sorry." He pulled to the shoulder behind the truck. The box's contents, some kind of sports trophies, littered the road. Other drivers swerved into each other's path to dodge them. The cars slowed. Geoff raised his hands to stop an approaching semi. He and the driver gathered the trophies before waving the vehicles on their way. He returned to the truck.

Savannah held her cell out the window. "Say cheese!"

"Provolone." Her camera clicked, and he laughed.

101

"Weirdo. I think I might want to learn how to take pictures, too. You never know when crazy people will run into the middle of a busy interstate to save the day." She giggled. "Are we close to Hamilton?"

"Yep." Her smile seemed genuine. He climbed in the truck and merged into the flow. "Mind if I ask a few more personal questions?"

She folded her arms. "I don't know."

Palming his leather wallet through his pocket, he visualized the picture Rose had given him—the vibrant smile. "What did you do after high school? Were you happy in Chicago?"

She shrugged, digging in her bag and removing a tissue. "I struggled on occasion. Like on my college softball team, where I learned to do eating disorder right."

"What major?"

She wet the tissue with her tongue and dabbed at her smudged eyes. "Business. What about you? Did you go to college?"

He nodded.

"What did you...?" She wadded the wet tissue and grinned. "Duh. Never mind. You majored in Ag. So, what have you done since college? Besides farming, I mean."

He tried to mask a wave of sadness by adjusting the radio station. Metallica. Perfect. "I married a Hispanic girl named Maria. She died in a bad accident, and they thought I sabotaged her car. She was pregnant." He glanced at Savannah through the rearview mirror. She bit her lip and wiped away fresh tears. "I didn't do it, but things got hairy until the court ruled in my favor. The company issued a recall about the same time, and they realized I didn't have anything to do with the accident."

Savannah flicked her gaze to the floorboard as though searching for words. "I'm so sorry. Losing her must have been terrible, and now you're enduring all this." She wadded the tissue and tossed it into her bag. "I guess they couldn't save the baby."

"No." His voice caught. "Afterward, I went to grad school, poured myself into building up the business and research side of the farm, and stumbled on a new process to hybridize crops. When I sold the patent to it, I invested a lot of the money. Now, most of the work we do is charity and the farm runs itself."

Savannah kicked off her shoes and hiked her knees against the dashboard. "Wow. I thought you planted crops and harvested them. I don't even know what hybridizing means."

"I told you, there's a lot more going on at the farm than you'd ever imagine. It needs to continue—for the benefit of the whole town. I hoped we could work something out, and you might keep some of the charity work going."

The touchscreen on her phone lit up, and a pop song played. "We'll see." She silenced the call. "Rose. She's called seventeen times in the last two days. I guess they heard I came back."

Geoff looked away. "Yeah, I think everybody knew."

"What about your parents? How are they?"

The sign for the Hamilton exit loomed overhead, and he signaled to change lanes. "They died a few years ago. Mona is the only family I have left, other than some cousins who live away. That's why I tolerate her."

He merged into the exiting traffic and eased behind a beat-up Nissan, signaling to turn into a Subway parking lot. Savannah pressed her lips thin and balled up her shoulders. Would things always be so awkward? "Okay, Dora. Looks like we're here."

"It's Savannah." She faced him, speaking through gritted teeth.

Geoff winced and palmed his face. Didn't matter if he hadn't meant to say it. He couldn't keep bringing up her wretched youth. At least he hadn't called her Panda. The horrid nickname came about in the winter of her eighth grade year, when she'd gone through a Joan Jett phase and dyed her hair black. What had she been thinking? The hair looked so ridiculous on her chunky physique. Not that it gave him any excuse.

Her favorite sweatshirt back then crossed between a Mondrian painting and a cow print, and she wore it several times a week. Rose and Phil had put her on a strict diet and sent celery sticks in her lunch every day. Geoff snapped a picture, hung it on her locker, and captioned it, "Panda."

She eyed his profile. Soft wrinkles spoke to his kindness, and the chiseled jaw clenched as soon as Dora slipped out of his mouth. Could he even be the same person? How could the guy who'd humiliated her be so benevolent and kind?

He took the keys out of the ignition and pocketed them. "I never thought the name Pandora fit your personality. Everything always came so easy for you—at least when we were younger."

Savannah shook her head. How could he say that? Nothing came easy. Ever.

They went in, hit the restrooms, and ordered fountain drinks. His regular, hers diet.

"You want a cookie?"

"No, thanks." She dropped her straw wrapper in the brown plastic trash bin. Did he not realize she struggled to eat in front of him? Did he have no memory of the embarrassment he'd caused her? It seemed time stood still for her, but kept moving for him. Then again, fourteen years was an eternity. Frank spoke truth. She needed to forget, too.

Back in the truck, she opened the journal. "I guess I should go to the next page." Slipping a fingernail through the garage sale sticker, she split the two stuck pages. "Here's an address and a map. That's all before the next seal. Frank says I can't read on until we get there."

Geoff studied Frank's drawing then plugged the address into his GPS. They drove through neighborhoods to the edge of a subdivision and parked in the cul de sac. On the other side of a chain-link fence, elementary school children climbed over rock walls and raced down huge plastic slides.

Savannah heaved her shoulders.

"Not what you expected?"

"No." She propped the journal against the truck and tore the sticker. "Let's see what Frank wrote about this place."

More monochrome pictures of smiling people surrounded an incomplete family tree. Frank had written descriptions below each person, including their occupations and personalities, birth and death dates.

Geoff leaned over her shoulder. His breath warmed her neck. Again. "Weird."

She frowned. "What?"

He pointed to the dates. "All four of these people died on April 14, 1920. Wonder if it's another bombing."

"That is strange." The following page yielded a newspaper clipping. "No. 'Disastrous storms reap harvest of lives in three states'," she read aloud. "'Hundreds of families rendered homeless, over two hundred dead, and millions of dollars in property damage.' It's sad."

On the next page, another article framed a photo with a woman clutching a baby. She stood in front of a pile of beams that looked like it once had been a house. Despair prevailed on even the baby's face, circled in red ink. Frank had printed his name below the picture.

Geoff brushed her arm as he reached and flipped to the family tree. He tapped a photo of a rundown house. "This must have been where they lived."

"And they were all killed in the tornado. He lost his father, brother, aunt, and uncle." She ran her finger over the name. "Carl T. McMillan, the uncle who was in the Klan. Guess he died before he got too involved."

Frank's handwritten scrawl filled the next page. "This one is a long entry. He says, 'The Sunday before Easter, the whole family

105

gathered at Gram's house for my cousin's birthday meal. We'd had to skip the year prior because of a dreadful flu epidemic, and my mother had been insistent everyone come.'"

"So the picture on the last page must be his whole family. Your whole family."

"I guess so." She took a deep breath. "'Of course, you must know this account is given by my aunt Marion, who tends to stretch the truth. She swore no one gave her or my uncle Carl an invitation. They showed up anyway and, as you can imagine, chaos ensued.'"

Geoff shut off the truck. "And...?"

"He continues, 'We were at the dinner table when the tornado hit. Ma drug the kids to the cellar, and her sister Sally went back in the house to beg Pa and Carl to join us. My little brother, Stephen, followed her. They didn't join us, of course.'" Savannah flipped to the next page. "'Ma went all crazy after they died. Marian says they had a big fight and Ma accused Marian of conning Pa to join the Klan. She said God paid him back for his hatred, and he got everything he deserved.'"

"Let's walk around and take some pictures."

They stepped out of the truck and paced the gravel at the side of the road. Geoff moved too close as Savannah paid homage to her ancestors. A light breeze blew around them, and she shivered. Wish she'd grabbed a jacket.

He draped an arm over her shoulder and drew her close. His breath tickled her cheek, and she lost her own. Her skin tingled for what felt like the millionth time, and she balled her fists. No. He would not get to her. "We should go."

His mouth brushed her temple, and an irresistible urge to face him, to meet the lips of her sworn enemy, consumed her. An enemy she hated less and less by the minute. She indulged the daydream for a moment. Then pictured him kneeling on the gym floor, slapping it with laughter as she sat in the middle of the mock panda habitat where he'd trapped her.

106

With an abrupt jerk, she pulled away and stalked back to the truck. Changed or not, she knew from experience he could turn on her anytime. She'd have to be more careful now.

Chapter Thirteen

Geoff finished the last bite of his fajitas and dropped the napkin on his plate. His lip burned from the spices collecting in a shaving gash. As he licked them, Savannah shifted in her seat and averted her eyes. Had she thought about kissing him as much as he'd thought about kissing her? Crazy, he knew, but amid the bright colors and festive music from the roaming mariachi band, it felt more like a date. Fine by him.

It had taken everything in his power not to kiss her in the field. She'd looked so beautiful and vulnerable. Dating her would certainly make convincing her to continue the farm operations easier. He could give her a job and put her on the board. Although… if things went wrong, it could be a disaster.

He picked up the bill folder and glanced at the ticket, then sifted through his wallet for a couple of twenties.

"You don't have to pay. I'll get it." Savannah unwrapped one of the complimentary mints and popped it into her mouth.

"If I'm out with a girl, I pay. Period."

A lovely blush pinked her cheeks. "Okay, fine. But I'll give you gas money."

"Nope. Not taking it." He held back a triumphant grin. Did he detect interest? "What's the next location?"

"Home."

Already? "Quitting?"

"No, I need to visit my parents before continuing. I should have done that first."

"Yeah. I'm sure they've missed you." He checked his cell phone. "It's five o'clock, but we're an hour behind Dreyfus. We could leave now and get there around one in the morning. Will they be okay with you getting in so late?"

She creased her brow. "I don't know...Dad used to get up at four thirty." Yawning, she bent her arm behind her right shoulder and stretched it, tilting her head against the left and letting her brown hair tumble to the side. "Could you drop me at a hotel? Tomorrow's Saturday. Phil might sleep later."

"Sure." His cell buzzed, a notification popping up on the screen. Mona again. Urgent. Call her. He flipped the phone over before Savannah had a chance to see.

"Ready to go?"

When she nodded, he waved down the waitress and handed her the cash. "Keep the change."

"I'm going to the restroom." Savannah pointed to a dark side hallway.

"Okay. I'm going to step outside and make a quick call."

"Meet you at the truck." She grinned. "You're not going to leave me, are you?"

"Nah. Want me to give you the keys?" He winked, dangling them over her head.

"Pest." As she sashayed down the long hall, he pocketed the keys. Even some flirting. Things progressed much better than he'd thought.

He thanked the hostess and headed to the sidewalk then sat on a stone bench where he could see the entrance. As he dialed, he could feel Mona's negative energy seeping through the phone.

"I've been worried sick." A growling dog masked his aunt's screech.

Geoff tapped his hand against his forehead. "Are you at the house? Is that Cyrus?"

"Stupid dog won't eat anything. I'm trying to feed it."

He blew a burst of air into the phone. "Zach's taking care of Cyrus. It's under control."

"Where are you? With that hussy?"

"She's not a hussy. You are so rude. Can't you leave people alone?" He held the phone away from his ear while she retorted. "I'll be home soon."

He disconnected, spinning to meet Savannah's blazing eyes. "Where'd you—?"

"Side exit. Who said that?" Hands on her hips, she moved closer. "Who called me a hussy?"

"No one important." He walked to the truck, slid behind the wheel, and slammed the door closed. Or, someone she needed to fear.

❦

Savannah scrunched her lips and shot a couple of blasts of air through her nostrils for good measure. Her sweater dropped to the floor, and she bent to retrieve it, bumping her head on the glove box.

She couldn't see a thing, not even with the dim glow of the semi lights shining through the rear window of Geoff's truck. Stuck two hours in utter darkness behind who knows what kind of accident, going nowhere with someone she couldn't stand. Here she thought she could get along with Geoff Spencer.

She straightened, casting a peripheral eye to his profile. So smug. So obnoxious. So annoying.

He snickered. "Hate much? Who are you mad at now? Me? Frank? The world?"

Do not engage. He couldn't get a rise out of her this time.

"Ahead of us, someone might mourn a wife or girlfriend. A husband or a child. Some hurt much worse than you."

Her eyes stinging, she blinked fast and turned to the window.

"Look, I'm sorry if I scared you. Church is important to me. I share my faith with everyone. I didn't mean to push you about it or make you uncomfortable."

"You didn't scare me." She stroked her scalp with her fingers, separating strands of hair and tugging out tangles. "You argued with me for three straight hours. That's not Christian." She flicked on the overhead light, spun to meet his gaze, and stretched out her upturned palms. "Who are you, Geoff? Are you the guy who makes sure the waitress knows you won't share a hotel with an unmarried woman?" She bounced her left hand then stilled it and shook the right one. "Or the man who will battle to make someone do what you think they should?"

He ducked his head. "I'm an imperfect man who makes a lot of mistakes. A man who is concerned about the souls of everyone he encounters and wants to share his faith. A man who cares enough about his employees and their families he'd do anything to help them, even driving across state lines with someone who thinks he's the enemy to convince her to keep his charities going."

Her sweater slid off again, falling between them.

As she reached for it, he covered her hand with his. "And I'm a simple man who can't figure out how to talk to a woman about the Bible without stirring up anger. I am so sorry I upset you."

She snatched the sweater and wrapped it around her shoulders. "You made me feel like a nobody. Like you were the righteous one and I wasn't worth the scum on your shoe."

"Not my intent. I meant you should at least visit. Give it another try. It would mean a lot to your parents."

"Why do you even care? Who am I to you? A girl you used to make fun of and now you feel guilty."

"I'd like you to be more." He swallowed hard.

Savannah pressed her fingers over her mouth. "What's that supposed to mean?"

111

"When I saw you the other day, I felt thunderstruck." The yellowed truck light cast a soft glow across his farm-chiseled face. "I thought about asking you out right there in front of all those old ladies and farmers."

She twisted her untangled hair into a loose braid, trying not to look at him. He wanted to ask her on a date? Did he think she would buy all of this?

"Stupid, I know. I recognized you, and—"

"Right. I repulsed you."

"You didn't repulse me. I didn't know what to say. Then, these last two days..." He shrugged. "I've enjoyed your company, that's all. Until we left the restaurant and you decided to get all hateful."

"You're the one who got hateful and wouldn't tell me who called."

"I didn't want to upset you."

"Well, you did." She kicked off her shoes. "Take the next exit and drive me to a rental car place. I'll find one on my phone."

Up ahead, the highway brightened as several cars in front of them flipped on their lights. Geoff started the truck, and she faced forward. Thank goodness.

Traffic made slow progress, and he eased into the farthest left lane. Nowhere near an exit.

She threw in another humph for good measure before leaning against the cool passenger window and closing her eyes.

The next two hours passed at turtle speed. Her neck ached from sitting in the same position, pretending to sleep. She massaged her temples. Why had she told him to take her home?

Because she put it off long enough. Like it or not, she had to face Rose.

"We're about thirty minutes away. You should call your parents and go straight there." Geoff freed her cell from the charger. "Give them a few minutes warning so she's not surprised."

Their headlights illuminated a green sign. Dreyfus, Thirty Miles.

"I should." Heart pounding, she made the call she should have made weeks ago. Someone answered, but no one spoke.

"Hey, Dad. You there?" She drummed her fingers against the leather seat. "It's Savannah. I'm in Mount Vernon. On my way home."

Instead of a response, shuffling and clanging preceded her dad's heavy breathing. "Sorry, I'm under a car. Who did you say?"

She gritted her teeth. Under a car at five in the morning. She should have known. "It's Sav… um… Dora. I'm on my way home. I'm with Geoff Spencer. You remember Geoff, right?"

More shuffling. Metal met concrete. "Dora? After all these years you want me to drop what I'm doing and entertain you? With no notice."

Savannah shifted the phone to her left hand. "I'm sorry. You're right. I should have called earlier." She moved her hand to her neck and massaged it. "Anyway, will you guys be home?"

"Why are you with the Spencer boy? Everyone in town has called about it. Did you spend the night with him? Have we taught you nothing?"

She huffed into the phone speakers. "It's not what you think, Dad. He's bringing me home in a few minutes. You want me to pick up doughnuts?"

Silence. A scratching sound, then more silence. "Okay. I'll get your mom to fry up some turkey bacon and eggs. Mr. Spencer can eat with us, and I'll give him a talking to about running off with my daughter."

That would be worth seeing. She chuckled. "After, not off with, Dad. We'll be there with doughnuts in about an hour."

"Your mother won't be awake for another hour." Click.

She shook her head. "He has the worst phone manners."

113

Geoff yawned as he merged lanes, sandwiching between two semis. "What did you commit me to doing?"

"Breakfast with the Barretts." She let out a nervous giggle. Would he even want to eat with them after such a rotten trip? "He hung up on me without saying goodbye. Like always."

Once they reached Dreyfus, Geoff swung by Lucy's Doughnut Shoppe and ordered a dozen. They were so close now.

Savannah's arm hairs prickled as she pictured herself walking in the house. She stuffed her phone in her bag and sat on her hands, taking a quick peek through the drive-thru bakery window into the restaurant, where two elderly ladies at the counter pointed her direction.

After placing his order, Geoff paid, accepted the doughnut box from the clerk, thanked her, and passed it across his lap.

One of the elderly ladies waved. Savannah groaned. "Busybodies. Some things around here haven't changed, I see."

"Wave back." Geoff laughed. He faced her, kissed her cheek, and turned back to the window, tipping his cap to the ladies. "Let them talk."

Their eyes widened, and grins smoothed their wrinkled faces.

Butterflies assaulted her stomach. She rubbed the spot where his lips had pressed, clinging tight to the doughnut box with her other hand. "Let's go. Dad's waiting."

Ten minutes later, Geoff sat with her on her parents' old wooden porch swing, rocking in a crooked pattern, completely out of sync. She pressed her body as far to the right as she could, leaving about sixteen inches between them. Did her cheek burn where he'd kissed her? Why wouldn't he go home?

Her father joined them, covered in oil and grease, lowering himself into one of her mother's pristine floral patio chairs. "Dora. Mr. Spencer."

She'd not prepared for this. Every inch of her body trembled. Waves of something passed over her entire being—Nausea? Fear?

Relief? How had she been so callous to stay away all these years? She leapt from the swing, rushed to his side, and bent down to hug him. "Daddy."

He might have put forth his fierce facade over the phone, but tears glistened in his eyes as he embraced her. "It's been too long. Your mom and I missed you."

"I've missed you, too." She averted her gaze. She'd been planning to set out again after getting the car, but her dad's strong arms felt incredible. For the first time since leaving Chicago, she realized what Frank must have already known. After coming home, she couldn't go back. She had to move closer.

Chicago had lost its glamor anyway. Her run-down apartment and dead-end job served as bookends to an empty, lonely existence. Phil would help her start over—she'd always known he would have if she asked, but he never would've left Dreyfus to do it. In the fourteen years she'd lived in Chicago, he hadn't done any more than call, not even when she'd been admitted into a mental institution for her eating disorder.

All these years, she'd punished him, and now, standing before him, she felt every ounce of the pain she caused him.

"I'll stay a couple days." She cringed. Too much time with Rose. How would Peter feel about it? Would he cut off her travel money? She couldn't worry. "Then I'll have to get on the road and finish this trip, and I'll come back for a while."

"Alrighty, then." Phil nodded to the house. "Let's get in there and fix us a big breakfast."

He held the kitchen door open, his eyes narrowing when Geoff placed a light hand against her back. She scuttled forward, resting the doughnut box on top of the plain white Formica counter. "I see Mom made you remodel."

Phil harrumphed. "Seven years ago."

Savannah swallowed. "Oh, yeah. I remember her telling me." She took her old seat at the oak table where she'd spent her childhood mornings. Her chest tightened as she eyed the sleek, black refrigerator and ceramic top stove.

Phil tossed a spoonful of butter into a flat pan on the stove and cracked several eggs, in his classic three-by-four pattern.

Savannah blinked. No wonder she'd had weight problems.

"Would you like any help?" Geoff moved next to Phil.

"You can do the turkey bacon." Phil opened the refrigerator. "Bottom drawer. Stupid nasty stuff."

Geoff chuckled. "How many pieces?"

Winking, Phil handed him a microwavable plate. "All of them. We can have half of it eaten before her mother gets home."

He'd finished setting the table when the screen door scraped against the threshold as Rose pulled it open. "Phil?" Her voice turned to a squeal. "Dora?"

Savannah steadied herself for the embrace, but it never came.

Rose dropped her hands to her side and marched into the kitchen "I see your father's got you supporting his cholesterol habit."

Gripping the edge of the table, Savannah tapped her feet and counted to ten. "I wanted to bring him doughnuts. Go easy, Mom. Don't ruin this."

Rose patted Geoff's arm. "Good to see you again, sugar. May Simpson called and said she saw you guys out for a ride together. Said you kissed my daughter."

Eyes covered, Savannah peeked between her fingers. May Simpson owned a cell? She had to be in her mid-nineties by now.

Geoff cleared his throat. "I caught her cheek while turning to pass her the doughnut box."

"That's not what May said." Rose harrumphed.

Savannah examined the paisley pattern in the carpet under the table. Could she disappear into the swirls? She picked a piece off the lemon-filled doughnut, rubbing it between her fingers until it shredded to crumbs.

Phil sunk his teeth into his sixth piece of turkey bacon. "Geoff? Are you and my daughter dating?"

"No." Savannah dropped the pastry.

Simultaneously, Geoff replied, "I'd like to be."

Good grief. She pushed her chair back. "I'm exhausted. Do I still even have a place to sleep in this house?"

"Sit down, young lady." Phil grabbed another doughnut then frowned as Rose snatched it from his hands. "You have some explaining to do."

"About what?"

He cleared his throat. "I understand you want to find your roots, and you had a right to pursue the ownership of Geoff's land." His stern look made her stomach churn. "I don't understand you didn't involve us in the process."

Savannah heaved her shoulders. "I guess I didn't want to hear what you'd have to say about it."

"Not involving us hurt more than telling us would have, since Frank McMillan already explained." Rose slammed the lid on the bakery box and carried it into the kitchen. "It hurt when people asked if we'd seen you and we didn't know you were home."

Savannah crossed her arms. "It hurt when I asked questions about the adoption and you didn't tell me what you knew."

Starting the faucet, Rose threw an egg-covered spatula in the sink. "It hurt when you didn't call this year on my birthday."

"Well, it hurt when..." Savannah glanced at Geoff, who propped his chin on his fists. "Never mind."

He scooted his chair back, slid out, and made his way toward the door. "It's been a pleasure, folks, but I've got farm business."

"You sit, too." Phil's voice came out sharp. "You haven't had near enough to eat, and I'm not finished talking to you."

Geoff bowed his head and returned to his chair.

117

Phil folded his hands. "What about the farm? Will you live there until she takes possession?"

"Mr. McMillan gave me six months to find a new place."

Rose filled Geoff's milk, and he took a big gulp.

"What about last night?" Phil leaned forward. "Did you sleep with my daughter?"

Milk sprayed the room.

Chapter Fourteen

"Excuse me?" Geoff slid his hand down his cheek and hid his mouth with his fingertips. Did he hear right?

"Phil!" Rose dabbed grease from the turkey bacon with a floral print paper towel, absorbing the milk droplets Geoff spewed across the table.

Phil rested clenched fists on either side of his plate. "I said, 'Did you sleep with my daughter?'"

"Dad. I went by myself to Alabama, and Geoff followed me." Savannah retrieved the tickets from the Civil Rights Institute. "We went to a museum. Ate at a couple restaurants, looked at a cornfield, and drove home. We didn't stay in the same room."

Phil snatched a piece of bacon, his elbow coming close to tipping Geoff's milk glass. "But you stayed at the same hotel."

"We did." Geoff set his cup away from the edge of the table. "But not as a couple."

Rose, hands on her hips, moved behind her husband. "Then why did you kiss her?"

Geoff sunk lower in his seat.

Savannah smirked. No sympathy from her. "Yeah. Why?"

"I don't know." Geoff picked up the kitten-shaped porcelain saltshaker and ran his finger over it from the bottom. He *didn't* know. He got caught in the funny moment. And to be honest, he just *wanted* to kiss her.

"Well, fun as this has been, I'm going to bed. See you, Geoff."
Savannah pushed her chair back from the table and stood. "Dad,
Mom, thanks for breakfast."

Geoff extended his hand to Phil. "Mr. Barrett, I meant no
disrespect. I've got to get home, but if you'd like to discuss things
further, you're welcome to come out this afternoon. I could take you
trap shooting."

Right. Guns and an angry father. Could he muddle this any
further? "Thanks for breakfast." He gave Rose a quick hug, brushed
Savannah's shoulder, and ducked out the front door.

The sun poked through clouds, casting an eerie red glow across
the Dreyfus skyline. He crossed the Barretts' driveway to his truck,
stopping when something glinted at his feet. A utility knife lay in
the gravel, inches from where he'd parked, and next to it a cracked
pocket mirror in a tarnished silver case. Weird.

Fallen leaves topped thick patches of green grass. He'd come
by later and rake them for Phil. It might help the situation. He'd call
sometime in the afternoon.

Geoff stood, lifting a foot to pivot toward his truck. Wait.

Under the carport, Rose's green SUV sat on four flat tires.

Glaring at Geoff Spencer's retreating truck, Avery brushed dust
from the case of Rose Barrett's passenger mirror.

Evidence. He snorted. He didn't need evidence to know who'd
attacked the woman's SUV. He'd seen this work before, and if Geoff
thought about it, he had, too.

Phil had gone over the entire car several times, listing of every
nick and scratch for the insurance. He'd get the money and get it
fixed. No need to upset the fruit basket, or in this case, the fruitcake.

So, why hadn't Mona called to gloat? She must be up to
something else. Could end up being a long day.

"Do you have any idea who could be responsible?" Rose paced the carport, pausing every two seconds to wring her hands. "I can't imagine someone doing something so horrid on our own property. We slept right through it."

Avery shrugged. "Some of the college kids are back in town. They had a big party out toward Lewis Road earlier this week, a three-day binge. They camped on an abandoned property and stayed high the entire time."

Phil felt under the carriage. "Those young fools think they're invincible. Have you had reports of any other cars being damaged?"

Stifling a chuckle, Avery pretended to scan the neighbor's yard. "There's been vandalism in other parts of town. I heard about a few break-ins down the street a couple weeks ago." The blinds rustled and hands separated them, forming a crack. Two sets of eyes peered out the glass. He needed to wrap this up before someone rushed over and started grilling him.

"Let me head back to the precinct. I'll go over security footage from the downtown bars and see if any groups of college students look suspicious. Sometimes a drunken kid doesn't need a reason, not if it's a fraternity initiation."

Rose circled the car, kneeling to examine the bits of tire in the gravel. "What about the mirror?"

"I doubt the owner will return for it." He walked to the curbside trash can and dropped it. "We already checked for fingerprints and couldn't find any."

Phil frowned. "I thought you were supposed to take it back as evidence."

Avery jiggled a Ziploc bag. "I have the utility knife, and I took a picture of the mirror. Sorry to rush on you folks, but if I'm going to be scanning hours of surveillance footage for you, I'd better get started."

"Thanks for coming." Rose turned to Phil. "I'm going to go in and check on Dora. Be right back."

Pandora? Avery glared at the SUV window, fighting to remain expressionless. When had she returned?

"It's been a long time since I've talked to Dora." He pretended to examine the brick wall separating the carport from the Barretts' kitchen. "Back when I still worked at the school, I think. She was just a kid."

Phil nodded. "She's still a kid. Nowhere near mature enough to own a farm."

Avery shook his head. "No, she doesn't look the farming type." He glanced at his watch. "I could go out there with you sometime and make sure she's got good security. At least you'd know she'd be protected from anyone coming in on her."

"I'm not sure she'll decide to live there."

On a scrap of paper, Avery scrawled his name and number. "Well, you can count on me if you need anyone."

Phil took the paper and extended his hand for a shake. "I'll keep it in mind."

Savannah woke at noon to off-rhythm hammering on metal. She sat up, pulled back the rose-covered curtains, and found Phil outside her bedroom window working the dent from a fender. Groaning, she dropped her head back to the pillow.

Flexing her toes and reaching her arms over her head, she stretched from one end of the bed to the other. She rolled over and rested her chin alongside a huge fabric rose, the pink thread faded to white. Other than that, nothing changed since she last stayed in this room. Nothing.

Geoff had gone home. Her shoulders gave an involuntary slump. Did she miss his company?

She hadn't even thought to ask for his number so she could text him if she needed to talk. About business, of course. The next stop on Frank's scavenger hunt. Although… she rather wanted to talk about other things. Did he have a girlfriend? Surely, he wouldn't kiss her on the cheek if he did.

She sat straight. What had happened to her? A few days ago, she would have dismissed the idea for a completely different reason. Had she already forgiven him and let go of the hurt? Could it be so easy? She smiled. Frank would be pleased.

She donned her old fuzzy slippers and a sweatshirt, and exited the back door to join Phil.

"Fixed your car. It's ready." His voice cracked.

Her heart melted. He thought this would be goodbye. Had she been such a jerk all this time? "I'm not leaving today. I thought I could help you some with the cars."

"Oh." He stared for a moment then handed her a wrench. "Then I'll teach you how to change a water pump. We ought to finish before your mom comes back, so we can go out and grab a late lunch." Winking, he patted his protruding belly. "Real food."

"Changing a water pump sounds interesting." In a paint drying sort of way. Savannah shoved the wrench in her sweatshirt pouch and leaned against his workbench. A white card with a phone number dropped to the ground, and she bent to retrieve it. The name below the number gave her chills. Avery Kaler. "Are you in some kind of trouble?"

Phil spit on the ground. "He came by this morning while you slept. You came out the back, so you didn't see. Someone slashed your mother's tires."

"What?" Savannah gasped, stumbling forward.

"He offered to install you a security system on the farm."

"Ugh. The guy gives me the creeps." She laughed. "Why would I need a security system? It's not like I'm going to be living there."

"Humph." Phil lifted the hood of an older Chevy Impala. "Where's the wrench I gave you? I want you to disconnect the battery." He tapped a terminal. "You're going to turn that one and loosen it."

She fumbled with the wrench, slipping it over the nut several times without catching it.

He set his jaw, took the wrench, and loosened it himself. Next, he disconnected the other one and tied back the cables.

"Okay, now we need to fix all this corrosion on the battery. Think I'm going to go ahead and clean it. Get me a cola out of that fridge."

"Dad." She waggled her finger. "Mom will kill me if I let you drink a Coke."

"I'm not drinking it." He grinned. "We're going to clean the battery."

"If you say so." Chuckling, she grabbed one from the rows of soda filling the fridge. Sure, he used them for cleaning.

He poured it over the battery, and the soda bubbled, eating away corrosion. He waited a couple minutes then attacked the battery with a wire brush. "Now hand me a couple paper towels then drag the water hose over here."

While he removed the gunk with the paper towels, Savannah scanned the shop walls. No telling how many thousands of dollars he invested in tools. When she'd left town, he still worked for Old Man Davis, making next to nothing. She stared at her fuzzy slippers, clean and bright against oil-stained concrete. She didn't even know when he'd branched out on his own.

"Here, throw these towels in the trash bin over there…" His gaze darted around the garage. "Oh, well, I wheeled it to the house so we could clean up the tire mess. Set it on the counter, and we'll throw it out later. Guess we'll do that after lunch if you want. Oh, and grab my cell if you will. I'm still waiting for the adjuster to call back about the insurance."

"I'll walk it over there."

In the carport, she stepped over forgotten pieces of tire as she approached the trash. Peering in, she dropped the paper towels on top, a cracked mirror glinting in the light.

Intricate carvings engraved the tarnished silver case. Interesting. The antique pattern not unlike her clamshell box. She scratched her finger on jagged glass fragments along the edge then stuffed it in her sweatshirt pocket and returned to the garage. Phil sat on the concrete floor, loosening bolts on the underside of the car.

"What now, Dad?"

The wrench slipped, fell from his hands, and landed with a clunk. "This aggravating model is next to impossible. Stuff's all crammed in there. Got to go underneath to reach everything."

She eyed the tire on its side next to him. Had he removed it in the two minutes she'd spent disposing of paper towels?

He worked more efficiently without her, so she settled in a lawn chair in the corner. "Where did Mom go this morning? I didn't hear her stirring in the house."

"Some local hoopla meeting. Your mother attends all these homemaker, craft maker, gossip maker meetings, and I never see her anymore."

Savannah stretched her legs in front of her and crossed her feet.

"So, be honest with me. What's going on with you and the Spencer boy? Everyone in town said you two ran off to Alabama together."

"I told you we didn't." She sighed. "I refused to come home and pick up the car, so the lawyer put me on a bus to Birmingham. Frank wanted me to go there. Did he tell you anything about the trip?"

"Not much." Phil grunted, stretching further into the cavity created by the missing tire.

"He's given me different locations and written instructions in a journal. I'm supposed to drive place to place and learn about my family. Like the last couple of days, I saw where Frank's dad and uncle died in a tornado in the 1920s."

125

A bolt rolled from under the car and rocked at her feet.

"Hand me that." Phil extended a grease-covered hand. "How does Geoff fit into it?"

She bent to pick up the bolt. "In his will, Frank ordered Geoff to go with me. He said some clues required Geoff's help. Otherwise, I'll lose the inheritance."

"Well, be careful. They say he's not been right since his wife died."

Plunking the bolt in Phil's hand, she frowned. "What do you mean, not right?"

"Pours all his time and energy into the farm. Gives away his money like candy."

"Tell me about his wife. Did I know her?"

"Nah. She came from California or somewhere. Snotty girl, if you ask me. She'd stroll into church wearing these little skimpy sundresses and walking around like she owned the place."

"How did she die?"

"Burned alive in a terrible accident. The brakes failed, and her car went over a cliff. Everybody thought he sabotaged the car. Had a big trial and everything. The company issued a nationwide recall, and the judge cleared his name."

"Oh, Dad. That's so awful. When did it happen?"

"Five years ago. He's gone around town like a robot ever since, throwing himself into community projects and stuff up at church."

Savannah sunk into the lawn chair, her chest aching like a heavy weight might burst through it. All this time she'd spent wishing he'd suffer, and it seemed like he had. "Well, anyway, he met me at the bus depot in Birmingham and took me to dinner. We talked about all his charities, and I agreed the community garden needs to continue."

"And?"

"Well, yesterday morning, I went for an early run."

"In the middle of Birmingham? By yourself? You could have been mugged."

"Dad. I used to run in Chicago every morning."

He slid from under the car and clutched his chest. "Don't tell me stuff like that. So you went out for a run...?"

"And there he stood, leaning beside his truck, holding a bag of fruit and bagels." She grinned. "Kind of sweet."

"He has changed. If you have to run around with him to get your inheritance, I can't stop you. But be careful."

As he crawled back under the car, Geoff cruised his Ford into the gravel next to her Prius. She laughed. "Good to know I have your approval, since he pulled in the drive."

Chapter Fifteen

Geoff forced his gaping mouth to close.

Savannah had tossed her hair into a loose ponytail, and a spot of grease dotted her nose. Had she been helping her dad? There was hope for her yet.

"What's wrong with you?" Zach spit a sunflower seed shell into an empty bottle. "It's not like she has three heads."

"I'm surprised at how much she's changed." Geoff pocketed his keys. "Come on, let's rake these leaves. Rose will make you some tea. You won't believe how good her tea is."

"Look, I know you want me to play wingman to your Romeo, and that's fine. Have you forgotten this is the girl who's ready to rip everything you own out from under you?"

"It's not her fault Herb stole the property. Who knows? We might end up together one day, and it won't be such an issue." Geoff reached behind the seat for a roll of lawn bags. He hopped out, tossed the bags in the middle of the yard, and snatched a rake from the truck bed.

Savannah moved beside him, close enough he could lean down and kiss her forehead. Would she smack him if he tried? He inhaled a breath of her rose-scented shampoo and stepped backward.

"Why are you here?"

He held out the rake, keeping his gaze trained on the fluffy greenhouse slippers accentuating her University of Chicago sweatshirt and silk pajama bottoms. She didn't have on a stitch of makeup. He liked it.

Zach punched him again. "You're out of control. Drooling over Panda."

Her eyes narrowed. "Who asked your—"

"Don't waste your time." Geoff scooted between them. "I'm sorry. You remember what an idiot Zach Allen is, right?"

"And proud of it." Zach bowed, though his smirk slacked as he straightened. "Sorry. I shouldn't have called you Panda. I find it ironic to see you two getting along so well."

Phil sauntered out of the garage. "To what do we owe this pleasure?" He winked. Her old man winked. Had she been able to reason with him?

Geoff caught his handshake, squeezing tight enough to let Phil have the greater strength. "Zach and I came to clear your leaves. It's the least I can do after upsetting you all this morning."

"Oh." Phil withdrew his hand and picked a piece of red plastic from his salt and pepper hair. "Carry on, then. Much appreciated."

Savannah, her gaze still honed in on Zach, stalked toward the house. Geoff sidestepped her, grinning. "I brought three rakes. Think you can outwork two farm boys?"

"No thanks." She planted a foot on the gravel driveway, winced, and jerked it back.

"Come on, tenderfoot. Put on your tennis shoes. Zach says you aren't cut out for farm work. Show him you can do it." He handed her his rake. "Then, I might take you out to dinner tonight."

Her cheeks reddened. She marched into the yard, piling leaves with vigor "I don't want to go out with you."

Laughter erupted from deep in his chest. Her spunk made him feel alive for the first time in… Had he ever felt this alive? He ruffled her hair, loosening strands from her ponytail. "Suit yourself. I'll ask again in about an hour, and you can be thinking about it."

Zach shook his head and worked feverishly on his pile. Within an hour, they'd cleared the entire yard and stuffed leaves into fourteen bags.

One big pile remained next to the fence separating the property from the Barretts' back neighbors. When Zach started toward it, Savannah raced past him. Rake hoisted, she crossed the yard, with Zach at her heels.

Geoff moved in a diagonal path, catching her in three strides. He scooped her up and dumped her into the leaves, laughing as she squealed.

Zach dove in next to her, showering her with brittle foliage. She grabbed a handful of her own and shoved them in his face, exploding with giggles and shrieks.

Chuckling, Geoff dropped to his knees. They hadn't played since they were kids. If he could only bottle that fire and make her drink it every day. He whistled, and they both faced him.

She wrapped her arms around a monstrous scoopful of the oak and maple leaves and lunged, sending a swirling spray of brown, red, and yellow into his chest.

Joining in his laughter, Zach hooked an arm around his knees and brought him to the ground. Savannah plopped on his legs, pinning him as Zach buried him farther in the pile.

"Well, isn't this interesting?" Rose emerged from around the corner of the house. "Never dreamed I'd see you guys wrestling around like you did when you were elementary kids." She scanned the yard. "Did you do all this?"

"Yes, ma'am." Geoff emerged from the leaves and scrambled to his feet, shaking foliage from him. "Least I could do after the morning you've had." He winked at her. "I've been trying to talk this daughter of yours into dinner, but she keeps telling me no."

Savannah averted her gaze. "I haven't been home in fourteen years, and I can only stay a couple days before I have to be back on the road. I'm sure Mom and Dad wouldn't want me to leave."

Rose beamed and engulfed him in an embrace. "Stay for dinner. You fellas could play cards with Phil later tonight."

Geoff squeezed her shoulders. "Sounds fun. How about you, Zach? Think you might be up for some of Rose's sweet tea?"

Zach crawled out of the leaf pile and pushed himself up on his knees. "I'm meeting the boys at Opal's..." He dodged Geoff's gaze. "Sure. I'd love to stay for dinner."

Savannah gathered clothes for after a shower and ducked into the powder-blue bathroom. She eyed Geoff and Zach out the window. They had such a weird relationship. Zach didn't want to do leaves, but Geoff must have talked him into coming. Zach didn't want to stay for dinner, but one look at Geoff changed his mind. And he wanted to do the same thing to her.

Why would he try to date her anyway? They had nothing in common. He'd be like her mom trying to push her into church. She did not need pushy.

She locked the door, turned on the hot water, and shimmied out of her sweatshirt as steam filled the room. Immersing in the spray, she let the scalding water ease her tired shoulders.

The shadow of her reflection mirrored her through the frosty glass, partly obscured by her bag, where Frank's journal poked out of the side. Would the steam damage the pictures? So much for avoiding Geoff with a long soak.

After a quick rinse, she cut off the water and toweled dry. She dressed, cracked the door, and set the journal in the hall while she styled her hair and applied makeup.

She emerged, finding only an empty hallway. No journal. She glanced down the hall toward the kitchen.

Phil and Geoff bent over the leather book, pointing at the pictures. Blood rushed to her temples as she stalked to their side. "Please tell me you didn't tear any of the stickers."

"We didn't. I remember what you told me." Geoff backed from the table. "Your dad found this in the hallway and asked about it. I told him about the exhibits in the Civil Rights Institute and showed him Frank's father and uncle."

Zach groaned from the living room armchair. "You've turned him into an outright bore."

"It didn't take much turning." She grinned then frowned. "Where's Mom?"

Phil held up his palms. "I have no idea. She muttered something about picking up some coleslaw from Opal's, but she's been gone over an hour."

"Do I need to start cooking?" Savannah scanned the counter and opened the fridge.

"Nah. Geoff's helping me grill some chicken. Baked beans are in the oven, and the potato salad is on the middle shelf."

Rose's potato salad. That alone would have been worth a trip home. A nervous tingle tickled the pit of her stomach. She'd have to be careful not to eat too much, or she'd put on every pound she'd lost.

Phil wrapped an arm around her waist and tugged her toward a kitchen chair. "Tell me more about this trip. Where's the next stop?"

"Washington, DC, I think." Here they went. He'd demand details and boss her about the plans. She peeked in the fridge and lifted the lid off the bowl, her eyes watering from the red onion. "To a place called the Knickerbocker Theater."

"DC is dangerous. Murders happen every day." Phil pointed to the flat-screen TV in the living room. "I saw it on CNN. They had a big protest there."

"Dad." Savannah flicked her gaze at Geoff, who gave her a bemused smile. "Someone slashed Mom's tires last night. In our carport. While you guys slept."

"Well, I don't like the idea of you in DC all by yourself."

"Dad. I'm twenty eight. I've lived on my own since eighteen. Now you want to tell me I can't travel by myself?" She covered her face with her palm. "Besides, Geoff's coming with me, remember?"

Phil slammed the table. "Everybody in town has called about your last overnight trip. No way will I let you take another one."

Geoff's already-ruddy cheeks reddened. "Why don't you come with us, Phil? See the White House."

Phil harrumphed. "This old body doesn't travel."

"Coming here—a total mistake." She scooted her chair across the light gray linoleum and stood. "I am an adult. I'll go where I want, drive where I want..." She glared at Geoff. "Eat dinner with who I want... I don't want to be treated like a teenager, and I don't want to date a farmer."

She ran out the front door, continuing down the sidewalk to the next street.

Geoff called after her, but she kept running, dropping over the hill into the neighborhood park.

She settled on one of the swings, tears streaming her face. What was wrong with her? Had she lost twenty years of maturity when she waltzed back into town?

A few seconds later, Zach's sandy hair popped over the hill, his bangs hanging over his eyes. He strolled to meet her, stopping a few inches from the mulch line surrounding the swing.

"You crushed my buddy."

"So?" She winced. Why did she feel like being so mean?

He shoved his hands in his pockets. "You okay?"

She swirled her feet around in the chipped wood, digging a groove. "No. I'm not okay."

"Look." He settled in the swing next to her. "I know you have every reason in the world to hate him, but you have to see he's a better person now. He's clearly into you. He's acting like an idiot."

133

"I don't hate him." She let the swing rock, pushing with her right foot.

"Your dad means well, too. I wish my dad had cared enough to put limits on me. He died about ten years ago, and the only indication I had he cared was the pizza he ordered me before he overdosed."

She gripped the chain tighter. "I'm sorry."

"I'm not. Geoff won't let me sit around and feel sorry for myself. I owe so much to him. You wouldn't believe everything he's done for me. He's made me to go to college, and now I'm just weeks from finishing my degree. I did those online classes."

She picked at a hangnail. "See? That's what scares me. He's bossy and pushy and makes you do what he wants. I don't want pushy."

"It's not like that." Zach twisted the chain on his swing a few times and let it spin, "He encourages me. Makes sure I have plenty of work to keep me out of trouble. Take tonight. He knew I planned to get plastered, and he dragged me over here instead. I grumbled about it, but I'm glad he talked me into staying."

"You are?" Savannah clamped her jaw shut.

"I don't mind. I do want better in my life."

"Me, too." She lifted her legs, crossing her feet. "It's hard to trust him after everything...you know."

"He's not that guy anymore. In fact, I don't think he's been that guy since you left town." Zach brushed a strand of hair from his eyes. "Remember when we were little kids and you beat us both in the big neighborhood race? I think about it all the time. You pushed yourself so hard. He did, too, and I sat back and let you both win. I didn't have motivation. Hanging around him makes me want to try harder."

"He said you managed the farm."

"Yeah. When I finish my business degree, he's making me a full partner in his operation. I'm finishing my last five classes this term."

134

The sun dipped over the horizon, filling the sky with vibrant reds and purples. Zach pointed at a fluffy white cloud standing out from the rest. "Beautiful sunset. You should be sharing this with him." He gave her a wry grin. "Most important thing about Geoff is he lives his life for others. I don't understand why or how, but I know he's the kind of man I want to be. You'd be crazy not to give him a chance. He deserves a good woman."

"I don't know if I'm that woman. I've got a lot of... baggage." She kicked back and pumped her knees. "And after he lost his first wife in such a tragic way, I wouldn't want to hurt him."

A scowl creased Zach's face, and he spit on the playground mulch. "Yeah. Maria. She was a real hoot, let me tell you."

"What do you mean?"

"Spoiled, rude, contemptuous..." He grinned. "Geoff teaches me all these big words, too. Says I need to go to graduate school when I finish undergrad, so I gotta brush up on them."

"And you called him a bore."

"He's like my brother, man. He's family." Zach kicked a clump of mud from the swing set frame, crumbling it to bits. "So you can see why I'd be interested in you not walking out on him and crushing his heart. He's been through enough already."

"If you're so sure he's into me, then I'll give him a chance." She stopped the swing and adjusted her ponytail. She wiped her eyes with her sleeve. "Might as well, since we're going to have to hang out together over the next few weeks anyway."

"You're a big girl. Make your own decision. If you decide not to, let him down easy. You don't need to drive daggers into his chest like he's your mortal enemy." He slammed his chest with his fist and pretended to fall backward.

She laughed. "I won't. What about you? Got a girlfriend?"

"Nah. Geoff works me sixteen hours a day." He chuckled. "Then I'm so tired when I go home, and I have to do all this studying... I cannot wait for Christmas when I graduate."

She rose from the swing. "I should apologize."

"Yeah. You guys can send me the bill."

When they arrived back at the house, Phil sat on the edge of the porch. A snarl twisted his whole face. He looked older. Much older.

She bit her lip, resisting the urge to reach out to him. If only she had known Geoff would have been so sorry about embarrassing her back then, she might have not left town, and she'd still be close to Daddy. It must have felt like abandonment to him for her to leave.

"I have an idea." Zach leaned against a porch column. "How about if you flew? It's what, three or four hours? You could arrive early in the morning, take care of business, and come home at the end of the day. Shew. I'd even chip in on the tickets at this point."

She shook her head. "Flying costs too much."

"And a hotel wouldn't? Gas? All those extra meals?"

Geoff scratched his chin. "I have money and some frequent flyer miles. Buying the tickets is not a problem."

"No. You're not paying for my ticket."

"Why not?" Geoff huffed. "You're going to let me keep the community garden. We could call it a trade."

"Let me at least text Peter and see if I can spend my Frank allowance on it. I have a prepaid card I can use for certain things."

She sent out the text, scowling when Peter answered flights were okay. She typed back with fury. Why didn't you tell me? His response? She didn't ask. He'd wanted her to ride the miserable bus. "We can fly on Frank's dollar. Both tickets."

Phil's face softened, but he held Geoff's arm in a finger-whitening grip.

Washington, DC with Geoff Spencer. She felt… giddy. Could she handle it?

Chapter Sixteen

Geoff emptied his duffle bag and slung it on the high closet shelf. He'd spent all night trying to process the leaf-raking debacle, but he could only think about how cute Savannah looked when he arrived.

Stupid. She had no desire whatsoever to be in church, and after his miserable marriage, he vowed not to fall into another relationship with someone who couldn't share his faith. But she'd awakened his passion to live and dream again. He'd given up on so many things—happiness, children, love. Even though she made it clear it would never work out, being around her offered him hope he might find someone who'd let him dream about those things again.

Regardless, he couldn't worry about this now. He had to hold back his feelings and help her stay focused on Frank McMillan's quest. And, keep her in a good mood with him so they could negotiate use of the property.

Pounding rattled the front door. He hurried down the hall, dressed in only his navy slacks and brown socks then returned for a white T-shirt. Who would visit so early on a Sunday?

The pounding intensified as he raced back. He peered out the front window. Mona. He should have known.

She'd parked her Camaro sideways behind his truck and left deep grooves in the lawn. Again.

He undid the latch and let her in, air blasting through his nostrils. He forced his lungs to fill. Patience. Kindness. "What brings you out this morning? Reconsidering my invite to church?"

"Nah." She fiddled with her jacket zipper, revealing her long, thin neck. Blotches of hair dye peppered her forehead. "Why were you at Pandora Barrett's house all day yesterday? I couldn't sleep for worrying."

Geoff took the ironing board down from the wall behind the kitchen door and retrieved the iron from under the cabinet. "I helped her parents rake leaves, and then we had supper. I enjoyed it."

Mona plopped into a kitchen chair. "Enjoyed? The evil woman stole my slot at Ava Tackett's salon for the third time this year."

Geoff grabbed his light gray dress shirt from the coatrack and smoothed it over the ironing board. "When? She just got back in town."

"Not Dora. Rose." Tapping the table with her red nails, Mona scrunched her nose. "Like I said, evil woman."

He flipped the iron switch to the highest setting and pressed the button to release a puff of steam. It sputtered and spurted. He set it up then turned off the steam.

"You forgot the water."

"Yeah." He headed to the sink for a cup. "Did she know the slot belonged to you? Rose isn't the vicious type."

Mona plucked an apple from his mother's Fostoria bowl and took a huge bite. "Oh, but she is," she mumbled between chews.

Geoff grimaced, picturing the hateful woman from fourteen years prior, who'd found out he'd humiliated her daughter. "Well, she's been vicious with me, true. I can't say I never deserved it."

"You should have heard her at the homemaker's meeting, ranting we needed to change the logo. Poor Stella Raney worked so hard on it, and Rose ripped the design in two and threw it at her. And..." Mona took another, smaller bite. "She told all the other women to vote her in as president and replace me. Called me unstable."

A snicker swelled his chest. Geoff swallowed it. Mona was unstable. He shut off the iron and poured water in, backing away as scalding jets burst from the holes in the steel. "You guys are middle-aged women. What's wrong with you?"

She stuck out her lower lip. "Insecurity? Loneliness. The pain from never marrying."

That again. Geoff unfolded the shirt collar and steamed it smooth. "So go to church. There are several single men there."

Mona snorted. "Church men. Not my type." She tossed the half-eaten apple in the trash. "Besides, you're missing the point. I hate that Barrett woman, and you're running around with her crazy daughter. The daughter who stole your farm, in fact. What's wrong with you? You're the one who's forgotten how much she's taken from our family."

"We'll talk later. I need to leave early today for a teacher's meeting before services."

"Tomorrow, then."

Geoff grinned, pressing the wrinkles out of his sleeve. "Not available."

"Ugh!" She pivoted, stomped her feet, and slammed the front door behind her.

He rested the iron and poked his head out the screen door. "Mona, it's my business. I'll run around with whomever I want. You stay out of it and leave Savannah alone."

She faced him, her eyes wild and fists balled. "So, it's Savannah now, is it? Not Dora? Not Panda? The little witch has completely charmed you. She's going to twist your heart in wretched pieces and destroy you, like that hussy Maria."

As she stalked down his driveway, Geoff clutched the hem of his T-shirt. Savannah talked revenge when she first came to town. Had she been kind so she could hurt him later?

No way. He'd seen it in her eyes. Nothing like Maria.

Time to finish getting ready and hand his worries over to God.

139

He spent the drive to church in near-continual prayer. When he walked through the custom mahogany doors, he met the concerned stares of three deacons.

"Geoff. You made it." They stood firm, a row of crossed arms in pinstriped suits and pastel dress shirts, like a church mafia. "We were worried."

He jingled the change in his pocket. "Why?"

Elmer Reynolds stepped forward, his face scrunched in a snarl. "People said you ran off with the Barretts' girl, and we didn't know if you'd be home to teach this morning."

"So, you're listening to the gossip mill, too?" Geoff rubbed the bulging veins in his neck. Simmer down, count to ten. The men were worse than the women. He eyed each of them. "I have been teaching Bible class in this church for over eight years. Have I missed even once?"

"No." Cory Baker kept his arms folded, yet relaxed his shoulders. "But to run off with a woman..."

"First of all, you're assuming a lot and speaking without all the facts." Geoff swallowed. Temper his words. Think before talking. Count to twenty. "I did not run off with her. I did follow her to Birmingham, because in his will, Frank McMillan indicated I'm to help her visit certain locations to find her biological roots. It's not anyone's business but mine and hers."

Arliss Thacker draped his arm across Geoff's shoulders. "Cut the guy some slack, fellas. You're treating him the same way everybody did during the trial for his wife's death. They found him innocent then, and I'm sure he's innocent now. He doesn't need our judgment; he needs our support."

Elmer cleared his throat. "But—"

Arliss moved between Elmer and Geoff. "You cannot take one of my best teachers from the rotation. Now, get in the conference room and let's have this meeting before parents start bringing in toddlers." He winked and gave a forced chuckle. "The women have already taken all the good seats."

140

Geoff found a seat next to Tom Hiser and looked over his class notes. Other than a few pointed stares and whispers, no one acknowledged his arrival. On a normal Sunday, they'd all be handshaking and patting his shoulder.

He survived his morning Bible class without stumbling, even though sparse comments and occasional glares strained the atmosphere. Next lesson he'd throw in a couple points about gossip and judging.

Between services, he sat on the short pew behind the pulpit and gripped the songbook, trying to steady his trembling hands. He hadn't been this nervous leading the singing since he buried Maria. He couldn't let busybodies get to him. This worship belonged to God, not man.

Dallas Brewer, the preacher, arranged his notes under the pulpit then patted Geoff on the shoulder. "This, too, shall pass."

Geoff gave him a wry smile. God had placed so many people in his life to keep him from falling. "Dallas, you're a good friend. How many times have you stood by me in tough situations?"

"Not a problem, son." Dallas hopped down the stage steps and joined his wife in the second row.

Only a handful of seats remained in the pews. Though it had its share of problems, God had also blessed the church and helped it grow into a community of workers.

Geoff studied the smiling faces, each carrying on in animated conversation. Amidst those eying him with curious stares, he found people he'd helped in various ways and those who'd helped him through Maria's death. Their smiles and waves filled him with encouragement. How could he continue to worry when blessings abounded from every angle?

The analog clock on the back wall ticked off the final seconds before turning over to ten a.m., and Cory approached to start the announcements. Geoff barely heard them, his gaze falling on Phil Barrett, whose eyes twinkled behind his stern nod. He'd won the man over with the leaves. An unexpected ally, for sure, but proof a good deed didn't go unpunished.

As Cory backed from the pulpit, Geoff stood and set up his songbook. He turned to the hymn he'd chosen. "Number six fifty-sev..."

Savannah stepped through the mahogany double doors at the back of the auditorium, her hair swept up and her eyes covered with celebrity-style sunglasses.

He sucked in a deep gulp of air and exhaled without swallowing. A long, black dress draped from her neckline to her toes, a walking rendition of Audrey Hepburn in *Breakfast at Tiffany's*. Thin, fragile arms emerged from short sleeves. It took all his strength to not run down the aisle and embrace her.

A hush passed through the fidgeting crowd as they made a collective glance over their shoulders. They followed with a series of gasps when she lifted the sunglasses and tucked them in her purse.

Geoff tightened his grip on the pulpit. By the time he realized his mouth still hung open, the collective glance had swiveled to him. He cleared his throat. "Um...six fifty-seven. We'll be starting with number six fifty-seven this morning. Let's all secure a songbook and sing." If he could form the words.

❧

Savannah stood at the back of the church, counting seconds between inhales and exhales. She met Geoff's stare for an instant, then ducked away, her frenzied heart flopping like a fish.

She hadn't thought about the church being full. Or having already started. They never started on time when she attended before.

As Geoff's strong baritone filled the auditorium, an usher linked arms with her and led her across the room. She ambled through the singing members with perfect posture and chin high. Each heavy step like walking on nails. Though her hands remained steady, her pulse rocked her body while everyone in her parents' pew scooted to the right to make room for her.

She sat next to Rose and folded her hands in her lap, looking straight forward at a spot on the wall. Whispers flew around her. She remained frozen in place. What a mistake. Why had she come?

A man strode forward and asked the crowd to bow their heads. She did, forcing even breaths while he appealed to God on the behalf of all the sick and afflicted in the church. When she lifted her gaze, Geoff returned to the pulpit.

"Now, turn with me to page one hundred fourteen." His strong voice wavered as he found the marked song in his book.

Rose gave Savannah a sideways glance. "Here." She shoved an open songbook in her hands.

"Christ for the world we sing..." Geoff's voice diminished into the crowd.

Savannah closed her eyes, the harmony sending chills to her spine. His baritone strengthened, and his words convicted her. "Sin sick and sorrow worn"—a perfect description for her time in Chicago. So much pain and worry from bad choices.

A sharp jab in her side made her jump.

"Stay awake," Rose hissed.

"I'm not asleep." Savannah bounced her right leg over her left, kicking the pew in front of her.

Rose narrowed her eyes and pinched Savannah's thigh. "Don't make me walk you to the back."

"Seriously, Mom. Stop it." Savannah's whisper came out louder than intended. How dare her mother humiliate her in front of everyone, treating her like a child? Didn't she know how much courage it took to walk into this building after so many bad memories?

Rose pinched her again.

Savannah huffed. She was so out of there. She stood then fled down the side aisle, through the lobby, out the door, and to her car.

The scenery blurred into angry swirls, but the drive seemed to take mere seconds. She skidded into the driveway, threw the car into park, and planted her heeled feet into gravel.

Ten stalks got her to the front door. Standing on her parents' porch, she eyed the deadbolt. Great. Just great. She'd completely forgotten she didn't have a key anymore. Now what?

Chapter Seventeen

Nine sympathy lunch invites—all rejected. In a church of 220 members. Even Rose Barrett asked, but Geoff'd had enough of her for a while. She didn't act sorry Savannah had left or anything.

Heart heavy, he unlocked his truck and set his Bible on the passenger seat. No wonder Savannah ran off like a skittish pup. Her parents tried to micromanage every inch of her life. Nagging her during the song service like a six-year-old, whispering to her loud enough for the whole church to hear—from behind the pulpit, he could see the sheen of her tears. Beautiful and fragile.

The thought stirred fire in his chest. After he'd stared like a fool, they all knew how he longed for her. He needed a break, not to fly across the country with her. If she'd still want him to go...

Bypassing the new part of town, he followed the series of neglected back roads twisting into little knobs and hills. The scent of fresh-cut pine drifted through his windows as he passed between stone fences through a series of horse and cattle farms. Trees dwarfed the fields in several places since the landowners, all aged or passed on, left the farms to uninterested children.

His chest constricted. The same fate would befall his property. Her property. No way she'd ever live there.

He approached the rear entrance to his farm for the first time in years. The rusty gate hung ajar, the lock sat busted, and trash covered the drive.

Blood pounded in his veins. Trespassers. He looked closer. Beer cans, junk food, and cigarette butts. College students? He got out, picked up the trash, and threw it in the truck bed. He'd have Zach fix the gate next week. They needed a college ministry in the worst way.

Four dilapidated barns topped the hills surrounding the valley he'd played in as a child. A few dozen acres away, an iron furnace loomed on the knob opposite his Nana Jean's former house. All abandoned. His fault.

He drove along the overgrown road through ragweed and thorn bushes between the barns, smiling. Well... Savannah couldn't sell him the property, but she might let him live in Nana Jean's old house if he promised to fix everything on this neglected side.

He opened and closed several gates, drove up to the farmhouse and rounded the corner to his yard. Two cars waited—Mona's Camaro and the Prius Frank bought for Savannah.

After a hard land in the mud, Savannah searched for a place to plant her feet, dodging the contents of her bag. She scrambled for the pictures and journal as her twenty-dollar foundation seeped from the broken bottle into the ground.

Geoff's crazy aunt stood over her, laughing.

"I don't know who you think you are." Savannah gripped the trunk of a close tree, her stiletto sandals sinking into soft dirt. "But I'm sure Geoff wouldn't be pleased with you threatening me."

Mona lunged at her. "You little witch! Do you think he'd take up for you?"

"Yes, I do." Savannah sidestepped, circling the tree as Mona chased her around it. She never should have come here.

A truck door slammed. She followed Mona's gaze to the side yard, where Geoff stalked toward them, his dress shoes sloshing in the muck. "See? Told you."

Eyes narrowed, he looked at both of them then focused on his aunt. "Mona, stop it!"

Mona grabbed for his sleeve. "Why jump me? This hussy thought she could drive up on your property like she owns it."

"She is not a hussy." Geoff jerked away from her. "Besides, she does own the place. She can come here whenever she wants."

He stepped closer to Savannah, lifting the legs of his slacks as he walked.

She hugged the tree, remembering the fire in his stare as he stood behind the pulpit. Fire the whole church had witnessed. Fire that shook her to her core.

Mona slapped clenched fists against her thighs and let out a childish scream. "I've tried so hard to raise you after your mama died. She'd be torn up by this. Torn to pieces."

"This is my business." Geoff eased a protective arm over Savannah's shoulders. "Leave her alone."

Tingles enveloped her entire body. More than anything, she wanted to fall into his embrace and give in to the sobs that threatened to wreck her makeup.

Mona waded through puddles to her car. She scraped her boots on the gravel, kicking mud toward the Prius. "You'll regret this. I can't believe you, of all people, would take her side."

"Of course I'm taking her side." He squeezed her tighter. "Give her a chance, Mona. She's not a bad person, and she didn't ask for any of this."

Snatching her car door open, Mona furrowed her brow. "I disagree."

Geoff scowled as she climbed in, slammed the door, and drove away. His grip slacked on Savannah's shoulder, and she rested her head against his chest.

They watched Mona to the end of the drive.

Savannah's tears wet his shirt. Cheeks warming, she pulled away and tried to take a step forward. Her shoe broke at the heel. She dropped to her knees and sobbed.

Strong arms scooped under her legs and steadied her back, and before she knew it, she'd rested her head on his shoulder again. He carried her to the porch and set her on the swing, his lips bumping her forehead as he walked.

"I'm so sorry." He kicked off his shoes and unlocked the front door. "I don't know what's wrong with her."

"It's fine." Her voice quivered. She dug through her bag, wiped her eyes and face, and tossed the dirty tissue in a side pocket. "I'm okay. I had a long morning."

"Well, come in the house. I needed to show it to you anyway."

She gave a shaky laugh. "I'm covered in mud."

"Me, too." He extended his hand. "Come on, and I'll grill us some steaks."

Their fingers interlocked, and she let him draw her to a stand. Should she cross his threshold? She treaded on dangerous ground. At this point, most of her relationships had taken a carnal turn. But Geoff was a Christian. Surely, he followed some kind of abstinence code.

Her heart raced. She let go and followed him into the wood-paneled entry. What would he do if she threw her arms around his neck and planted her lips on his? Did Christians even kiss?

According to Rose, no. Back in middle school, she'd chided Savannah for watching soap operas, spouting off about sinners and adultery every time two people kissed on the television. Savannah had fired back kisses were innocent. She knew better now, but from a Christian... Then again, the smoke in Geoff's eyes when he looked at her made her shiver. Not so innocent.

If she let herself, the familiar temptation would take over her senses. She could picture her hands clinging to his bare muscles.... No. She couldn't indulge the thought.

He nodded to a leather chair. "Give me a second, and I'll find you some dry clothes. Maria had several things that would fit you."

She settled into the seat as he sprinted past the worn oak banister up the stairs. Did she want to wear his dead wife's clothes? She picked a muddy blade of grass from her dress. Guess she had no choice. Wonder how the town gossips would feel.

Kicking off her shoes, she inspected the house she'd inherited. It needed work. Lovely hardwood covered the floors, but years of nicks and scrapes marred the surface. Shelves of trinkets, smothered with a thick layer of dust, filled each corner of the living room. Cobwebs hung from the rusty ceiling fan.

She peered through an opening to the right. A fraying couch faced a big screen television. She grinned. Bet she knew where Geoff spent most of his time. A flicker of guilt surged her heart. He could still come over and watch TV.

To her left, an old piano rested against the wall, several ivory keys depressed. She walked over and played a couple chords, the hint of a smile forming on her lips. In spite of herself, she could see happiness here.

Geoff rushed down the steps, a wad of clothes in his hands. "I don't know if any of this will fit you. You can change in the guest bathroom, second door down, before the kitchen."

He dumped the clothes on the table and darted to the front door. "I'm going to… um… check the cattle. Be back in a few minutes."

Savannah sorted through the pile of embroidered jeans and wrinkled cotton blouses. A couple pieces seemed right. After about twenty minutes in the bathroom, she'd freed her hair from the mud and slipped into a T-shirt and a soft pair of Maria's jeans.

After she emerged, Geoff returned carrying a bag of cucumbers, peppers, and zucchini. "Ready for lunch?"

"Sure." She plopped her purse in the kitchen chair, her fingers lingering on the pocket where she'd stuffed Frank's pictures. Shuffling through them, she frowned. "All these trees and a couple barns. I have no idea why Frank wanted me to have pictures of trees."

Geoff set down the knife and pepper he'd grabbed and placed a light hand on her shoulder as she laid them on the table. "I know why. This is the farm."

He rearranged them into a rectangle, overlapping some of the edges. "They're old pictures, but definitely the farm. Taken from overhead, too. From a helicopter?"

She ran her finger along one then flipped it. "There's something written on the back. I can feel grooves from the pen." She held it up to the light. "But I can't tell for sure what it says."

He reached into a kitchen drawer and retrieved a pencil. "Shade the back with this. Something might surface."

As she did, letters and numbers formed. 20-H4, 22-KT, and 32-MI-2.

"Here." Geoff shuffled in a junk drawer, coming out with a legal pad. "Write it down, so you won't have to keep handling the pictures." He chopped the vegetables as she worked on the rest of them.

Frank wrote most of the codes on the four corner pictures, although a few photos had strange marks in the center. All jumbles.

"Did you enjoy church? Seemed like you did. Other than the obvious awkward moments."

"I liked the song leader." She stared at the pencil. God Loves You spiraled from the eraser to the tip. Right. More like God is sorry you were ever born.

"No kidding?" He nudged her and winked. "Next time won't be so bad."

"How can I go back and face all those people after what happened?"

"Trust me." Geoff tore a piece of aluminum foil from the roll and spread it on the counter. "You can hang with me. Don't sit with her anymore."

150

She giggled. "On the stage?"

"No, not on the stage."

"But you're the song leader."

"Not every week. I just fill in when others are away."

She puffed her cheeks and gathered the pictures. "I don't know if I'll be ready to go to church again for a long time. It's hard, you know."

Besides, she needed to back off from him. Focus on finishing Frank's quest and moving on with her life.

Something in his eyes told her he wouldn't quit trying.

Chapter Eighteen

Savannah paced the sidewalk of the SunTrust Bank, eying the uneven storefront roofs across the street. Pockets of people rushed by, some dressed in sweats with earbuds, others in high-class business attire. A suited man riding a bicycle winked as he swept in front of her, forcing her to take a step backward, stumbling into Geoff.

He'd driven to their six a.m. flight. Her arms had stayed so cramped from scooting too close to the passenger door they ached when she boarded the plane. At his insistence, she'd taken the window seat and maintained her space. Now, she'd come close enough his breath warmed her neck. Too close. She'd expected anger toward him, even hatred. This attraction? More than she could handle.

He steadied her, laying a light hand on her shoulder, his touch sending a shiver coursing to the tips of her toes. "Sorry. We flew all this way, and there's nothing here but businesses. Should we go inside and ask if anyone knew Frank?"

"No." She unzipped her bag and removed Frank's journal. "I'm supposed to break the seal now anyway. He'll explain. At least he'd better."

Geoff guided her to a brick bench topped with a concrete slab, and they sat. Again, too close. A light breeze ruffled her ponytail as she ripped through the garage sale sticker. She grasped the page's top corner, her body tensing when he looked over her shoulder.

She turned to request space, and his cheek brushed hers. Her entire body blazed as her lips made contact with his baby-smooth skin. She inhaled his sporty aftershave and exhaled through an involuntary pucker. If he turned… a fraction of an inch… Why did her heart have to ache for a kiss that could never happen?

He cleared his throat, and she jerked her gaze to the wintery pictures covering the page. After a couple minutes, she dared a glance. Jaw clenched, he stared at the McDonald's across the street.

"Aren't you curious?" About the sensation of his lips on hers? About the possibility of a future with her? She hoped so. But she couldn't. Besides, she'd meant the journal. Hadn't she?

His stomach growled. He snickered. "I'm curious about eating. Don't you ever get hungry?"

Always. Deny self, keep off the weight. She'd never be Panda again. As her stomach rumbled, too, she forced a laugh. "You're such a goof. We'll go eat in a minute."

"Fifty-nine, fifty-eight..."

"Fine. Be stubborn." She giggled. "It's mostly pictures on this page. I'll tell you what the captions say if you're too hunger-struck to read. This label reads Stepfather, but there's no name or anything. There are several pictures of this man with Frank's mother. I guess she's my great, great-grandmother. Most of the photos are dated 1922, and I think she had just remarried."

After she flipped the page, Geoff traced his fingers across the captions. "I can read them. A honeymoon trip?"

"Maybe. Louisa. I like her name." The flannel of his shirt tickled her arm. She closed her eyes for a second. Speaking…impossible with him so close. "Look at her short skirt. I didn't know they wore stuff like that back then."

"Check out the old-time cars." Geoff slipped his arm behind her back, resting his hand mid-torso. "And their coats and hats. I've seen similar ones in old movies."

She could fight this no longer. Scooting so her shoulder rubbed against his chest, she tucked her head under his chin. How could he have grown to be so perfect? "You watch old movies? I mean, I love them, but you're a guy."

He drew back, hiding his eyes under his palm, and peeked through his fingers at her. "I'm a sucker for them. What can I say? This mean old bully has a tender spot." Giving her a playful nudge, he met her gaze with an intensity that made her tremble. "We can watch a couple together sometime."

"Sure." Her heart spun like it had a motor; her eyes remained fixed on his face. She'd always managed to keep herself detached in relationships, but not now. Not with him. Had these feelings always been there? She'd had a crush on him in middle school, sure, but even in youth, he'd been her preferred playmate. He hadn't started being mean until he began running around with the other sixth-grade basketball players.

Even in hating him over the years, she'd thought about him all the time. Geoff Spencer had always been a presence in her life.

He brushed three fingers over her cheek and cupped her chin. "We'll have a lot of movie nights."

"Maybe..." She stood and sat cross-legged, creating a more comfortable space, and then set the journal between them. A single 8x10 filled the next page, a snow-blanketed street. She squinted at the print on a yardstick stuck in the drift. Twenty-eight inches. "Wow. I've never seen this much snow. What a disaster."

"DC is kind of south for so much coverage." He stood. "I'm going to run over and get lunch. Be right back."

She watched him cross the street before reading on, shaking her head. He hadn't even asked what she wanted.

The next photo revealed a group of men standing around debris, obscured by mounds of snow. Steel beams jutted from all angles. January 21, 1922. The caption listed the SunTrust Bank's address, but referenced the Knickerbocker Theater. Interesting. She searched her phone browser until Geoff returned holding sodas and a stuffed white bag.

"Wow. This must have been the place to be back in the day. Look. Neoclassic architecture, vaulted ceiling, orchestra pit— amazing and beautiful."

He handed her a soda and examined the screen. "What happened? A bomb?"

She sipped her diet cola and smiled. He'd remembered. "The snowstorm collapsed the roof. What you're looking at now is where the orchestra had been playing. No wonder it's not here anymore."

"I think I know what happened." Geoff's husky voice lowered. "He lost his mother in this collapse. He lost his father in the tornado. Frank McMillan became an orphan that day. Could have been adopted, like you." He handed her a grilled chicken wrap.

"You're right. So sad." Filling her mouth with a bigger bite than she'd intended, she dribbled ranch on her chin and wiped it away with her fingertips. He'd guessed right, exactly what she would have ordered, except without the dressing. On the page, the black-and-white men in thick coats made piles of jagged boards and fragmented steel. "It says here ninety-eight people died and a hundred thirty-six were trapped. They had a hard time rescuing the patrons because so many people stood around watching. Like when the old Dreyfus Elementary burned down, a couple months before I left town. Everyone came out to see it burn. Remember?"

"Yeah. I helped them build the new playground. Dad made me work on it after school every day. It might have been what saved me." He blew across his straw, whistling like he'd done in grade school. "Well, the guilt from hurting you might have saved me."

Tight chested, she scanned the paragraph on the page before the next seal. "Now we'll go to Fletcher Chapel. Frank said the Metro from Columbia Heights puts us straight there."

"Sounds good." Geoff grinned. "After we finish eating."

"Of course."

About fifty minutes later, they arrived at the small white church. Savannah, carrying the open journal, looked between the pages and the building. "Built in 1854, and thought to be a stop on the Underground Railroad." She eyed Frank's tiny letters. "Okay, he's making a point about slavery and civil rights, but I don't understand what he wants me to know."

155

"You'll understand soon."

"I hope so." She made notes and clicked a few pictures. "There's a name here. Andrew Jackson Downing. Ever heard of him?"

Geoff shook his head.

"Bah!" Savannah swiped the screen of her phone. "My battery is at four percent. I wish he would have told me."

"What good is a family mystery if all the answers come easy?"

"Okay, it's loaded. He was a designer. I guess the building is his style. The clue must relate to Downing's architecture, because there's not much else here. It's at the end of the section and says the next place is near Lake Michigan. Dad's going to love that." She closed the journal. "Let's check out the places you wanted to visit before we fly back to Dreyfus."

<hr />

Quaking concrete warned of an upcoming train. Geoff tugged Savannah closer to the waiting crowd. "One more time."

She laughed. "You've ridden this thing all over town, Geoff. You're bad as a kid."

He couldn't hold back his smile. "I think it's kind of cool. It would be neat to live here."

"Next you're going to tell me you want a man purse. You're hysterical."

The young man in front of them adjusted the leather strap securing the bag at his waist and glanced over his shoulder. He moved several feet away.

She covered her mouth, masking stifled laughter. "Oops! Should we wait for the next train?"

"Who's the bully now?" Geoff clamped his jaw. Ahh! Idiocy. Why did he mention bullying?

She smiled. "It's fine. I'm over it."

The train stopped, and they climbed aboard, choosing the side opposite the man with the leather satchel.

Savannah slid into the seat next to Geoff, and her breath quickened when he draped his arm around her shoulders. She melted into him, a yawn stretching her face.

Attraction? Contentment? She'd appeared to feel it all day. Was it real? Enduring?

His nose sunk into her hair. She smelled like a garden, like paradise. If only the ride could last forever.

At their stop, she blushed as she met his gaze. Words unspoken made his chest ache. How much longer could they go on in awkwardness?

He followed her off the train, and they traveled for blocks, taking in all the federal buildings and the White House. They spent forty-five minutes meandering through the World War II Memorial, reading every inscription and studying each granite pillar with only stilted conversation. Something had to give.

He knelt, tracing words etched in stone. "This is incredible."

"Twentieth time you've said so." A jogger sped past, and Savannah stared after him for a second before a wide grin breached her face. "It is incredible." She cast a teasing wink over her shoulder and jetted toward the Lincoln Memorial.

Ignoring curious stares from security and passers-by, he chased her, catching up on the last step. As he wrapped his arms around her, he tripped, sending them both to the marble floor.

"Ow!" She rubbed her hip and stuck her tongue out at him. "Will you please stop embarrassing me in front of hundreds of people?"

He sat with his knees bent. "Will you please forgive me a second time?" Snorting, he touched the tip of her nose. "In fact, will you please forgive me the first time?"

She giggled. "Fine. I will."

They scooted to a spot between two monstrous marble columns. The sun shone above the reflecting pool at the tip of the Washington Monument.

"Amazing." He snapped a picture with his phone, then examined Lincoln's statue. "So much history here."

"Not incredible?"

"No, amazing." He slipped the phone in his pocket and moved closer. "As beautiful as all this is, it's not the most beautiful thing here."

He brought his face close to hers. Her eyes glossed, and her heart raced against his chest.

"What kind of line is that?" She looked away.

He puffed a blast of air. He'd thought... he'd hoped. Not yet. Maybe not ever.

Pointing to three bouncing children coming up the steps in their direction, she chewed on her lower lip. "We should go and let them have their turn. We haven't even scratched this city's surface yet, and the plane leaves in hours."

Though his shoulders slumped and his mouth turned down, he nodded, and they headed toward the Korean War Veterans Memorial. Tears welled as they passed the statues and walked along the mural wall.

His chest burned, air sticking in his lungs. He'd considered military service. Why hadn't he joined? Everyone in Dreyfus thought him a hero because he threw vegetables their way every so often. He didn't even come close.

Savannah started for his hand, but withdrew. He stared at her profile. He hadn't felt this much emotion since losing his mom. He shouldn't have come with her, scholarship or no scholarship. Or did Frank want to unsettle both of them?

As they left, a man dressed in fatigues led his young family in the opposite way. "Thank you." Geoff extended his hand.

The man raised his brow, and Geoff withdrew. Why had he been so compelled to approach the man? Did his heart find its own tongue? Nevertheless, he couldn't stop himself from saying it again. "Thank you for serving."

The soldier nodded, but didn't speak. His two daughters gazed wide-eyed at Geoff.

After holding the man's gaze for a moment, Geoff offered a hundred-dollar bill. "Take your family out for dinner."

The soldier raised his hand as if to protest. Geoff slipped the bill between his fingers anyway. "Please. Take it."

Tears streamed his wife's face, and she embraced Geoff. "Thank you so much. You have no idea how much we needed that."

"It's nothing." Geoff withdrew two more bills. "Here. Wish I could do more."

As the couple walked away, Geoff shifted. Savannah studied him. Did he see admiration in her eyes?

"Think we could have dinner, too?" Her voice wavered. "Our plane leaves soon."

He shoved his wallet back in his pocket. "Sure."

While she went to the restroom, he looked through the gift shop. He needed to give her a gift to capture what he felt but couldn't say. When he left the store, he found her waiting on a bench.

"I'm glad you came with me." She smiled, friendlier than he could have ever hoped. "I've had a good time."

He lifted a green sweatshirt from the white plastic bag, and grinned. "It's not silk, but I bet it's warmer than those blouses you always like to wear. I, um… thought you'd wear a small."

"Oh. Thanks." She lifted the sweatshirt, her brown eyes widening as he held out the snow globe hidden underneath the heavy fleece. "A miniature Lincoln Memorial. It's beautiful."

He joined her on the bench and placed it in her hands. "I wanted to thank you for giving me another chance." Lame. Wincing, he leaned closer and kissed her cheek.

"You're welcome." She blushed deep. "We'd better go."

They grabbed burgers at the airport and made the plane in perfect time. Hours later, they stood in her parents' driveway at the base of the porch.

"Good night." She started up the steps.

He spun her so she faced him, and met her lips in soft hesitance. After barely brushing them, he left her side. "Good night."

She bounded to the door, as though she couldn't escape fast enough. Enough with the awkwardness. How could he let her walk away? He had to tell her.

Now or never. "Savannah..."

She rested her hand on the doorknob, her shoulders heaving.

His outstretched palm quivered in the cool night air. "I wanted your forgiveness, but the truth is I want so much more. Be my girl."

Chapter Nineteen

Savannah faced her blotchy reflection in the mirror above the dresser, her eyes burning from two straight hours of crying. Why had she been such an idiot? Geoff put his heart on the line, and she crushed it for no good reason.

Seven heartless words: *I don't want to be your girl.* Words meaning nothing, because her entire soul screamed she wanted to be his girl. Image after image flashed through her mind—enjoying the sunset from the farmhouse porch, breaking beans, and chasing his dog across the crop-covered fields.

Savannah studied the pictures of her friends pinned cockeyed under the ribbon on her corkboard. She'd abandoned them when she left town. They must hate her.

She plopped on her middle-school comforter, rubbing her fingertips over the quilted octagons. Fourteen years to the day, she collapsed on this bed, sobbing over the same boy. Hating him all this time had turned her into a monster. Could loving him be the cure?

Clutching her collar button, she blew air over her upper lip in short bursts. He'd given her his number. She should text him.

After ten minutes of staring at her blank cell screen, she pressed the button to wake up her phone. She thought for a minute then typed. *Hey.*

Hey. His response came seconds later. Had he been waiting for her message?

She took a deep breath and tapped the letters with her right pointer finger. *I'm so sorry. I'm overwhelmed.*

Minutes ticked by like months. No response. Should she try again? Tell him everything? *We've moved so fast.*

He needed to understand. *I've dated over fifteen guys in the last two years. Some overlapping; others one night stands. I'm not the settle-down-on-the-farm kind of girl.*

Could she be? She swung her legs against the bedframe. Would he even have an answer?

Another ding.

Don't care about your past. I'm crazy about the girl you are now.

Her heart soared, but something squelched it. Crazy about her? Did she want him to be crazy about her?

Ellipses dotted the chat box. She tapped her toes until the text appeared.

One of these days, I'll kiss you longer and harder than you've ever been kissed, and you'll beg me every single day because you can't live without another.

More ellipses. *If it means not living on a farm, I can handle that.*

The phone fell to the mattress. Was he for real? She plummeted to her pillow, her lips turning upward.

She eyed her corkboard then the journal resting on her white, flowered desk. Frank's words rang in her ears. Make things right. Geoff needed a real, heartfelt apology. She should stop making excuses for being a rotten person and try to be a better one. Didn't Frank want that for her?

The journal. She'd completely lost track of her purpose, to follow the scavenger hunt to the next place, a cabin at Lake Michigan. This time, Frank had written a phone number.

Should she call it?

Only nine thirty. Most people wouldn't go to bed so early.

She sat straighter. Yes, she should.

Mona waited at the door with a plastic bowl filled with cantaloupe, berries, and watermelon. "Morning, nephew." She pushed past Geoff and set the bowl on the kitchen table. "I've been thinking."

Geoff grimaced. Mona's thinking usually meant disaster. "About fruit?"

"About Pandora. If you want to date her, fine. I'll try to give you space."

"We aren't dating, not that it's any of your business." Not yet, anyway.

Mona waggled her finger. "You don't go on a cross country trip with a woman—"

"Frank..." He looked at the muddy clumps left on the floor by his worn leather boots. "Okay, fine. I'm attracted to her. Why change your tune?"

She shrugged. "If the two of you were to fall in love and get married, you'd own the farm again. Problem solved."

"Problem solved, huh? What if she doesn't agree to marry me?"

"She's an idiot."

"What if I don't want to marry her?"

"Then you're the idiot." She hung her purse over the kitchen chair. "But you should definitely work that angle. It's a win-win for everyone, right?" A bitter chuckle escaped her throat. "Well, except me."

"You're not involved."

"True." She rifled through a stack of bills on the counter. "Have you started looking for another farm?"

He carried the bills to his desk in the living room corner. "Zach's trying. He's found three properties, and we're going next week to look."

She lifted the coffee mug of ink pens next to the bills and set it back on the counter. "What did you do in DC?"

"Not much. Toured places. We went to the spot where Frank's mother died." Geoff grabbed an Ale-8 from the fridge.

"I can't believe you still drink such nasty stuff. Soda's bad for you. Haven't you read all those articles about sugar?"

He popped the cap, took a long swig, and swallowed. Ginger flavored bubbles tickled all the way down to the pit of his stomach. "Frank has an obsession with slavery and the Underground Railroad. He sent her to the Civil Rights Institute in Birmingham, for example. Then, we visited this little church, Fletcher Chapel. No idea of why it's important, other than a man named Andrew Jackson Downing created the design. Do you know anything about any of that?"

"Hmm. I can tell you the connection, I think. Your farmhouse is Downing's style. I remember studying his designs in college and coming home amazed to see one in person. The long front porch and balcony over top of it are classic examples. When Frank had this house built in 1939, he used one of Downing's floor plans." She clamped her mouth shut.

Geoff jerked to face her. "I thought you didn't know any details about this place. You told me you only knew Frank worked as a photographer and he disappeared after the war."

She shrugged. "I didn't think the house design mattered."

"Frank did."

"Frank was insane. He thought fence posts mattered." Mona replaced the refrigerator magnet she'd been holding and hurried to the front door. "You two lovebirds enjoy the fruit."

He locked the door after her, rocking on his feet, and then removed his cell from his pocket. He should text Savannah.

Hey. Lame, but she used it.

Hey.

Would they ever get over the awkwardness? He retreated to his den and flipped on the local news. *Found out from Mona that the farmhouse has one of Andrew Jackson Downing's floor plans.*

It does?

164

Then nothing.

Geoff rubbed his temples. He should go kiss her right now. Get it over with and see how she'd react. He chuckled. Her dad would shoot him.

He stirred around in the kitchen for a while, cutting up vegetables and packing them in foil. When his cell alerted him of another text, he jumped, knocking diced celery to the floor.

Do you remember Cindy Smith? She was our babysitter.

Cindy Smith—the eccentric, fun-loving woman who taught him to love old movies. *Yeah. What about her?*

We need to go to Lake Michigan to see her.

His pulse quickened. She'd said we. *When?*

Leave Thursday morning? Stay with her for two days or a couple more.

Okay.

Zach would have to manage things a while longer.

Geoff ran to his truck and drove out to the field where his men repaired storm damage along the fence. When he stepped out, a pang seared his heart. They looked sorry to see him. No wonder. He'd given them nothing but bad news lately.

"Wish I could find a girl and take off with her. Stop working, do whatever I want." Cole, his newest help, leaned against a post and whistled.

"Yep." Zach dropped the roll of barbed wire he'd been holding and laughed. "Glad you showed up to help. Thought you quit on us for good."

Geoff slapped his shoulder. "I haven't taken a vacation in five years, fellas. Surely, you guys could afford me one."

Zach picked up an old, partly buried bottle cap and pocketed it. "Take as much time as you want. Where to this time? Got a hot date across the country?"

Geoff smirked. Tools stilled, and all six men stared at him.

Grinning, he shook his head. "We're not leaving until Thursday morning. I'm taking her to visit our old babysitter. We're staying in a lake cabin with an older woman. Sound like a hot date?"

"You're weird, brother." Zach spit in a muddy tuft of grass.

"I pay you not to notice. Don't you guys have a fence to mend?"

Zach fake-coughed and cleared his throat. "Don't you?"

His men laughed. They kept their gazes trained on the truck as he drove away. He did have a good crew. They deserved better than this. When he returned from Michigan, he'd focus on finding a new farm so they wouldn't have to worry.

Back at the house, he tossed a few clothes in the washer. After some thought, he went into the old master bedroom and filled a cardboard box with more of Maria's old clothes. Might as well start packing her stuff. Time to get rid of it.

He packed until church time, taking note of things he'd repair for Savannah. The house needed so much work. She hadn't mentioned living there, or even staying in town, but if he fixed it up, she might stay.

He changed out his laundry then straightened the kitchen, groaning when he saw Mona's purse hanging over the back of a chair. An intricate comb poked out from a pocket. He picked it up and traced the grooves in the plastic, the same pattern as the mirror left at the Barretts' house.

"What?" He turned the comb over in his hands a few times then dialed the police station. Mona'd spiraled out of control. "Ryan Chambers, please." Maybe his old high school buddy could watch her.

Chapter Twenty

The threat of his promised kiss hung between them the whole ten-hour ride to Michigan. Geoff didn't care. She needed to squirm for a while.

Savannah ran her fingers over the journal page in her lap, scanning Frank's painstaking print. "I'm going to call Cindy and tell her we're close. Then I'll call Dad and apologize for sneaking off without saying goodbye." She frowned. "Or I'll wait a day or two. He's still mad I wouldn't go to church last night."

"He'll be fine." Geoff squinted at a road sign, obscured by trees, and turned right. After she made the call, they came to a gated lake house community and followed a dim, winding road to a two-story log cabin. Lights beamed from every window. Made perfect sense. Cindy never had been a fan of the dark.

He parked his truck behind a rental sedan and followed Savannah to the porch.

Before they had a chance to ring the bell, Cindy swept the door open and waved with a flourish. The scent of menthol cigarettes and stale coffee mixed with her musky perfume. Yellow sunglasses matched her cardigan, and a silky black scarf wrapped her hair. The bluish porch light spotlighted her, illuminating the bare shoulder peeking from beneath her sweater.

"Geoffrey Spencer." She engulfed him in a hearty embrace. "You haven't aged a day since I last saw you. How is your sweet mama?"

He forced out a deep, slow exhale. "She's been gone for about seven years now."

"Right. I remember. Frank told me. I've missed her so much."
She turned to Savannah. "Don't you know who I am?"

Savannah searched Cindy's sun-wrinkled face. Not even a hint
of recognition crossed hers. She ducked her head and traced a terra-
cotta porch tile with her toe. "I think so."

"I'm supposed to tell you a lot of things." Cindy ushered them
into the cabin. She squeezed Geoff's hand. "I suppose you're ready
to find out where you fit into his plan."

"I'd like to, yes." Geoff set his luggage by the door.

Cindy grinned. "Well, you'll have to wait. I promised Frank."

Savannah patted the journal through the pocket of her bag. "Yep.
I read all about it."

"Well." Cindy swiveled, her cigarette hanging from her lips. "I
guess we'd better get inside and I'll show you your rooms." She cast
Geoff a pointed look over her shoulder. "I hadn't planned for two
guests, so it's going to take a while."

Savannah studied the old rotary phone on an antique accent table.

Cindy reached around her and dialed the phone. A man's
annoyed voice came through the speaker.

"Miller, they're here. I need you to come up and take care of a
couple things in the morning. Yes…" She sighed. "I know you don't
want to get out of bed that early. Don't forget how much I'm paying
you for this."

A mumbled protest blasted through the speaker.

"I don't care how early it is." Cindy picked lint from her jogging
pants. "Get your lazy self up here. If I don't see you in the morning,
I'm going to cut off your Internet access."

Savannah walked to the porch and sat on a dainty wrought-iron bench. She leaned closer to the armrest, inspecting the complex interweaving of French curves. She'd seen this bench. When had she last seen Cindy?

Geoff joined her, sitting way too close. His racing heartbeat matched hers. Did he feel it? Did he know how nervous he made her? How long had it been since they'd been comfortable around each other? Decades, at least.

A much younger Geoff came to mind, sitting on the same bench in a different house. Several other kids ran in diapers at their feet.

"It's been years since I've thought about our childhood." She peered into the kitchen window.

Cindy gestured animatedly to the person on the phone then disappeared from view.

Blood roared in Savannah's ears. "I wonder if Cindy is my real mother."

Geoff's arm crept around her shoulder. "She doesn't look anything like you."

"Maybe not..." Savannah nuzzled closer, pressing her cheek against his, feeling his heart pounding even faster. Could this be the kiss? Was she ready?

"My guess is they were childhood friends. They'd be about the same age." He brushed his lips across her temple.

She scowled as he smirked. How dare he tease her after their history?

He scooted away and pointed to a paved drive circling the cabins. A short, stumpy guy with wayward brown hair shuffled their way. "That must be Miller."

Cindy blasted out to the porch and waved the guy closer. "Get over here." She wrinkled her nose. "My useless nephew. Textbook image of a sloth. He's coming to give me a piece of his feeble little mind, no doubt."

"What's his first name?"

"Come here, Miller. Meet your cousin." Cindy's expression hardened.

Savannah gasped. "My cousin?"

"Oops, I can't tell you yet. Never mind the connection, because he's my lousy ex-husband's sister's child. No blood relation to you. Nate Miller, Savannah Barrett-McMillan and Geoffrey Spencer."

Nate gave a long yawn, nodded to her, and lifted his wife-beater tank to scratch his hairy stomach. "I'm not getting up at dawn."

"It's good for you."

Savannah shifted to study Cindy's profile. "So, if Nate and I are related by marriage, you're related, too."

"I'll explain everything in Frank's time." Cindy balanced her phone, a lit cigarette, and a can of soda against her chest and fished an envelope out of her purse. "First, we need to go on a short walk in the morning. Nate, here's the key."

Nate disappeared into a shed behind the cabin, and Savannah followed Geoff and Cindy into the entry. Cindy showed them where to find towels then headed out to her nephew, nagging so loud it drifted through the closed window.

Geoff lingered beside Savannah's door for a moment and cupped her cheek before disappearing into his room. She glared after him, then stomped into her room and got ready for bed, her stomach in knots. He enjoyed this too much.

An hour before sunrise, surprising brightness streamed through the curtains. Savannah stretched and yawned to the rhythm of tinkling wind chimes playing the tune of "Amazing Grace". She rolled out of bed, tiptoed to the bathroom, brushed her teeth, and twisted her hair into a loose ponytail. Cindy waited downstairs at the kitchen table, nursing a cup of coffee.

"Let's walk."

"Shouldn't we wake Geoff?"

Cindy snickered. "Nah. Let him sleep."

"Okay." Savannah looked down at her flannel pajamas. "I'll go change. Where are we headed?"

Cindy nodded to three pairs of muddy boots by the door. "How do you feel about worms?"

Savannah's stomach churned. "Worms?"

Geoff cleared his throat. "You're going to take her fishing?"

She eyed the boots. "I can fish. Why couldn't I fish?"

"You're not a settle-on-the-farm type of girl, remember?" He winked. "This will be a true test."

"Morning, Geoff." Cindy laughed. "We catch our own dinner around here. She has to earn her meals. Think you can teach her?"

"I can try."

After a quick breakfast, they took a brisk walk through fog to the fishing dock. Savannah shivered in the cool morning air. The mist made her lungs ache.

Nate stood at the end of the dock under a thatched roof, leaning four poles against the railing. He glowered at Cindy then smiled at Savannah.

"Morning." Cindy strolled over and slapped his shoulder. "Did you get enough?"

"I'd say so." He tapped a monstrous bucket of night crawlers with a muddy boot. "Help yourselves."

Geoff readied a rod, and hooked a wiggling worm. He passed it to Savannah.

"Do you think I can't do it?" Worm or no worm, he wouldn't get the satisfaction of watching her fail. No way. She snatched a different rod and plunged her hand into the worm bucket. Slimy creatures slithered around her fingers. A chilling wetness spread over every surface and crevice of her hand. Shuddering, she pinched one between her pointer finger and thumb.

She slipped it over the hook and brandished the assembly. The grin left her face as the worm shimmied and dove to the ground.

Cindy cackled. "Good try. Let Nate show you."

Nate groaned. "You're going to scare away the fish."

"Pshaw." Cindy dropped into a lawn chair and crossed her legs at the ankles, casting chunks of old mud to the dock.

Several tries later, Savannah hooked a night crawler, and they flung their lines into the water. Her lips turned upward. "First try for casting."

Geoff grinned. "Not bad."

Her line tugged. Already? She stood straighter, brought the pole to her chest, and gripped it with whitened knuckles. Steadying herself against the dock's old, wooden railing, she shivered, releasing the cool metal handle and dropping the pole.

"Here, let me get it." Cindy rescued it and reeled in the tiny flapping fish. She pulled the hook out of its mouth and tossed the fish into the water.

Savannah covered her gaping mouth. "I..." At Nate's frown, she lowered her voice. "I just caught it! Why did you—?"

"Half the fun of it." Cindy laughed. "We always throw the small ones back."

Fifteen dinner-sized trout later, Nate dragged a bucket to the cabin, with Cindy nagging at his side. Geoff squeezed Savannah's hand tight. "You did well today."

"I know." She giggled, bumping his shoulder as they walked.

When they reached the house, he leaned to her ear. "You stink like fish."

She nudged his chest. "You stink."

Cindy lit her fifth cigarette for the morning. "We all stink. Miller, go home. Geoff and Savannah, go change, and I'll show you Frank's trophies. He used to win the Dreyfus Fisherman's Club competitions every year."

"I think I remember. Herb used to get so angry." Geoff nodded to the bucket. "For a first-timer, Savannah didn't do half bad."

"What can I say? I've got skills." She trekked ahead through the kitchen, disappeared upstairs, and soaked in a bubble bath for a full hour. Intense savory smells greeted her when she emerged. Her stomach growled as her nose led her to the stairwell. She peeked through the rails.

Geoff stirred something in a steaming pan.

Cindy tapped her fingers on the kitchen counter. "Sit down a minute and let me talk to you."

He adjusted the stove burner and faced Cindy, his gaze landing below Savannah's line of sight. Would Cindy give real answers?

"It's been a long time since you were in Dreyfus." He lowered himself into a kitchen chair. "I didn't know what happened to you after you left."

Cindy dug through her purse. "Frank felt terrible for filing for ownership, but he knew you'd handle it with grace. I'm so sorry your sweet mama isn't here to help you through it."

Geoff's shoulders heaved. "Yeah, Mom died about six months after Dad. You'd think it would get easier after all this time, but it hasn't. She was my rock."

Savannah, her heart aching for him, put her weight on the railing. It wobbled, and she jumped, trying to land soft enough to not be heard.

Geoff glanced toward the rail, and she stomped past the stairs to the bathroom. Then she tiptoed back.

Cindy had moved out of her line of sight. "Frank also said you hadn't even tried to date or anything. Wonder if he expected you two might find each other, and that's why he asked you to come."

"I wondered when you'd bring up our relationship. Mona already has."

"So, why Dora? Why now?" Cindy moved into view and patted Geoff's arm. "It's about the farm, isn't it? Or are you after Frank's fortune?"

173

Geoff tilted his head toward the floor. "At first, I wanted to tag along because Frank promised the scholarship money fund. But the more I get to know her..." He exhaled. "I mean, she's a beautiful, single woman. Of course there's a level of attraction."

Cindy narrowed her eyes. "I think it's more."

Geoff's cheeks pinked. "My sun doesn't rise these days until she's in the room. I never expected to fall head over heels. If I thought she'd say yes, I'd propose tomorrow."

Savannah's stomach knotted. Heat covered her cheeks. Marriage? She'd never considered it. Geoff—he was a family man. He'd expect her to birth him twelve strapping boys and tug them around on her hips. No way would she fall into such a simple, archaic life.

"I, for one, think it's a great idea." Cindy slapped his shoulder. "You're a good man, Geoff. It's a real shame you've been lonely for so long."

"I've not been lonely. I've been busy." His words came out too fast.

Savannah's heartbeat quickened. How could she push him away and cause him more pain?

"Sure, you've been lonely."

Geoff brushed crumbs off the table. "I don't think she wants the same things out of a relationship as I do. She's already said she doesn't want to settle down with a farmer. I doubt she even wants children."

Exactly. Savannah twisted the collar of her shirt in her fist. Did she want children? Ever?

Cindy scoffed. "Give her time. She'll adjust. Now tell me more about all this charity work. What is it you do, exactly?"

"We buy school supplies for needy children. We support missionaries across the world, sending Bibles and medicine to third world countries—all kinds of stuff." A grin resonated in his voice. "We sent a big shipment of medical supplies to Honduras. It ended

174

up being about fifty-thousand dollars' worth of materials. I still can't believe we collected so much."

"I told your mama you'd turn out okay. I remember the year of your baptism. Right before I left town. Well, the second time." Cindy inhaled her cigarette. "Forget about the romance for now. The girl has bigger things to consider. Be supportive. It'll happen."

Cindy called it. Savannah felt the pulse of romance compressing her heart in all directions every time Geoff walked in a room. She couldn't hold it back if she tried. But her track record of destroying men—how could she be sure she'd always love him? Better to break both their hearts now, than to crush his after building a life together.

Cindy tapped her cigarette over an empty glass. "Has she found Frank's riddles yet? Did she figure out the cryptogram clues?"

"She found puzzles, but I don't think she's solved any of them."

Savannah knelt, and pressed her hands into the carpet fibers. She knew who could help her. Rose had been solving cryptograms since high school. Everyone knew about her obsession.

Geoff checked the sizzling pans and cut the heat once more. "Do you know what they mean?"

"No. I helped him develop the pictures. I didn't know about the puzzles until he told me."

Savannah snuck to her room then clomped to the steps.

Cindy met her gaze through the railing. "You're ready for answers."

Savannah joined them at the table. "Please."

"We lived in Dreyfus for years." Cindy exhaled, puffing a ring of smoke over her cheeks. "When Frank told me we had a family connection, I wanted to run and give Rose a piece of my mind for sending you away to her aunt. If I'd known, I would have taken you in myself." She paused. "Frank stayed in a mental institute for a while. Did he tell you?"

"No."

175

"I think they called it drug-induced psychosis back then, although according to my mother he had a history of mental illness. You can't take everything he's told you at face value."

Savannah bit her lower lip. "Speaking of mothers, are you mine?"

"Oh, no." Cindy braced herself against the table. "That baby was stillborn. This is a different one."

"What baby? You're not making any sense." Savannah looked at Geoff, who shrugged, lifting his palms. She turned to Cindy. "Are you my grandmother?"

Cindy's jaw dropped. "Excuse me?"

"I'm sorry. Of course you aren't. You aren't old enough." She looked old enough. Savannah inspected her own tanned arms. Would she look like that someday, too? "What baby? Who is the mother?"

"The way I heard it, the girl seduced him. Of course, he left the hospital and joined the army, and the scandal disappeared. I'm not quite sure how."

"Scandal? What scandal?" Savannah rubbed her eyes and yawned. "Geoff, do you understand any of this?"

"No. Cindy, who had a baby?"

Cindy gripped the edge of the table. "The babies changed everything." She sucked in a gush of smoky air. "Go get your journal. Since you've been fishing, you're ready for the next part."

Chapter Twenty-One

Geoff devoured a plate of tortilla chips smothered in Monterey Jack Queso while Savannah broke the next seal. Cindy sat wrapped in a wool blanket on the front porch. The journal must have disturbed her. Something else disturbed him.

He'd brought up marriage. Was he crazy? Maybe not. They fit, like pieces to an unsolved puzzle. Still, he couldn't consider marriage unless she cultivated her relationship with God. Shouldn't consider dating.

Speaking of puzzles… Savannah had laid all Frank's farm pictures out face down on the table. Geoff picked up the corner one, inspected the codes, and laid it back in its spot.

Her eyes widened. "Well, look at 20-H4, for example. Hamilton in the1920s. Four deaths."

"You're right." He skimmed the legal pad with her notes. "Knickerbocker Theater, 22-KT-2. Two deaths in 1922."

She scribbled at the bottom the pad. "Frank would have been here in Michigan around 1929. That matches 29-MI-2. Two deaths?"

"Guess we'll find out later. Where's the next stop?"

"Sand dunes." She glanced over her shoulder at him and grinned. "We have to jump off a cliff. Hope we're not the two deaths."

"I doubt going over a sand dune would be too traumatic."
He pulled the chair next to her, his lungs constricting when she smoothed his hair.

"I've wanted to do this since age seven." She traced his sideburn and rested her hand against his cheek. "You know you were my first and only Dreyfus crush, right?"

"I didn't." His heart grappled for hope. "After middle school, you acted so weird around me. I had no idea how to interpret it. That's why we picked on you so much. Not that we had any excuse." He scratched his scalp. "I need a haircut. It feels gross."

"It's soft." She scooted her chair ninety degrees and faced him. "I owe you an apology."

"Why?"

"I never meant to hurt your feelings." She wiggled her toes and sat on her hands. "I have a terrible track record with relationships. If not for Frank, I'd still be sitting in Chicago in my lousy apartment, working at my dead-end job, and having one night stands with whatever men pay me the least attention."

"That's not you."

"It is me." She held up her right palm, fingers spread. "Part of me wants to jump in your arms and scream yes. Let's be together. But you deserve quality. I'm not quality."

"No." Geoff spoke through gritted teeth. "Don't say that. It's not like I'm any better." He pushed the journal away and rested his elbow on the table. "I dated only the prettiest girls. Found myself married to a snob. She didn't care enough about me to bring a glass of water when I got sick. I didn't know anything about humility until after she died."

"You learned it." She reached for his hand. "I'd be lying if I said I didn't want to try. You're so different now. I mean, back there in the courthouse. How were you so calm? You didn't even yell at me."

"I found God." He stared straight into her brown eyes, which had grown darker. *Please, let her hear me.* "When I became a Christian, I did change. Before you returned, I made things right with everyone I bullied—except you. I wanted to find you."

178

He toyed with loose strands of her hair. She stared at the table. If he wrapped her in his arms, would she stay?

Touching the tip of her chin, he made her look at him. "We all make mistakes. Neither of us is immune. But together, we can help each other be better."

"We can." She cast him a tentative smile.

"You know, church helped, but not just attending. I learned how to serve others instead of myself. A lot of people go to church and never change."

"Yeah, like Rose." A snarl flickered across her lips. "She told me she'd rather I die skinny than ever get fat again. How's that for a Christian attitude?"

"Let it go. Part of changing means we turn the other cheek."

"I'll try." She pushed her chair from the table. "Ready to visit the dunes?"

❋❋❋

Savannah's breath caught as her gaze swept across panoramic blues. Lake Michigan gleamed below a clear sky, with two smaller lakes beside it, as if she perched atop a perfect tiny island.

On the beach below, waves lapped the colorful sand, swirling red and black crystals into a paisley pattern.

Shouts rang to the left. A teenage boy leapt over the edge of the dune. He dropped several feet and landed with a skid. "Awesome!"

Another boy followed. "Again!"

She tucked her sandals in the knapsack she borrowed from Cindy. "You game, Geoff?"

"Sure." He laughed and removed his socks and shoes. His callused toes were no match for her manicured ones. "How many times have you wanted to push me off a cliff with no consequences?"

"You have no idea."

179

"Hardy, har, har. Let's jump. One, two..." He whistled and poked her side. "I'm not sure this is a good idea."

"Stop it." Savannah giggled and lunged. "Three!"

She closed her eyes as they sailed through the air in free fall. It took seconds to hit the lower sand, but it felt like flying through time. If only it could erase her mistakes.

When they landed, she found his face only an inch away. He touched his cheek to hers, and she shivered.

Breathe! Her body didn't listen, instead responding with trembling. She wanted to kiss him so badly she couldn't stand it. But she wouldn't.

The intensity in his stare made her think he might do it. This might be the moment he'd promised.

He withdrew.

Of course, he did. She blinked away stinging tears. "Let's go again."

At the bottom, granite rocks littered the beach in sparkling reds, browns, grays, and whites, tumbled smooth by the waves. She pocketed a handful and found a dry spot feet away.

She broke the next journal seal. "Here's a family picture. Looks to be a birthday party. Several smiling people." She flipped the page. "And here's the cake on the floor, smashed to bits."

He straightened his crouch, letting lake water spill between his fingers. His feet sunk in the wet sand as he neared. "Frank's birthday?"

"I think so." She held up the page. A dark-haired boy sat crumpled on the floor next to the cake, with his head buried between his knees. "Foster dad dies of heart attack. But it's only one death. There's no caption after this page."

Geoff studied the pictures. "Could the numbers represent people he lost, not just people who died? What if his foster mom couldn't keep him after her losing her husband?"

"Could be." Savannah pressed her hand against her lips. "So..." She puffed a blast of air. "Next is Chicago." Her filthy apartment. Blood rushed to her temples. "I think I should go alone."

"We can talk about that later." He pointed across the lake. "Look at the lighthouse. We could explore one tomorrow before we leave."

"Yeah..." She averted her gaze, Chicago oppressing her already. "Sounds great."

"Hold still." He readied his phone camera. "Sit up another inch if you can."

She loosened her hair, letting it tumble over her shoulders. She forced a smile for the camera then stretched across the beach when he lowered his phone. "I'm resting."

The flood of memories raged behind closed eyes. Adam Capesi, in an intense late-night make-out session at the realty company where she worked. Todd, her boss, and the inappropriate touches she'd allowed when she brought him paperwork. Heat surged through her cheeks. Geoff had no clue about her real identity.

"This weather is perfect. Too perfect for being a beach bum all day." He pulled her mind to the present.

She opened her eyes as he leaned over her again, his knees pressing into the sand next to hers.

"You are so beautiful." He kissed her forehead, then both cheeks.

She wiggled out from beneath him. "Agh! Would you please stop tempting me and not delivering?"

He laughed. "I tried, but I couldn't bring myself to do it. Not yet."

"So, let me get this straight." Her brow creased so tight it ached. "Last night you were ready to propose, and you can't bring yourself to kiss me?"

Geoff sprung to his feet and crossed his arms. "How do you know that?"

181

"I heard what you told Cindy." She stood, brushing sand from her capris. "I've been with more men than you have cattle. There. It's out in the open. I seduce men and leave them, smirking in the distance as their hearts fall apart. It's a game to me. My continual revenge on the male species, you might say."

He reached for her, chuckling. "I haven't dated any cattle."

Couldn't she shock him away? Why wouldn't he listen? "No, you need to hear this. I'm not wife material. I'm ruined goods. As much as I'd love to kiss you right now, as soon as it happened, I'd be ready to move on to some other guy. I can't promise I wouldn't end up hating you again tomorrow."

"You aren't that person anymore. At least, you don't have to be. The blood of Christ covers everything, Savannah. Even sexual sin."

She stomped her feet in the sand. "I don't want to hear another word about the blood of Christ. You and I will never happen. We can't happen. End of story."

He remained still, only a flicker in his jaw. As she made her way back up the hill, her chest constricted until she gasped for breaths. Tears spilled onto the sand. She hadn't meant to be so cruel, but she had to be honest. She'd never be good enough for him.

At the top of the dune, she glanced down once more before running to the truck. He had dropped to his knees, his head bent over and his wrists buried in the sand.

He'd buried her heart with them.

Chapter Twenty-Two

Sifting through ingredients in Cindy's kitchen, Geoff hummed "Amazing Grace" and remembered his mother's creativity.

Savannah hadn't spoken since her confession. He should have taken her in his arms right then and explained he had no right to judge anyone about sexual sin. Why hadn't he?

While he mixed raspberries into custard, she connected the farm pictures with clear packing tape.

Cindy puffed on cigarettes as if they provided her life-sustaining air. "Any progress?"

Savannah nodded. "We discovered these clues were places, dates, and I think number of deaths. Like the next date is 1929 and NP. He wants me to go to Chicago, so NP is Navy Pier? Then 1934. His eighteenth birthday?"

Geoff snatched a few spoons and slammed the drawer. Great. She would talk, but not to him.

Cindy clapped. "Smart girl. The numbers don't always mean deaths."

"Yeah."

"And the letters don't always mean locations. Navy Pier is right."

He cleared his throat. "Cindy, did Frank say anything about the Underground Railroad or the Klan?"

She concentrated on a spot on the ceiling, her lips moving as if amid conversation. After a few moments, she rubbed her forehead with her palms. "Here's what I can tell you. Frank suffered from post-traumatic stress disorder."

Maybe she did, too. Apparently, Cindy didn't want to talk about the Underground Railroad. Did she even know anything about Frank's curiosity? He grabbed three bowls from the cupboard and spooned custard into them. He shouldn't be here. This was Savannah's life—her conversation.

Cindy sipped water from a tall, thin bottle. "Frank had a romantic tryst with a lovely young nurse at the mental hospital. She miscarried, but they married. Nine months later, the young lady bore a child, Arthur."

Savannah scribbled notes. "Did Arthur die? He couldn't have lost contact with the lady or he would have put two lost, right? One doesn't make sense. Or, it might not be the right point in the timeline." Dropping the pencil, she tangled her hand in her hair. "Ugh! None of this makes sense. Is this Arthur my grandfather?"

"Yes." Cindy withdrew two more cigarettes from her purse. She placed one in her mouth and lit it, blowing the smoke toward him. "He married the young lady. Your great-grandmother Belinda."

Dodging the thick white cloud, he set the custard bowls on the table and jammed spoons into them.

"Thanks." Savannah started a new page, drawing several circles. One, she captioned Military Service, another Deaths, and another Births.

Cindy balanced her cigarette on the tip of a cup and started eating heaping spoonfuls of his pink, creamy concoction. She passed him the empty bowl, her eyes trained on Savannah. "After Frank married, he returned to the mental hospital for a stint, and Belinda left him. Then he left for the war."

Savannah tapped her pen against the legal pad. "They helped him, right? He couldn't have gone into the draft mentally unstable."

Cindy shrugged. "I'm not sure. He never returned. Herb told everyone Frank sold him the land and left town to ease his broken heart."

Savannah scooped a tiny bit of custard and tested it with the tip of her tongue. "Poor Belinda." She abandoned the dessert and captioned another circle Marriage.

Geoff ran hot water in the sink and submerged Cindy's bowl. "What does the BB represent?"

Cindy gripped the edge of the table, her face blanching. "Baby born." She sucked air through puckered lips, whistling. "Birth dates of family members and deaths. A family tree, more or less."

"Didn't you like it?" He reached for Savannah's custard.

"It's good." She scooted the bowl closer and scraped her spoon around the edge, collecting a tiny bite. "Cindy, why didn't he tell me?"

"Schizophrenia." Cindy clasped her fingers, sounding clinical. "We should have known. Frank talked to fence posts and feared government takeovers. He reappeared, disappeared, and reappeared again. That's Frank's normal."

"And?"

"Two years ago, he contacted me." She gazed at the floor.

Geoff chuckled as Savannah wrote furious letters with one hand and took absentminded bites with her other. All her quirks intrigued him.

"Wait a minute. One baby born in 1934—Arthur, my grandfather…" She pointed to the journal, where several men posed in fatigues. "Frank served in World War II around 1944. So in 1944-P-+++ the pluses are casualties. The P represents the Pacific Ocean?"

"Yep." Cindy pivoted and marched out the front door.

He took the seat across from Savannah and gestured to her notes, bringing his hand next to hers. She didn't jerk away. A good sign. "Did you see anything significant about the birth years or slavery related? Hmm, 1934, 1955, 1981, and 1987. Nah, too modern for anything to do with slaves."

"Well…" She drew a timeline on the legal pad and tipped it to him. "I was born in 1987. My biological father could have been born in 1955. It would have had to be my father, right? For me to be a McMillan?"

"I was born in 1955, too." Cindy's voice drifted through the porch window. "Same day, same mother..."

Geoff leaned out the open window. "You're her dad's twin?"

"Arthur and Belinda McMillan were our parents."

Savannah stood at the edge of the porch, hands on her hips. "Did you know?"

Cindy's eyes glazed and Savannah knelt to face her. "When you babysat me as a child, did you know you were my aunt? Did Arthur know?"

Moving the swing back and forth with her toes, Cindy inhaled the remainder of her umpteenth cigarette and tossed the butt to the gravel drive. "I didn't. I should have suspected, because you bear such a resemblance to Carrie."

"Carrie." Savannah chewed her lip. "My mother?"

Geoff propped himself against a porch column. "Cindy, you weren't a McMillan, and neither were your parents."

"We had a hyphenated name. Levi and I decided to keep the Smith. I guess that's why it mattered so much to Frank to see you take on the McMillan name. None of the other off spring kept it."

"So my dad is Levi Smith." Savannah braced the notepad on her leg and uncapped her pen. "Okay, here's another question. In 1981, it says BB-3. Three babies born?"

Cindy's eyes bulged. She covered her mouth with quivering fi ngers then lurched and darted down the sidewalk toward the beach.

Savannah tried to follow, but he caught her arm. "Wait. Give her space."

"But I've waited so long for… fine." Savannah ducked inside and cleared her notes from the table.

He returned to the dishes, his jaw tight. "Think I'll go to bed soon."

She tucked her pencil into the side pocket of her purse. Should she make a peace offering? She moved behind him and put her hands on his shoulders. "Want help?"

He pivoted, loosening from her grasp, looking so deep into her soul she shivered. "I'm finished now." Hooking his thumbs in his belt loops, he stuffed his hands in his pocket.

"Maybe I'll kiss you." She tipped her head upward to meet his lips. Her heart thundered as she pressed against him like a vixen, waiting for his response.

He sidestepped her. "I'm sorry for playing with your emotions. I won't do it again."

What had she done? She fled to the second floor. "My mistake." She gripped the wooden bedroom door, poised to slam it. "Go back to Dreyfus. There's no point in you being here."

He switched off the lights and bounded up the stairs, running his hands along the intricate carvings lining the banister. "I'll leave in the morning. I take it you can find your way home."

Slamming commenced. She set the alarm, called a rental agency, and cried herself to sleep.

At 3:30 a.m., Savannah rolled out of bed, muttering to herself. She slid her feet into tennis shoes, slipped into the hall, and peeked into his bedroom. Soft snores drifted from the bed.

She grabbed her clothes and stuffed them into her bag, then raced to the sidewalk. The agency charged extra for redeye pickup, but it was worth every penny. The driver had parked a short distance down the street like she'd requested. He even agreed to wait through one last stop at the beach.

Water pounded the coastline in unending rhythm. *You could be made new,* the drops seemed to whisper. *A new life, a new beginning... forgiveness and hope.*

Once she settled the rental paperwork, she drove like a demon, making the five-hour trip to Chicago in outrageous time. When she arrived at a parking area close to the pier, she checked her bag. She'd forgotten the journal. Great. She'd have to call Geoff.

As she dialed, she got out and locked the car door, swinging her bag over her shoulder.

"Hello?" After several rings, his voice came out groggy. "Savannah?" Shuffling sounded through the speaker. "Where are you?"

"Were you asleep? It's nine thirty."

His lips smacked, and he yawned heavy into the phone. "Are you serious? Where are you?"

"Navy Pier."

Silence. Then slow breathing. "A six-hour drive? What time did you leave? And how?"

"Five-hour drive." She puffed her cheeks. "I left about four and took a rental car. They brought it by at three forty-five this morning."

"Stubborn woman. Are you in trouble?"

"I left the journal." With her cardigan sleeve, she brushed a dusty spot off the window of the white compact car.

"Oh."

"I need you to break the next seal and tell me what's there."

"Okay, wait, and I'll go downstairs and get it." The cabin stairs creaked.

An apology hung on the tip of her tongue. Would it matter at this point? How could she face him again after making such a fool of herself?

"Let me tear the seal." More shuffling. "Frank wants you to leave Chicago. Quit your job."

"Frank's words or yours?" She dropped her bag to the blacktop and sat on the front fender. Did Geoff say it so she'd stay in Dreyfus? "Can you text a picture to me?"

His breath blasted the speaker. "Wait a second." He disconnected, and two minutes later, he texted four images.

Tears stung her eyes. He'd been telling the truth. Why had she doubted? She dialed back. "I can't read all of it. What does it say on the second page?"

"Same as the first. Live where you want. Find a better job."

"Oh." Where would she go? Not back home, for sure. Not to the farm. Lexington? "What else?"

"He wants you to ride the Ferris wheel with a stranger."

"Okay… but why?"

"Oh. I think I missed two pages in the middle. I'll send you the picture in a second. He visited the Pier after his foster dad's death. Thought about killing himself, even had a plan, but decided to use the last of his money to ride the Ferris wheel before calling it quits."

"Wow." No wonder. Frank's life had been terrible. "Did it mention the trigger?"

"I'll check."

She yawned, lulled by the soft rhythm of his breath and synchronizing hers to it. She tapped her feet against the pavement and shifted. Looming towers stood prominent against the bright blue skyline. Would the possibility always haunt her?

Geoff coughed. "Ugh. This smoke. The gist is his unhappiness in foster care after losing his first family meant he couldn't fit in with anyone else. He hated living up north." More pages. "This entry is long. No pictures. He's noted several different incidents with police and included a folded excerpt from his medical file documenting mental illness."

Savannah eyed the distant amusement ride. "What does the Ferris wheel have to do with it? Does it say?"

"Years ago, a woman waited in line with him, and both would have ridden by themselves, but she offered to share the seat." He cleared his throat again, harder. "Oh, wait. Another page has stuck. Here you go. She'd lost her husband. Turns out, she lived in Dreyfus. She told him she'd do whatever it took to arrange to be his foster mom or even to adopt him if she could. And, she taught him photography."

After a long pause, he coughed again. "I can't take any more of Cindy's cigarettes. Anyway, he went to live with her. She taught him how to develop pictures and got him into church."

"Hmm..." Savannah shrunk against the car as three middle-grade kids dashed by, all wearing ear buds. Was it the cigarettes, or had he been trying to hide his feelings? Agh! She doubted him again. Why couldn't she have let things go? Let him kiss her in his time? "Frank wants me to lift someone's spirit, I guess. Like she did his."

"And to move out of your apartment." Geoff swallowed. "Do you want my help? I could stay with Zach, and you could go to the farmhouse."

"No." Her eyes burned and damped at the corners. She didn't want him to leave the farmhouse. Not after she'd hurt him. "I'll manage. Is that all?"

"One more thing. The woman sent him to Oneida, a school for troubled youth."

A suited man on a motorcycle pulled into the space beside her and glanced at his watch before hurrying across the parking lot. She eyed the time on her cell. Nine fifty. "Well, I'd better go if I'm going to get all this done." She sighed. "I'll meet up with you in Dreyfus for the journal."

Chapter Twenty-Three

Geoff fumbled with his clothes, half-folding, half-wadding them into his bag. He straightened the bedding and wiped toothpaste out of the sink.

Lingering by Savannah's room, he memorized the soft hint of her perfume. He could drive to Chicago. Reason with her.

He nixed the thought. She'd be long out of town by the time he arrived. At least she would return to Dreyfus, though he doubted she'd stay. No reason.

Cindy had left a note on the kitchen counter. She'd gone fishing. Of course.

He popped a couple cinnamon rolls in the microwave and scrawled a return note telling her goodbye.

A drive to the sand dunes drew him once more to the top. If he'd kissed Savannah, would things have been different? Would she have been like Maria, trapped, bored and depressed? With the lakes in his view, he dropped to his knees.

Lord, you are all-powerful, and you know all things. You understand where our hearts are, and why we make our choices. If there is any sin on my part—anything I've done to glorify myself rather than you, please grant me your forgiveness.

My heart has been empty for so many years. Her presence in my life is a gift, I know. If it's a temporary gift, please help me accept your will.

Watch over her and protect her.... He opened his eyes. He'd forgotten to warn her about Mona and the mirror.

Lord, please help me continue in service to you, with the right mind, the right heart, and the right spirit. Amen.

He raced to the parking area, squishing into the sand. It seeped into his sneakers, scratching his feet through the socks.

Back at the truck, he reached under the seat for his hidden cell and dialed. "Ryan?"

"Yep. Geoff, I meant to call you, but it's been hectic. Give me a second."

Geoff turned the ignition and drummed his fingers against the steering wheel.

"Okay. I stood at the spot where they found the mirror and looked from all directions. At a forty-degree turn, I found a brown, melted spot on the house."

"Like she wanted to catch it on fire with the mirror?"

"Well, we think the spot came from a cigarette lighter. It's a tiny dot of melted plastic." Chambers spoke to a person in the background and shuffled more papers. "I think... I mean I don't think she tried to start a fire. She wanted to scare them."

"Kaler threw away the mirror, so there'd be no evidence she was there."

Chambers made a guttural sound. "He's on my last nerve. I'll watch her though, and have the Barretts' house watched, too. If we can catch her in the act, it's better."

"Yeah..." Geoff backed out of the parking space. "I'll be there in about ten hours."

Savannah people-watched from a bench a few feet from the Ferris wheel. She tapped her feet against the concrete, wrinkling her nose at the stale smoke wafting from the ashtray beside her.

Smoke like Cindy, who'd be mad she left.

A teenage girl in black clothes rounded the corner. Two tall men in hooded sweatshirts scowled as they scanned the tourists. The girl ducked behind a trashcan, jerked her hood over her head, and wrapped herself in her arms.

When the men passed, the girl remained balled up beside the plastic receptacle, whispering to herself. Could she be the one?

Savannah walked to the trashcan and dropped an imaginary piece of paper. She looked at the Ferris wheel. "Man, I wish I had someone to ride with me."

The hood moved a fraction of an inch.

Savannah knelt to the girl's eye level. "Would you want to join me? I'll pay for it."

"I can't." Black fingernails picked at the frazzled hoodie string.

"Are you in trouble?" Savannah offered her hand, but the girl shrunk against the concrete wall.

"I need to disappear."

"Who were those men?" Savannah scanned the sidewalks. "Do they want to hurt you?"

"My foster dad and his brother. They want to send me to a boarding school. I'm too much trouble." The girl brushed dust from her pants and stood. "You mean it? You'd pay and let me ride with you?"

"Sure." Savannah smiled. "Look. There's not even a line."

She bought two tickets and returned to the trashcan. The girl had disappeared. Brow scrunched, Savannah pocketed the second ticket and walked to the ride entrance.

A fingernail dug into her shoulder, and she faced a jet-black ponytail. The girl had tied the sweatshirt around her waist and pulled a ball cap over her eyes. She tapped the rail with her palms while Savannah handed the operator the tickets.

"Let's go." Savannah pointed to the open car. The glass had fogged on the outside, and she left fingertip prints as she steadied herself against the door to climb in the seat. "You're going to love this view."

The girl cast a tentative glance around and ducked into the car. After the attendant closed them in, she gripped the bottom of the seat. "I'm crazy scared of heights."

Savannah laughed. "Are you?"

"I'm crazy scared of everything." The girl twisted her feet over each other, pointing her toes at forty-five degrees. "What's your name?"

"Savannah. What's yours?"

"Kim."

The wheel advanced a notch, swaying the car back and forth. Kim clutched her chest. "I can't do this. I can't ride this thing."

Savannah laughed. "Too late now. They won't stop until we've finished."

Kim scraped her teeth forward like her tongue itched and needed scratching. "Why did you buy me a ticket?"

The car lurched forward another notch, swaying even more this time. Kim trembled, and Savannah took her hand. "I'm exploring the idea that life is about more than me."

Kim gave a nervous giggle. "Bill's always telling me that. You know, my foster dad."

Savannah grasped Kim's other hand, turning her in the seat so her focus would stay on the conversation as the car passed another spoke. "Listen, I understand how you feel. I'm adopted, but I ran away fourteen years ago."

"You ran away?" Kim's eyebrow rose. "Why?"

"Well, I didn't exactly live on the streets." Savannah flicked her gaze to the ceiling, tears pooling. "My adoptive mom can be a real nag. Even downright mean. She got hateful with me about my weight."

"Bill told me I look like a vampire."

194

Suppressing a chuckle, Savannah eased her grip on Kim's hands until black nails rested on Savannah's palm. "I hate to tell you this," the chuckle escaped, "but you kind of do. At least an attractive one. Look at yourself."

Kim caught her reflection in the glass door. She burst into boisterous laughter. "I look ridiculous. You are so right."

Savannah reclaimed Kim's hands as the wheel made another lurch. "I know it's hard to imagine this, but one day you're going to regret shutting them out of your life. On my fourteenth birthday, my parents agreed to let me stay with an aunt in Chicago."

Kim leaned forward.

"So I did, and a month after I graduated high school, Aunt Nellie got sick. She couldn't help much anymore." Savannah sucked in a deep breath. "I went to college for free, because I had a high ACT score, good grades, and a softball scholarship. So, I didn't need anyone besides myself... or so I thought."

Turning her face toward the fogged window, Kim rubbed her cheeks.

"Let me tell you this, sweetheart. The worst day with my mom was better than any of the rock-bottom days I spent alone." Savannah's voice wavered. "Imagine every birthday and Christmas since graduating high school lonely—with no presents. Having to rely on yourself to buy a ride or find a place to live."

Kim snatched her hands free. Her sobs shook the car as they neared the cusp.

Savannah wiped her eyes with her sleeve. "I know it's hard to live with certain family members, but it's harder to live with regret. Oh... Kim, look out the window. Look at the lake."

She rubbed the glass, clearing a space in the fog, revealing a line of skyscrapers across the crisp, blue water. She'd missed this last time she'd rode the Ferris wheel, the view wasted in a make-out session with Adam Capesi.

195

Kim's gasp echoed her own. Savannah draped an arm over the girl's shoulder. "When we get down, I can help you find your dad."

Kim's chest heaved. "Okay."

They sat in silence as the wheel filled the rest of the way, and held tight hands as it spun. When the ride ended, they climbed out together, and Savannah walked Kim over to a popcorn kiosk. She bought two bags and two sodas, and they ate on a gray metal bench.

"Do you have Bill's cell number?" Savannah popped a handful of puffed buttery kernels in her mouth. The salt burned her lower lip where she'd been chewing it.

"Yeah." Kim folded the top of her popcorn bag. "In a second."

After she called, Savannah faded into the crowd, watching Kim wait from a distance. The two men rushed to the girl, and they embraced in tearful hugs. Savannah's heart burst with longing. She had to go back to Dreyfus and repair her relationship with her parents.

The forty-minute drive across town to her apartment felt like an eternity. She kept an eye trained on her cell. She should call Rose.

The cell lit with a text. She parked and swiped the screen. Adam. The lover she could catch, but never land. Her stomach sank. Did Geoff see her that way?

Heard you were back in town. Dave spotted you at the Pier.

Minor annoyance replaced the butterflies and flutters she might have felt a few days ago. She'd burned for Adam so many times, and he'd used and dismissed her. She should use him for once. *Moving out of my apartment. Need help if you have time.*

Come get me. My ride's out of commission.

Of course it was. Two miles later, she found Adam leaning against the front window of his pawnshop. He'd dressed in full leather, with a smirk playing across his face.

When she emerged from the car, he engulfed her in a tight embrace. He'd thinned and grown a mustache, spotted with gray, like

196

his once jet-black hair. What did she see in him, other than the thrill of the chase?

"Savannah!"

He met her lips before she could protest. Unable to stop herself, she returned the kiss, releasing the fierce passion building for Geoff. Harvey, one of Adam's workers, whistled, and she jerked away, refusing to meet Adam's hungry eyes.

"You'd better look at me. You'll never believe how much I've missed you." He forced her face back toward his.

She traced along his shoulder to the palm of his hand, wishing she could stop the barrage of X-rated memories assaulting her. She'd never squelch the fire building in her belly. Texting him back had been a bad idea. "Let's go, then."

He drummed his fingers on her thighs, conjuring images of every possible temptation.

"Stop!" She got in the car and scooted as close to the driver's-side door as she could. "Listen. Help me move. No—"

"Got you another fella?" Adam laughed. "You wear guilt well, sister."

"It's not guilt."

"If you say so."

Back at her apartment, she retrieved the broken-down cardboard boxes she'd stowed in the trunk when she'd unpacked months ago. She carried them to the apartment and set them on the ground while she unlocked the door. Dizziness overcame her. She took three stumbling steps across the threshold. "I mean, I've kind of been seeing someone, but we..."

"Good." Adam stood behind her, wrapping his arms around her, leaving only a thin layer of air between their bodies.

She shivered, slipping free. "I don't have much time. I need you to help me pack."

"There's always time." He planted kisses below her chin.

Her shoulders rose and fell in a deep sigh.

"So, who is this guy? You've never mentioned him, right?"

"I didn't. I've been back home. In Kentucky." She snatched a flattened box and focused on taping the bottom. "Remember the bully from middle school?"

Adam snorted. "Him?"

She shoved a stack of her college textbooks into the box and started on another. "He's different now. Nicer and all."

"You know..." Adam stole the book and set it on the coffee table. He tapped his pointer finger against her chin and drew her closer. "If you were into this guy, you wouldn't have brought me here. It's not like you didn't know what would happen."

He captured her lips, lifting the hem of her shirt as he lowered her to the couch.

She held up one hand in protest then dropped it to her side. He'd been right. She'd known exactly what would happen. Wanted it, even.

Yet another reason Geoff deserved better.

Chapter Twenty-Four

Geoff sprayed ammonia over the interior of his truck windows, covering the remaining hint of Savannah's perfume. He pressed so hard against the glass his fingers ached when he finished. Why had he let himself believe she'd return his feelings?

He wanted to tuck his tail and crawl into the doghouse with Cyrus, but he had to worry about more important things. How could he protect her from Mona?

Though he needed sleep, he tackled the house next, dusting every inch of the living room and cleaning the barrister bookcase's glass. Her bookcase. Her great-grandfather's cameras. How many times had he'd stared at them as a youth and never thought to look more closely?

His Nana Jean had protected them, insisting Herb never toss them. Even when Herb went to the nursing home, and Geoff's parents took over the farmhouse, she came in every week to dust them until she could no longer stand.

Papa Lee died early. Nana Jean would have been young enough to remarry. Had she known Frank? Did they share a bond?

Geoff finally showered and crawled into bed, forcing his weary eyes to skim over his Bible class lesson. He'd flipped off the lamp and lowered his head to the pillow when his cell rang.

"Hello?"

"Ryan Chambers." A desk squeaked. "Can you think of any business your aunt might have on the edge of your property? She came by the station today and talked to Avery Kaler for an hour.

They were thick as syrup, weird like she had control over him."
Another squeak. "He acted strange when he left. I had one of my
deputies tail him, and he went by Mona's townhouse to get her, like
a date. You remember Nathan Smith, right? He followed them to the
edge of your property."

"Where did they go? The back side?" Geoff jolted, bumping his
shoulder on the headboard.

"Close to your Nana Jean's old house. The side entrance with the
rusted-out gate by the iron furnace."

He'd forgotten to have Zach fix the lock. "What would she be
doing there?"

"I don't know, but Nathan said they went up the drive, sat in the
car for about thirty minutes, and then left."

"Guess I'll have to get out and replace the gate tomorrow."

Savannah lay twisted in her pilled cotton sheets. Adam had left, as
usual. She told her feet to move, but they remained fixed, as if glued to
the mattress. How could she face Geoff?

She sat up, the morning chill assaulting her bare shoulder. Why
did she feel so guilty? It wasn't like they'd been committed or
anything.

Her cell dinged. Not Geoff —he'd be in church. She palmed her
makeshift nightstand. No phone.

She glanced all around then through the upturned crate she used
as a nightstand. There, on the fl oor.

The lewd image on the screen heated her cheeks. The phone
dinged several times as Adam sent her pictures from previous
interludes. *Thought you might want to remember the good times.*

No. She wanted to forget all of them. She tugged the sheet
around her shoulders. As if forgetting the embarrassing things she'd

done could even be possible. Instead, they flashed through her mind like a slideshow loop.

Adam had helped load her car up tight the night before, so she took a quick shower and stuffed her remaining possessions in the last small box. Her landlord could have the furniture. He'd sell it at the flea market.

One last pass through the kitchen led her to a note from Adam, scrawled on the bottom of the box of the pizza they shared.

You talked in your sleep all night.

"I didn't." She pursed her lips.

I know when to exit stage right. I'll miss you, Savannah. Good luck working things out in Kentucky.

If so, why did he still text her? To taunt. She stumbled to the door and locked it, her chest so tight she could barely breathe. She'd sworn she'd never give in again. What had she done?

The six-hour drive to Dreyfus seemed to take twenty. She programmed the CD to repeat and replayed her entire life to the soulful voice of the Bob Seger mix Adam made for her when they first met. Every mistake, every broken heart, every ounce of pain, pushed to the forefront of her mind.

Before going home, she drove by the elementary school playground where she and Geoff had chased each other around the trees. So much joy and happiness. Whatever happened?

A woman pulled into the parking lot, and two little girls hopped out of the backseat. Curls bouncing, they raced to the playground holding hands.

Something inside Savannah's chest stirred. She'd not considered having children, or if she'd even want to be a mother. What would her future look like in the long term? In Rose's words, she couldn't keep flitting between casual relationships. How could she make things right?

She knew what Phil and Geoff would say. God could get her through anything.

201

Another memory overcame her senses—her twelve-year-old self, standing in front of the church, shivering and sopping wet. She'd beamed as the entire congregation joined hands in a circle around the room, singing in celebration with her.

She turned off the radio, creasing her forehead. What were those words? Tears streaming, she sang in a shaky voice. "But we never can prove, the delight of his love, until all at the altar we lay...."

That's what she needed to do. Lay it all at the altar. Confess everyone in front of God, Geoff, and her parents. Even if it killed her, she had to commit to the change.

She glanced at her watch. Five fifty. If she hurried, she could make it before the evening service started.

Misty-eyed, she backed onto the main road and made the three turns to her to the church. She clutched the steering wheel as she entered the lot, blowing a light stream of air between puckered lips. She could do this. She had to do this.

An older couple got out of the car beside her. They nodded and smiled, as if they knew she needed encouragement. When she crossed the threshold, she collapsed on the carpet in tears.

"Dora?" Rose swept her in a tight embrace. "Dora, you okay?"

As leathered feet gathered around her, Savannah groped for a clear space of carpet. Someone helped her stand, and she met the concerned gazes of many familiar faces. "I..." She swallowed, taking Rose's trembling hand. "I don't know what to say."

As a new wave of sorrows engulfed her, Phil's strong arm linked hers and led her to a side office. Rose followed, her finger poised to waggle, and he gave her a stern glare. "Leave us."

A younger man with bushy black hair entered as Rose huffed away, followed by Dallas Brewer, who preached for the church as long as Savannah could remember. Dallas wrapped thick arms around her and squeezed. "Eli, think you could teach our class on short notice?"

"Sure." The younger man hurried toward the auditorium.

She puffed her cheeks with forced breathing as Dallas led her and Phil to his office.

"Something weighing on your heart, young lady?" He pointed to a brown leather sofa and plopped into a linen armchair, resting his arms on his knees.

She sat next to Phil, who remained standing, rocking on his heels.

"When you ran off running the other day, I told your mother we were way out of line." Phil fiddled with his tie. "She has to stop badgering you. I can't let it go on any longer. I have to stop treating you like a child."

Dallas held out a tissue box.

She accepted one and patted her burning eyes. "It's not you or Mom. It's me." She shoved her hands between her knees. "I can't do anything right these days. Nothing. All I do is hurt people who love me. She shouldn't have badgered me, but I should've tried harder to listen."

Dallas went to the bookshelf and traced his finger along the spines until he came to a bright green photo album. He removed it from the shelf and set it in her lap. "All have sinned and fallen short, Dora."

"It's Savannah. I legally changed my name when I lived in Chicago."

"Right. Savannah." He opened the cover, revealing pictures of fifteen smiling middle school kids, with her in the center. "I remember the night I baptized you. It stormed for hours. We feared we wouldn't make it out of the building alive. Do you remember?"

Phil chuckled. "Yeah, and your mom wanted us to wait. She thought you'd be electrocuted. You told her getting struck by lightning in baptism would earn a one-way ticket to heaven."

Savannah let out a small giggle. "I do remember. I felt sure I could conquer the world. Instead, it's conquered me."

"It overcomes all of us at times of weakness." Dallas adjusted his tie. "Do you want to talk specifics?"

She shook her head. "I've not been living right in a lot of ways. Go through a list of every sin, and I've committed all of them. Well, except murder. I haven't killed anyone."

Phil gripped the seat next to her. "We should have been there for you. Helped you more."

Sighing, she squeezed his hand. "I don't want you to feel blame for it. This is all on me. I've been the selfish one. I've been the stubborn one." Her voice cracked. "I shouldn't have run away."

Dallas returned to his leather chair and folded his hands in his lap. "What sin do you struggle with most?"

A sob bubbled out of her throat. "Sexual." She averted her gaze from Phil. "I don't know how to stop."

"Rob, our new associate minister, is a family therapist. He would be willing to meet with you for free if you'd like, and help you with strategies to overcome it."

Phil knelt, grabbing her knees with both hands. The hard man who never cried hunkered before her, his eyes blotched and his cheeks wet. "You know there's nothing you could have done so bad I wouldn't forgive it."

"I know" She hugged his neck. "It feels good to be home." They hugged for a couple minutes, and she straightened. "I hurt Geoff. He's been so kind, and I've been cruel. How do I fix that?"

"Baby steps." Dallas extended a hand. "The same way you can make all this right with God. We take baby steps to the front of the church, and I'll announce your wish for restoration to the faith. You take baby steps home and repair the relationship with your mother. Small changes, daily prayer, and help from all the people who love you." He winked. "And I don't think you're going to have a problem with Geoff. I saw the way he looked at you from the pulpit last Sunday when you lit out of here."

"Okay." She took a deep breath. "When do I go in front of the church?"

"After Bible class. Now, why don't you come with me and hear Rob teach? He's fresh out of college and has great ideas."

They all hugged once more, and Dallas led her to the auditorium doors. He pulled the right one open, and Phil linked arms with her.

She took careful steps down the side aisle, cringing as the crowd showered her in over-the-shoulder glances.

Phil accompanied her to Rose's pew. He eased in first, leaving her the outside spot, and planted a kiss on her forehead. "I'll walk with you if that will help."

His whisper gave her the assurance she needed to sit straight and smile. For the duration of the class, she read the notes in the margin of Phil's Bible, next to the heading of Galatians 5. Humility, patience, self-control—could she achieve all these things? For the first time since leaving Dreyfus, she wanted to try with all her heart.

As if reading her mind, Phil rubbed her forearm. She wasn't alone. She'd never need to be alone again.

Geoff had taken the front pew, his focus forward, occasionally nodding. Her soul aching, she fixed her gaze over his head until Rob finished the lesson.

When Rob stepped down, Dallas smiled from the pulpit. She gripped the back of the pew before her, paralyzed, as a bustle of children raced into the auditorium.

The crowd settled, and Dallas adjusted the mic. "Good evening."

The congregation's echo sent chills down Savannah's spine. So many people. Could she do this?

He opened his Bible to a marked page. "Tonight, for our short devotional, I'd like to remind you of one simple thought. All have sinned and fallen short of the glory of God. Though our sins vary, we each find ourselves alone in iniquity, and He extends his Son to us, offering grace and mercy."

Heads bobbed, and the room resonated with amen.

"Savannah Barrett, Phil and Rose's daughter, has expressed her desire to be restored to the Lord's church. This young woman wants and deserves God's grace and mercy. She deserves not our judgment, but our love." He beckoned. "Savannah, come forward, and we'll lead a prayer on your behalf."

Geoff tucked his songbook under the pulpit, his eyes never straying from Savannah's frail, tearful form. He'd waited an hour to talk to her, his mind racing with different ways to bare his heart.

When he returned to the front of the church, she'd caught his gaze, her eyes blazing with emotion he couldn't discern.

The last trickle of well-wishing women left her side, leaving her parents and a handful of the men. After she'd hugged them, she dropped to a pew. Rose sat beside her, still clutching and crying.

He bounded down the three steps and paused beside the carpeted stage. He couldn't bring himself to approach her. Not yet. Not in front of her parents.

Phil caught his glance and gave a nod. "Rosie, let's leave these kids to talk." He pried her arm away and led her out of the room.

Dallas patted Savannah's shoulder. "Proud of you. What you did tonight takes courage. Hope we'll see you Sunday morning in Bible class. We have one for new converts and restored members you might enjoy."

"I'll be there." Her voice rasped, and she cleared her throat, flickering a peek Geoffs way.

Dallas started down the aisle, and Geoffstood as she peered after his retreating figure, her chest heaving.

She rose, her knees knocking as he neared. Two feet from her, he stopped, holding his palms up in front of her hands. She raised hers and pressed her fingers to his before sliding them to interlock in a tight grip.

"Hi." Involuntary wetness crept down his cheeks. He wriggled free from her hands and embraced her as he'd dreamed of doing so many times since her return.

"Hi." She punctuated her whisper by a squeeze of her own.

He guided her to the pew. "Want to talk about it?"

She glanced toward the auditorium door, where Rose clutched the trim. "Can we go somewhere more private?"

"If you want." He spoke in her ear. "I don't care about your past life. I want you, in my life, at my side. For the long haul. Please, give us a chance."

Her eyes shimmered. "I want that, too. I do. But I'm afraid I'll hurt you."

"We could start small, with a date. You know, like normal couples."

"Okay." She shifted. "What did you have in mind?"

Grinning, he reached in his wallet and handed her a shiny folded paper. He straightened it to reveal the charity barbecue flier. "All the money goes to building a playground for the special needs kids."

She giggled. "I heard about that. Sounds great."

"Pick you up tomorrow night at six forty-five?"

Glancing back at Rose, she shook her head. "It's at Georgia's, right? I'll meet you there."

Chapter Twenty-Five

Savannah carried a box of clothes from her trunk toward her bedroom, sidestepping her hovercraft mother.

"I have questions, Dora. I want specifics."

Of course, she did.

"It's her business, Rosie." Phil followed with another box. "Give her space."

"It's late. You should wait until the morning to unload." Huffing to her armchair, Rose picked up her knitting and attacked a half-finished sweater.

"Your mother is a complicated woman. It'll take her time." Phil set the box on her bed, kissed Savannah's forehead, and left.

Her cheeks warmed as she sifted through a myriad of silky sleeveless tops Rose would never approve. She tossed them in the giveaway pile and opened the box containing her casual work clothes. Nothing suited for a night out with Geoff.

She settled on a bright floral piece that flattered her bony figure. Great. It had a stain on the stomach. Her modest-necked black silk would work. Nope. A hole had worn in the underarm stitching. Tossing the shirt into the trash pile, she flopped onto the bed and stretched her arms.

Why did she worry? Geoff wouldn't care what she wore. Her heart fluttered. Of course. Everyone in town would be watching them the entire date. It would be the middle school dance all over again.

She could go shopping. Her gaze fell on the rectangular gift box in the corner of her room, resting in the top of a crate holding her college textbooks. Her eyes flooded. The birthday gift from Phil and Rose. Never opened.

She slipped off the ribbon. Inside, shimmery lace covered a soft cotton dress, dark teal with quarter-length flared sleeves. The modest neckline gathered at a dainty teardrop opening secured by a glittering silver-and-black button. Every handmade stitch aligned exactly. Modern, beautiful, and perfect.

She raised the dress to her shoulders. The hem landed past her knees, ending in a taper. She even had matching stilettos.

After several hours sorting clothes, sleep came without effort, and she rested until well after noon the next day. Finding both parents gone, she fixed herself a sandwich and flipped through old photo albums until the clock chimed five.

She spent twenty minutes applying makeup and another thirty curling her hair before the lock in the front door clicked. Smiling, she smoothed the dress and stepped into the living room.

Rose gasped, swatting the front door behind her. "You look so beautiful."

Savannah rushed to her mother. "Amazing dress. I can't believe how perfect it is."

Dropping her knitting bags on the couch, Rose blinked away tears. She tugged at the waistline and adjusted the sleeves. "I'm glad you like it. Where will you go tonight?"

"Georgia's." She sucked in a mouthful of air. "I'm going with Geoff to the charity barbecue."

"So I'll have grandchildren after all." Rose rubbed her thumb along Savannah's lower lip, coming away with a smudge of plum lipstick.

"It's a date." Savannah laughed. "No promises."

Rose disappeared into her room, returning with a perfume bottle and a white gold earring and necklace set, studded in tiny topaz stones.

"He likes this one." She sprayed then held out her wrist to Savannah's nose. "He always bought it for his mama when I worked at the drugstore."

"I don't want to smell like his mama. Besides, I'm already wearing perfume."

Rose shook her head and placed the bottle on the mock-granite counter. "This necklace belonged to my grandmother. She would have wanted you to have it."

Savannah let her fasten the necklace around her neck and swap out the earrings. She touched the chain and whispered, "Thanks, Mom."

Rose hugged her. She lifted the ends of the dress out and let them fall back to Savannah's legs. "It's a twirling skirt. I should make me one, and maybe your dad will take me out, too."

They shared a chuckle. Phil wouldn't notice a dress if his life depended on it.

Savannah returned to the bathroom and applied a final coat of lotion to her sun-kissed legs. Spinning and grinning, she twisted her mom into the hallway and nearly knocked over her dad.

"Hot date? Should I give you a sample of eau de auto?" He waved his greasy hands below her nose.

"We'll see." She ducked his grasp, snickering. "Why don't you bring Mom out to Georgia's tonight?"

"Meh..." He winked. "Did I hear your mother mention grandchildren?"

"Good grief. It's one date." She brushed a piece of cut grass from his hair. "By the way, I'm going to stay in Dreyfus, at least for a while. But I want my own place."

"Good. I don't want you keeping me up all night." He wiped his oily hands on his canvas work pants. "Dora, please don't let the past get in the way of your future."

"I won't." She waved a finger toward him. "Don't forget I go by Savannah now."

He shoved his hands in his pockets and shuffled down the hall. "You'll always be my sweet, special Dora."

She melted. "I'm counting on it."

The grandfather clock chimed six thirty, and she set out for Georgia's Restaurant, which had been a hopping joint as far back as she could remember. Proud of herself for getting there without directions, she maneuvered her Prius into the lot full of gas-guzzling trucks and monster SUVs.

The smell of Georgia's sweet-n-spicy barbecue sauce poured over charred pork overwhelmed her senses, bringing back memories of Sunday afternoon dinners with Rose and Phil. Standing by the front porch where Geoff said they'd meet, she frowned. No sign of him. She settled into a rocking chair, watching through sunglasses as girls her age streamed into the restaurant, linked arm-in-arm with denim-clad dates. Great. She'd overdressed. Well, maybe not. Another group came in wearing what might have been prom attire.

At 6:58, he still hadn't shown. The butterflies in her stomach multiplied. Would this be another opportunity for humiliation? She stood to leave. Then strong hands covered her eyes.

"Savannah." Her name sounded lyrical in Geoff's deep drawl. "Walk with me. I have a surprise."

He led her to the side of the building, pausing twice to open gates. "Okay, now you can look." He lifted his hands.

"Dreyfus Charity Barbecue." She eyed the fifteen-foot banners lining the courtyard behind Georgia's. Smaller banners featured local "celebrity" sponsors—the mayor, the state governor, and a couple musicians. In the center, a picture of herself hung in her college softball uniform, holding a trophy.

Geoff beamed. "I made a contribution in your name. A big one. Hope you don't mind."

She hid her face and peeked through her fingers. "Are you serious? Where did you find the picture?" Dropping her hands to her side, she laughed. "Let me guess. Rose."

"Yep."

As he slid his arm around her waist, she stepped back. "Wait a minute. You donated on my behalf? Why?"

"I didn't want you to suffer anything from people afraid of you taking over the farm. They're nervous the charity work will stop, and I wanted to reassure them you'd never let it happen."

She forced her mouth closed and slipped beneath his arm. "Thanks."

"You look fantastic."

"Thanks." She examined her feet.

"You said that."

Laughing, she rested her head on her shoulder. "You, too."

He did. He'd worn a three-piece suit, complete with a suspicious teal cummerbund and bow tie.

"We match."

He grinned, tugging the cummerbund away from his waist. "Your mama is a good seamstress. A fast one."

"Are you serious? She acted like she didn't even know about our date. I didn't tell her I chose this dress. Not until about an hour ago." Savannah spotted several couples with familiar faces. She snorted, waving at her parents. "She is fast."

"Ready?" At her nod, he reached for her hand and led her past rows of plastic lawn chairs and tables. Conversations died as they approached two empty seats. "I'll do the talking, if you want."

"I'll be okay." She examined the circle of faces, familiar, but changed with time. Lisa Abner, Melissa Ashley, Kevin Henry. None spoke. All gaped.

Geoff kissed her cheek, drawing warmth and soliciting hoots from his friends. "Yes. We're involved. It's not anyone's business but ours. I would appreciate you making Savannah feel a part of this little group."

"Savannah?" Robbie Davis scratched his head. "Not Dora?"

212

Geoff squeezed her fingers. "She wants to be known as Savannah now. You guys have two minutes for questions. Who wants to go first?"

The awkward silence dragged on, other than the bustling of the surrounding people. When the two minutes passed, he grinned. "Last call."

Melissa's eyes brightened, and she smiled big. "Okay, Savannah. I'm dying to know where you got those stilettos."

She felt herself glowing as she launched into a tale about a mom-and-pop shoe store in the heart of Chicago. She'd be fine.

Music blared through the speakers, and Lisa jumped from the table. "We're starting."

Georgia took the microphone. "Welcome, humble and generous citizens of Dreyfus, to our charity barbecue. Darla Evans and Kira Maze are up here with the sign-up sheet for the first round of our competition. Eat plenty ribs, drink gallons of tea, and open those wallets and give, give, give." She waved Geoff forward. "You, boy. Make us a speech, and tell us why we're collecting this money."

"Um..." He walked to the podium, met Savannah's gaze, and pressed his lips together under the twinkling paper lanterns hanging from a clothesline across the courtyard. "Welcome, everyone, and thanks for your support. Many thanks to Georgia for hosting and our spectacular emcee, Mr. Drew Monroe!"

Drew activated an applause sound byte, and the patrons erupted into laughter as he made several dramatic bows.

Savannah squinted at him. She remembered Drew, the class clown who'd taken a far greater bully beating than she'd ever faced.

Drew raised a tie-dye-covered arm and pointed to Geoff. "There's the man, ladies and gentlemen. Mr. Geoff Spencer."

Geoff bowed as Drew set off a drumbeat. When it finished, Geoff shoved his right hand in his pocket and withdrew a folded paper. "This special needs playground has been in the works for two years now, and we're about five-thousand dollars shy of the goal."

He tore the wrapping from the paper. "Four thousand, eight hundred and sixty-two dollars, to be exact. So, come up here, see Shelia Morgan, and make your donations. Sign up for the competition. It's twenty dollars per couple, and the winners get two free plates of Georgia's famous ribs once a month for the next year."

Leaning to the mic, he gripped the stand. "Although, I'm planning to enjoy those ribs myself. Sheila, go ahead and write my name. Geoff Spencer, plus awesome date, Savannah Barrett."

Savannah's neck warmed as everyone's gaze swiveled to her.

"Geoff! Geoff!" Screams and chants echoed through the restaurant.

She slunk in her seat, peering between fingers as hands patted her shoulders. Tingles spread over her body. He'd claimed her. Right there in front of her parents, God, and everyone. Embarrassing, but... amazing.

"Y'all have fun." He marched to her side while the music changed.

"Line dancing!" Lisa squealed, tugging Savannah toward the temporary wood floor in the courtyard center.

Savannah stretched her free hand to Geoff's, catching his fingers and dragging him after them.

He grimaced. "I have no idea how to do a line dance."

She kicked out her foot and pivoted on the other one, then stomped twice. "This one is easy. Follow my lead."

Her spirit soared as he joined her on the dance floor, his awkward moves pitiful copies of her own. As they laughed together, passion for him built in her soul. How could she have ever doubted loving him would be anything but good?

Geoff stayed off a beat the entire song. Contagious laughter spread over the dance floor. He made his way to the sidelines, clapping for the other line dancers. One by one, they backed away as the steps became more complicated, eventually leaving only Savannah.

Eyes closed, a mystic smile splayed from her cheek to cheek. His lioness seemed more like a gypsy, the tails of her skirt swaying around her legs. Catching her was one thing, taming her another. Did he even want her to change?

She finished alone, and her blush radiated, but when the crowd clapped for her, she curtsied and met his gaze.

Hushed whispers filled the room, and Drew switched the music to a slower song. "I don't know about everybody else here, but I'd love to see Mr. Spencer give this lady a congratulatory couples dance."

"No way." Geoff shook his head. "I don't slow dance."

She took a step toward the sidelines, her shoulders slumped.

"Come on, Spencer." Drew stretched the mic cord across the floor, catching her by the arm. "You can't leave the lady hanging like this. Help me encourage him, people. Geoff, Geoff, Geoff…"

The entire room leaned closer, their hands cupped and eyes twinkling. "Geoff, Geoff, Geoff, Geoff…"

His breath caught as she scanned the room, her frown deepening as she faced him. He'd humiliated her before, and here he stood about to humiliate her again. How could he? Just one dance couldn't hurt. Middle school style.

Couples gathered as he walked closer and placed both hands on her shoulders.

"The waist, man." Drew took his arm and lowered his hand. "Surely you of all people haven't forgotten how to hold a woman."

The soft music resonated in his very soul as he tugged her closer, burying his face against her strawberry-scented hair as applause and whoops filled the room.

For a few moments, he grinned, holding her tighter as they swayed in a slow circle. Her breath tickled his neck, and he slipped his cheek against hers. "I could hold you like this for hours."

When he pulled back to look at her, fire blazed in her eyes. He swallowed. What had he just done? Dallas had warned him. Dancing created temptation for her, and he needed to be considerate. And, no question, it tempted him as well.

"What are you doing?" Five long fingernails sunk deep into his left wrist.

He let go of Savannah, and the fingernails took a swipe at her face.

"You trashy little gold digger!" Mona's raspy voice sounded loud and clear, even over the speakers. "What do you think you're doing with my nephew?"

The music died. The crowd stopped dancing, and the other couples backed away.

Savannah clutched his arm. "Leave us alone. We're not bothering you."

"You told me you were fine with this." He folded his arms. "What is your problem?"

She pointed to the banner, where Savannah's college picture hung in two jagged halves. "That gold-digging girl. What's she trying to prove?" She waved a finger at him. "You need to stay away from her."

"Mona, I'm a grown man." He pushed away her finger. "This is my business and her business, but definitely not yours."

Mona made a noise resembling an evil cackle. "I get it." She sneered. "You think you can charm her and marry your land back."

The crowd gasped. He scanned them. Did they all think the same thing? "Mona, those were your words, remember? What you suggested Sunday morning. I thought you gave us your blessing."

"Changed my mind."

"I'm crazy about her." He planted his feet between Mona and Savannah. "Get to know her. You'll see."

Mona glared over his shoulder. Savannah trembled against him, and her heavy breath tickled his neck.

"It's only been a week, Geoff." Mona stepped around him and grabbed Savannah's arm. "He will never love you." Her dark eyes narrowed into slits. "It will always be about the land."

Savannah drew a deep breath. "It might. I don't care. I'm crazy about him, too. What we have right now, even in its infancy, is deep. Perfect, even. I will not give up on our relationship. So… back off, and leave us alone."

His heart stopped. She'd said it in front of everyone. Did she mean it?

Mona shoved him before stomping through the gaping crowd. At the courtyard exit, she pivoted, pointing her finger at Savannah. "I will put a stop to this."

Drew started the music again, a fitting Jason Mraz song, and before long, couples danced next to them. Geoff wrapped Savannah in his arms and kissed the bright red spot where Mona slapped her. "We should go."

She shook her head, leading him into a sway. "You owe me a slow dance, and you promised me barbecue, remember? I'm not quitting on this date. No way."

"That's my girl." He pressed his cheek against hers. "Love this song. I'm not giving up on us, either. I'm so sorry she spoiled our night."

"Nonsense." Savannah squeezed tighter. "I've made friends with a couple of people, and I'm in your arms. Five percent unpleasant, ninety-five percent perfect."

217

"And you haven't even had the food yet."

After the dance, they returned to the table, and Geoff waved over a server. "Hey, Laney. We'll have the Trio for Two Platter." He stacked the menus beside the ketchup and turned to Savannah. "It's all healthy stuff. Smoked brisket, pulled pork and chicken, baked sweet potatoes, and barbecued black beans."

"Wow. Sounds great." She reached across the table for his hands. "So, is it true? Are you crazy about me?"

"Certifiable." He traced a circle around her ring finger. "There's no good reason I should want to be with you right now."

She snorted. "I get beat up by your aunt, and now this?"

"Okay, okay. Forgive me. I have every good reason to be with you right now."

Zach planted two fists on the table and leaned close to Geoff's ear. "Dude. Your aunt slashed your girlfriend's tires. She's wigging out in the parking lot. Georgia called the police."

Geoff scowled. "This situation is out of control."

Chapter Twenty-Six

Savannah paced the living room while Phil, Geoff, Ryan Chambers, and Nathan Smith downed full glasses of Rose's tea. Though their attention flattered her, she longed to be on the road, far away from their smothering concern.

Ryan set his glass on the coaster and rested his elbows on his knees. "We believe Kaler helped Mona clear out of town. There's no one at her house, and her car is still parked there."

Geoff balled his fists. "Where is he?"

"Not sure. He's off duty tonight." Nathan chomped on a piece of ice. "No one has seen him. The two of them have been tight lately."

Phil reached behind him, catching Savannah by the hand. "You should go ahead to the next stop on your trip. She can't be a threat to you if you're out of town."

Rose came in from the kitchen and set a plate of cookies on the coffee table. "She could be more of a threat then. What if she follows Dora?"

Savannah dug the journal out of her bag. She placed it beside the cookies and sat cross-legged on the carpet. "The next location is Pigeon Forge. It's only four hours from here. I could leave early in the morning."

Geoff snagged a cookie and broke off a small piece. "Mona's a morning person. Rose is right. It's better if you stay put a few days and let things settle."

Phil stood, moving behind her. "Sounds like a good idea."

"I wonder..." Nathan knocked an afghan off the couch arm. "She kept going to the farm while you were away the first time, right?"

219

"Yeah." Geoff shrugged. "She's on the farm all the time, though. So no big shocker there, other than the time when she went out by the old furnace with Kaler." He wrinkled his nose. "Ugh. Hope they weren't... frisky. I used to catch college students out there until we got too busy to care."

"Stop, man. I just ate." Nathan picked up the afghan and aligned the corners. "I wonder if they chased away students together. Kaler's been letting her act like a cop lately. They've been doing things like target practice and bow hunting."

Savannah shivered. If Mona attacked her with a gun or bow, no way could she defend herself. "Were they alone?"

Nathan shrugged. "I didn't see anyone else."

Yawning, she collected the empty glasses. "Why attack me? I mean, it's Geoff's farm. Not hers. He's the one standing to lose something. What if she decides to attack him, too?"

"She's always been ultra-protective of me." Geoff fished a business card from his wallet. "In fact, this is the info on a life insurance policy she took out on herself, naming me the beneficiary. She's acted like my mother ever since Mom died. I don't think she'd hurt me."

Savannah narrowed her eyes. "She shoved you."

Pots and pans crashed in the kitchen. Savannah rushed in, sliding into the table. Rose had crumpled on the floor at the base of a stool.

Sweeping in from behind, Ryan lifted Rose from the floor. "You okay, Mrs. Barrett?"

"I'm just a little shaken. I wanted to put this skillet on the high shelf." She waved toward the space above the cabinets.

Ryan hoisted the pan over his head and slipped it above the upper cabinet trim. "There you go."

"Thanks, son. Goodness knows Phil isn't going to help me get anything up there." She placed her fists on her hips and hobbled into the living room.

Phil flipped his palms. "You never asked."

She slid into the armchair, grabbed one of her puzzle books, and addressed Nathan. "Have you boys found anything?"

"No, ma'am." Nathan ducked his head. "We're still discussing the situation."

Savannah eyed Rose's cryptogram magazine. The letters on the farm pictures! She'd forgotten.

She retrieved them from the bag, unfolded the taped pictures, and copied the shaded words onto a piece of paper as the men peeked over her shoulders. "Here, Mom. Try this one."

Rose's pencil flew over the page, pausing at certain letters and making notes to the side. She wrote a phrase below the coded words, her brow creased tight.

After about fifteen minutes, she set it aside, frowning. "I don't know, Dora. I can't figure out what it spells. Are you sure it's a cryptogram?"

Ryan reached for the page. "We could have a go at it." His cell rang at the same time Nathan's did.

Nathan answered. "Yes. Chambers is here with me. Okay, we'll be there right away."

He glanced at Geoff. "Someone said they spotted her standing down in Pritchard's Gulley, right where Maria went over the hill. Said they stopped to see if she needed help, and she told them to get lost."

"No kidding?" Geoff's jaw clenched.

"Well, it gets worse. Apparently, Kaler's had an accident about a tenth of a mile from the site, an hour after the man spotted her. They found him scowling behind the wheel. Bad injuries. Not life threatening, but he missed going over by a hair." Nathan shoved his phone in his pocket. "I wonder if he's the one who answered the call about her being in the gulley."

Savannah pressed her fingers against her temples. "Could she have caused his accident? Is she capable?"

Geoff emptied his chest. "When Maria died, they thought I'd tampered with the car. They had a huge investigation, and for a while, everyone thought I'd..." He swallowed. "They thought I'd killed her."

Ryan nodded. "Turns out, the company recalled the car. A faulty ignition switch. The pavement had crumbled in the curve—we guessed rain washed it out, but one investigator suggested Geoff might have busted up the blacktop with some kind of tool. Maria dipped off the road while making the turn. The ignition shut the power down, locking up the steering wheel and rendering her helpless to keep the car from spinning over the edge."

Savannah clutched her collar. "Could Mona have done that?"

"She excelled at technical stuff. I even let her work tool and die for me a few years back." Geoff stared at the floor. "Mona pulled up behind Maria. She drove past and parked on the side of the road, then hiked down to the accident." He rubbed his left eye. "A year ago, she confessed she got there before Maria died. She spoke to her, but didn't try to save her."

He clasped his fingers tight, squeezing them so hard they popped. "I asked her why." His voice caught.

"I told her... I understood she hated Maria. Why couldn't she at least try to save my unborn child?"

Savannah grabbed a tissue from the end table and dabbed at her eyes. Black smudges soaked through to her fingers.

"She claimed fear." He exhaled, long and hard. "She said she thought she'd be caught in the explosion."

"And you forgave her?" Savannah gritted her teeth.

"The Bible says forgive everyone." Phil patted Geoff on the shoulder. "Son, I'm so sorry for your loss. I'm not sure we ever told you so."

Rose dropped the paper she'd been cyphering on and eyed the officers. "You boys had better get on out there. Be careful."

Geoff stood. "I'm going, too."

Savannah's heart walked out the door with him.

The week ticked by at a snail's pace while Savannah sat in what she'd dubbed her protection cell, sorting through her belongings and Frank's clues. Rose put her to canning and cleaning. Geoff hadn't told her what they'd discovered at the accident scene, but his silence gave enough of an answer. Even Peter told her to put Frank's hunt on hold until they could ensure her safety.

Geoff set Zach and the others on double watch at the farm, ordered them not to drive out alone. Then he insisted on staying at the Barretts' to protect her and Rose. On Saturday afternoon, Phil offered to drive Rose to the grocery.

"Now listen here, Geoff." He rested his shotgun beside the front door. "You two need to keep your hands to yourself."

Savannah imagined melting into the carpet as heat flooded her cheeks. "Daddy."

Phil waggled his finger. "I mean it."

Geoff chuckled as he closed the door behind him. "Are your parents always so intense?"

"Yep." She examined a torn fingernail. "All day long, every day. The man needs a hobby. You should try living with him. Oh, wait." She giggled. "You are."

Geoff gave her a gentle push against the wall and leaned close. "Then I guess we'd better do this now," his voice deepened, "so we don't destroy his natural order."

He met her lips in swift tenderness, his soft touch growing firmer while the emotion of the week channeled between them. She gasped when he pulled away and brushed her hair out of her eyes.

"There you go. The kiss I promised you. Okay timing?"

Savannah gave a slow nod and touched her tingling lips. She traced the stubble covering his chin. "Perfect."

He kissed her again, longer and deeper. "Savannah Barrett, I like you."

"I like you, too." She backed away, breathless. Carnal thoughts flashed into her mind, and she closed her eyes. "But we need to stop."

"Sure. I have to get something out of the truck." He bounded out the front door and glanced over his shoulder.

She placed her fist over her pounding heart. Could she already be in love with him?

He returned with a box of old-time, bulky cameras. "I bet these belonged to Frank." Picking up the top one, he pretended to snap her picture. "I used to stare at these all the time as a kid."

"Wow." She palmed a different one. "Have you ever thought about trying them?"

He shrugged. "I never took the time. Photography served a minor interest. My real love has always been cooking."

She traded cameras. Turning to him, she winked. "Say cheese!"

"Provolone." He indulged her with a goofy grin.

"I can't even figure out how to make it work." She squinted. "Does this kind even work on batteries?"

"If it did, the film would still be too old to get a good picture."

"Do you think Mona will come after me again?"

"I hope not." He walked her outside, hand in hand amid dancing fireflies.

"You know..." She winked when he met her gaze. "I've decided I don't care if you're in this for the land, as long as you kiss me like that every day for the rest of our lives."

"It can be arranged." He wrapped an arm around her waist. "Not for a while, thought. I don't want to cause you to stumble. But I did want you to know what I felt."

They went back in the house and started dinner. When Phil and Rose returned, Geoff kept a careful distance, and she refused to meet his gaze. Still, she sensed Phil watching. He must have known.

As he'd done the previous two nights, Geoff slept in a chair by her window, with the door open so Phil had a clear view from his room across the hall. A shotgun hung over the edge of the chair, and Savannah dreamed of it going off while he slept.

After restless sleep, she woke early Sunday morning to a symphony of soft snores. Rose had curled up beside her. She chuckled. When?

Geoff stirred.

She put her fingers to her lips and motioned toward her mother. "This is ridiculous," she whispered. "Why?"

"A dog barked at three a.m.," he whispered back.

"I've never felt so safe in my life." She restrained a giggle, slipped out of the bedroom, and headed for the kitchen. As she popped the lid off a dingy yellow Tupperware, the aroma of dark roast coffee filled the room.

He handed her a carton of eggs. "I messaged Ryan earlier. He's going to get us an escort out of town, so if anyone follows you, we'll know. We're going to take you in Cole's truck."

Savannah threw biscuits on a pan. "You know, you're not the only one who likes to cook." She grabbed an onion and pepper from the fridge to chop. "Omelets are my specialty."

He moved behind her, guiding her wrist. "Like this. You're going to cut off your fingers."

"Well, it's going to taste good." She dropped the knife and pivoted, sticking her tongue out at him.

He leaned forward, kissing her nose. "Not if it has blood in it."

From the hallway, Phil cleared his throat. "Y'all getting ready for church?"

"I'll go now." Savannah dashed toward the bathroom then lingered in the hall.

Geoff took over chopping the vegetables. "Not yet. We've been working on breakfast."

Phil poured a cup of coffee. "Listen, when you leave today... I have a lot of respect for you, son. Your mama and my wife were church friends, God rest her soul. But many a good man has fallen to temptation." He glanced at the knife. "Fast chopping."

Laughing, Geoff set the knife down and cracked eggs into an iron skillet. "I don't suppose you're a fan of peppers and onions in your omelets?"

"Meh..." Phil shook his head.

"Then we'll save these for the girls." He broke eggs into a bowl and poured milk into them. "Phil, you and I have gone to church together for thirteen years now. You've sat in my Bible classes, and I helped you build the big old ark for Vacation Bible School." Stirring with a whisk, he added pinches of salt and pepper. "You can trust me. I'm going to do right by your daughter."

She heaved a long sigh.

Phil rested in a kitchen chair and picked at a woven placemat. "I know I can."

Geoff winked. "Besides, I have every intention of marrying her within the next year."

The gasp escaped before Savannah could stop it. Her heart exploded.

"Are you serious?" Rose bounded past her into the kitchen.

"You can trust me." He flipped the sizzling omelet with one swift lift of the pan, his eyes boring into hers. Their intensity left her shivering. "You'll have a son-in-law before next Christmas."

Chapter Twenty-Seven

Savannah tapped her head against the car window. "Mom, Let it go."

"Well, I think he should have proposed first." Rose picked at loose tendrils of hair spilling around her cheeks.

"We haven't dated long enough for him to propose."

"Then he shouldn't have talked marriage."

"I thought you wanted grandchildren. Shouldn't marriage come first?"

"You know what I mean."

"Girls." Phil cleared his throat as they arrived at the brick church building, a relic compared to the modern one the church now occupied. An old iron furnace towered above a thicket of trees. Geoff's farm. Her farm.

Savannah traced the fence line in her mind. She should have brought Frank's pictures. Frowning, she glanced at her dad. She could take a short walk and get some with her phone. "How does this service work? Does it start right away?"

Phil shut off the ignition and climbed out, turning toward the hillside, where suited men and sun-dressed women in cardigans surrounded the stone amphitheater. "We have a regular church service outside, like they did in the old days. Then Dallas will give a sermon inside about how things were back then. He'll tell us we need to go back to the Bible and rethink our worship—do we please God or ourselves? After that, the guest preacher will speak about the Israelites and returning to God. Same as every year."

Rose glared at Phil. "Why don't you let them tell it?"

They joined a flock of families trekking across the disheveled lot, moving alongside a line of overgrown bushes to a vine-covered gate. They passed the front of the church, and Savannah's heart stopped when she read the sign. Stony Grove Church of Christ. Why hadn't Rose told her?

She paused mid-step, staring at the crumbling concrete porch. Reaching for Phil's shoulder, she teetered. "This is the place. This is where my real mom left me."

"Yes." Rose ran a manicured hand over the railing. "I used to walk over this spot every week and pray I could handle the responsibility of raising you." Her eyes teared. "Guess I failed."

Savannah bit her lip and hugged her mom. "All wasn't lost. We still have time."

Geoff waved to a tall gray-haired woman as he came up beside them. He wrapped his arm around Savannah, dodging a slivered glance from Phil. "Let's find a seat while there's still room."

Their hike over softened ground drew whispers and curious smiles. Geoff slipped his hand in hers, and she tried to stand straighter, a challenge with her stilettos sinking in the mud.

While Phil and Geoff shook a line of hands, Rose flitted between fluorescent print dresses and beauty-shop curls then settled on the front stone bench. Savannah took the place next to her, sitting on her hands.

"Sit straight. Be confident." Rose squeezed her leg. "Wow them with your singing and make them forget the gossip."

Savannah nodded, intending to comply, but when Geoff started singing beside her, she could only listen. His rich baritone voice sent chills down her spine.

Rose nudged her. "Sing!"

Savannah sucked in air. "When other helpers fail and comforts flee..." Her voice, tentative at first, strengthened with each word. "Help of the helpless, O abide with me."

She'd forgotten her passion for singing hymns. How had something she loved so much slipped so far away?

When the song ended, Rose patted her shoulder. "Good job, Dora."

Savannah's shoulders slumped. Her mother's breath warmed her neck, but a chill cooled her heart. Would Rose ever let her be Savannah?

Geoff balanced his Bible in his lap. She scooted closer, widening the space between her and Rose.

Men carried around the communion trays, and when the bread passed in front of her, she hesitated before accepting.

"You're forgiven." Geoff's whisper made her heart soar.

She was forgiven. If only she could leave the past and sin no more.

Hand shaking, she reached for the flat, brittle bread, breaking off a tiny piece. She closed her eyes as she placed the piece on her tongue. *Dear Lord, please help me remember what I've committed to you. I pray for your strength and guidance as I figure all this stuff out again.* She chewed a piece of skin off her bottom lip. *I appreciate your sacrifice and your forgiveness....*

She folded her hands in her lap, feeling awkward. As a child, she'd prayed often—for the wrong things, of course, but she still felt comfortable with the words she'd said. Did God hear the prayers of people who'd messed up as badly as she had? Though she'd asked forgiveness, guilt still consumed her, and her chest tightened.

When communion ended and the visiting preacher took the stage, her thoughts drifted to Frank. Years ago, he sat in the opposite pew, her biological past mere feet away. If only she'd known. What would he think if he saw her now, an arm linked with Geoff's, and entertaining the thought of spending a lifetime with him?

Something told her he'd have been pleased.

230

Savannah waited on the porch when Geoff arrived at the Barretts' following a quick check on his animals after church. She ran to the truck before he could get out. "Let's go."

Rose and Phil waved from the kitchen window as she climbed in and dropped her bag on the floorboard.

"Why the hurry?"

"Phil says he has a bad feeling, and he wants us out of town."

Geoff backed down the drive. "Okay. Ryan's going to tail Mona and make sure she doesn't follow us. We'll be in Knoxville around four."

"I Googled the address. It's Norris Dam State Park, and it's only about two hours from here. You'll never believe this. They changed the name of the town to Rocky Top, Tennessee a while back."

"I heard about it."

Savannah rested her head against the leather seat and closed her eyes. She fell asleep within minutes, and he spent most of the trip making sideways glances at her profile.

How had he been so lucky? He eyed his Bible in the console between them. Luck had nothing to do with it. God had a plan.

He arrived in Rocky Top in record time, swinging through a drive-thru for a couple of barbecue sandwiches and crinkle-cut fries. As they left the restaurant, Savannah stirred.

"Hey, you." He grinned. "Smell of the food woke you?"

She smoothed her hair and sat straighter. "Yep."

"Sorry. It's not healthy, but this little roadside place looked so good."

He drove through fallen leaves and bare trees to the monstrous concrete dam. Savannah gripped the edge of her seat as he crossed.

"There's a picnic area where we can eat."

Her stomach rumbled. "Good. I'm starving. I don't mind unhealthy as long as it's a rare occasion."

The radio crackled into static, and he adjusted it, settling on an old-school country station. "I used to come to Tennessee with my parents three or four times every year." He gave her a rueful smile. "Dad would drive around, Mom would shop, and I'd daydream about being in one of the shows."

"You are a good singer." She shifted in the seat to face him. "When you stood up the first time I came to church, I couldn't even open my mouth to sing. You blew me away."

He parked and handed her a sandwich. "I guess I could have pursued singing if I'd wanted. Mom entered me in a local talent contest at sixteen, and I won. Thing is, I don't like singing in front of people—strange, I know, since I spent my whole life in the spotlight. On the ground, as a matter of fact."

She snickered, unfolding the wrapper. "Let me guess. Football."

"Yeah. Remember? I played in eighth grade, the first year Dreyfus had a team." He passed her a bag of fries.

She sniffed the fries before taking one. "You stand up in front of the crowd at church."

"I do, but I don't sing for the crowd. I sing for God. It's different."

A swarm of people migrated to a lower lot. She arched, looking toward the entrance. "You know, I think we can see the dam better from there."

"Okay, I'll drive down and see if there's a spot."

She clutched her sandwich with one hand and the dash with the other, her eyes widening. "Cool. There it is! Can you believe the crowd?"

"They must be getting ready to open the gates."

They finished their lunch then joined the throng. As they approached the dam, he reached into a bag he'd swung over his shoulder.

"Wow. Awesome camera. When did you get it?"

He couldn't contain his grin. "I bought it on the way back from Michigan. Thought we could learn to use it together. I guess I hoped things might work out between us."

He snapped her picture as an older couple walked by, holding hands. The woman chuckled. "Let me guess. Newlyweds."

Savannah's cheeks turned a lovely pink.

"No." He draped the camera strap back over his shoulder. "We haven't been dating long, but we have a history."

"We do, too." The man kissed his wife on the cheek, his wispy beard brushing her chin. "Today's our forty-seventh anniversary."

"We've come here together every time they've opened the spill gates for as long as we've lived here." The woman nodded to the dam. "You're right on time."

"Forty-seven years. Wow." A siren blared, and Geoff winced.

Water poured over the top of the dam, beneath the roadway in a solid white sheet. He zoomed closer, and Savannah leaned over his shoulder to see the image on the digital screen.

The man gave Geoff a hearty backslap, jostling the camera. "Incredible, isn't it? We dropped everything to get here on time. Right, Mari?"

"Sure is." She chuckled. "We left our beans on the stove and had to call the neighbor to turn them off for us." Extending her hand, she smiled. "I'm Marietta, and this is David. Where are you from, dear?"

"Chic... um... Kentucky." Savannah showed Mari the journal pictures. "One of my family members helped build the dam, back in the thirties. I'm trying to learn more about it."

For the next twenty five minutes, Geoff stared at the falling water while David explained how the dam changed the area's culture.

When he finished, Savannah hugged both David and Marietta. "Thanks so much for everything. You were such a big help."

They wandered closer to the dam as Geoff led Savannah to the truck. "What a sweet couple. Think we could ever...?"

Savannah tucked her arm around his waist. "I'm willing to try." She climbed in the passenger side. "Hope we make it to the church before their service starts."

"We will."

She consulted the journal. "I see pictures of the dam, but nothing more. A couple featured men in hard hats. None with captions. I'm not sure what he wants me to know about this one, other than I think he became a skilled builder at a young age." She tugged at the corner of the page. "Ahh. Here we go. This one's stuck, too. I wonder if he glued them." She flipped to more family pictures. "The woman who brought Frank to Dreyfus adopted him. Lizzie Noble. Her husband served in the Army Core of Engineers and managed to get Frank a job running errands for the workers and contractors. He proved useful, and they took him under their wing."

Geoff started the truck. "I could have guessed. A master carpenter built the farmhouse. There's not a single room out of square or with shoddy framework. Parts of it need restoration, but the craftsmanship is near-perfect."

She stuffed the journal in her bag and buckled the seatbelt. "I don't want you to leave the farmhouse. It's your home."

He jerked. "What?"

"I want you to stay in the house. I'll find somewhere else to live." She wrinkled her nose. "And a job in Lexington where I could use my business management degree."

"Well..." He turned the key in the ignition. "I could use someone with a keen eye for business to help with the books."

She smiled, fake-fluttering her eyelashes. "Think you're clever, do you, Mr. Spencer? Hoping to keep me underfoot? How flattering." Her cheeks reddened. "I could manage a job keeping your books."

He flicked his gaze to the sky and gave a quick thanks. He owed God a long grateful, prayer as soon as he had a chance.

Chapter Twenty-Eight

Savannah couldn't stop smiling over letting Geoff stay on the farm. Who cared if she owned it on paper? It had always been his. They'd draw up an agreement, and she'd let him help her build a house on a different part of the property. She'd even stay with her parents until he finished building it.

Geoff signaled, merging into the passing lane. "It's strange how Frank's mind worked. We've spent all this time trying to understand him, but could it be possible there's not any significance to his ramblings? Like he just wanted you to know about his carpentry skill?"

"I know." She flipped through her notes. "I've been thinking about this list of locations and dates. They don't have anything in common. Deaths in the tornado, people who left him in Michigan, all these plus signs might relate to the war—other than loose family ties and it being sequential, some of it doesn't fit the puzzle."

"It's like we're missing something." He lowered the radio. "I wonder if we haven't skipped a clue."

Savannah held up a half-filled page from her legal pad. "I think he wanted to leave mystery. Like the church in Washington, DC. Did he leave out the details on purpose or did he mean to explain and forgot? And now, we're going to another church, and there's barely anything on the page."

"Have you Googled it yet?"

"I will." She searched on her phone. A vintage country gospel song started playing, and he sang along, giving her chills.

"Okay, Pavarotti, hush for a minute, and I'll tell you what I found."

He stopped singing and chuckled. "As you wish..."

"C'mon, Wesley. Next thing I know, you'll be calling me Buttercup and rolling down a hill. Can't you be serious?"

He turned off the radio. "What did you find?"

"The Greater Warner Tabernacle was the oldest black church in Knoxville history and a station on the Underground Railroad. Again, the slavery theme."

Geoff slowed as he came up on a minivan letting the driver beside him pass before changing lanes. "Frank was too young to be an abolitionist, so was it someone in his adopted family? Did he attend this church while his family lived here?"

"Could be. There aren't any pictures or anything to document it. Besides, I think it was an African American church. You never know, though." Her shoulders slumped. "I feel like we keep going in circles. Every new answer leads to more questions."

He pulled up to the front of the church. The door opened, and a middle-aged woman emerged, carrying a handful of stark-white tablecloths.

Savannah hopped out and ran to her. "Hi. This might be an odd question, but could you let me see inside the church?"

"Got to do the washing." The woman looked closer. "You must be Miss Savannah. Your great-grandfather told me to watch for you." She extended her hand. "Name's Mabel Harper, but everyone calls me Miss May. How is Frank these days?"

"He passed." Savannah's chest heaved. "Died of a stroke a couple weeks ago."

"Sorry to hear it." Mabel shifted the tablecloths to her right hip. "I liked Frank."

"Did you know him well?"

"I knew him as a traveling photographer, well into his eighties, and he'd lived in the Knoxville area in his early teenage years." Mabel shrugged. "I met him same as I met you. He rested on the foot of these steps, reminiscing. Said he'd sat on these same steps years ago with his aunt and uncle, listening to stories about the Underground Railroad. He talked about it like he'd been through it himself."

Interesting. Savannah eyed a line of ants scurrying into a crack in the stone sidewalk. Odd for late October.

Mabel lost hold of a tablecloth corner and rearranged the bundle. "I told him what I knew. In exchange, he took the most beautiful pictures of my grandchildren and didn't charge me a penny. He built us a magnificent dollhouse. All carved out of wood. He sat out here on the porch and whittled on it for a month straight."

"Did he tell you anything about me?"

"He said you'd be passing through, and he wanted to leave you this envelope of photographs."

Savannah rocked on her heels. "Is there any way I could see the dollhouse, and take pictures of it? I don't mean to pry. I'm searching for my biological roots, and it might give me a clue."

Mabel smiled. "I thought you might like to see it. Follow me. I live a few blocks down, off Oakland Street. Won't take us but a minute to get there."

Savannah trailed behind her to a white brick house. Struck by its character, she stumbled on the concrete steps leading up the walk. She held the tablecloths while Mabel retrieved the keys to the rustic wooden door.

"The interior is prettier." Mabel closed her purse. "I keep after Thomas to get me a new door, and he won't hear it."

"It's lovely." Savannah ran her fingers across the smooth red paint covering the doorjamb. "It's got character."

Mabel led her over hardwood floors through the cherry-paneled entry into a living room, which still bore the olive and goldenrod shades of years before, although Savannah suspected they'd been recently painted. Following her gaze, Mabel grinned. "Thomas thinks he's a preservationist. He wants to make things like they did back in the old days. He and Frank got along fine."

She lifted a quilt, revealing the dollhouse atop an antique oak table. "I have to keep it covered. It gets real dusty here."

Savannah circled the house, snapping pictures with her phone. "Beautiful craftsmanship."

Frank had decorated the outside with stones like the bridges she'd passed driving into Dreyfus. He'd shaped the house more like a barn, with arched windows and a loft, and thick wood trim lined each room. All the décor bore carvings, painted murals, or wood stain, from the toilets, to the spiral staircase connecting the floors.

Mabel swung open the plastic roof, revealing two hinges in the back.

Savannah knelt to get a closer look. "I can't believe the detail. Frank made this all for you by hand?"

Mabel nodded. "At first I thought he might be mentally ill or homeless. In fact, I started to call the police on him a time or two. But when I talked to him, the man was a walking Bible. I've never known anyone who knew the Book as well as Frank.

"About three days in, he showed me the plans he'd drawn. Both his talent and generosity amazed me. He arrived at about seven a.m. and worked until three o'clock every day. He came in summer, so the kids all gathered around and watched him, and he told Bible stories. One day he finished, and he up and disappeared, leaving me a note saying you might be by and to give you the envelope. I tried a hundred times to pay him, but he wouldn't take my money."

Savannah tipped her cell phone to the portrait angle and zoomed in on the finer details.

"I forgot." Mabel reached into a drawer. "He also made the neatest little dolls. Carved all of them from the same branch."

She removed a bag of four wooden figurines, each decorated with bright, detailed paint, and stood them up one-by-one in the dollhouse. Savannah recognized Cindy right away.

"This one resembles you." Mabel pointed to the brown-headed one. "He must have loved you."

Tears filled her eyes. She picked it up and ran her fingers along its smooth edges. Etched letters crossed the bottom of the feet. Her mother's name. Carrie.

"I should go." She tucked her phone into her pocket and wiped her eyes with her sleeve. "Thanks for letting me see this."

Savannah waved to Mabel and walked onto the steps, the white brick blinding her in the bright sun. She made her way to the church, where Geoff sat on the truck bed.

He hopped down and opened the passenger door for her. "Learn anything?"

"Not much. I did take a lot of pictures, though." She passed him her phone. "Look at these dolls he's carved. Here's Cindy, but much younger. This one is my mother. He carved her name on one of the feet. This third one—I wasn't sure." She turned toward the house and sighed. "I should have checked. He etched the names into the feet."

"I know who it is." Geoff's eyes darkened. "It's my mother. I've seen a picture of her wearing the same outfit about age seventeen."

"I'd like to print these." She clicked the button, darkening her screen.

"I saw a drugstore on Chapman Highway. I bet it has a one-hour photo."

"This dollhouse had odd construction. You take steps down the side to get into the door. No windows on this bottom floor, so it's more like a basement. Then the top of it looks kind of like a barn."

He signaled and nodded. "What's the envelope?"

"Pictures of a life-sized room like the one he built for the little girl. There's not a room like this in the farmhouse, right?"

239

He shook his head. "Well, as far as the upper part, Frank may have drawn inspiration from places he recognized. We've got stone barns on the farm, on the far corner where it's overgrown." He backed out of the parking space. "And as far as the room, he moved around a lot. Maybe he stayed in that bedroom when he moved in with his foster mom."

"Maybe..." She tucked the seal flap inside the envelope. "Are stone barns common to Kentucky? I don't think I've ever seen one."

"In places. I researched them a long time ago. The original owner kept horses. I've thought about fixing them up and getting horses of my own, but we've spent so much time on the hybridization project. There's also an iron furnace out there I've been meaning to explore. It's on the northern edge, close to Nana Jean's house. I'll show you when we get back. It's in the spot on the map where Frank wrote his riddle."

"Yeah. I saw it. Hmm... Wonder what the significance is between the dollhouse and our mothers. It has to mean something."

A shiver raced up her spine. Everything else Frank had written about had been a disaster. What had she stumbled on now?

Chapter Twenty-Nine

"Is this the right place? We've been driving forever." Geoff swigged a sip from his water bottle and set it in the cup holder, his chest swelling with contentment.

She pinched her fingers across her cell screen, magnifying the image. "Yes! Service. It's not too much further. Less than a mile."

"I'm surprised Frank didn't have Cades Cove as a stop on your list."

"Yeah. It's a neat place. Phil used to take me there every summer."

A brown sign poked out of a grove of trees a few feet ahead, and she leaned forward. "There's the drive. Make this right, take one more left, and the cabin is down a gravel road."

Thick mud spun under the tires, and he grimaced. "Gravel, my foot. This place is more like a swamp. Good thing you didn't try to drive your car."

"Yeah. I'm glad you're with me. It would be scary to visit a strange man in a cabin by myself."

"Speaking of old men…"

A diagonal shadow crossed the cabin's front exterior wall, darkening the features of the camouflaged man who approached. Tufts of wild gray poked out beneath a Tennessee Volunteers cap, inches above a shotgun resting on his right shoulder. The man sat on a handmade rocker and gripped the forestock with a withered hand, aiming straight at the truck.

She shuddered. "Did Frank want to get us killed?"

"You stay in here. I'll talk to him." Geoff eased out of the driver's door, holding up both hands. "We don't want trouble. Frank McMillan sent us."

"Frank McMillan didn't say nothin' 'bout no us." The man lowered the gun an inch and walked to the truck. He stared through the glass, and his scowl slacked. "She's the girl?"

Geoff winced as Savannah rolled the window down a crack.

"I brought you something." She held out a plastic bag. "Peanut butter fudge from the store by the Old Mill Restaurant. Frank called it your favorite."

Dropping the gun to his side, the man snatched the bag. He pinched a tiny piece of the fudge and popped it into his mouth. "Eli Dawson." The words came out muffled. "Like Millie's. I suppose you wanna come in and visit."

"Sure." Savannah handed him the rest of the bag and climbed from the truck.

The cabin's interior starkly contrasted the mud-covered disheveled outer walls. Cedar paneling framed the room, and contemporary appliance clocks blinked. Eli led them to a leather couch, framed by white lace and thick, green curtains.

"Millie." Eli gestured to a picture of a ponytailed blonde wearing a UT sweatshirt and a bright smile. "My granddaughter. She died a couple years back."

"Sorry to hear that." Geoff scanned the room. "Can we help you with anything?"

Bushy white hair sprung out as Eli removed his cap and hung it on a hat rack. "Where do you want to start? I haven't been able to get to the store in days. All this rain's turned the drive into mush, and I'm having trouble with the toilet leaking."

Geoff removed a business card from his wallet. "Hmm... I know a man who can help with the gravel. This guy used to live in Dreyfus, but he moved to La Follette a few years ago. I'm sure he'll be reasonable. Believe it or not, I might have a toilet repair kit in one of my toolboxes." He slipped outside, leaving Savannah in the entry. Surely, the guy wouldn't hurt her.

Savannah paced the small cabin, her gaze focused on Eli's gun cabinet.

"Sit, young lady. Let me tell you about your great-grandfather." Eli coughed into a yellowed handkerchief, thick and bronchial. He settled into his plush blue-velvet armchair. "Frank and I served overseas together in the Cigarette Camps toward the end of the war. I trust you've read about them in your schoolbooks."

"Sorry." Her cheeks warmed. "I don't know anything about the Cigarette Camps. I didn't pay as much attention in history class as I should have. World War II, I guess?"

"Right. In the forties. They sent us to a place called Le Harve with the promise of women and smokes."

"Frank chased women? He had a wife and kid back home, right?"

Eli folded his handkerchief and tucked it into his shirt pocket. "A handful of soldiers found a brothel close to where they stationed us. You know what happened. It bothered Frank, and after a while, he put a stop to it."

"How?"

"First, he studied languages like a madman—French, Spanish, Russian, Chinese. You'd never believe how fast he learned to speak them." Eli shuffled to a built-in bookshelf and retrieved an old photo album. "Here, I took pictures—they're toward the end. If you find them, you can keep them."

She accepted the album. A few brown-spotted photos of Frank in military attire filled seven yellowed pages. She peeled them away from the sticky backing and stacked them on the coffee table. "Thanks."

Eli slid the album into its spot on the shelf. "After learning the languages, Frank started meeting the girls. We used to tease him about it. He'd go every night. Turned out he wasn't even as much as kissing them. He interviewed them, finding out where they came from and how they got there. Turns out, most had been trafficked."

Savannah took her legal pad out of her bag. "Do you mind if I take notes? I'll never remember."

"Sure. Frank had a hard time getting the girls to talk at first. Fright, as you can imagine. After a while, one of them talked." Eli pointed to a photo of Frank and a thin girl in a flowery hat and knee-length dress. "As a small child, she'd been kidnaped from a family with a long line of nobility. Frank helped her return home, and her family rewarded him." He cupped his mouth and whispered, "I'm talking more money than anyone around here's ever seen."

"So that's where he got his fortune."

"Sure is."

She scribbled on her legal pad. "Whatever happened to the other girls? Did he help them escape, too?"

"They shut the place down faster than the bank at closing time. Her family put a stop to it."

"And Frank?"

"He sat by the train station and watched every one of them board for home, and then came on back to our quarters and served the rest of his time. He never complained, never asked for anything. When they sent us home, he told me everything. He promised he'd take care of me and thanked me for being a good friend."

"And did he? Take care of you?"

"We lost touch for years. When we reconnected, he followed through with his promise." Eli jerked his thumb toward his cook top stove. "He paid for everything in this cabin, and for the boat and car in the drive. Wouldn't take no for an answer."

Eli focused on the TV while she mulled over what he told her. She read the journal entry, and a few things started making sense.

244

"So, while he served, a man named Herb Spencer moved into his farmhouse and took over his property. Did you know?"

"Not until recently. He never talked about where he lived. So odd. He disappeared for decades. Not a word from him. I figured he'd forgotten his promise. Then one day he showed up and started throwing money at me like candy."

She flipped the journal to an old photograph of them dressed in helmets and wielding submachine guns. "I think Frank wanted me to keep taking care of you, since Millie can't anymore. You work on that list for Geoff. We can arrange to have all this fixed up for you, and then we'll come back and check on you every now and then."

Geoff tinkered with loose trim as she bustled around Eli's house, scrubbing the corners and baseboards. "When Frank's money is released, I'm going to hire him a housekeeper."

"Let's go ahead and hire him one." Geoff tapped a nail into the trim. "I'll pay for it." He turned to Eli. "How would you feel about a live-in caretaker? We could put up a wall here and fix it so they'd have their own apartment."

Eli scoffed. "Who'd want to come live here and take care of an old coot like me?"

"I know of a couple living in the area that lost everything to a fire. They're churchgoing people, my contact for charity work here in town. Their kids are grown. I'm sure it would be perfect for them."

While Geoff made the call, she inspected Eli's pantry and refrigerator and wrote a grocery list. Later, she climbed into the truck, beaming, as Geoff slid into the driver's seat.

"Kindness becomes you." He reached across and tucked a loose tendril behind her ears. "Will you tackle the farmhouse when we get back?"

She shrugged. "I'm not domestic."

They both laughed.

"But I could learn to be, I guess." Interlocking her fingers with his, she scooted closer. "It did feel good to help him. I'm glad we can take care of him."

"You know, there may be hope for you yet."

Savannah's cell rang, the glow pulling her out of her peaceful daydream. "Er... Um... Hello?"

"It's a double code."

She stretched her legs. "What?"

"It's a double code. Your puzzle."

She grinned. "Hi to you, too, Mom."

"It's after ten. Are you guys on the way back?"

"Yeah. We've driven all over the country in the past hours. I'll pass out when I get home."

"Where are you?"

"About forty-five minutes from Corbin. We toured Cades Cove, met up with an elderly man Frank knew, and went to church in Sevierville. Geoff's paying for gas right now."

Her mother rattled in the kitchen. "Sounds like you're having a good time."

"I am. Back to the puzzle."

"Took a while to solve this one." Rose cleared her throat, and shuffling papers crinkled. "First, I deciphered the words into a meaningless list of scrambled letters, but I realized those words matched cryptograms for the real ones."

"Wow, Mom." Savannah reached for her notepad. "Awesome."

"The words are strange, though. What kind of puzzle is it?"

Savannah had to laugh. Rose had long forgotten the map, and she would never put two-and-two together to realize the relation to Frank's mystery. "Tell me the message slow, so I can write it."

"Well, I've only done one of them," she said. "Two babies left in the hay..."

Rose paused, and Savannah printed the riddle on the notepad above where she'd written the cryptic clues.

"One father made them."

One father? Savannah frowned. Herb?

"Three mothers, a daughter, two sons..."

"One child died; the mother cried," Rose continued. "One child lived; the mother ran. The third child lived where it all began. Such a strange poem. A riddle?"

"Okay, say the last part again. One child died; the mother cried." Savannah read over the lines once more. "I'll let you know when I figure it out, I promise." She took a deep breath. "Love you, Mom."

She shut off her phone as Geoff got back in the truck. "Mom figured out the cryptogram. We still have to solve it."

"What is it?"

"More baby talk." She read the words aloud, pausing at the end of each line, the way Rose did.

"The woman who ran could be your mother." He handed her the diet soft drink. "You could be the daughter."

"A real possibility." She added it to her notes. "There are three babies here, two sons and a daughter. I guess the third mother must have kept the baby."

He groaned. "I hope the hay doesn't mean there's a baby buried on the farm. We need to find out when a child died."

"He didn't put dates on it, so I guess it could be anyone."

Geoff turned the air conditioner down a notch. "I don't remember hearing about anyone losing a child, although it could have been before my birth. Weren't there three BBs on the code list?"

247

"Yeah, from 1981." She scrolled through her cell pictures to the wooden dolls. "I know two women who do not have any children, who never married, and who could've made a pact to leave babies in the hay."

His eyes widened. "Mona and Cindy. Could be why Cindy moved away. She could be the one who ran."

Savannah straightened. "Mona and Cindy are the same age. This makes more sense. We need to go talk to Cindy again."

He snorted. "Call her. I can't handle those cigarettes."

"True. This phrase about one father made them—it could be a religious undertone. Or... maybe not. What if they all became pregnant by the same man? By Herb..."

He nodded at the glove box. "Get the photo album out of there. I found it at the house in Mom's stuff. It has several pictures of Carrie in it. Meant to give it to you this morning." He glanced in the rearview mirror then changed lanes. "The word *left* bothers me. Did they not want the babies, or leave them and intend to come back for them?"

"I guess we need to consider the possibility Frank meant himself here, too. Could he have been the father? Or, since there's no date, the son?"

Geoff upped his speed and set the cruise control. "If not, why didn't he include this event here? He told you about his mother in good detail, and nothing about fathering a bunch of kids."

For the next hour, she scanned the pictures, which chronicled the lives of the three girls into their teens. One set of photos all featured the same stone wall, the girls standing in the same pose. Her mother frowned in every picture. Cindy started out a happy child, then a giddy girl, and at last she morphed into a brooding woman. Geoff's mom always wore smiles, though defiance shone in her eyes. "I wonder... if this clue does refer to Cindy and our moms..."

Geoff handed over her phone. "Let's call her."

"I doubt she'll tell me anything over the phone. I'll try." She dialed and launched into her questions as soon as Cindy answered.

"Are you crazy?" Cindy's voice resonated, followed by several crashes and bangs as the phone clattered to the floor. Sobs overtook the line.

"Hello?" Savannah cradled the cell to her ear, straining to listen. "Cindy?"

Muffled noises, heavy breathing, and then a long sigh drifted through the speaker.

"Cindy. Are you okay?"

Metal clanged, and Cindy cleared her throat. "I'm shocked. I thought no one knew, not even Frank."

"Knew what?" Savannah held her breath. Cindy had lied. She'd even talked about babies earlier. "All we have are his words and the stuff you told us."

"I need to… help Miller. Catch you later." Cindy ended the call.

Savannah raised her brows. "Strange. Now what?"

"Her reaction is an admission she's involved."

"Right. What if..." Savannah searched the puzzle again, trying to take the words as literally as possible. "What if my mother, Mona, and Cindy all had babies around the same time by the same guy? We know my mother ran, so I might be the living one. Cindy's baby died. What if Frank didn't know what happened to the other baby?"

"Or," Geoff tapped the brake and swept around a slow truck before resetting the cruise speed, "Cindy said she's your aunt. She's your father's sister. The boy and girl babies are her and your father, not twins. Born on the same day to two different women."

"It could be, but I don't think so. Her reaction seemed more like a big secret she didn't want anyone to know. If she had a baby and it died without being discovered, she'd want to keep it hidden."

Geoff yawned. "Go on. We can revisit theories later."

"Well... Rose told me my mother dropped me on the doorstep of the church a few hours after giving birth. They found blood all over the bathroom, and a broken window where she entered to clean herself. I was never near any hay. I still say I'm not one of the two babies in the hay. Could those babies be the ones born in 1981?"

"I bet you're right. Mona would've never cried over a baby." His lips twisted in a frown. "She's not the mourning type, so she would've been the one who ran away, which means Cindy had the child who died."

"So, who is the third mother?"

Savannah eyed the photo album, the three teenage girls staring intently at the camera. "Yours?"

"I don't have any siblings."

"That you know." Savannah's cell rang. "It's Phil. He never calls." She answered, her pulse roaring in her ears. "Dad, what's wrong?"

"Get home quick. We're taking your mom to the hospital."

Chapter Thirty

"Have they found Mona?" Geoff dropped into the waiting room chair next to Ryan Chambers.

"No." Ryan stretched out his legs. "But we've got a lot of men out looking. They'll arrest her as soon as we spot her."

"What about Kaler?"

Ryan twisted his lips. "He's still on a leave of absence, recovering from his injuries. I don't think he's helping her."

Geoff gripped the chair arm. "It's not like Dreyfus is a huge city. Where could she be?"

"We believe she drove a stolen car and abandoned it to hitchhike out of town. Nathan found one a few miles from the extension office where their homemaker's group meets. Rose lay outside the office door, face down in the mulch."

The wall clock ticked. A pregnant woman waddled by, her husband towing two toddlers behind her. An elderly couple held hands and prayed in the opposite corner.

Geoff sifted through the magazines on the table beside him. Nothing appealing. He tapped his boots together.

Phil came out of a secured hallway and walked to them. "Dora wants you to come up for a few minutes. They'll only let in two at a time."

"Yeah. She told me earlier." Geoff stood. "What's the extent of Rose's injuries?"

"She..." Phil's lower lip quivered. "She..." He fell into a seat.

Ryan leaned forward. "Mona hit her head and struck several times on her legs, arms, and back. She has multiple contusions and may have internal bleeding. They're watching her overnight."

Geoff patted Phil's shoulder. "No broken bones?"

"No." Phil clenched Geoff's arm. "But she's going to be in a lot of pain for a while."

Kneeling, Geoff slid off his cap. "Let me pray with you, Phil."

Savannah kept one eye on her mother's sleeping form as she read the next journal section. Dates and images coursed through her mind. Three babies, born in 1981 by the same man to different mothers. Two lived. She gritted her teeth. Cindy had to spill her secrets.

She slipped into the hall and headed to an isolated corner to dial Cindy. As the phone rang, she brushed dust from the windowsill.

"Sorry I haven't called." Cindy sniffled. "This is such a challenge. They say the truth always comes out with time. I should have come forward back then, but I was scared."

Down the hall, a nurse pushed a teenage boy in a wheelchair, rolling him into the room next door to Rose. His bloodied face broke Savannah's heart. She gazed at the parking lot, her breath leaving a spot on the window.

"I'm not going to tell anyone." She dug through her bag for her notebook. "I need to solve Frank's puzzle. That's all."

Silence. Cindy tapped against the phone speaker. "Where's Geoff? Have the two of you reconciled?"

"Yeah. We went on a date the other night." She couldn't stop her spreading smile. "I'm excited to help his charity work. It's a good change for me, and he can be great company when he wants to be."

Cindy struck her lighter, the sound hissing. Savannah pictured her taking a deep draw from one of her long, thin cigarettes, a ring of lipstick on the filter. Okay. Enough small talk. "In fact, our biggest problem is Mona. She's threatened me. I'm at the hospital right now because she attacked Rose."

Silence filled the deadly pause. Had Cindy dropped the phone?

"We were raped." Cindy's rasp came out tiny and weak. "The three of us, and Mona watched the whole time."

Savannah gripped the window ledge, her stomach churning. "Ra—she watched?"

"Photographed."

Even worse. Saliva caught in the back of Savannah's throat, and she forced a gulp. "By whom?"

Silence.

"Cindy?"

"Herb Spencer."

Geoff's great-grandfather. Savannah fanned her face, as though it would slow her thundering heart. "Which three? You, Geoff's mother, and my mother?" She shivered against the cool glass.

"Yes." Cindy's whisper barely sounded through the speakers. "Carrie Harman, me, and April."

Harman. Her maternal grandparents would be Harmans. Could they still be living? A light hand touched her shoulder, and Savannah pivoted. Geoff. She held a finger to her lips, and mouthed Cindy.

"Our parents dropped us at Herb and Leila's house for a week every summer and went on vacation together. That's how Carrie first met Levi."

Resting her notebook in the windowsill, Savannah jotted a few words. Cindy sobbed for a few minutes until Savannah could wait no more. "Anything else?"

"Other times, too. Occasional Fridays they'd have us spend the night. We'd go to big dinners on Sunday afternoons. Herb would make us play in the barn—he built us swings and a beautiful life-sized dollhouse."

Savannah's jaw dropped. The dollhouse. Cindy'd mentioned it. Did the rapes happen there? "Where can we find the dollhouse?"

"On the farm somewhere. He put blindfolds on us before bringing us there. Acted like he wanted to surprise us." Cindy sniffled. "Our parents thought he treated us so well. For the most part, he did, other than he photographed us in lingerie. He told us he'd help us become models. Except one night… "

Savannah shuddered. "What about Frank? Did he help Herb?"

"Herb treated him like a servant, making him run errands all the time. At first, we all thought he made money like the other farmworkers, who worked in slave-like conditions. Long hours, hard labor. Not Frank…" She clucked her tongue. "So strange. Frank could come and go, but Herb… had a strange power over him. They fought often. Frank usually caved."

After a long pause, Cindy cleared her throat. "And then, Frank stopped working on the farm, and Herb decided to leave him alone after we had the babies."

Savannah wrote Herb's name on the page and marked Xs in it, over and over, until the groove wore through the page. How many people had the horrid man terrorized?

Cindy blasted air into the speakers. "Herb had a hidden underground room in one of his barns. That's where the dollhouse was. He let us bring boyfriends and have alcohol, but he'd always drive us there and make everyone wear blindfolds. He said he didn't want anyone to break into the place."

"On the farm?" The lead had thinned. Her pencil screeched on the pad. "Cindy, I—"

"Mona claimed the dollhouse as her own. In our youth, we'd all do skits together, us four girls. Herb would stand in as all the male characters. We enjoyed ourselves. No discomfort at all. He brought us all kinds of dress-up clothes. Then, when we got older, the clothes became more… um… risqué."

"So next he talked about the modeling, right?"

"Yes. One night, he decided to take things to the next level. He tied us up back to back and made us watch while he… well um..."

Savannah shivered. She could only imagine.

"Mona helped him. She called it a role play and said if we told our parents, she'd tell them about our parties."

Savannah chewed a loose fingernail. "Why?"

"I don't know. April and I both discovered our pregnancies on my sixteenth birthday. Carrie found out a couple months later. We made a pact to hide the babies and get rid of them. We did well, too, dieting and exercising to keep from gaining weight. We couldn't hide from Herb, though. He figured it out when the babies started kicking.

"Close to her delivery time, April decided to tell her parents, but she never got a chance. He arranged for them to take a two-week vacation with my mom and dad and kept us in that underground room the entire time. He managed to get his hands on oxytocin and induced our labor. He made Mona take the babies up to the barn and cover them with hay so they'd die."

Geoff paced the hall. "I'm going for a walk."

"Okay." Savannah flipped to a new page. "So, Cindy, Herb didn't take my mother down there when you delivered your baby? Right?"

"No. Carrie snuck into the barn and found the babies. Mine had already died. I cried and cried."

"April's lived then?"

"Yes, and Carrie snatched the baby from the barn and ran with it. She wrapped it in her coat. She had money and hitchhiked. She told me an older man picked her up and helped her hide the baby in another town."

"Frank, no doubt." Savannah glanced down the hall to the stairwell Geoff had taken. "So what does it mean?"

Cindy sighed. "You and Geoff both have brothers you haven't met. Carrie told her parents she was pregnant, but refused to name the father, and they sent her away until after Brent's birth. They put him up for adoption, but she ended up taking him back from the family after she married Levi." A drawer squeaked, and things rattled in it.

"So Geoff has a brother, fathered by his grandfather?" Savannah slid down the concrete wall to the floor. Why had Carrie sought custody of Brent and not her?

"Sweet David." Cindy breathed heavy into the phone. "He had severe mental disabilities. He's been in an institution his entire life." The drawer closed. "Here, I found the addresses for you. Your brother, Brent, expects a visit soon. And I'm sure Geoff would want to meet David, his brother. Someone will need to take care of him since Frank is gone."

Savannah scrawled the addresses, her letters jagged from her unsteady hands.

Geoff walked to her side as she ended the call.

"Well, the good news—she gave me answers."

"And the bad news?"

She rubbed her left temple. "You don't want to know them."

He talked her into letting him buy her lunch at the hospital cafeteria. Twenty minutes later, her food remained untouched.

"I still can't believe I have a brother. Or that Mom never told me." He folded his hands in front of him on the table. "So, there's a dead infant body hidden on my farm. How many times has Mona gotten away with murder?"

Savannah tapped her fingers together. "The underground room shouldn't be too hard to find if it is in one of your barns. Do you know where it might be?"

"The back side of the property hasn't been touched in years." He frowned. "Mona and Kaler have been seen there recently. I need to catch Ryan if he hasn't already left and let him know all this, too."

Savannah speared a couple bites of lettuce and swirled them in salad dressing. "Out of curiosity, how did Herb die?"

"He had several stroke symptoms, and then his doctor diagnosed him with Lewy body dementia. He went down fast."

"Interesting. Is it possible someone exposed him to some kind of poison? My boss's uncle in Chicago got sprayed with pesticide and had similar symptoms. Don't you have a lot of pesticides on the farm?"

Geoff brushed dust from the windowsill's marble ledge. "You're saying Mona might have been responsible for his death, too? I don't see how she could have."

"Well, he lived to be an old man, so I doubt it."

"Did you bring the farm pictures?" He picked up her straw wrapper and wadded it into a ball. "We still haven't figured out all the puzzles yet. I think we're close to the end, don't you? I wonder if the dollhouse is labeled there, and we've missed it."

She retrieved the pictures from her bag and laid them out on the table.

"I can Google instructions to how to solve cryptograms and figure out the rest of them." She opened the browser on her phone. "I doubt Mom is up for it right now."

He traced his fingers over several barns. "My guess is one of these four. There are twenty-six barns on the property. Ten are modern, eight are abandoned, and the rest are storage."

"Okay, here we go. We try to solve the one-letter words." She flipped the picture and examined the list. "Great. There aren't any of those."

"You're doing this the hard way." He winked, sliding her phone closer. "Online cryptogram solver."

As he typed, she smiled. "I knew you had a dark side, you big cheater."

He ducked his head, laughing. "What can I say? Just give me the first letters."

"V-U-R-O-B-B-D-X-J."

A circle swirled on the screen, and then it flashed to a new one. He raised his right eyebrow. "Potassium?"

"Weird." Savannah squinted at the shaded letters. "Okay, the next one is Y-G-N-N-O-Z-S-O-K-D-Q-G."

"Ferricyanide."

"Potassium ferricyanide. Poison?" She took the phone back and typed it in a search box. "Oh, it's a chemical used in developing photographs."

"Ahh. Gotcha. Type in the next letters."

She switched to the solver screen and typed. "Sodium thiosulfate. Another developing chemical. I saw it on the ferricyanide website. He wants me to learn about photography."

Geoff pointed to her bag. "Let me see the dollhouse pictures again."

"I need to go to Virginia and meet Brent and read the next section in the journal." She reached for the journal, but it slid from her grip. The pictures tumbled to the tile floor, and as she scrambled for them, one poked out of the sealed pages, showing Frank standing in the life-sized dollhouse. "How did this get in there?"

Geoff squinted at the picture. "Wait. This isn't the same room. Or... Herb redecorated?"

"Oh." She covered her mouth. "Look at the wall. All those pictures of Carrie and Cindy from your mom's album... taken right there. We'd better call Peter and Ryan. It's time to turn this over to the police."

"What about the chemicals?"

Stacking the pictures in a neat pile, she puffed her cheeks. "I bet the rest of this is a recipe and instructions on how to develop them. Why would he give me the recipe, if he's giving me the pictures?" Her breath caught. "Oh."

"What?"

"Whatever this mystery leads to, he's caught it on film. I bet there's an old film canister hidden on the farm."

Chapter Thirty-One

Back in the waiting room, Geoff peered over his magazine at the racy picture on Savannah's forgotten cell. Her, casting the photographer a provocative smile, revealing body parts he shouldn't be seeing.

Another buzz. A naked man popped up on the screen, draped across a four-poster canopy bed. Ugh.

The veins in Geoff's neck pulsed. Count. Breathe. Don't get mad. She'd explained her past life. He turned the cell facedown.

It buzzed again. He stared at the plastic case for a minute, flipped the phone, and loaded her texts. Twelve new messages from a guy named Adam. All lewd.

After another quick side-to-side glance, he scrolled through the messages. Dozens of exchanges, all screaming inappropriate. She hadn't been kidding. Her responses were distant....

Except the ones from the past week.

She'd been involved with this guy right after leaving the lake house. Surely, it triggered her tearful response at the church. Why, if she'd changed, was she still communicating with the guy? Why had she kept the images on her phone?

He turned the screen down once more and resumed his perusal of a racecar article. Carnal thoughts fought to the forefront of his mind. He couldn't yield to them. But, yet how could he see her now and not think of those images? He never should have looked the first time.

His phone dinged in his pocket as Savannah burst through the double doors. "Hey." He checked the message. "Ryan is headed his way. Still no sign of Mona."

Savannah's phone buzzed again.

"Mom is better. She's eating." After a quick scan of the table, she snatched the cell, glanced at it, and shoved it in her pocket, her cheeks blazing.

A scowl fought to cross his face. Count again. Think. Don't let anger consume him. He relaxed his muscles.

She huffed, slamming her hands against her hips. "You've been on my phone."

He held up a hand, opened his mouth, and clamped it shut again.

"Did you go through all my texts?"

The magazine slipped to the floor. As he swooped to retrieve it, he shifted his gaze from hers. "I thought it was an emergency. You kept getting messages."

She stepped forward, forcing him back into her direct line of sight. "Did you go through my texts?"

"Yes." He palmed his cheeks. "I'm sorry. If I... I mean, we've agreed to be exclusive, right? And I—"

"Look, I saw this guy before I came home. As in seeing, not dating. Having sex. I ran into him, and we had one last night together. Nothing more."

"One last night together last week. He's still messaging you."

Her fist balled. "Yes, last week. If you recall, we weren't dating last week. Funny how things change. I regretted every second of it. I could only think about you."

"Well, if I understand the timeline right, you agreed to date me the day after this happened. I don't understand how you could be thinking about me and—"

"I cried all the way home. Did you see where I asked him to stop sending pictures? I doubt it." She paced the waiting room floor, pausing in front of a painting of a horse and jockey. "My problem has never been a secret."

"You're right." He clenched and unclenched his hands. Knowing she'd warned him didn't make it any easier. He forced his hardened jaw to slack and tried for a softer tone. "Why didn't you delete his messages after going forward at church?"

There, the crux of the matter. Did she still want the guy? Did she long for the sin? Could she be faithful? He searched her face, trying to find the truth there. If he believed she'd repented, why did he think she'd lie?

"I don't know. In case you haven't noticed, I've been worried about other things." Tears brimmed her eyelids. "Here's what I do know. I'm going to Virginia to meet my brother. By myself."

The tiny freckle sitting beneath her lower lip jiggled. She dropped into the chair across from him, bringing her feet up and landing in a fetal position. She wrapped her thin arms around her bony knees and ducked her head.

She'd never looked so vulnerable. Well, she had looked that vulnerable. Once, long ago. He could still picture her tormented face from years before as she sat amidst the humiliation he'd created for her as his cruel friends chanted, "Panda!"—Her face haunted him for so long. How could he forget so much of her pain originated from him?

Right now, could he sit in a car with her for ten hours? Even with his hurt pride, he owed it to her to try. He moved to her side, knelt, and placed a light hand on her shoulder. "I'll go with you. Frank wanted me to be with you."

"I don't want your company." She slung her bag over her opposite shoulder and ducked around him to climb out of the seat. "I wanted to give us a shot. But I'm not anywhere close to perfect, and I can't promise I won't walk out of this hospital and be tempted by the next guy I encounter. It's how I'm wired."

A portly middle-aged man entered the waiting room. "Excuse me. Have you seen anyone from the Roberts family?"

Geoff shook his head. "No, sir. I'm sorry. Other than us, this room has been empty for the last hour."

The man left, and Geoff smirked. Humor might help. "Well, were you?"

"What?"

"Attracted?"

Savannah huffed. "Can't you be serious? Trust me. It's better we part ways now."

"Savannah, I was—"

She pivoted, stalked to the exit, and cast him a glance over her shoulder. "Bye, Geoff."

When the door slammed behind her, he felt it in his heart. Love. But she spoke truth. He couldn't get involved in another relationship with a woman who refused to put God first. Even before seeing those pictures, he fought the intense temptation to think carnal thoughts. If they got married, how could he trust her not to cheat? Holding on to those messages could only mean nostalgia for the lifestyle.

He'd leave her good and alone. Things would work out better that way. He squeezed his teeth together and drew in a deep breath. Bad as it hurt.

Time to find this dollhouse and move on with his life.

Grateful for the suitcase she'd left in her trunk, Savannah signaled right out of the hospital lot and merged straight onto the Interstate. Virginia or bust.

She found conviction in the lyrics of every Bob Seger song on the CD Adam made for her. Yes, she was a beautiful loser. She, too, had been a guest who stayed too long and needed to leave.

Where could she go? Anywhere but Chicago and anywhere but Dreyfus.

Yawns overtook her, and she got a room at a hotel overlooking the Kanawa River. When she'd settled in, she curled up on the bed and tore the remaining seals from Frank's journal.

She skimmed the descriptions of the family she never knew. Words she'd waited to hear her entire life, now dribble on Frank's pages. Levi Smith, Carrie's husband—her father, had been a civil engineer. He'd studied at the University of Kentucky and worked for the Transportation Cabinet. Frank included several pictures of him in various colored hardhats, standing beside bridges in different stages of completion. Bridges she'd driven across many times in her life. Why had he chosen to burn bridges with her?

Frank painted her mother as a gifted musician. Carrie dreamed of studying at Juilliard, until Herb Spencer made sure it would never happen. Instead, she'd gone back to school later in life and become an accountant. She'd spent years in therapy. Long after taking Savannah's brother, Brent, to Virginia and leaving Savannah, a crying infant at the steps of the church, Carrie found peace performing in the orchestra of a Richmond theater.

Savannah's chest tightened. Why hadn't Carrie made peace with her? She flipped the page.

Pictures of a sedan twisted beneath a semi filled the entire space, captured in a black and white sheen with a few colored enhancements. Had Frank taken them? Red blood oozed from Levi's monochrome forehead as he slumped against the windshield. Carrie's outstretched arms splayed across the crunched hood, her body draped like a ragdoll over the broken windshield.

Savannah blinked her dry eyes. She pressed her left fist against her heart and imagined she could reach inside herself and pinch. Then she could feel something—anything. She jerked the right page to the left, ripping the last sticker in two.

What? A page of scribbles? Frank had a twisted sense of humor, for sure. He'd left no words, only penciled lines intersecting in odd, comb-like formations. Another map? Tunnels? Walking paths? Was the journal incomplete? There had to be more.

She snapped pictures of the scribbles. She should text them to Geoff. Would he even talk to her?

Adam's smirking face popped up on her screen, naked on his motorcycle. Enough. She jabbed her pointer finger at the phone, tapping the letters one at a time.

"Stop... texting... me." Her lungs filled with regret, and she blew it out hard. Tomorrow, she'd figure out how to block him.

She tossed her phone on the bed and dug through her bag for Carrie's Bible. Since Kathy had given it to her at the Dreyfus Bank, it had been dead weight. Maybe she'd find answers there.

Fragmented pieces of leather fused the spine, and the paper had stiffened. Every page contained underlined and circled phrases and notes from sermons. Every page.

Salty tears rolled over her lips. She devoured her mother's notes on peace and forgiveness, on how Christ's blood covered all sins. Same words Geoff insisted she hear. When she could read no more, she turned to the front, where the red tassel of a bookmark hung over the worn leather. A paper, folded in fourths, nestled in the crease.

She opened it, tears assaulting her. The penmanship nearly matched hers.

> *Frank,*
>
> *Levi and I will meet you in Dreyfus on Saturday. He's in agreement. I trust you've already arranged things with the adoptive parents. We agree if they do not keep her in their custody, we will take her into our home. It's time to make things right, as I should have done back then.*
>
> *See you in a few days.*
>
> *Carrie*

Hands trembling, Savannah lowered the letter to the crumpled bedspread. Her mother planned to pursue custody? At the time she'd missed her most. Why hadn't Phil and Rose mentioned it? Had Carrie not wanted to give her up in the first place?

If only she could talk to someone. She needed Geoff.

No.

She needed God.

Sliding off the bed, she dropped to her knees and clutched her mother's Bible behind folded arms. She sucked in a deep breath and rested her forehead against the velvet bedspread. The mustiness caught in her nostrils, and she sneezed.

"God... um..." She sucked on her upper lip. It had been so long since she'd uttered a true, deep prayer. If she'd ever. "Dear Lord..."

The Bible slipped to the paisley carpet.

"God, please help me be the kind of woman Geoff deserves. Help me overcome sin and put you first in everything."

She swallowed. "Um... I guess, Amen."

The room teetered as she returned to the bed. Why had her mother left her at the church? She found Levi's picture on the journal page, holding the scissors to cut a ribbon in front of a new tunnel. His eyes, warm and friendly, bore into hers. Had he forced Carrie to leave her? Had he even known about her birth? Did he not want her?

Carrie—had she known about Rose? Had she seen the terrible nagging and constant pressure to be perfect? Had she heard about Geoff and the humiliation? Geoff's mom and Carrie grew up as friends. Savannah, even overweight, shared distinct features with Carrie. Had his mom pieced together her identity?

What about Frank? Memories flashed of him greeting her, passing along his Teaberry gum and squeezing her arm. Loving gestures? Compensation for what she'd had to tolerate from Rose? Had he tried to help her the only way he knew how?

Her stomach gave a low, deep growl. Had she eaten today? She grabbed a pack of peanut butter crackers from her bag's side pocket. As she ripped into them, her cell dinged again.

Adam. This had to stop. How could she block his texts? A tap of her phone opened the browser, and a few pecks gave the answer.

Click the contact app and scroll all the way to the bottom. Block the caller. Easy-peasy.

She deleted picture after picture, her tears wetting the screen. There. She'd cut Adam from her life forever. Would it be enough for Geoff to believe she could be trusted?

Chapter Thirty-Two

Geoff sat with Ryan Chambers at his mother's solid oak dining room table, studying Savannah's notes from the legal pad she'd left at the hospital. Around him, red-and-white striped wallpaper peeled away from the drywall, and cobwebs decorated every corner. Maria had been right. The place felt more like a haunted house than a home.

She'd begged to redecorate, and he'd protected his family heirlooms with fierce resistance. He should have let her. He could have found what Frank had hidden much earlier and saved Savannah the pain of it all.

He lifted another leather-bound notebook from the pile Savannah's attorney had brought. "I wish she'd waited and let us make a copy of her journal before she left. My guess is all the clues to the dollhouse are there."

Ryan marked a dot on the topography map in front of him. "We'll find it. There's not a ton of ground to cover here. The years of exposure have surely left part of it uncovered. I have friends who might pull strings with equipment."

Vibrations from Geoff's cell surged through the table. Savannah? He eyed the screen and answered it on speaker. "Hello, Mona."

Ryan raised his brow.

She huffed. "Where are you? You sound like you're in a tunnel."

Geoff pushed the pictures aside and moved Savannah's legal pad within reach. "Working out on the farm. I guess you've talked to Cindy."

He could hear Mona's sneer through the phone. "Stay out of this. It's not your business."

Ryan pointed to the map.

Geoff nodded. "Where is Herb's dollhouse?"

Silence.

He drummed his fingers on the table. "Where is David? My brother."

More silence.

"Mona, please. Talk to me." A spider dropped from overhead, landing on Geoff's left boot. He scraped across it with the right one, sending the spider scurrying across the 1970s carpet. Mona was like the spider. Scared. He scratched his chin. "Look, we know Herb did terrible things to Cindy, Mom, and Savannah's mom. Even to you. Ryan wants to talk. He's not going to arrest you. We want to find the dollhouse and put all this negativity behind us for good. Then we can move on with our lives."

She ended the call.

Geoff dialed back, but no answer. "Can you trace it?"

Ryan reached for his cell. "We can try. If she's close, her phone should be pinging cell towers." He glanced at the screen. "Nathan texted. He and your crew have started on barn numbers three and four. Still haven't found anything but junk. I've sent a Michigan deputy to try to talk to Cindy, but she's disappeared, too."

"She could be out on the lake." Geoff unsnapped the Velcro fastener and opened the journal. More family pictures. This time of a man whose profile identically matched Savannah. Possibly her brother. Nothing of use in finding the dollhouse.

"I'm going to call the station and get Maria's accident file faxed here. I'm starting to wonder if Mona was more than a victim. What if she befriended the girls and helped Herb lure them? If Cindy's right and he held them captive for days, he would have needed help. I can't picture any man handling two births at the same time, not even your great-grandfather."

Geoff eyed Savannah's flowing scrawl, then flicked his gaze across the room to the oak curio cabinet and the cameras sitting on a quarter inch of dust. "I think Frank has all this documented on an undeveloped film. If we can find it. And if it's not too old."

"There's nothing in the cabinet?"

"Not that I've seen. You're welcome to check it, but most are relics with no film." He stood. "I'm going to go help Zach with the search."

Ryan walked over and picked up one of the old cameras. He held it overhead then set it back on the shelf. "Okay. I'll hang around here and go over the accident report, and I'll be out later."

Geoff drove to the rear side of the farm. The ground had solidified since the last rain, and he jostled through the deep grooves along the dirt road. All these barns—so much neglect. He'd let the back be overtaken with growth. After all, his father had done the same. Had he known of Herb's atrocities? Had they been involved, too, and kept it hidden?

Not finding Zach, Geoff sent him a quick text and stopped at his Nana Jean's vacant house. She'd always been protective of the cameras. Now, knowing they belonged to Frank, it felt odd. Had she been close to him? Had she known about any of this?

He brushed away cobwebs and stepped through the chipped doorframe, into the wood-paneled entry. Mud had collected around the threshold.

"Hey, Nana." He crossed into the living room and straightened a picture hanging cockeyed from a loose nail.

Guided by his flashlight, he inspected the kitchen. Nana Jean's copper pots still dangled from nails around the hood of the stove. Grit had collected in grooves of the seventies linoleum and the dishes felt sticky from dust. Dead insects crunched beneath his boots.

In the den, an old school, boxy television occupied a crate, the two antenna rods still tuned exactly thirty-eight degrees apart, as his grandfather had insisted. Nana Jean never watched TV. This room hadn't been touched since his grandfather died.

Or, had it? A Crystal soda can set on the coffee table in front of the TV, a product marketed in the early nineties, after Nana Jean died. Had Frank lived in the house? Someone had been there. How had Herb not known?

Geoff traced the edges of a hole where the drywall crumbled. No way could he salvage the place. He'd have to tear the whole house down and build a new one from scratch. Savannah wouldn't want that, even though she'd already said it would be fine. She'd want him gone. He kicked at the foot of a chair.

Zach's truck rattled in the drive, and Geoff went out to meet him.

"Dude. I've been looking all over for you. You owe me. Your great-grandfather was a total slob. Didn't anybody ever clean anything up around here?"

Geoff eyed the tips of the barns over the horizon. "Apparently not. Have you found anything?"

Zach shrugged. "Lots of old equipment. Antique tractors and old yokes. I bet we could sell it to Mr. Sullivan for a ton of cash and put it all in the scholarship fund." He held up blackened hands. "And tons of trash. I don't think Herb ever threw anything away."

"Yeah." Geoff broke a chunk of mud off the caked-over gutter. "Dad said he'd piddle in one barn until he filled it with junk and build another. Reminds me of this guy in the Bible."

Zach paused at the crooked screen door, inspected the screws, and entered the house. "This place is a tomb."

Geoff followed him, a loose floorboard springing under his feet. "Yeah. Have a look in the den. See anything odd?"

Zach walked to the TV, wrinkled his nose, and sneezed. "There's an old newspaper from the Gulf war. I don't see anything."

"Right. The newspaper. Nana Jean died in 1989, and this house has been empty ever since then." Geoff pointed to the soda. "And that can. Remember the commercial?"

Zach lunged for it.

"Wait. Don't touch anything. I'll have Ryan print it so we can see if it belonged to someone besides Frank."

Geoff left the den and started upstairs, creaks accompanying his paces. At the top, he eyed a bulging wet spot in the floor, and lifted his gaze to the swollen, dripping ceiling. Shoulders slumped, he lumbered back to the first level. "The upper floor is compromised. Looks like a bad leak from the roof."

"We can build a support." Zach brushed a thick layer of dust from the stairwell base.

"Message Cole. He said we had plenty beams left over at the construction site." Geoff wandered around the kitchen, his flashlight beam falling on a bag of leftover trash. The food, long since decayed, emitted a faded bitter odor. He focused the beam. Petrified chicken bones and a lump that might have been a roll in a box from the old Druther's Restaurant, which closed in 1992.

Geoff found the cellar key hanging outside by the back door. He jiggled the rusty metal in the lock and tugged hard to swing the dry-rotted wood on its hinges. Inside, plywood boards sported layer upon layer of newspapers. An odd pattern of circled words and connecting lines obscured each page. Definitely Frank.

How? And why?

"Thanks, Peter. I'll drop by your office and sign the paperwork when I get back." Savannah ended the call and tore Frank's list of financial restrictions to shreds. The money he'd promised—hers at last, to spend however she wished.

She could buy anything—new clothes, new shoes, new house. But helping Eli made her hungry to do more. Geoff had been so worried about his charities and the scholarship fund. No way would she let a silly deed stand in his way.

She smiled all the way to Richmond. Geoff was right. Service made all the difference. She couldn't share her life with him, but she could share her money.

"Take exit 181 to North Parham Road." The sultry woman's voice on her GPS gave her shivers. So close now. All this time, and finally she would meet the one person who could give her legitimate answers.

Merging onto a road lined with trees, she scanned the horizon for a place to pull over and call her brother. She'd grab a diet soda. Nothing surfaced. No McDonald's or anything. She drove past a bank and a large church, keeping her eyes peeled for the next road.

Her entire body shook, her hands struggling to keep their grip on the slick leather steering wheel. She glanced to her right, out the passenger window, meeting the friendly wave of a woman standing alongside a white picket fence. Casting the woman a nervous smile, she focused her attention on the road.

The radio announcer's voice cut off a commercial to tell her the next song would be Bob Seger. No. She couldn't stand the thought of her old life. Not now. Not when her future stood only miles away. She tapped the seek button on the dash, grimacing at the notes of a country song—one she and Geoff had danced to at Georgia's. Could she get no mercy?

Finally, she came upon a gas station and pulled into the parking lot to make the call.

The phones connected on the first ring. "Hello? Brent?"

She frowned when his end went to voicemail. "This is Savannah. Your sister. I'm in Richmond, close to your house. Frank said…"

A beep. Did she want to rerecord? Sighing, she pressed one to send and snaked through traffic to the main road.

She passed the McDonald's she'd hoped to find. The trees obscured even it. Maybe she didn't need a diet soda after all.

A few miles later, she made a couple of turns to Brent's street and parked in front of the two-story red brick home where her

273

mother had raised him. Her vision blurred. She blinked twice and stepped out of the car, planting her feet next to a fence overtaken by vines. White trim and columns framed a bright red door. Rose bushes sprouted from several different places in the lawn.

The hairs on her arm stood on end as she strolled up the walk and tapped the doorbell. Footsteps thudded on the other side, and the lock thwacked as the deadbolt released.

"Can I help you?" The tall blond took a step backward. "Savannah."

"Brent? I tried to call..." The tears she'd been holding back spilled. Her knees knocked, and when he reached for her hand, she nearly fell into him.

"You look like Mom. Beautiful." His smile softened the sharpness of his chiseled chin and pointed nose, features they didn't share.

"Thanks." Savannah's chest tightened. Her mother had stood in this hall. She'd slept under this roof.

"We've had the guest bedroom ready for a while. From what Frank told me, I expected you earlier." He gestured to the staircase behind him. "Let's take your bags up, and then we can visit."

"Okay." She inwardly cringed. All this time waiting, and she could only manage one-and two-syllable words.

Her cell buzzed. The device slipped from her grasp. When Brent caught it, his eyes widened.

A picture of her scantily dressed had popped up on the screen, her face frozen in horror, bound to a large wrought-iron bed. Adam? She'd never posed like that. Had he photoshopped it? Did the block not work? No, wait. Carrie? "Oh, no. I need to call the police."

"Why?" Brent's jaw clenched. "Who sent this? Is it Mom?"

"I don't know." She dropped to cushioned bench in the entry. "I have to text Geoff, so he can let the Dreyfus police know about this."

Carrie's long brown hair matched the shade of hers exactly, and the freckled face, twisted into a scream, could have been her own. Who sent it?

"Geoff? Husband or boyfriend?"

"It's complicated." The phone buzzed again. Tension pulsed through every muscle in her body. *Like mother, like daughter. Come home, Pandora.*

Savannah trembled, stumbling forward. Brent helped her to a linen chair in a pristine beige sitting room.

The creases in his brow had deepened. "What's wrong? All Frank said was I had a sister, and you'd be coming to visit. He said Mom abandoned a baby, and Dad moved her here."

"Oh." Savannah gripped the chair arm, the stiff stitches scratching her fingers. "It's a long story. She… our mom…" How much should she tell him? Veins bulged in his neck. "I'll call the Dreyfus police. They're already working the case."

A perky blonde rushed around the corner, dusted in white powder. "I'm so sorry for my rudeness, but I'd decided to try out a new recipe for Brent tonight." She offered a sheepish grin then frowned when she made eye contact with Savannah. "I'm afraid I'm not managing well."

Brent gave a stiff laugh and kissed the top of the blonde's head. "Savannah, this is my wife, Emily."

Metal clanged in the distance. "Oh, no!" Emily took off running down the hall.

"We can always go out," Brent called after her.

"It's under control!"

"I don't want to alarm Emily. Let me get you settled and I'll make those calls."

"And then, you can tell me about Mom and Dad."

"He…" Brent furrowed his brow. "Dad was a politician. You know, I—"

"What?" Savannah braced against the doorjamb.

"Well, Frank said you belonged to Mom. But he didn't say anything about Dad. I thought she might have abandoned you because you weren't his."

"No." Her purse slipped off her shoulder to the floor, and she dropped after it. "Are you serious?"

"Later, I asked him. He said Levi is not your father."

Her words came out a whisper. "If he's not, then who is?"

"Frank wouldn't say."

Chapter Thirty-Three

Geoff propped himself with the tamper as Zach and Phil eased the fence post into the rain-soaked ground. "Glad you're helping, Phil. I might as well sell that bull to the neighbors."

Zach laughed. "Think he's cheating on you, eh?"

Phil gave him an awkward glance, and Geoff cleared his throat. "Zach, why don't you go back to searching barns? We've got this." A drop of sweat rolled down Geoff's forehead. As he lifted his forearm to wipe it off, his cell rang. He rested the tamper against the fence and brushed dirt off his hands before answering. "It's Savannah."

A deep crease formed in Phil's brow.

Geoff swiped the screen to answer, greeted by sobs instead of her voice. "Savannah? What's wrong?"

"We made a big mistake."

He glanced at the clouds. What now? "A mistake?"

"Kissing you... it was... we shouldn't have." More sobs.

"I..." Drawing a nervous look from Phil, he walked a few feet away and inspected a rusty nail in another part of the fence. "Wait a minute. Start from the beginning."

"Levi..." She gasped for breath. "Levi is not... my father."

Phil stepped closer. "Is she okay?"

Geoff shook his head. Please, Lord, no. "Levi is not your father. Do you know who is?"

Grasping the tamper, Phil clenched his teeth as if it might disguise their chattering.

Sniffles resonated through the speaker. "I think...Herb."

Geoff's chest tightened. He kicked mud off a fencepost. "Herb can't be your father."

"It would explain Carrie giving me away." She sniffled and took another deep breath. "Why she ran."

He grimaced. It made sense to him, too. Carrie could have kept the pregnancy a secret and given her up when she delivered. Still... "You can't make assumptions."

Although, what other possibility existed? If he dated Savannah, he'd be dating his... what? The equivalent of a grandmother? Was it possible? Surely not.

Savannah dropped to the floor as Brent freed the phone from her fingers and switched it to speaker.

"This is Brent Smith, Savannah's brother. Are you her boyfriend?"

"It's complicated." Geoff cleared his throat. "I'll come get her."

Savannah whimpered as she sucked in a breath.

"Hey." Geoff's deep baritone shook her. "Listen, don't get upset until we know for sure. There has to be another explanation."

Brent laid a light hand on her shoulder. "I can drive her home. I need to give my boss a heads up, but we could leave tomorrow."

"Might be better. Has she told you about her danger? She's going to need protection from my aunt."

"She got a threatening picture in a text a few minutes ago. We started to call the police, and then all this happened."

"Hey. Ryan will track down whoever messaged you. He tells me it's easy to find someone who's using a cell. Let Brent bring you home, okay?" Geoff spoke in a soft tone, but each syllable ended with a crisp pause. "Hang in there, and I'll call you later."

"I... bye." She'd come close to blurting unfathomable words. She didn't know the point where she had started to love him, but now she couldn't picture life without him. She'd hoped he would eventually forgive her. If Herb ended up being her father, she had no hope.

"You okay?" Brent knelt beside her.

"I need to rest a while."

He led her to a guest bedroom, and she lost herself under a blanket.

A couple of times, Brent interrupted her sleep, offering food. Savannah couldn't make herself emerge from her velour cocoon. In her waking moments, she cried until she had no more tears. In her sleeping ones, nightmares assaulted her.

"Hey, Savannah? If you still want me to drive you back to Dreyfus, we can leave in an hour or so. We'd arrive around three in the morning, but I don't mind driving overnight."

Savannah sat up, steadying herself against the cherry sleigh-style headboard. "What time is it? What day is it?"

Brent chuckled. "You looked exhausted. We let you sleep on through the night and all of today." He handed her a couple towels. "You can shower if you want. It's two doors down on the right."

"Okay." She gave a drawn out yawn and planted her feet on the cool hardwood. She dug through her suitcase for her toiletry bag as Brent backed out of the room.

After dressing in jeans and a floral V-neck tee, she met Brent and Emily on the front porch. "Thanks for your hospitality. I'm sorry I haven't been much of a guest."

Emily smiled, rocking the wrought-iron swing with her toes. "It's fine. You've been through a rough patch. We're glad to be here to help." She kissed Brent on the cheek. "Love you. Be careful, sweetheart."

"I will, babe. Love you."

Emily disappeared into the house as Brent loaded two suitcases into the Prius trunk.

Savannah handed him her bags, and he stuffed them in as well before taking the driver's seat.

"Tell me about Carrie." Savannah slid into the passenger side and stretched so her toes brushed the edge of the floorboard.

Brent started the car and switched the station to a classical one. Rich, perky music featuring a violin drifted through the speakers. "Picture this. All day, every day. When home, she played. Continuous torture."

"Frank wrote about her musical brilliance." Savannah glanced at the pack of legal pads she'd bought at a drug store on the way to Virginia. Should she document as he talked? It felt wrong. "When did she get custody of you?"

Brent found a country station and turned the speakers down a few notches. "I don't know. She left me in foster care for several years. I think in 1986, a year after Mom married Levi. Frank gave me pictures he'd taken at my kindergarten graduation."

"So, the next year she conceived me." Savannah removed the plastic from the legal pads. "I have to write all this in my notebook. I'd never remember."

Brent laughed. "You're so much like her."

"When did you meet Frank?"

While signaling to turn left out of the subdivision, Brent squinted and looked both ways. "Somewhere around 1998, I think. He showed up at my high school graduation, too, and college." Brent frowned. "Mom and Levi didn't get to attend the college one."

Tears stung Savannah's eyes. "Frank left me a picture he'd taken at the accident."

"Yeah." Brent's knuckles whitened on the steering wheel. A vein in his neck throbbed. "It happened in Dreyfus, you know."

"Yeah." Savannah drew in a deep breath. "When they came for me."

In the awkward silence, she studied Brent's profile and then examined her reflection in the visor mirror. He and Geoff looked enough alike to be cousins. She, on the other hand, had a smaller, daintier nose, and a softer jawline, exactly like Carrie.

She cleared her throat. "Did you happen to have Frank's address? I don't even know where he lived in Dreyfus."

Brent nodded and handed her his cell. "It's in my contacts list. He left me the house in his will. I'm going to sell it, but you can stay there a while if you want."

"No kidding." She tapped the screen and found Frank's name. "State Street? Right next to church."

"He said he bought the house in 1993, but he's done major renovations in the last five years. New cabinets and everything. I think he hoped I'd move back to Dreyfus."

Savannah frowned. "Hmm. The year they moved into the new church building. Close to my sixth birthday. He showed me a picture of him giving me a piece of Teaberry gum taken around the same time."

The memory focused in her mind. Frank hadn't disappeared. She'd known all along in her heart. Surely, Herb had, too. So, why had he left Frank alone? Why didn't Frank go after his property then?

Savannah yawned and nestled in the passenger seat.

"Sleep if you want. I can tell you're still exhausted." Brent reached into the back seat for his jacket. He handed it to her, and she spread it over her shoulders. "I'll be fine. I'll get you up when we stop."

"Okay."

She slept most of the trip, waking once for a pit stop, and again when they passed Lexington. She sat up and stretched. "We're already in Kentucky?"

"Yeah." Brent pointed to the rolling hills on the horizon, where the trees had become shadows against the setting sun. "It's beautiful here."

"It is." She checked her phone. "Geoff said go on to the police station, and they'd meet us there."

"Will do." Brent glanced at her through the rearview mirror. "I wish I could tell you more about your history. All I know is we lived in Dreyfus until your birth, but Mom and Dad never talked about it."

Savannah scrolled through her phone at the pictures of journal snippets Geoff had sent her. "According to Frank, they were both too intellectual for their neighbors. He wrote even though she didn't have a college degree at the time, she was well-spoken and loved science and math."

"Sounds like Mom." Brent laughed. "Yeah, you might say they had high expectations when I attended school."

"Slow down," she said. "The old hospital used to be right there. The new one is across town and three stories taller. Now this one is a church-sponsored school for migrant children." Tears filled her eyes. "Geoff helped them remodel it."

"Remind me about the turn. We're close now, aren't we?"

"Not yet." She nodded to a narrow road bypassing the downtown shops, along their rear entrances. "This is a shortcut. It's winding, but it comes out right by the station."

She tried not to cringe as Brent jerked the car wide to make the turn. He dipped off the road, leaving a trail of gravel and dust. Blue lights flashed in the mirror.

"Great." Savannah grimaced as both cars slowed to a halt.

Brent pulled his license out of his wallet as the tall officer with salt-and-pepper hair walked up and tapped the glass. Brent flashed a TV-personality grin and rolled down the window. "Hello, sir. I apologize for my sharp turn. I'm not from around here, and I was confused."

Savannah shivered as Avery Kaler traced his finger along the edge of the car window then brushed dust off his finger with his thumb.

"I see you've found Pandora." He leaned across Brent and into the car. "I take it you're back to cause more trouble."

She straightened, thankful the darkness hid her trembling hands. "I want to go home."

"I thought you dated the Spencer boy." Kaler's upturned lips seemed as though they might pop off his face as his mouth stretched from cheek to cheek. "I'm going to have to search your car."

"Why?" She glared.

Brent stepped out and folded muscular arms across his chest. "Search it if you want. We have nothing to hide."

Savannah got out as well, holding her breath as Kaler rummaged through the glove box. Brent came to her and put his arms around her shoulders. "We haven't done anything wrong, Savannah. What can he possibly find in your car?"

"There's nothing." She clung to her purse, the journal poking out of the side pocket.

Kaler searched the floorboards, whistling a strange tune.

She tried to figure out the notes—F? Next, a sharp F, a G and G sharp—it hit her. The gibberish at the top corner of Frank's map. The letters flashed through her mind, FFGGBCCCGGFC, and she could clearly hear it. She had no doubt. Kaler whistled the same tune.

She'd heard him hum once before, in middle school. He'd harassed a group of kids at a baseball game and walked away with a smirk. Identical notes. She shook in earnest.

Brent clutched her hand. "Officer, my sister is not well. Please, if you don't mind, can I take her home?"

"Sister?" Kaler aligned his Glock with Brent's skull.

283

"Leave us alone." Brent lunged sideways, knocking the gun through the car window.

Kaler wrapped his arm around Brent's neck as she raced to the passenger side. Within seconds, Brent slid to the ground.

Savannah fumbled with the door handle, lifting it as Kaler stuck his hand inside the window and locked it.

She dove toward a ditch and winced as gravel scraped into her cheek. Trickles of blood dripped onto her jeans.

Kaler planted a boot against her back when she tried to stand. "Stay quiet, and your friend might stay alive."

"My brother."

"Carrie's brat. I should have known."

"Geoff knows I'm in town. He's waiting for me."

Kaler jerked her arms behind her back and cuffed them. He swept her up and dumped her into the back seat of his cruiser. After a few seconds of shuffling in his pocket, he retrieved a tiny white pill and forced it in her mouth.

Savannah bit at his finger and tried to push out the pill with her tongue, but most of it dissolved before she could spit.

He pointed to the dumpsters behind a crumbling building, the shell of an old pizza restaurant. "I need to hide the car. Where are your keys?"

"I don't have them." She scooted to the other side of the car as he lurched closer, snagging her right arm with another set of cuffs.

He twisted her body sideways and hooked the cuffs around a metal bar. After slamming the cruiser door, he popped the lock on the Prius, and retrieved his gun.

Brent stirred on the ground. Her heart sank as Kaler forced him into her car at gunpoint. They drove behind an abandoned pizza restaurant to a parking lot surrounded by thick forest.

The ground shook as a train rattled the old, rusty tracks. The metallic grind of its wheels reduced a single gunshot to a soft pop.

She choked on her sobs, coughing as she tried to turn her contorted body. A stream of tears dampened her cheeks, and she tried to wipe them on her shoulder. She'd just found Brent. Why did Kaler have to take him away now?

Carrie. The one word played on a loop in her mind. The sick excuse for an officer had called her mother by name. What else did he know?

Long minutes passed before Kaler's shadowy form emerged in the streetlights range glow. As he approached the car, she gritted her teeth. How could she stall enough to give Geoff a chance to find her?

"Solved that problem."

"I haaaate you." Savannah shivered, her words slurring. She fought for clarity as confusion overtook her consciousness.

Kaler's tires spun gravel as he pulled onto the narrow road in the opposite direction from where she'd come. He made several turns, ending up on a dark country road she'd never seen. Double images of his smirk overlapped in the rearview mirror.

He swung the car left, onto a gravel road, and they disappeared between thick trees. After a couple miles, he parked inside an old barn. "Pandora, your dollhouse waits."

Savannah tried to frown, though she felt no control of her facial muscles. "Where are we?" Was the dollhouse not on Geoff's property? "Please, don't kill me."

She fought the cuffs. If only she could use her cell! She had to tell Geoff.

"You worry too much." Kaler closed the barn door. The dim moonlight converged into a tiny sliver, leaving only the interior light from the patrol car. "I'm not going to hurt you, Dora. What kind of monster would hurt his daughter?"

Bile built in Savannah's throat. His daughter? "I don't believe you." But she did. She stumbled out of the car and pawed at the ground. She needed to stand. "Are you the one who gave me the wretched name?"

"Mona did." He snorted. "She thought it fitting for the situation. The little Pandora's Box made Herb give up his hobby. Levi felt certain Herb was your father."

He whistled the tune again, and she swung at him, crashing—no, melting—into the ground at his feet. Kneeling beside her, he planted a wet kiss on her cheek.

Her stomach churned, but her resolve strengthened. She'd be the Pandora who put a stop to him, too.

Chapter Thirty-Four

When Savannah opened her eyes, the beautiful canopy from Frank's pictures hung above her, and the thick damask curtains draped the wall. Perhaps it would have even been comfortable, had she not been tied to the bed.

The fog had yet to lift from her brain. Where was Brent? How long had she been here?

Tightness claimed her chest as she remembered the gun shot and Kaler's smugness when he promised her brother had breathed his last. She gurgled, a sob catching in her throat. *Poor Emily.*

Sweet vanilla tobacco filled the room.

Her clothes lay in a neat, folded pile on the nightstand, and soft silk caressed her skin, the hem falling way past her knees. A slide show appeared on the wall in front of her, from a modern projector, depicting college-aged girls in various states of trauma and undress. Gasping, she averted her gaze to the other side of the bed, where Kaler smoked a cigar in a high-backed chair.

"Hello, princess." His tone, eerie-yet-gentle, came out pitches lower than normal. "Daddy is here."

Daddy? He oozed insanity. She tugged at her hands, causing the old bed to squeak while he covered her forehead with a headband made from thorny vines. She strained her bonds to lift her arms and knocked it to the floor.

"Oh no, Dora." Kaler shoved the band back on her head so hard the bristly vines dug into her flesh. "Don't lose your tiara, princess. I went to a lot of trouble to make it for you."

287

"You're insane." She mashed her body against the mattress as if she could melt into it. With her crossed wrists, she picked up a pillow and moved it in front of her face. Holding her breath, she peeked over the lacy trim.

Kaler used a remote control to switch to another set of pictures, depicting him much younger, taunting three teenaged women tied back to back on the same bed. Cindy, Geoff's mother, and her own.

"Beautiful Carrie...she didn't compare to you." Kaler advanced the pictures to ones featuring her mother. "It's a shame she died before I had a chance to love her again."

Savannah gasped. Even in her terrified state, Carrie's exquisite face resembled porcelain. Brent had been right. She and her mother could have been twins.

Though the gruesome, heinous display nauseated her, she kept her eyes trained on the only pictures she had ever seen of the woman. Frank's photography notes nagged at her. Had he taken these pictures?

Kaler sat on the edge of the bed, leaning closer as she inched away. He slid his fingers under her spaghetti straps, easing one off her shoulders.

She writhed. "Don't touch me."

He pulled a roll of duct tape out of the nightstand drawer. Then he removed his boot and pointed to his sweaty sock. "You can chew on this, or you can be quiet. Your choice."

Savannah gagged. She closed her eyes. Think! Think of anything else. Happy thoughts.

As she balled her fists, relief swept over her. If Kaler was her father, Herb wasn't. Things could work out with Geoff after all. If she could only make it out of this alive and tell him. If only he would forgive her.

A sharp prick struck her neck. She blinked. Kaler tapped her nose with a switchblade. "Don't close your eyes."

Her repressed bile surged forward, and she felt a crazy urge to laugh as she covered him in her vomit.

He snarled, retrieved a needle from the nightstand drawer, and jabbed the syringe through the green silk into her thigh. While he paced, the drug rendered her paralyzed. And alert. She could only watch as he unbound and uncuffed her arms and carried her to a claw foot bathtub opposite the bed. He dropped her on the floor and tore the sheets from the mattress.

Pacing, he opened and closed various drawers, tossing new bedding and silk garments in a pile. "Why did you have to ruin the green one?"

Savannah tried to move her lips, but no words came. Within minutes, she sensed the paralysis fading, but remained completely still. If he thought the drugs still clouded her mind, she could find a way to escape.

"Avery!" Mona's shrill voice sent chills down her spine as he dumped her into the tub, gown and all.

He cranked the cast-iron handle of an antique water pump. A few frigid drops landed on her feet.

Mona shoved him against the wall. "Are you out of your mind?"

"Would you deny me what I've dreamed of for decades?" He lunged, driving Mona across the room.

"She's not Carrie." Her slap resonated through the basement. "We need to get out of here, you idiot. Do you want to get caught? Here, move, and I'll clean her."

Mona pumped two inches of the frigid water over Savannah's convulsing body and scrubbed her with a hard-bristled brush.

"Please. Once more. For old time's sake." Kaler's lower lip jutted forward.

Shrugging, Mona met Savannah's stare. "You have an hour. Then this place will burn. With or without you."

Savannah's mind raced. After making the connection between Kaler's whistle and the map, she knew exactly where the dollhouse rested in relation to the edge of the farm—on a piece of land nestled between the old church and Geoff's property. The entrance was on a different farm, across the access road. They'd never find her in time.

If she could figure out where Kaler put her phone... if she'd have service.

Kaler's cell rang, and he answered with a gruff hello.

She hid her smile. He had service. Her cell would work, too. If she could find it.

He listened for a moment. "I'll be there in a few minutes." He approached her, and she shrunk, her bared shoulder rubbing against the dead spider.

"I'm sorry I scare you, dear." He traced her forearm with his fingers. "I wish it didn't have to be this way."

"Get me... out of here.... Save me." She swallowed. "We could go... Chicago... together."

"Princess." His raspy voice sounded desperate. "I wish I could. I need you to take care of me—to heal my wounds. The loss of your mother."

"You can." She blinked, her stomach lurching. "Daddy... leave everything... stop Mona.... Let's go to Chicago."

Kaler stroked her cheek. "You're right. I've wanted to kill her for years, anyway."

He returned to the nightstand drawer and tossed her the folded clothes. Her cell clattered to the floor, and he kicked it under the bed. A few more paces, and he paused at the door to the stairs. "I'll be back for you soon."

"Okay." Fighting shivers, Savannah hurriedly changed and fished for her phone. No service. No time to cry. There had to be a way to escape.

She scanned the room. All Frank's clues. Compassion and forgiveness. Pain and misery. What had he been trying to tell her?

To trust God? She lifted her gaze to the ceiling, and stenciled words above the headboard snagged her attention. The verse—the passage from the Birmingham Civil Rights Institute Geoff read from the Bible. *You will go out in joy and be led forth in peace; the mountains and hills will burst into song before you, and all the trees of the field will clap their hands.*

It fit the setting. Where, Frank? Where could she go out in joy?

Savannah tapped her thumb against three fingers on her left hand. The slavery, the maps, the weird lined pattern in the journal… The Underground Railroad? "Secret passages!"

Her quavering voice filled the entire space. She glanced over her shoulder. Lord willing, Kaler would stay gone for a while.

She circled the room, lifting damask curtains from false windows—nothing but concrete blocks. She felt all over the wall, finding no openings, not even a crack. Then she faced the bed. A tiny, clear stone glinted from the middle of the headboard, below the Bible verse.

Her pulse quickened. Not a stone. A peephole?

Pivoting, she spotted the mock-fireplace where Carrie stood with Cindy and Geoff's mom in the pictures. Had they been taken from behind the wall?

She knocked on the headboard in several places, the thunder from her racing heart roaring in her ears. The headboard was fixed, and not at all hollow, though it appeared sunk into the wall.

Could it be? An opening under the bed? Behind a piece of furniture? Her eyes settled on the air vent in the corner of the room, obscured by an artificial tree at its left. Maybe…

She examined the white metal cover. The screws hung loose in their grooves, and it lifted on a hidden hinge. It caught, suspended ninety degrees from the wall. A crawlspace opened into a much lighter room, lit by a slim skylight. Was it already past dawn?

A flashlight rested against the crawlspace opening, next to a plastic box filled with D-cell batteries, all leaking acid. What were her options? To go into the dark tunnel and pray for an easy escape? To wait for Kaler or Mona to unlock the door?

What if they started the fire without coming into the room? Had they planted explosives?

She checked her phone battery. Down to 35 percent. It might provide enough light. Her jaw clenched, she poked her head into the space and planted her hands on the cool dirt floor.

She crawled into the dark chamber and set the vent back into place, then attempted a text to Ryan. Kaler took me to the dollhouse, but I've escaped. Battery low.

An error message came up on the screen. No service.

The tiny room more closely resembled a narrow hall, about ten by four feet. Thin glass windows at the ceiling added slivers of light from the main room. A high stool backed up to the wall, where someone could sit and peer through an old camera fixed to the back of the headboard. Shivers coursed through her spine as she peered into the room. No wonder Frank suffered from mental illness. Had Herb forced him to watch while he did things to his victims? Had he been a victim?

Perhaps Frank found the secret room by accident when Herb forced him to build the dollhouse. It could have been Frank's secret. At any rate, she hoped Kaler and Mona didn't know it existed.

Guided by her cell, Savannah approached a wooden door hanging on rusty hinges bolted into the stone wall. It led to another dark hall, then several others, none of them branching into paths. Brushing aside cobwebs and critters, she trekked on for an eternity.

The tunnels must have built in the 1800s. Frank discovered them and outsmarted Herb to escape.

As she turned into another chamber, a set of stairs culminated with a metal hatch. Light poked through rusted holes around its perimeter. She stood about eight feet underground. Savannah climbed up, opened the hatch, and crawled through, emerging beside the old iron furnace. Makeshift skylights provided ample luminosity, and a cast-iron fountain offered much-needed spring water. She pumped a handful and sipped, wrinkling her nose at the metallic taste. Water would have to wait.

Mona tapped a heeled toe against the concrete church porch. "Why on earth would you greet your favorite auntie with a gun?"

Geoff kept his tone even and cool. "Where's Savannah?"

She pushed past him. "Am I your girlfriend's keeper? Surely, that's your job. Why would she leave you in the first place? Has she found another man?"

He hopped to the ground and grabbed her shoulder, keeping the gun trained on her forehead. "You're insane. They've called in FBI agents with sophisticated radar devices to find underground locations. It's a matter of time before they find evidence connecting you to her disappearance."

She swatted, and he caught her arm. "You're out of time. Savannah's brother is missing; her car is missing—I talked to her a half-hour outside of Dreyfus. We've been on this for several hours."

Mona's lower lip jutted. "You're the one who is out of time. Kaler will burn her alive. I barely escaped myself."

"Not the first time you've let someone I love burn alive."

"Touché."

"Where is Kaler? Where's he hiding Savannah?" Geoff glanced at the horizon. She'd come to stall him. Savannah was close. He could feel it. "Get in the truck and take me to her."

"I can't. Avery will kill us both."

As if in punctuation, a police cruiser sped along the drive, skidding to a stop at the old church parking lot.

Mona smirked. "Here he is now."

Her shoulders slumped when Ryan Chambers stepped out of the car, running a hand over his shaved head.

"We've been looking for you, Mona Spencer." Ryan nodded to Geoff. "Got a text from Savannah. Kaler captured her, but she escaped."

A snarl distorted Mona's face, and she held out her hands. "Go ahead. Cuff me. Avery's the one you want. He's already shot her brother and left the car out by the old Milano's Pizza Parlor. He'll shoot Pandora, too."

Ryan's cell dinged. "Sorry, Mona. They've already picked him up, too."

Chapter Thirty-Five

Savannah pushed hard on the hatch, nearly stumbling when it opened. She climbed through the space, pulling herself onto a rocky, yet grassy hillside. To her left, the old iron furnace towered. Crumbled white-stone bricks lay in piles beneath falling arches. In the center of the structure, a rectangular doorway led to the inner chamber.

A few feet inside, up a thirty-degree incline, a crate of tiki torches rested. Savannah crawled into the nook and swept away cobwebs in search of matches. A box sat next to a bottle of paraffin oil, which she poured into the torch with quivering hands. Three strikes sent a blast of sulfur tickling her nostrils, and the torch burst into bright flames as she touched the match to its wick.

Light danced over a rotting wooden door and disappeared into a shadowy crack. Savannah nudged the door open wider and gripped the torch tight as she entered the chamber. Inside, remnants of history littered the planked floor. A dusty steam engine sat on a table to her right, behind a deep cemented ditch where iron must have flowed. To her left, a cot hung from two thick pipes, and several wood crates had been nailed together to fashion a makeshift desk.

A piece of silicone, like Rose used for her sewing, topped the desk. Fragments of paper scattered around where Frank had trimmed the edges of photographs, and several empty bottles of rubber cement lined the spot where the desk rested against the wall. On a close shelf, a basket hosted more bottles—chemical names, like the ones she'd deciphered from Frank's cryptogram, labeled these. A clothesline spanned from one side of the room to another, pins marking where photographs once hung.

Pictures from the dollhouse papered every wall. Herb, interacting with the girls in their makeshift costumes. A young Kaler, holding a beer and standing hugged up to Cindy next to the stone fireplace. April and Carrie, grinning ear to ear as they made provocative poses in camisole tops and bikini bottoms. All smiles and no terror. Nothing like the picture of Carrie Mona sent over the phone.

Savannah knelt beside the cot and peered below it into a cubby Frank fashioned from one of the iron-flow channels. Could it be? Answers?

She lodged the torch in a straight pipe made for holding it. The leather journal bore more wear than the one he'd given her, and fifteen more waited beneath it in identical condition. She reached it, spidery silk tickling her hand. When she brought it close to her, the musty pages triggered a chain of sneezes.

Inside the cover, Frank posed hand-in-hand with a beautiful white-haired woman. Below the picture, he'd printed, "Beloved Jean." Geoff's grandmother.

Frank dated the opposite page May 28, 1989, and filled it with his scrawl.

> *My dearest Jean,*
>
> *I watched today as they lowered your body into its final resting place, next to your husband on the hill. Where you belong. Our secret is safe. I thank you for many years of blessed companionship, and for protecting me when I couldn't protect myself. Though I'll carry on, I will miss you forever.*
>
> *Please forgive me that I could not abide by your wishes. Herb is determined to see me institutionalized. To pursue the farm would be of nothing but detriment to me. He does know, however, that I know all his secrets. He is aware I have proof, and should anything ever happen to me, there's a lockbox in the Dreyfus bank with enough evidence to prove his guilt. We are at a stalemate, I believe.*

I've made an offer on a piece of land next to the new church, and I'm planning to stay off the farm. New beginnings, right? I wish it could have been ours.

A piece of the brittle page came off in Savannah's fingers as she flipped through several other entries. Frank had made a decent income with gallery photos and wedding photography. He'd traveled all over the country in search of Eli and the other men who'd served with him.

Dearest Jean,

Another burial today, and a beautiful sunset. Who could have believed ol' Herb would outlive them all? I sit here, overlooking the funeral procession as they approach the graveyard. Only a handful of people gathered to pay their respects, and even those came only on the boy's behalf.

I've decided to file the claim for the farm. It grieves me. That boy has seen more pain than he deserves.

He has a benevolent heart, and he uses his fortune to serve others. Perhaps he'll come to understand.

All my love,

Frank

Savannah grabbed a pencil and twisted her hair into a loose bun. She wiped sweat from her nape and dropped to the crate that must have served as Frank's seat.

The last entry in the book dated July 7, 2015. Two weeks past her twenty-eighth birthday.

Dearest Jean,

I must be quick. Peter waits in the car as I grab the ledgers, and then we will go to the courthouse. We missed that dreadful Avery by minutes, but I had to come back here one last time and bid you a final goodbye. I labored to even push open the door.

My beloved Savannah could not give me her trust. I press forward with the claim to the farm, hoping she changes her mind before I succumb to illness.

If she will follow my instructions, justice will be served, and she will become the heir to the McMillan line. If not, all our secrets will be buried, and she'll receive a modest compensation.

I have lied to her, Jean. I know you would have begged me to do otherwise, but if she had not believed the family connection, I may have never convinced her to hear me. With all my heart, I wish she could have been Levi's daughter. Our lives might have ended quite differently.

Yours,

Frank

Savannah swallowed the drainage collecting in the back of her throat as she blinked away tears. She didn't belong to Frank. Though she should have realized it as soon as Kaler admitted to being her father, it felt surreal. Brent didn't belong to Frank, either, at least not in his eyes. Did that mean there were no other relatives? Cousins? Aunts or uncles? Regardless, Frank chose her—his beloved her—as the sole heir. If only he were still alive, so she could thank him.

The brittle page dampened from her tears. "Frank, I would have claimed you," she whispered to the stone wall. "I would have accepted you as a grandfather and loved you as you deserved."

With trembling hands, she drew her cell from her pocket. She'd shut it off to preserve the fragment of remaining battery. Would it be enough to send one more text?

Geoff. I'm at the furnace. Come get me.

The screen died as she pressed send.

Geoff followed Ryan through a canopy of trees along winding roads leading to the entrance of the adjacent property where the deputies spotted Kaler's cruiser. He tapped an impatient steel toe over the gas pedal, fingers tightening on the wheel. If he'd driven in front, he'd already be there.

They maneuvered through three gates, and sped down a gravel drive, coming up on a hill overlooking his farm. Geoff barely took the time to shut off the truck before racing up to the officers surrounding Kaler.

"Where is she?"

Kaler shrugged. "Find the hatch, under the floorboards."

Geoff lunged at him, but Ryan caught his sleeve. "Let's go find her." They followed another officer into the barn and searched the concrete floor for openings. "Over here." Ryan lifted a rusty metal door, revealing light from a lower room. "It's like she said. The place has electricity."

He passed Geoff a pair of gloves. "Don't touch anything. Let us know if you see something belonging to Savannah."

"Okay." Geoff followed Ryan down the steps, his breath catching. The room looked exactly as it had in the pictures. Officers descended like ants, scouring the walls for an opening. Geoff eyed a pile of silk in the corner, hands fisting, teeth grinding. If Kaler had touched her...

He walked around the bed, nearly tripping over discarded cords, and opened the nightstand drawer with the hem of his shirt, careful not to touch the handle. "Wow. Needles and drugs in here. Kaler's?"

"Could be." Ryan nodded to the projector. "Shall we look?"

"Ugh. I know. But it's necessary." Geoff reached up and switched the machine on, wincing as Carrie's tormented face appeared on the wall across from him. "Where's the computer?"

With a gloved hand, Nathan Smith traced a cable from a faux window to an armoire. "In here." In a few clicks, he advanced the slideshow to pictures of Kaler in compromising positions with unconscious girls. "Wow. Get a load of this guy. I always considered him a jerk, but… "

"You never know about people." Ryan shook his head.

Geoff crossed to the claw foot tub. He winced. Water droplets clung to its surface, and several dark brown hairs had clumped at the drain. "I think Savannah's been in this bathtub. Did she text anything else?"

"No. Her phone died. We need to find the tunnel." Nathan uncapped the lens of his camera and aimed at the computer.

"Here's the crawlspace." Ryan waved Geoff over to the artificial tree in the corner, where he'd taken off the vent cover. "But it's empty." He shined his flashlight to the opposite end. "There's a door."

Geoff peered into the opening. "What's on the wall?"

Ryan's light danced over grooves etched into the stone. "A map? That looks like the church." He pointed to a rough sketch appearing to have a steeple. "The boxy one is the iron furnace?"

"If that's right, then this tunnel appears to lead straight there. I bet she's already made it through to the other side." Geoff straightened. "I'm going to search it."

"Okay." Ryan passed through the crawlspace. "We'll text you if we find her first."

Chapter Thirty-Six

Savannah stood atop the hill while Geoff sped toward her, down the old dirt road at the rear of his property. As he drew closer, she sat on a stone bench and picked through tangles in her hair.

A crumbling brick-lined walk led to the gravel road. He parked and hiked up the incline.

"Hey." He sat next to her, wrapping her in his arms.

"Hey." She toppled into his embrace. "I would've tried to walk, but I'm dehydrated."

"Paramedics will be here soon." He stared toward a road in the distance, where a fire truck and ambulance headed their way. "When I saw the text you sent Ryan, I... I couldn't lose you.... "

"Oh, good. You did get it. I thought it never sent. I kept praying I'd get a chance to apologize again and beg your forgiveness. I'm so sorry I hurt you."

"It's forgotten." He freed a dust bunny from her hair and let it drift to the ground. "I guess you know they caught both of them."

"I saw the arrests from here. It's quite the view. Frank must have lived in this furnace. You wouldn't believe all the pictures he left."

He reached for her hand. "I'm sorry about your brother. I know you hoped he could give you answers."

Tears wet her cheeks. "Yeah. Have they called his wife? I don't even have her number. It's in the journal, I think in Kaler's cruiser. Her name's Emily."

"Ryan heard he was shot. We'll call her as soon as we can."

"So awful. All of it." She shivered. "At least I know my parents. Carrie Harman and... Avery Kaler."

Geoff's eyes widened. "You're kidding."

"So Kaler says." She dislodged the brick at her feet with her shoe as she told him about the hummed notes. Beneath it, a bronze plate rested, etched with lettering. "It makes sense. I have his nose."

"Your nose is much cuter." Geoff kissed the tip of it.

She mock-punched his arm. "You're such a goof."

"What is that?"

She kicked away another chunk of dirt. "I'm not sure. I saw a couple of other plates like it on the other side."

Kneeling, Geoff freed the bricks next to the one she'd loosened and blew away dust. "Established 1844. About the same time as the Underground Railroad. I bet that's when all the tunnels were built."

He lifted the cover, revealing a metal trunk. Inside laid a pile of pistols and short swords.

He whistled. "Look at all these old weapons."

"That pistol has to be from the Civil War era." She picked up the gun and held it flat in her palm.

"Careful. It could still be loaded." Geoff took it from her and inspected the barrel. "An old Remington. My dad would have loved it."

"Frank wrote a lot about treasure. Could these be his treasures? Old Civil War guns would bring a lot of money."

"Could be."

Sitting cross-legged on the bare dirt surrounding the path, she propped her chin with her fists. "I know there's more to his puzzle. I have to solve it. I feel like I'm missing something big."

"We found the dollhouse. It's exactly like the replica." Geoff massaged her arm as she shuddered. "What if there's something else in there?"

"Could be, but I don't want to return anytime soon." She gripped her head. "Whew. I'm dizzy."

"Well, you can rest. I'll keep looking."

"No. I want to look." She examined the furnace's old sandstone walls, badly weathered with multiple striations. "There's another tunnel here. The last page of the journal…" She glanced at her phone. If only she'd had battery left. "I think it's a network of tunnels, rather than one."

"Yeah. There's a map in the one behind the dollhouse, carved into the wall."

"I think there might be a path leading to your Nana Jean's house. Frank wrote her a journal full of love letters."

"I suspected they might have had a relationship." Geoff tugged at a loose brick, freeing it from the wall. Behind it, a cubby bore several empty whiskey bottles. "Look at these. Maybe from the 1800s, too."

They combed the furnace floor. Still nothing. Savannah, shoulders slumped, dropped to her knees. "What if I did find everything? I felt like there should be more. Like Frank had an end game other than me locating the dollhouse. He had no way of knowing Kaler would trap me there."

"Here." Geoff rubbed his palm over a heart-shaped brass knob embedded in the ground outside the furnace entrance. "Wonder why this is here?"

Savannah knelt beside it. "In the dollhouse, I saw a dresser with heart-shaped knobs. One missing." She traced the heart.

They brushed away the dust around it, finding another hatch. She tugged at the knob. No luck.. "Agh!" Her knees pressing into sharp pebbles, she doubled over and hugged herself.

"You don't have to keep being strong for me, you know."

She puffed her cheeks and padded the ground until she found a long, thin rock. "I can't cry now. I need to solve his last riddle. Can we pry it?"

"I think it has screws." He grabbed the handle with both hands. As he twisted, the heart shifted a half turn, and the rusty door popped up from its frame.

"Another tunnel! I knew it!" Tears streamed her face as the blaring sirens approached. She grimaced, reaching through spider webs to shine her light into the space. It opened to a chamber full of ceramic dishes and worn leather sandals. As she bent forward, a wave of dizziness overtook her. Geoff's strong arms enclosed around her as her world faded to black.

Two days later, Geoff tapped the doorjamb of Savannah's hospital room, holding a small cardboard box and watching her with a bemused smile. As she sat up, he strode to her bedside and handed her a silver treasure chest, engraved with organic swirls. Even tarnished, the silver piece rivaled the beauty of the two halves of her friendship heart. "Found this in the dresser drawer inside the dollhouse. The knob is the key."

"Makes perfect sense...." She traced the key's edges and eyed the box she and Geoff found at the furnace. "That Bible verse. Where your treasure is, there will your heart be also."

"Right."

She held her breath, eased the key into the hole, and exhaled when the treasure box popped open to reveal a pocket-sized notebook. As she flipped through the pages, an index card dropped. "These look like bank account numbers."

He inspected the pages. "I think it's a summary of his state of affairs, and here are phone numbers. You need to call Frank's lawyer and get an accurate list of Frank's assets. From the looks of this, it's more than you could fathom."

A folded page fell from the back of the book and dropped to her bed. "Another letter?"

Geoff leaned over her shoulder. "Looks to be."

My dearest Dora,

If you have found these words, then you have discovered all of your terrible family secrets. I am so sorry such atrocities mar your roots. Had I been a stronger man, perhaps I might have fought harder to bring justice to those girls. Had I not been such a coward, I might have let the system work as it should. I pray you'll do for me what I could never do and set all of these things right.

I'm sure you've already figured out we have no biological relation, and the birth certificate I showed you is fake. Carrie named Levi as your father, but he knew better. That's why he refused to let her keep you. The truth is she left you on the steps of that church with nothing but a blanket.

Savannah gasped. "All these years, I've thought my mother wanted me to have the heart as a memento to her. And all along, it was Frank."

I couldn't bear you having no remnants of your past, so I left you the roses and gave you half of the heart-shaped box. I dreamed of the day you'd decipher my clues and find your way back to me. Then, I could give you the life you deserved, free from the evil leading to your conception.

Carrie returned to the church on your thirteenth birthday, her heart full of guilt. She begged me to find you. I told her I already knew where to find you, and you belonged to me.

"I believe that, too." Savannah wiped away a tear with the hem of her sheet. "Frank is my family, more so than if blood joined us. He has loved me all of these years, greater even than Rose and Phil."

Geoff dragged his finger halfway down the page. "Listen to this. 'I hope within this time you've found peace with Geoff Spencer. Not only peace, but perhaps love. At the least, a friendship love to let you fulfill my wishes in unity. My dream is you'll share my fortune. I trust it to you for helping the helpless and serving others, with Geoff at your side. Perhaps you'll pass the land on to your own children. Spencer children. True heirs.'" He folded the page. "Have you found love?"

"I will share his fortune." Savannah sat straighter in the bed. "I want you to use it for your charities."

"You didn't answer my question." He reached for her hand. "You know everything is forgiven, right? We can start fresh. Have you found love?"

She sighed. "As friends, yes. But I can't—"

"I love you, Savannah, as my soul mate. Not just a friend. With all my heart, I love you. Now and forever." He bent and captured her lips in a swift kiss.

She jerked away. "I'm sorry, Geoff. I can't."

"Why not? Will you at least stay in Dreyfus? Do you want me to move out of the farmhouse so you can live there?"

"Goodness, no. I'll stay with Mom and Dad until we..." Her cheeks grew bright red. She scrunched her forehead and clutched the sheets, tugging them close to her neckline. "I think I want to open an exercise studio. I'd like to work with young girls and teach them to embrace inner beauty and find self-confidence."

"I could build you a studio on the property I bought for my restaurant. There are four extra storefronts." He winked and dropped to his knee, still holding her hands. "Until what?" Marriage? Forever?

She held her breath, then released it in short bursts. "Until I don't know."

Fine. He'd wait. But not long. "Let's get you home, and we'll talk about it when the time comes." Geoff's cell rang. "Oh, it's Ryan." Standing, he answered and put it on speaker. "I'm here at the hospital. Savannah's listening."

"Good news. Mona and Kaler can't stop confessing each other's sins. We've identified girls from the pictures—they recognized him."

He shook a tight fist, as if in victory.

"In a fit of anger, Mona even confessed to tampering with Maria's car. Those two will be in prison for a long time."

Chapter Thirty-Seven

Sitting on the edge of her bed, Savannah held the pillow Rose made for her in preschool—the one that sent all the monsters away. No amount of monster-busting pillows could prepare her for this morning.

Rose tapped at her door. "She's here."

Savannah dropped the pillow on the bed. She walked toward the front of the house, her feet shuffling as if made of lead. Pausing at the screen door, she closed her eyes a few seconds before she swung it open and entered. Lord, please help me know what to say.

"Hey." Emily dabbed at her puffy red eyes with a tissue. Blonde wisps surrounded her face.

"I'm so sorry." Savannah stepped forward, reaching to hug her, but then withdrawing. "I can tell you really loved each other."

"I don't know what I'm going to do." Emily dropped to the porch swing, burying her head in her hands. "I finished with the medical examiner. We have plots in Virginia, so I'll have the ceremony there. I understand if you can't—"

"I'll be there." Savannah took the spot next to her on the step and massaged her back. "I didn't even get the chance to know him, but he seemed like a great guy."

"He was." Emily erupted in sobs. "I loved him... so much."

Cloud after cloud rolled by as Savannah cried with her, the hint of a thunderstorm hanging on the horizon.

"I'd better go." Emily nodded to the skyline. "But I'll be in touch."

Back in the house, Savannah lingered in the shower, wishing the hot water could erase her nerves. She'd promised Geoff she'd meet him to talk. A mistake?

She spent an hour choosing an outfit, and another to style her long, brown hair. After a while, she gave up and headed to the kitchen, where Rose stood peeling potatoes.

"Mom, would you mind going with me to April's Salon? I think I might try the layered look you suggested."

Her mother's eyes sparkled. "Okay." Rose filled a bowl with water and put the already-peeled potatoes in the refrigerator. "I'm making a salad for our Ladies Group, but it can wait."

Savannah rubbed her stomach. "You know, afterward, we might go check out the new boutique next to Opal's and have a late lunch. I'm starving."

When they got to the restaurant, Megan Carter waved from her smoking bench. She stood and ran to Savannah, nearly knocking her over from the force of the hug.

"I can't believe Mona Spencer tried to kill you. I'm so glad you're safe."

"Me either." Savannah hugged her again. "We need to hang out next week. We can go to Georgia's one night."

"Please do. It's good to reconnect with friends." Rose waggled her finger. "But none of that trouble you two used to stir."

"We'd never dare." Megan chuckled then frowned. "Is it all true? Did she and Kaler trap you in a basement and try to set the place on fire?"

Savannah nodded, fresh chill bumps covering her arms. "It's true."

"And you're still dating Geoff?"

Rose beamed. "Yes. I'm going to have grandchildren."

"Oh." Megan blushed. "So you're expecting?"

"Mom. No, I'm not pregnant." Savannah flicked her gaze to the ceiling. "And as far as Geoff, I'm not sure where things stand right now. I'm going to meet him tonight, and we'll go from there."

"Well, you look fantastic." Megan turned to Rose. "She does, doesn't she? I love the haircut."

Rose grinned. "My idea. I thought it would suit her."

"A good one."

After their meal, Savannah waited with Megan as Rose went to get the car. "You know..." Megan peeked over both shoulders. "I haven't done a good prank since you left town." She met Savannah's gaze with a sardonic grin. "Geoff has been on my list for years."

Savannah laughed. "We'll see. Oh, there's Anabelle. That reminds me. Will you go the reunion?"

Megan shrugged. "Not sure. It's not for months, though, right?"

"We've got to go. See you later." After one more hug, Savannah headed to her mother's car.

As they turned into the driveway, sun glinted from Savannah's Prius. Phil worked on a lawnmower with the neighbors. When she got out, he stood, backing away from it, and she wrapped her arms around his neck. "I love you, Daddy. So much more than you could ever know. Thanks for everything."

His cheeks flushed, and he glanced at each of the neighbor men before his gaze landed back on her. "I love you too, sweetheart."

She left him, returned to her bedroom, and removed the black silk dress from her shopping bag. Rose had been right again. It screamed classy—exactly her plan. With the light lace overlay and modest neckline, it fell from her neck to her toes.

Rose insisted on buying her jewelry and a new purse to go with it, and by the time Savannah finished dressing, she felt like a million dollars. She climbed into the Prius and tapped her text icon. "Okay, Geoff. Hope you're ready."

His response gave her shivers. *Meet me at the restaurant property. It's at 3540 State Street. I have a surprise.* State Street. Where Frank had lived.

She plugged the address into her GPS, following it to an old warehouse, where a half-constructed facade promised modern renovation. Dialing Geoff, she checked the road sign. "I'm here. Where do I enter?"

"I see you." He stepped out of the warehouse front door appraised her with a tentative grin. "Wow. Incredible."

"Thanks. I've missed you." She held her trembling hands at her side.

"I've missed you, too." He looped a lock of her hair around his pinky and gave it a light tug. "I went to visit my brother yesterday. He's in a home about thirty miles from here."

"I'm glad you found him." She gave a tentative smile. "How was he?"

"He has a severe mental disability, but he's happy. At least that's what the woman at the desk said. I'm going to keep visiting as much as I can."

"Good." She swallowed, a single tear streaking her cheek. "Listen, I—"

"Savannah, we—"

"I..." She let out a nervous giggle. "Can we try again?"

Geoff put his fingers on her lips and led her into the warehouse through a narrow hallway and a thick metal door. It opened to a bright room with windows obscured by a privacy film. Mirrors lined one wall, and unassembled exercise equipment spread across the sprung floor, waiting to be installed.

"I'm not sure how much business you'll get in Dreyfus, so I put in three studio rooms and a kids play area. There's space to expand. You might want to hire an assistant. Of course, you'll want a connection to my restaurant." He gestured to the door they'd entered and pointed to one a few feet down the hallway. "And your father's new garage will go there."

"How did you do this so fast? Did you even sleep the last couple of days?" Savannah blinked, waving her hand in front of her face, as though that could dam the flood of emotion spilling from her heart. "I can't believe this. It's incredible."

"That's my word." Winking, Geoff took her hand. He tugged her through another door, into a posh, yet unfinished lobby. "Over there I'm building a shop for your mother. She can sell her candles and crafts when she feels like it."

"She'll love it."

He led her to a tall counter, where a CD player rested on a high-backed leather stool. Pressing the play button, he looked up to the ceiling, and then faced her as the music started. He dropped to his knee and held out a dainty blue box. "Savannah, be my wife."

"I..." The first lyric struck her. Like the singer, Geoff had been waiting by the phone for her to reach out to him. And she hadn't.

She'd heard the song before—beautiful, one of her favorites, written by the grandson of a man who had attended their church. She smiled. Rose had gushed to tell her all about it. "Hurry home," she whispered, tumbling into his arms.

"It doesn't tell your story, but the chorus applies." Misty-eyed, Geoff helped her stand, leading her into a slow, easy sway.

As the singer crooned, Geoff's message sounded loud and clear. He'd forgiven everything, regardless of her horrible actions. And he loved her still.

As they moved in slow circles, she glanced at the vaulted ceiling. Below it, silvery lettering stenciled her name onto the wall. *Savannah Spencer Exercise Studio.*

He grinned. "Sorry for being presumptuous. The guys said I should wait until you accepted. Do I need to ask again?"

"Of course, yes." She could feel herself yielding to him, step by step, sway by sway. She poured her heart outward into his, melting into the kiss that matched his promise.

His lips, both tender and wanting, captured hers, spreading warmth over her entire body. He cupped her cheeks with both hands, daring her to withdraw. "I love you, Savannah Barrett."

His murmur between kisses sent tingles though her every nerve. "I love you, too," she gasped, clutching him harder.

When they parted, she ducked her head. "I don't deserve your forgiveness."

He tipped her gaze to the ceiling. "My mother taught me compassion every day of her life." He rubbed the scar on his chin, the one he'd worn to school the day after locking her in the panda habitat. "She taught me everyone deserves forgiveness, even my great-grandfather after all those horrible things he'd done to her. It's what Christians do."

"I wish I'd known her." Savannah kissed her fingertip then traced the scar. "I wish I could be as compassionate as she was."

"You will." He led her to an outside door, propped open with a stone. "One more thing."

They walked along the sidewalk to a two-foot hole next to a shovel. Frank's silver treasure box rested in its center.

Geoff withdrew a yellowed paper from his pocket, secured in several layers of plastic. "If it's fine by you, I'd like to bury Pandora's Deed. Let's leave everything behind us and move forward together."

Savannah accepted the deed, knelt, and tucked it into the box. "With all my heart."

THE END

The Series

PANDORA (Savannah Barrett), after fleeing childhood bullies, settles for empty relationships and believes no one could desire her for more. She blames Geoff Spencer, her former tormentor, the man who could love her anyway. When she inherits his farm, she returns to claim his property and face her dreadful past.

MEDUSA (Megan Carter) cannot stop crossing paths with the ruggedly dashing Zach Allen, who resents her for brushing him off in high school. Her heart's so full of bitterness toward him that she cannot love anyone, especially herself.

ATHENA (Athena Lewis), a single mom, regrets past mistakes but cannot seem to stop making them. Now she's pregnant from a one-night stand, and believes she's not worthy of love. Officer Nathan Smith hopes to change her mind.

CASSANDRA (Cassie Davis) follows her psychic aunt's New Age religion, and searches the cards for her soulmate. She finds handsome and overly zealous Christian lawyer Kevin Henry, who pursues her in a witch-hunt lawsuit.

NIKE (Nikki Denton) must rely on attractive coworker Mark Harris to help her team when an accident sidelines her starting players and assistant coaches. While she aims to win the championship, he tries to win her heart.

IRIS (Iris Chambers) blames God and her husband, Ryan, for losing everything to a flood. When she turns to a neighbor for support, she just may ruin her marriage.

APHRODITE (Anabelle Cooper) obsesses over beauty, which leads to severe, crippling anxiety. When type-Z personality Drew Monroe helps her escape a teenage stalker, he offers an imperfect love that she must humble herself to accept.

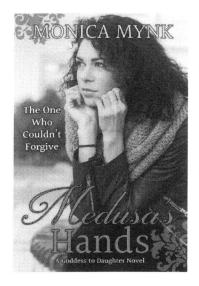

Twenty-eight year old waitress Megan Carter dreams of a different life, far away from Zach Allen, who's wanted to date her since high school.

Zach truly loves Megan, but he can't let go of his party boy persona long enough to show her he's serious. As soon as she graduages beauty school, she plans to walk away and leave him behind for good.

When Zach's stepsister disappears, her teenage daughter, Kelsey, shows up on Megan's doorstep asking to crash for a few days. Convinced Kelsey's mom is in danger, Megan begrudgingly enlists Zach's help and discovers Kelsey's dad, Warren, is their biggest threat.

She starts to trust Zach and opens her heart, but before long she realizes he's still struggling for sobriety and clinging to his past mistakes. How can she forgive him when he refuses to change?

Will Warren find Kelsey and lure her into his life of sex trafficking and degradation, or can Megan and Zach overcome their differences to help them?

Available on Amazon

Medusa

Please enjoy this sneak peek from *Medusa's Hands*, book two of the *Goddess to Daughter Series.*

Larissa Nickell tucked a frayed wool blanket over her fifteen-year-old daughter Kelsey's tiny frame, covering her up to her neck. She held her breath, counted to one hundred, and crept to her chain-locked door. The peeling paint caught under her index fingernail as she lifted onto tiptoes to see out the peephole. Her neighbors stood in a semicircle in the dimly lit hallway.

The apartment doorbell chimed three times, a pause, and then another, just as it had moments before. Hank. It had to be. But how? Why?

Mrs. Applewood's screech shot through the quarter-inch crack separating the heavy metal door from the jamb. "Get outta here! Told ya I'd be calling the police if I saw ya poking your nose 'round here again. They're already on the way!"

Footsteps thudded away from her apartment door.

A door creaked across the hall. Her pulse thundering, Larissa brushed her stringy hair from her eyes and looked out again. Mr. Gaines, with his faded old-school marine tattoos and Hank, with his wanna-be thug ink, seemed ready to face off in a wife-beater tee contest. The elderly man waved a golf club in Hank's face, his frail frame almost an even match to Hank's heroin chic. "The lady's right. You've got no business here."

Larissa wiped her sleeve along her wet cheek. How lucky she was to have neighbors to watch out for her. But this couldn't go on forever. He'd hurt one of them eventually. Hank could strike viciously, unprovoked, like a pit bull, and she had the scars to prove

316

it. She'd have to talk to him sometime. Why now, when she was getting ready to graduate beauty school?

She tied her robe sash tighter and stepped barefoot into the hallway, grit and dirt sliding between her toes.

He faced her, his cool gray eyes narrowing then lightening as his features tightened into a smirk.

"Hello, Hank." Hands on her hips, she formed her best scowl. It didn't feel near mean enough.

"Larissa." He dropped to his knees, grabbing at her feet with his needle-tracked arms. "I'm so sorry, love."

Too late. Did he think she was a fool?

"A century of apologies wouldn't cut it. I told you I never wanted to see you again." She crossed her terrycloth-covered arms, glancing at Mrs. Applewood, who held a silver candlestick over Hank's head. "When did they let you go? I thought you had to serve two more years."

He palmed her calf, the grip so tight she wobbled. "Six months ago, for good behavior, baby. So you spent all my money on this swanky place?"

"I told you, Nelson called the police." Mrs. Applewood inched the candlestick closer to Hank's receding hairline. Her husband stepped into the hall with his pistol. No wonder Hank was acting so penitent. Without the gun, he'd have pummeled poor Mr. Gaines into the wall, ex-marine or not.

"Thank you." Hands on her hips, Larissa glared over her nose at her poor excuse for an ex-husband. She wriggled from his grasp to the right. "Did they let your girlfriend out, too?"

"Please." Hank tried to stand. Mr. Abrams smacked his shoulder with the golf club, and he dropped back to his knees. "Larissa, I just need the coins. Let me have them, and I'll leave you alone for good."

"No." She clamped her teeth together. "Those coins belong to Kelsey now. For college. Remember? Your daughter? Would you steal from your own child?"

"I have to pay Mac. He's going to—"

"You should have thought of that before you decided to get yourself thrown in prison."

Police sirens blared. Hank ducked around the golf club and squeezed his fingers over her arm. "Larissa, you have to help me. He's going to kill me."

"I don't have to do anything." She jerked away, willing her tears to stay put. "Maybe if he kills you, it's for the best."

Pivoting, she reentered the apartment, twisted the deadbolt, and fastened the chain.

Kelsey sat straight up, her eyes wide, and her hands cupping her mouth.

"I'll be back. You can't run from me, Larissa." Hank's retreating footsteps pounded the hallway floor moments before the sirens cut short and police doors slammed.

"Kels. Get bag out of the closet. I'm taking you to Megan's."

Megan Carter sat in the intersection of Barlow Avenue and Searcy Street, her temples developing a sudden throb. Her mustard-smeared apron lay crumpled in the passenger seat beside her, a handful of coins and cash spilling from the pocket. At least she'd managed to drop her electric payment in the slot before her ten-year-old Sentra stalled out.

She tilted and hid her face, her springy-curled ponytail flattening against the headrest. Grease-spotted leather shoes stretched to the gas and brake pedals. She imagined herself sinking into the floorboard. This was not happening. Not again. Not at the busiest intersection in town.

Abrupt honks and long blares insisted others would like to turn. She squeezed her eyes shut and tried the ignition. Nothing happened. Not even the hint of a click or scrape. She tapped her head against the headrest. Why couldn't she disappear? When she opened her eyes, Geoff Spencer's face pressed against the window.

She opened the door a crack. "Sorry."

"What's wrong?"

"I don't know. It was making this jittery sound while I was idling, and it doesn't want to respond when I give it gas. And it kind of lurched forward before it stopped." Her voice cracked. "It's done this on me four times this week."

"Bet it's your sparkplugs." Geoff waved to his truck, which he'd parked on the median. The passenger stepped out, scowling beneath a sandy colored mess of uncombed hair. Zach Allen. Heat overwhelmed her cheeks. Maybe she could pull the carpet over her head and hide under it.

"Okay, Zach and I are going to push you out of the road. You put it in neutral and steer, okay? Think you can do that?"

"Yeah." She puffed her cheeks, trying to keep her focus on the steering wheel. Zach's narrowed eyes glared through the rearview mirror. When her glance caught his, he deepened his scowl.

Twenty minutes later, she begrudgingly climbed into Geoff's truck. Zach squeezed in beside her, keeping his face pressed to the passenger window.

"Want me to have it towed somewhere?" Geoff pulled his cell out of his pocket. "Phil Barrett can fix it for you. He's trustworthy."

Megan hid behind her palms. "I can't afford to have it fixed right now. I barely have enough to cover my rent." She jabbed her elbow into Zach's side. "If certain people would ever tip…"

Zach grunted. "If certain people would bring the steak sauce when I ask for it."

"I had two parties. Call me human, but I forgot."

"That's no excuse not to tip her, Zach." Geoff huffed. "I'll take care of the tow for you."

"No." She dragged her fingers over her forehead. Could he not just drop it? The last thing she needed was for Zach Allen to know every embarrassing detail about her life. "You've already done too much for me."

"You can pay me back with free haircuts when you have your own salon." He winked. "Don't forget, I've got plans for you in that last little corner of the restaurant plaza. Savannah would kill me if I didn't make a way for you two to work close together."

Her cheeks warmed again. "That would be awesome."

He merged into the now-flowing traffic, tipping his cap to an older man who let him in the lane. He signaled left and pointed across the street, where a group of students kicked a soccer ball around in a field. "Can't believe they're practicing in all this mud."

"I know." She shifted. Dark clouds swirled in a menacing spiral to their south. "Wonder if it's ever going to stop raining."

"Weatherman says probably at least another week of heavy rains. We're headed toward a pretty big flood, I'm afraid."

When the light changed to green, the truck surged forward, and she braced herself against the dash, her hand landing inches from Zach's. She drew it back, pressing it into her pilled polyester pants.

"You always smell like steak." Zach folded his arms.

"I wonder why." She flicked her gaze to the ceiling then returned it to her lap. Could the five-mile drive take any longer?

Geoff stopped at a crosswalk, letting four college students pass in front of him. A pretty brunette with bushy curls smiled her thanks as she flounced by the truck.

"You should wear your hair down like that." Zach tugged at one of Megan's curls.

Megan lunged toward Geoff. "You should mind your business."

"Behave, you two." The truck started rolling again, and Geoff eased through the line of traffic, pulling between the two monstrous churches at the intersection leading to Main Street.

"You guys should get married in that one." She pointed to the Presbyterian church on her right, with its Corinthian columns and arched wooden doors. "It's so pretty."

"It's not our church home." Geoff tapped the dash, waiting to make the right turn. "Savannah and I have a long history in our church. Didn't you attend there, too?"

"Yeah. When I was young."

Zach snorted. "You went to church? You're mean as a snake."

She responded with a snort of her own. "I'm not mean to everyone. Only people who treat me bad."

Geoff found a space in her apartment complex and shut off the truck. Zach didn't budge.

"Dude." Geoff reached over her shoulder to nudge him. "Let her out."

"I'm not moving."

"Stubborn jerk." Megan lurched for the door handle, slinging it open. She swung her legs up and climbed across Zach to get out, contorting her body in a painfully awkward twist to avoid contact. When her feet landed on the pavement, she grimaced. Her purse rested on the seat beside him, out of her reach.

She grabbed for it as he lifted it high above her head. He leaned out of the truck, balancing his feet on the side step.

Zach dropped to the seat, tossing the purse at her.

Geoff cleared his throat. "Sorry about that, Megan. See you later. I'll text you about the car when I hear back from Phil." He gripped the gearshift. "What are you, Zach, fourteen? Seriously. Give the girl a break."

321

She stared after him, open-mouthed, as Zach slammed the truck door closed. No kidding, give her a break. She'd thought things might get better with Zach after she'd driven him home on a drunk night a few weeks ago, but they'd gotten worse. And now she was starting school and couldn't work as many shifts as she used to… She didn't care what Opal said. Next time, somebody else was waiting on his table.

As she closed the distance between the parking lot and her apartment door, her cell rang. Savannah.

"Hello, best friend." Megan smiled for the first time all day. "Your knight in shining armor saved me."

"No kidding?" The grin came through in Savannah's voice. "What's Mr. White Horse done for you today?"

Megan let herself into the tiny apartment she called home. She kicked off her shoes and placed them neatly in the closet, then hung her apron on a hook by the door. "My car died in the middle of the road again. Can you believe it? Geoff helped me push it out of the street. Him, and stupid Zach Allen."

"What's wrong with it?"

"Geoff thinks spark plugs." The rent notice glared from her kitchen door. "I don't know for sure. He's taking it to your dad to be fixed. I told him no, but he didn't let me have an option."

"You should have told me." Savannah clucked her tongue. "Dad wouldn't have charged you anything to fix it. You get the daughter's-best-friend discount."

Megan laughed. "Well, tell your dad so he doesn't charge Geoff all that much, then."

"Truth be told, he's probably going to make Geoff do half the work. He's been trying to steal him from the restaurant construction all week."

Squirting lotion into her hand, she eyed the fading wallpaper around her room. "When's the restaurant ever going to get finished? He promised me I could work there when it opens."

"There's probably about four weeks of construction left, and then all the inspections and stuff. I'm excited, though, to see how it's all going to come together. Did he tell you? It will be pay what you can, and the community garden will supply a lot of the food ingredients."

"He's told me a few times." Megan chuckled, dropped to her armchair, and rubbed the lotion on her tired feet. The smell of raspberries filled the room, her mom's favorite. Misty-eyed, she capped the lotion and set it on the TV tray beside her. "Things are getting pretty serious between you two."

"Actually, that's what I called about." Savannah's lips smacked. "He proposed to me last night."

"Are you kidding?" Megan jumped from her seat. "That is awesome! You have to come by Opal's tomorrow and let me see the ring."

"I was hoping you might agree to be my maid of honor."

"Of course." Despite her wide smile, a pang struck her heart. She'd probably never get married. Just like her mom, she'd die sad and lonely. She probably wouldn't even have a daughter to keep her company and take care of her.

"One thing, since you've already agreed." Savannah's breath drifted through the speaker. "Geoff is going to ask Zach to be his best man. Think you can live with him walking you down the aisle?"

Tears stung Megan's cheeks. How could she say no? "For you, anything."

Zach Allen stared out the truck window at a beat-up red Chevy in Megan's apartment lot. He tried to notice every detail—the right-wing sticker on the dash, the rip in the leather seat—anything to keep his mind off her.

"Feel like explaining?" Geoff signaled, raising his eyebrow.

Zach shrugged. "I just get tired of bad service."

"You go in her restaurant seven nights a week and run her like a crazy person." Geoff made the left turn, dipping into the gravel. "I've seen how you treat her. She can't even manage her other tables for doing stuff for you. If all you guys tipped her like you should, she'd have plenty to get by. How long are you going to make her pay for something from when you were teenagers?"

"Dunno." Zach rubbed the window trim until it shone.

"It mystifies me why you keep going back to hang out with those boys anyway. Do you honestly think you can sustain drinking so much every single night until you're an old man?"

Zach stretched his legs out and bumped his head against the back window. "Not your business."

"If you're going to help manage my farm, it is. I don't want an old drunk handling my important decisions."

"What else do I have to do besides manage your farm?"

Geoff grinned. "I do have a wedding coming up, bro. And even if I don't approve of your night activities, you're still the best friend I have at the moment. So, I was hoping you might fulfill the role of best man."

"A wedding? You proposed?"

"Last night. And she said yes."

Zach straightened, scooting his back against the seat. "I guess this means I need to wear a tux."

"Yep. And maybe wash those stinking feet." Geoff turned down the narrow side road leading to the farm. "So, Savannah's planning to ask Megan to be her maid of honor."

Zach snatched his hat from his head and threw it against his knee. "No way. I'm not walking down the aisle with th—"

"Are you asking me to tell my fiancé she can't have her dream wedding with her best friend?"

324

Meeting his scowl in the passenger mirror, Zach took a few breaths. "I hate that stupid girl."

"Savannah or Megan?"

Zach crossed his arms and slapped his elbows against his chest.

"Suit yourself." Geoff stopped the truck. "Ride stops here."

As if punctuating Geoff's insistence, bulky water droplets pelted the windshield. Zach glanced at Geoff, then the mired road. "You want me to get out? Now?"

"I want you to agree to be my best man and get over who's a bridesmaid. All you have to do is play nice for two nights—the rehearsal dinner and the wedding. Think you can?"

Jerking the handle, Zach lunged into the door and shoved it open. He slid out of the seat and slammed the door shut before stomping toward the trailer Geoff loaned him.

Rain splashed around his feet, cold and wet. It pummeled his head and shoulders, probably leaving dents it struck so hard. Within seconds, his too-long bangs clumped against his forehead, and his plaid flannel shirt stuck to his chest.

He kicked at a loose stone as Geoff's truck disappeared around a corner. No way was he going to cut that crazy girl any slack. He'd poured his heart and soul out to her time after time, and she crushed it again and again. She was getting what she deserved.

He walked the road along the yellow line like a tightrope, holding his hands out as though he needed balance. A honk sounded behind him, and he stepped aside, imagining the asphalt crumbling under his feet. He followed the curves in the gravel shoulder, occasionally stopping to snap off a protruding branch from the hill on his right. Across the valley to his left loomed the old iron furnace where Geoff found Savannah after she'd been captured. The place still gave him shivers.

Two miles later, when he reached the ten-acre property Geoff deeded to him, his pant legs clung to his boots. He approached the house he'd been building.

Gloppy mud surrounded the brick perimeter. Who knew when they'd be able to pour the concrete for the driveway? Wiping water from his eyes, he let himself inside. The interior lacked a few details —carpeting, painting, and installing the cabinets and appliances, and putting down the hardwood floors. But the exterior... If it would ever quit raining, he could finish in a few weeks.

He peered out the window at the dismal gray sky. That was a big if.

A quick pass through to the right side of the house left a trail of mud on the subfloor. He stood in the center of his great room, glanced at the vaulted ceiling, and shook his head. They'd painted the loft rail and completely missed one side of three of the posts. Geoff was right. Those guys he hung around had no ambition. They half-did everything, and he had to go along behind them and redo it.

So, why couldn't he turn his life in a different direction?

An empty glass bottle taunted him from a plastic bucket in the corner. He knew why. It wasn't the boys he had trouble turning away from.

Young Adult Christian Fiction
Dystopian Suspense
The Cavernous Trilogy

A Christian Teen battles for her soul against an extremist leader--her father

In a divided America, several secessions lead to the formation of a new nation, the Alliance of American States. Fueled by extremists who solicit members via social media, the Alliance has one weak point: Callie Noland, daughter of deceptive leader Adrian Lamb.

When he snatches her from the man she's always called dad, he forces her into a suppressive life, training to serve in the Alliance military. Can she maintain her faith in God and stand up to the man who calls himself Lord and Master?

Available in print and on Amazon Kindle. Find more information at
https://monicamynk.com

Bible Studies for Ladies
Ungodly Clutter

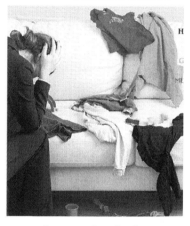

UnGODly Clutt

MONICA MYNK

Have you ever been embarrassed to invite someone into your home? Cobwebs in the corners? Laundry piled to the ceiling? Mile-high dishes in the sink? If it's true that cleanliness is next to godliness, does that mean those of us too stressed and over-worked to maintain a clean home are ungodly?

Perhaps, God would be appalled to enter many of our homes... but not for the reasons we might think! Today's world is full of distractions and many litter our living space without us giving them a second thought.

How can Christian women cleanse their homes of the idols and temptations that hinder salvation?

Available for print and Amazon Kindle. More information at https://monicamynk.com

329

About the Author

MONICA MYNK is a high school chemistry teacher and author from Eastern Kentucky. She spent her early years reading books with her mother, acting out plays with her brother and sister, climbing in corncribs, and helping her dad on the farm. Periodically, she loves to tell corny science jokes

Monica comes from a long line of preachers, elders, deacons, and Bible class teachers, and hopes to live up to their example. She clings to the hope that God's promises are new every morning. A favorite hobby is writing devotionals, which can be found on her blog.

In her spare time, Monica loves spending time with family, especially her husband and beautiful children. They've been known to hang out at the soccer field, and they are active participants in the Lads to Leaders program She is an active member of the American Christian Fiction Writers (ACFW).

NEED A SPEAKER?

Monica enjoys conducting ladies days and writing/editing seminars for women. If you're interested in booking, more information is available on her website.

https://monicamynk.com/speaking/

Acknowledgements

Thanks to the Deirdre Lockhart for going the extra mile in editing.

To Christa Holland of Paper and Sage Design, for another beautiful cover. And to Amy for bringing Savannah to life.

To Kathy Cretsinger and Diane Turpin

To my Scribes girls, Audrey, Deb, Julie F, Julie K, and Angela.

To my ACFW friends, especially Nadine, Angie, Gregg and Hallee, Ralene, Vicki, Angela, Rose, Audie and Betty for their guidance.

To Callie for your friendship and legal advice.

To Charanda and Jeannie, for listening, reading, and believing.

To my beta readers—my sisters—for helping make that final polish perfect. I've so enjoyed our discussions. I love and appreciate all of you!

To those on writing forums and social media. Through your critiques, brutal honesty, and friendship, I've been able to turn a dream into a reality. Special thanks to my friends at LegendFire, and my Spiritual Warriors group, Rebecca, Paylor, Jordan, Viktor, and Patrick.

To friends and family, especially my brother Nick and sister Micki, who were great partners in pretending, and my wonderful in-laws, Terry, Sue, Lindsay and Joseph. Love you all!

To my parents—my heroes. Mom, who nicknamed me Florence, and Dad, who taught me to always search the Scriptures.

To Lane, Matt, and Dana Kate, my beautiful family. Every day, my love for you grows even more.

To God, for His enduring patience and benevolent forgiveness. I pray that my stories will inspire others to delve into Your truth.

64471077R00199

Made in the USA
Lexington, KY
09 June 2017